BELOVED DAUGHTER

ELLIS BRIGHTWELL

Winter Blood Moon Harvest Publishing

eBook ISBN: 978-1-7369827-2-3

Print ISBN: 978-1-7369827-0-9

CONTENTS

Part I
KING'S OATH

1. Ardelle — 3
2. Accusations — 13
3. Aldorman — 25
4. Flight — 41
5. Isadora — 53
6. Imprisonment — 66
7. Sisters — 80
8. Myrah — 95

Part II
SANCTUARY

9. Evensong — 115
10. Inquisitions — 128
11. Desire — 144
12. Pleas — 156
13. Secrets — 167
14. Betrayal — 185
15. Battle — 200
16. Freedom — 217

Part III
THE HIDDEN WORLD

17. Burdens — 237
18. Proposal — 252
19. Daughter — 262
20. Constantine — 277
21. Sithebad — 288
22. Reunion — 301
23. Beloved — 317

Part IV
SHE WHO MAKES KINGS

24. Kinship   335
25. Rosamond   352
26. Oathbreaker   369
27. Gerahard   381
28. Wedding   392
29. Dreams   408
30. Death   420

Part V
A MOTHER'S LAMENT

31. Life   441
32. Frijona   452
33. Mildred   468
34. Farewell   479
35. Remembrance   495

I

KING'S OATH

ARDELLE

When an unyielding length of wood bests my blunted ax and marks its own unbroken life by splitting itself into oaken slivers, the boy from the neighbouring fields steps out from behind mother's weaving house and wipes the last of summer's sweat from his forehead with the sleeve of his dung-hued tunic. Alfred's reedy eyebrows look as though they might hide themselves in the thick brown thatch he wears on his head as hair.

"Ardelle," he says. "Did you see that lightning from the heavens?"

"I did not," I say. "I can not see the tales within your mind half as well you. I do, however, see you twice as often as your father, who takes in the harvest."

"He does not trust me with a scythe after I sheared a bull between its hind legs and it did not live to become an ox," says Alfred.

"What in the world do you mean?" I say.

"We had to eat it," says Alfred. "Do you know what we ate for our first meal?"

I take another length of wood from a heap of its slain kindred and set it upright on the oak stump.

"Bollocks," I say.

I hew the wood down the middle, sending one of the halves between Alfred's ox-brown leggings. He clutches himself where the wood struck him.

"Forgive me," I say.

I strike my ax into the stump and set a hand on his shoulder.

"I will tell father of what you have done," he says.

"I did not mean to," I say.

"You did not mean to call lightning from the heavens? I think you know what you do."

"I have only read—"

I have only read of such things in the books mother's friend Isadora keeps in her house of stone. Isadora would never share them with one such as Alfred, whose wild thoughts take him further afield than any steed. Or does Alfred follow me when I go to Isadora and listen to what we do?

"Your face brightens with redness when you do not wear linen on your head in the summer sun," he says. "I think this makes you look even fairer."

"What?"

Alfred stands before me as if for the first time: his clothing still bears the hue of horse dung; his hook-toed feet wear more of the earth than mine do; his claw-like fingers grasp my elbows where they hang beside my waist. When he looks up at me, he may as well look at the clouds—his forehead stands little higher than my ribs.

"Give me a kiss and I will not tell," he says.

"I am not your mother," I say.

"Not that kind of kiss," he says. "The other kind."

I breathe out sharply, sending a gust of harvest wind through the straw of the bird's nest on his egg-shaped head.

"If I do this," I say, "you must never ask this of me again. You must leave at once and not return to our fields unless your father is with you."

"I will," he says.

I bend down to kiss Alfred as mother did me when I had not yet learned how to run without falling. No sooner have I drawn away from him than his hands grasp the back of my neck and pull my lips onto his. His thumb opens my jaw, giving me the gift of a breath laden with ale-water, half-cooked barley, and three-day-old fish. He breathes loudly with his eyes closed as I shove against his shoulder with my palm, yet he will not free me. Something is on my hip—I take his wrist there and his fingers from my neck and throw his hands at him as I step away.

"I think I am in love with you," he says.

I wrest my ax from the oak stump and wield its edge above my head. Alfred's eyes widen; his lanky legs take him through the stalks of our wheat fields so swiftly that the earth flies from the bottoms of his feet. I wake three lengths of wood from their sleeping brothers and give them each a swift death. When Alfred returns, I will have set the lot of them around mother's weaving house and burned it to the ground so that he can never again hide himself behind it and watch what I do.

When the sun burns brightest among the clouds, its warmth floods my face so well that I must wrap my head in a length of linen to ward my cheeks against the reddening Alfred worships. Father comes in from the fields with a welcoming grin for the high heaps of hewn wood I have made for winter's hearth. His short brown hair lies wet with sweat as he pulls a two-handled cart as long as a horse laden with stalks of wheat.

I step into our house, careful not to wake mother, and walk our heavy stone quern with grunting swings over the earthen floor. I lift it through the opening and bear it to the oak stump, where I set it down. Father and I strike the wheat stalks with wooden rods to loosen the seeds, whereafter we pour them thrice into a great wooden bowl to winnow the chaff. I sit with the quern on top of the green woollen gown between my legs and begin the burdensome work of grinding corn for the giving of harvest thanks: we thank ourselves, on the king's behalf, for harvesting his fourth of our fields by eating the other three fourths. Alfred and Harold, who now walk through the stunted stalks of our fields pulling a small cart of their own in matching earth-hued clothing, have made it their wont to give their own thanks to us for being such close neighbours by trading some of their oats and barley for more than some of our wheat and rye.

"Does your daughter never braid her hair?" asks Harold with a loud laugh. "Or do you not mind those long yellow strands in your bread?"

"Her hair gives her strength," says father, "as does her mother's. Have you come to give thanks for the harvest before it is half-done?"

"That hair must give your daughter greater strength than you know," says Harold. "Alfred has seen how she hews timber without an ax."

"Alfred wields no scythe and yet your crops are harvested," I say.

"Had he a wife," says Harold, "he would learn swiftly."

"Such tales he must tell you," says father. "You are a good man for looking after him. Shall I load your wheat stalks?"

"Alfred has a told me a tale I could not but listen to wholly," says Harold. "It is one in which he and Ardelle are wed and live in happiness among the king's fields." Father sets the bundle of wheat stalks he had lifted back down on the ground. "The king shares in this happiness, for he thinks not on what your daughter does when Alfred brings him his many carts of wheat."

The round stones between my knees have stopped their grinding. I sweep the ground wheat into a small heap behind the quern. Father stands upright, taller than I have seen him since my head came up to his knees.

"Ardelle is not old enough to wed," father says.

"Seventeen winters have made her a woman, Gildewin," says Harold. "And Alfred has seen how they have made her something more than that."

"Young Alfred's tales must send you into a wondrous sleep at night," says father. "Ardelle's mother will be the one to choose Ardelle's husband when she is ready to take one, much as you are the one who shows Alfred best how one *becomes* a man."

Harold sets his hand on his son's head and smiles.

"Alfred looks up to the king's aldorman as well," he says.

Father breathes out loudly and looks to the clouds as he runs his hand through his hair. He takes a bundle of wheat stalks and throws them into Harold's cart. Many of them land on the ground.

"How is it that you worship your son's tales of things unseen in the heavens so blindly?" father says.

"So you know of things unseen," says Harold. "The king's aldorman is unwed and does not yet know of Ardelle."

"We help you scythe your fields and share our harvest with you," father says. "My Branwen weaves flax and wool in the same house with your Hilda. Is it your wife who sends you to battle with your own kith?"

Alfred takes up the wheat stalks from the ground and sets them in the cart. He lifts the wooden handles to his waist and would turn the cart around did his father not steady his keen offspring with a hand on Alfred's shoulder.

"How many carts do you want?" I say.

Harold's eyes follow a path from my earth-caked feet to the top of my braidless hair.

"When we have harvested everything," I say, "I will go with the carts to the king's men and tell them of what Alfred said."

"Good," says father. "Shall I have Ardelle grind your oats, Harold?"

Harold eyes father for a time.

"Will you not ask your wife?" Harold says.

"You may ask again when Alfred has grown as tall as you are," says father.

Alfred takes a small bundle of wheat stalks into his arms and sets them in the cart. His father grabs him by his tunic and shoves him before me.

"Tell Ardelle how faithful you will be while her father and I load the first of our three carts," Harold says.

Alfred's shoulders sink beneath the weight of his thick head. He opens his mouth to speak, but nothing comes from his throat. When father has filled Harold's cart with more than it can bear, Harold claps one hand against Alfred's shoulder and shows him the gift of wheat the king has given him.

"Forgive me," Alfred says to me.

"You are forgiven," I say to our quern. "Farewell, Alfred."

As the sun makes ready to bed down beyond the western river, I take the linen from my head, step down onto the earthen floor of our house, and hand my cloth to mother, who has risen from her bedding to wipe the sweat from her brow. She unbinds the strands of her waist-length brown braid and reweaves them with shaking fingers. I wet the ground wheat with boiled river water and knead the dough into a bread cake for the cooking stone.

"Set it on the embers," mother says in her tongue. "I am hungry."

When her bread has cooked and cooled, she bites into its

crusted, meaty end with teeth as white as winter's snow. The bread falls from her hand at the sound of father in the fields greeting our good friend and neighbour, Harold.

"He does not come for his second cart until the sun goes down," I say.

"Help your father," says mother. "I will need your hands on my back when you return. Give me a kiss."

I set my lips against her forehead and hasten without to where father stands before Harold, Alfred, and a man wearing a rich blue woollen tunic, leggings of the same hue, and shoes made of leather. His waist-belt bears a sheathed sword held against his hip by another belt over his shoulder. Around his neck rest thin links of silver that gleam softly in the setting sun.

"Why do you wear a yoke on your neck?" I ask him.

The man frowns as he looks over the two boar tusk shoulder pins that fasten the wool of my sleeveless green gown to its long-sleeved linen sister dyed yellow beneath it.

"This is the aldorman's thane, Ardelle," says Harold. "He is a man of might and wealth. He has come here on the aldorman's behalf to help us."

"Were you a man of might, Harold," says father, "you would speak to me yourself, man to man, rather than running off to fetch another to do it for you."

"It is my understanding," says the aldorman's thane, "that Harold asked your daughter to show him how to hew timber without an ax, and she could not do so. Might you show us again, young woman, so that I may tell the aldorman he has no need to keep you in his thoughts?"

Neither father's eyes nor his words tell me what I am to do, so I swing my flattened hand downwards twice, then show them the many dead lengths of hewn wood near the oak stump. The thane grins and laughs.

"There," says father. "She has shown you what you could

have seen for yourself, Harold, had you but looked with your own eyes instead of believing your son's tales so blindly."

"I shall tell the aldorman of this," says the thane, "though your daughter bears no mark of fairness that would give my words any more weight in his mind than the wind that blows between the legs of your oxen."

"I have heard Ardelle reading runes in a stone house," says Alfred.

"You allow your son to wander from your fields so that he may follow my daughter about and tell tales about what she does," says father. "Have you nothing to say for yourself, Harold?"

"She whispers these runes to herself when nobody is around," says Alfred.

"Nobody but *you*," I say.

"Tales and truth are often more alike than not," says the thane. "What do you know of books, Ardelle?"

"She knows nothing," says father. "When summer's sun floods her face with sore redness, my wife sends her to our friend Isadora, who lives near a river in which Ardelle cools herself. They tell tales to one another when they wait for sleep, nothing more."

"I have heard the name Isadora used among those who come from Hispania," says the thane. "That is the birth place of the king's thyle, who keeps his words and histories from eyes that have no need to see them. I think your Isadora and the king's Isadora must be one and the same. If this is true, to show the king's writings to another would be a great misdeed unless the king's thyle, in her wisdom, wishes to learn for herself whether Ardelle's words are more than mere tales when the king leaves his battle to come and meet them."

The thane's silver neck links glow as they draw near. The bearded man who wears them hooks his thumbs over his belt at his hips. Father puts his arm around my waist and draws my back into his breast. That word the thane used, *histories*, opens a door within my mind that should not be there. My own words leave my mouth before I know I have said them.

"They are dark dreams, not histories," I say.

The thane smiles.

"The aldorman was wise to send me here," he says. "He saw through the mist of Harold's words to the unclouded truth."

"My daughter goes with the harvest to the king," says father. "That is the unclouded truth."

"Did you not hear me when I said the king is away at battle?" says the thane. "He needs fighting men, even now, and the aldorman is the one who seeks for him those who bear shields and spears as well as they do scythes and knives."

Harold looks as though he might hide himself behind his son were Alfred tall enough. Alfred clutches his father's tunic.

"I will not leave my wife," says father.

The thane's cheeks and jaw harden. He sets his hand on the hilt of his sword. Something swells within me. The gold-wrought buckle on his leather belt falls to the ground, leaving his sheathed sword swinging freely from the shoulder belt at his hip. The thane stares at me, as do Harold and Alfred. Father looks at his own bare feet.

"Where is your mother, Ardelle?" the thane says.

"In our house," I say. "She does not move well. Her limbs ache."

"The aldorman's herbs can help her," says the thane. "They might take the redness from your cheeks as well. You may ask him of this when you go to see him tomorrow."

Father's arms tighten around my waist and shoulders. He kisses my hair.

"If mother needs more than what I can give her," I say, "I will ask it of the king when I bring his wheat to him."

The thane takes his golden buckle from the ground, looks

at the rough-edged leather of the broken belt on both ends of it, and closes his fingers around it.

"Again, you have not heard me when I say the king is away," says the thane. "The aldorman makes ready to see you tomorrow."

The thane meets father's eyes, then walks through the shortened stalks of our wheat fields. Harold and Alfred follow many steps behind him, their heads hung low as if burdened by ox yokes. I hold my own head upright.

"See to your mother," says father as he takes up his scythe. "Her back needs your hands."

Alfred turns from his father and rushes towards me—what does he think to do as both our fathers watch? He hugs me and lightens the dark green wool of my gown with snot from his nose. I set one hand on his hair; the other, I set on his back.

"I told you I am not your mother," I say, "nor shall I be anyone's mother for many years. Let your own mother look after you while I go to look after mine."

Alfred leaves me as swiftly as he came to me. I find mother in the house, where she lies face down on her woollen bedding with her fingers balled into fists at her sides. As I kneel astride her waist and knead the flesh of her back through her linen gown, I find my thoughts wandering to Alfred and what tales he must have told his father about how I kissed him. No, I must forget these things and the memory of what has happened this day. I will instead give my mind to soothing mother's aching spine that I might take from her, when she rests peacefully, her bright-cheeked smile, the glow of her brown eyes, and the warmth of arms that have given me strength for as long as I can remember.

2

ACCUSATIONS

I wake with the sun to find father gone from the house, and from the wooden walls in which we keep our pigs and oxen, and from the wheat and rye fields ready for harvesting, and from the oak stump beside which our bread-grinding quern lies idle. I spend that day and the next spinning wool onto spindles for mother's loom as she threads the yarn holder back and forth through upright strands. When she tires of working the shed rod and beating the weft, I work my thumbs into the flesh of her hands and arms and back. On the morning of the third day, when father has not yet returned, mother sends me into the northern birch groves to carve the bark with which she scrapes blood into her aching legs. I bear a full basket back to our fields, where I find brown-clothed men with scythes sweeping our wheat stalks to the ground without having first asked us whether they may do so. I hasten into the house to tell mother, only to find her kneeling with her linen-sleeved arms raised as she takes a brown woollen gown from a fair-faced young woman wearing dark blue over white. Her shoulder-length yellow hair is less than half as long as moth-

13

er's braid but glows twice as well in the light of our hearth's fire.

"A gift from the aldorman," says mother.

The young woman smiles and sets her hands on my shoulders as she turns towards me in stepping through our house's opening not wide enough for two. My eyes follow her leather shoes through the furrows of our eastern rye fields.

"You could have stepped aside for her," says mother.

She lies down on her bedding of wool-hidden hay with her old green gown bundled beneath her head. She shows me the bright white teeth she says drew father's eyes to her when he first met her in Powys.

"Your father will be back within the next few days," mother says in her tongue. "He is needed here more than elsewhere. He would not have you fret while he is gone. Come here."

I lie down in mother's arms. The warmth of her breath on my hair slows the blood that sets fire to my face and breast.

"When your father returns," she says, "you may help him slaughter that sickly ox that limps about. We also have a young bull ready to be tempered."

"I can make him into an ox better than Alfred," I say.

"Your father told me of what happened," mother says. "Is that young man still in your thoughts?"

"No," I say as I sit up from her arms. "I will help with the harvest."

Mother takes my wrists. I still her brittle fingers.

"Leave the men be," she says. "Help me sleep. When I wake, we will cook bread with the oats from your little friend's fields."

"Little is how much I think of him," I say. "Can you not sleep at night?"

"The sun has always been a better bedside friend to me

than the moon," says mother. "And you must have someone to watch over you in your dreams."

Tufts of smoke from the hearth's fire whirl about in the morning light as they follow winding paths towards the roof's thatch. When mother's breaths sound softly through her nose, I leave her to her sweet dreams. In the fields, the men have felled large swathes of rye. I take up a scythe.

"That blade is not meant for you."

A lean-limbed man with ruddy cheeks takes my scythe's haft and wrests it from my grip, throwing it to his idle brothers where they sit and stand among tall stalks.

"These are our fields," I say.

"Are you the king's daughter?" he says.

Laughter bellows from the handful of men who yield their share of the harvest by holding scythe hafts against their shoulders as they watch their friends work.

"You are not," he says, "and yet you and she will eat of the same bread without thinking about where it has come from."

"It comes from our fields," I say.

Their sweating, shirtless brothers come in from the harvest and rest among the furrows. After a time, the ruddy man with arms stronger than mine leads his well-rested friends out to the stalks, where they begin sweeping their scythes through the rye near the ground. A bearded man with an otherwise hairless head looks over my gowns.

"Have you a man?" he asks.

"Mother calls me."

I hasten into the house without a thought for anything but waking mother and telling her of this. The stray strands of dark hair beside her thick eyebrows are wet with sweat; the elksand beads she wears strung between her shoulders rise and fall with her soft and steady breaths. Seeing her like this, I can do nothing more than take her ankles in my lap and knead the flesh of her legs below her knees until her life's blood warms them once again. When she wakes, I will do likewise to her back; and when I have done, she may find herself in need of an eventide walk with her daughter.

I spend the next month doing my best not to fret as I grind wheat and bake bread with mother, whose legs are only sturdy enough to bear her to the weaving house. The scythe-men wield their blades in slaughtering our sickly ox and helping us smoke its meat, as do they show Harold's dear son Alfred how to temper a bull without having to eat it thereafter. I wake, one morning, to its weeping cries within our house though our oxen sleep elsewhere—it is mother who calls for me from where she lies beside the far wall. Ground wheat and water spill from the leaning wooden bowl that rests against her shins.

"Fetch the healer for me," she says.

The men who spent so many days harvesting dwell among our empty fields long after their scythes are no longer needed. The king's share of the harvest lies heaped in thirty carts that stir little more than they or mother do, yet I would rather listen to her tell me which of those men would make the best husband for me than have to ask among them for the aldorman's healer. I take the wooden bowl from her legs, unfasten her woollen gown's shoulder pins, and turn her over onto her back, finding with my fingertips those places where her flesh has become stone so my elbows may ask it to soften. The ridges on both sides of her spine flatten as I weigh down on them with my palms. Mother grunts at the sound of twigs cracking on the hearth.

"Child, you have broken my bones," she says.

"I have only helped you to breathe better," I say. "Rest your arms so I can stretch them."

"Give me some of that oat bread bearing the healer's herbs."

I take a hardened cake from the leaves beside the hearth,

dipping it into the last of the wooden bowl's water to soften it for mother. She chews loudly as I feel along her back with my fingers—something stirs in the house's opening. I meet the eyes of a brown-haired boy who hides himself from our sight.

"The men heard yelling from the house and asked me to come here," he says.

"My mother feels better," I say.

"I will feel better when I have seen the aldorman's healer," says mother. "My daughter goes to ask the men where he is."

I lean over and speak to her ear.

"Why does the healer not stay in one place so we may find him?" I whisper.

"I am not the only one he heals," mother says.

"I have no wish to listen to what those men will say to me."

"So hold your hands over your ears," mother says in her tongue.

I sigh and hang my head.

"Would you fetch the aldorman's healer for me?" I say to the boy.

"I must help the men, as they drink mead today to give thanks for the harvest they will bring to the king tomorrow," he says.

"Good," says mother. She lifts herself onto her elbows. "The healer will make me well enough to go with our wheat."

"You were well enough when the stalks lay ready seven days ago," I say.

"Come in here, young man," says mother.

She sits up, sending me from her back to kneel beside her. The boy stares at us from our house's opening but does not step through it.

"What is your name?" mother says.

"Aldewine," says the boy.

"Aldewine," says mother. "You look like a young man who could wed my daughter if he were older."

"*Much* older," I say.

Aldewine steps into the opening. He stands as short as Alfred.

"Is there something Ardelle could do in your stead while you go and fetch the aldorman's healer for me, Aldewine?" says mother.

"The men did ask me to bring them water from the lake three fields away," he says. "They will drink it when they have no more mead. And I am to wake them with it tomorrow if their eyes will not open on their own."

"The river is nearer," I say. "Why do they need water from the lake?"

"The aldorman has told them not to shit there," says Aldewine.

Mother smiles to herself. Aldewine looks at us with one hand clutching the timber. His clothing bears the same brown hue as Alfred's tunic and leggings and earth-caked feet. If Aldewine tells tales of thunder and lightning half as well as Alfred, the men will have no need to talk to me of husbands and wives. I walk to the pots in the back of the house and take the one with the widest mouth and narrowest bottom. Three soft ridges are home to two fish bone snakes that wind like mother's spine as they slither along the dark brown clay.

"Do you like it?" says mother. "It is a gift from the king. The aldorman has told him of us. We are in the king's thoughts even before he meets us."

I frown—I should not think ill of mother's words, but I do not believe that she would so readily trade a pot for father.

"Give me a kiss before you leave," mother says in her tongue.

I set my lips to her forehead; she sets hers against my cheek. Aldewine stares at us from the opening.

"I have no kiss for you," I say to him.

"Why are you so tall?" he says and runs off.

Around the oak stump, scytheless men stand in a ring and drink from a wide brown pot, which each of them threatens to set down on the ground thereafter. When they do not and instead hand it to the next man, they win loud laughter from some and cursed oaths from others. I keep my eyes on my feet as I walk towards the southeastern fields.

"She has a pot as well," says one of them.

"She is as tall as Ceolmund."

"Yet which of them is fairer?"

Beyond the drunken, laughing men, a wan shape runs along the northern edge of the harvested fields. A whooping yell greets the clouds as the man lifts his arms. No tunic, no leggings. This must be Ceolmund.

"What in the world is he doing?" I say to myself.

"That is our game," says one of Ceolmund's clothed friends. "The one who drinks last or sets the pot down runs around the fields."

"Or the one who forgets to drink."

"Or the one who is too drunk to hold the pot."

"Who is drunk? See here, man: I hold on to this blade of grass and do not fall from the earth."

The men laugh loudly enough to wake the neighbouring oxen. Their eyes fall on me.

"Will you drink with us?" one says.

"I go to fetch water from the lake," I say.

They send roaring laughter to their friend Ceolmund, whose running has slowed along the western fields. A palm claps my shoulder—I smile at its hairy, mead-breathed owner as well as I can and hasten towards the lake. Should any of them follow me, I will hide myself among one of the many groves of elm trees along the way.

When I have left the easternmost of our fields, only

Aldewine follows me, flattening himself against empty furrows that do nothing to hide him. The aldorman's healer must not dwell far from here, unless Aldewine told those men the same kinds of tales that Alfred tells his father. I am a mother to neither of them, and as long as Aldewine does not ask me for a mother's kiss, he may as well be a wild cat hunting mice.

I make my way through thick elm trees whose snaking, tooth-leafed boughs I sweep aside with one arm. The lake stretches as long as five houses and as wide as two horses with water so clear that its mossy bed stares up at the sun unhindered. I fill my pot from amid tall reeds and bear its heavy load in both arms. Water spills from its mouth—I nearly trip over my own feet at the sight of Aldewine hiding behind a thin hedge near a grove of wych elms kin to those through which I came here.

"Aldewine," I call.

Again, he flattens himself against the ground. When I reach him, he hides his face in the earth: if he can not see me, I can not see him.

"If you lie here long enough, the aldorman's healer may find you and think you beyond healing," I say.

Aldewine stands in haste and runs back towards our fields. How long will it take him to find the aldorman's healer now? My return to our oak stump takes twice as long under the burden of a heavy pot made even heavier by the cold water that soaks into the wool of my gown. Our mead-drinking harvest helpers are gone but for three of them who sleep in the fields without their shirts. Whether they have won or lost their game, I do not know. Mother is not in our house; the weaving house's opening has taken a door, before which stands a wide cooking pot as high as my waist that will not yield to my shoulder. I set my ear against the timber: low grunts weave themselves between raspy breaths. I strike the door with my hand.

"Mother?" I say.

The sounds stop.

"Mother."

"I am feeling better," mother says from within. "We will not be long."

"Aldewine followed me to the lake," I say. "How did the healer find you so quickly?"

"Aldewine must have asked one of the men to fetch him," says mother. "Their legs are longer. They run better than he."

I have no wish to see Ceolmund's unclothed, flailing limbs a second time, so I close my eyes.

"Leave your water in the cooking pot until it is half-full," mother says.

"Why does it stand before the door?"

"To keep it from opening with the wind," says mother. "Go, child. The healer has work to do."

My steps are slower as I walk to the lake this time, for I will need ten pots of water to do what mother has asked of me. Aldewine has grown taller and wears a beard—this must be one of the men who comes to see that I take water from the lake and not from the river in which he and his friends empty themselves. I return to the cooking pot to find that all of the drunken men have won their game, for they have fallen asleep without their shirts next to whichever blade of grass they held to keep them from floating away into the heavens. Who, then, are those three men in brown that watch me from beyond the fields on my third walk to the lake?

When I kneel among the reeds to fill my pot, they have gone, yet on the northern bank of the water, a fleshy face stares up at the clouds. Did one of the drunken men come here to sate his thirst and fall asleep after having done so? I set my pot down and creep beside the tall grass to better see what he does here. This is no scythe-bearing man: he wears his yellow hair in a brass-bound tail; his leggings are blue rather than brown; his neck bears a thin strand of silver links; on his belly above his beltless leggings writhes a reddish-blue snake akin to Isadora's ink. My fingertips search the flesh of his arm for the warmth of life.

"What is this?" bellows a man.

It is not one man, but three. They stand over me in their brown clothing and leather shoes with knives hanging from their belts. The tallest of them grabs my arm and nearly takes it from my shoulder as he lifts me to my feet.

"What are you doing here?" he growls.

"Filling a water pot," I say. "For the men who drink mead."

"And what has this man to do with the water pot you do not bear?"

"I left it over there. I thought he might have fallen asleep. I came to wake him."

"Do you not see that he sleeps forever?"

He grasps my neck and shoves my head at the sleeping man. Fear and fire flood my arms and ribs. In my thoughts, I call to father, but he does not come.

"Why do you think he sleeps forever?" says the man.

"It may be that a dead bough from one of those elm trees fell on his head," I say.

"Did an elm tree put its mark on his belly?"

"I do not know."

"You *do* know, for the men of these fields along the stone path talk of a woman who calls the heavens to do her bidding. Show her."

A golden belt buckle with rough leather edges on both sides falls to the ground before me.

"Tell me you did not ask the heavens to strike down the aldorman's thane," he says.

"I did not," I say. "He walked away from me. If I had done that—"

His foot strikes the back of my legs. I fall to my knees with his fingers still squeezing my neck. I vomit on his shoes. He shakes them at the grass, sending bits of filth onto my gown as he does.

"Does your father have enough oxen and pigs and carts of wheat for the life of the aldorman's thane?" he says. "Do you even know how many he would need?"

The man unsheathes his long knife and sets its sharpened end against my throat. My mouth tastes of ashen ale-water; my innards threaten to empty themselves anew onto my legs; my face burns hotter than the sun. Fire and ice swell within me, gripping my breast and driving all breath from me. Before I can vomit on the man's shoes a second time, the knife he holds shatters into shards that bury themselves in the grassy earth around his feet.

He and his two friends run from me as well as any horse would. I take up one of the iron shards—its edges draw blood that darkens the yellow sleeves of my undergown. Aldewine comes to me wearing a face of stone that might only be softened by a thousand years of rain.

"How did you do that?" he says.

"I do not know," I say. "Have I done something?"

"I am to ask you whether you go to see the aldorman tomorrow."

"Is that why you came to our house?"

"I wished to see the woman as tall as a horse who breathes fire and walks with thunder."

"Who told you this?"

"My father. Everyone talks of it."

Aldewine steps past me to look at where the aldorman's thane lies in the water. I stand before him and turn his chin to me with the fingertips of my unbloodied hand.

"Tell whomever will listen to you that they need not speak of me," I say. "I will go to see the aldorman tomorrow."

Aldewine runs off—not towards our fields, but into the elm trees where those men must have awaited me. I take my pot from the reeds, leaving it empty of the lake's befouled water, and walk without stopping through our fields, where those shirtless men all snore the same song of dreamless drunkenness. No sooner have I set my clay pot down on the earth of our house than mother sits up from her bedding and washes my bloodied fingers. I tell her, in her tongue, what has happened. She looks at me from the side of her eyes with a frown for my many misspoken words until a sound from her tongue stops my speech.

"You did nothing, daughter," she says. "I do not know who those men are. I will go with you to the aldorman tomorrow and make him ask your forgiveness for keeping your father from you for so long."

"But your legs will not even let you go for a walk with me in the evening," I say.

"Would you rather have me welcome the aldorman into our home while I lie in bed and let him think that he might give you a little brother like Aldewine?"

"What? No."

"Lie down with me now. You do not leave the house again until tomorrow."

As I lie beside her, I think not on what the aldorman will say when we meet with him, but on how mother will speak to him in light of what she has said to her own daughter this day. As for me, I shall tell that boy Aldewine to find another older sister to follow around so that I may abide in peace.

3

ALDORMAN

My eyes open so often to ember-lit darkness that I know not whether I have slept when mother wakes me with the sun. She smooths and straightens my hair with her fingers as I tell her of my dream: I hid among our wheat stalks, where I watched those drunken men stand in a ring and send a ball of stone as tall as Alfred between themselves. Each man slowed the stone with weakening arms and leaned against it to stop it from flattening him. The stone grew heavier than an ox and taller and wider than Isadora's house. They saw me and sent it to me—it threw me to the ground and took the wind from my lungs. I woke to gasping breaths and cheeks wet with fear.

Mother rests her palm on my neck; she runs her thin-toothed comb of bone along the back of my head and down my matted strands of hair. My shoulders sink.

"I was awake all night," mother says. "Every time I looked at you, your eyes were closed. When I set my hand on you, your breaths did little to stir it."

"You should be too weary to see the aldorman, then," I say.

25

"I will sleep in the wheat cart drawn by our limping ox," she says. "He will make good meat for the aldorman and his men."

Men who draw knives and tell me I have killed. My head sinks along with my shoulders as their thorned words and faces burn themselves into my breast anew and grip my heart with icy fingers.

"I would not have you wear your own blood before the aldorman," mother says. "Take off your yellow and wear my old linen. The aldorman will think no less of you."

I sit upright and fold my arms. Mother's words float with the hearth's smoke into the thatch, where they hang over my head. A string of yellow elksand beads hangs over my left shoulder.

"Did your mother not give you these?" I say.

"Isadora calls them amber," says mother.

"What will shield you if you do not wear them?"

"You will."

Mother takes my bloodied sleeve between her fingers and shakes it.

"Let the aldorman see what men have done to me," I say.

Mother sighs. She ties the ends of her leather-strung amber beads around my gown pins and fastens my green wool to the yellow linen beneath it anew. As she stands, I stand with her; she leans against me so she does not send herself to the floor.

"Take me to the cart," she says. "You will only need to lead the ox. He will do the work for you."

Beyond the oak stump at the inner edge of our empty eastern rye fields stands our limping ox with one leg wrapped in linen. He is bound by leather straps to a wooden, wheat-laden cart as wide and long as he. I help mother onto a bed of dried stalks that crack as they take her back. I bundle her old green gown and set it beneath her head.

"Take the wooden bridge over the river and walk along Harold's fields until we reach the stone path," she says.

Under greying clouds I lead our ox through the furrows his brothers ploughed last year and will plough again after the long row of wheat carts at the outer edges of our fields has been given to the king by men who hide themselves as well as Alfred. Harold's empty fields are also empty of carts and the oats and barley his wife Hilda grinds from dawn to dusk for seven days so she may spend the rest of the year talking as she watches mother weave. Whether her husband has learned his idleness from her or she from him, mother has never told me. Our ox blinks slowly and hangs his head, as though he is ready to fall asleep.

"How far is the aldorman from here?" I say.

"Follow the path beyond the great grove of ash trees until the grass becomes sandy," mother says. "There you will find his house of stone."

I pull on the leather strap against our ox's unyielding neck. After some grunting, he steps forwards into the chalky grass with a sharp breath that stinks of the same.

"Is his house anything like Isadora's?" I say.

"I have never seen it," mother says. "The healer has only told me that it stretches further than any house we have seen among our neighbours' fields."

"What else has the healer told you?"

"How to sleep well when my head aches," says mother. "Do not wake me until we have reached the aldorman's mansio."

Isadora sits beside me in a candle's light as I read this word *mansio* from one of her many parchment sheets. When I turn to ask her of its meaning, she is without her gowns on her bedding and takes to her breast an unclothed man whose face I do not see. I shake my head and give our ox the rest he wishes. Mother opens her eyes and sits up as misty rain begins to fall.

"Why have you stopped?" she says.

"Do you lie with the healer in the weaving house as you do with father?" I say.

"No," she says. "He is a man of learning who shares with me what he knows of how to soothe the aching in my limbs and the swarming bees within my head."

I clutch mother's beads until my palm and fingers ache. From beneath her head I take her green woollen gown and spread it over the wheat heaped on both sides of her to shield her from the rain. With a kiss for her forehead, I bid her sleep so well that she will have forgotten her dreams when she wakes.

Our ox's steps become swifter when his hooves find the rain-smoothed stones of the old path laid by men from a dead kingdom that lives on in the thoughts and dreams of those who come after them. Where my gowns lie soaked with the heavens' gift against my chilly flesh, our ox's damp hide stinks even worse than his breath. Row after row of harvested fields at last give way to spindled birch trees whose leaves drink deeply from showering rain, then to great groves of bushy ash trees, then to meadows of sleeping red and white flowers, then to dewy green grass whose sandy earth I take between my toes.

Striking hooves sound somewhere in the mist further along the path. A hooded man in blue clothing rides his steed towards us in haste, slowing to a stop that leaves his horse's nose close enough to our ox to smell him and stamp backwards even as his master tells him not to. The rider greets us with a loud sigh.

"The aldorman awaits a young woman," he says, "not an ox and a cart."

"Does he not want these things?" I say. "My mother does not walk well and needs a bed."

"She may stay here while you come with me," says the rider. "You will not take much of the aldorman's time."

"You would have me leave my mother here?" I say. "Get out of my way."

His horse stamps its hooves. Its rider does not draw back his hood to show me who he is. Mother says nothing of what I should do—she must sleep in peace as the healer taught her. Or is this her nightmare that stands before me? I greet the steed with my fingertips and stroke its hair between its eyes until it bows its head to me, then greet its thick skull with my own, sending it backwards at a slow walk while I set my fingers to my hair where it has become bloody.

"Are you mad?" bellows the rider and throws back his hood. I wish he had not, for the flesh of his face unhidden by his beard is not as fair as his horse's. "If this is how you behave, your mother may rest with the cows in the wooden stalls at the aldorman's *mansio*."

The rider turns his horse around and runs off into the mist without waiting for us to follow. As I lead our ox along the stone path, the sun shows itself in the heavens for the first time this day and takes the rain from our heads. I give thanks for the warmth that dries my clinging gowns by muddying my feet with as much of this rain-drowned sand as I can so that I may give the aldorman a fitting greeting when we reach his *mansio*.

In the east, where the sun has risen from its bed, stands one of those old stone towns with many of its halls unbroken. Mother sits up in her cart, holding her green wool over her head, and tells me to walk on the stone path instead of the grass. I keep my head down until my feet are met by six more: three women in blue gowns wearing linen wrapped about their hair stare at me.

"Is she the mother?" one says to me.

"Here," says mother.

As one, they help mother from her wooden bed. The sturdiest of them lifts mother onto her back and bears her through the opening of a great hall whose walls are as tall as a man and half again. Brown and grey stones rest on top of and beside one another held together by that same clay between the stones of the path beneath our feet. Why anyone would build a dwelling from stones that stink of horse dung and set a roof of timber on top of it, I do not know. A brown-clothed man without a sheathed knife on his belt leads my ox into thatch-roofed wooden stalls against the western wall of the mansio. I follow the blue-gowned women through the mansio's opening, only to be met by a beak-nosed, yellow-haired man who sets a wide-mouthed pot of water at my feet.

"You may wash your feet before the aldorman sees you," he says.

He shows me teeth as yellow as his hair; the water in the pot is no clearer. I go to my knees and take in the rainwater's stench. As I rise, I wave my hand before my nose and cough.

"Did you stand astride this pot and fill it from between your legs?" I say.

The blue-clothed horseman who met us greets his friend with a clap on the shoulder and a loud laugh.

"You have given her the horse's pot, man," he says.

Together, their laughter fills the small room of stone. They are at once still—the honeyed speech of a man calls to them as though he sings a child to sleep.

"Send that young woman to me when you have seen to her salutary needs."

The horseman strides off into a great, open room, where rainwater lies in a pit. The pot-bearing man chokes on his own mirth.

"Forgive me," he says. "I shall gather water from the baths. Wait here."

When he has left, I walk through the opening in the wall before me and find myself lost in four neighbouring rooms that house wide brown pots bearing ground wheat, rye, barley, and oats; tall handled pots of shining red stone whose water stinks worse than the horse's pot; smoked fish and meat hanging from hooks fastened to beams of timber; and floors that have become smooth, white-grey, and somehow warm beneath my feet. I wander in search of that man who uses Isadora's words until I come to a long oaken table set with many chairs brought to life by the eastern sunlight streaming in from the broad, roofless room in which the rainwater pit lies. The walls behind the table are home to sunken shelves whose brass-bowled candles watch over ring-haired, rainbow-hued men with bearded faces so stern that they need carved stone to master their earnestness. On the other side of the table stands a man no taller than father with his back to me wearing a dark blue tunic trimmed with gold. His brown hair hangs between his shoulders in a tail bound by a long, thick clasp of golden snakes on a field of black.

"Why do you live in a house of stone?" I ask.

His cheeks and jaw are those of a newborn; his brown eyes are dim even in the sun-brightened wax-light; his silver-ringed fingers sound on the table as he sets his palms against it.

"Some of us are yet mindful of the old ways," he says. "The king and I are alike in this. You are Branwen's daughter?"

"Ardelle."

"You are as keen as your name declares." He looks over the table. "Did my men not offer you water for your feet?"

"Do your men wash their feet with a horse's urine?"

The aldorman grins.

"You may not believe this, but men once washed their clothing in such a way."

"And these are the old ways of which you are mindful."

"I am mindful of many things, not least of which the way in which you greeted my horse." He raises his chin and eyebrows towards my forehead. "Sit while I see whether my maids have heated the baths well enough to wash away what the rain has not."

No sooner has the aldorman left me than his faithful man, the master of the pots, kneels beside my chair and offers me his water once more. He takes my bare feet without asking and washes the mud from them, whereafter he dries them with white cloth. He is as silent as these men of stone, whose bodies and clothing end below their shoulders. Beneath all but one of them, words have been carved from the letters found in Isadora's books. The aldorman's nameless forefather bears a pear-shaped nose and sallow cheeks.

"What is the aldorman's name?" I ask.

"That is only for his dearest friends to know," says the man as he stands bearing his pot. "You will not have been the first to become friends with him so quickly."

He smiles without opening his mouth and leaves me. When the aldorman returns, the face of his stone forefather has become friends with the floor. The aldorman sets one of those tall red handled pots down on the table and makes a sound with his tongue.

"Did you two see battle while I was away?" he asks.

"He would not tell me his name," I say.

"And so you have broken his nose." The aldorman takes his forefather from the floor, leaving the shards of his face behind, and lays him to rest on the wall shelf. "You have won, yet so has he, for you still know nothing of his name. If you had shown him the kindness of friendship, he might have given it to you ere you left."

"My mother has given you her name. Does that mean that you and she are friends?"

"That man you overthrew was Marcus Aurelius, the last of the Roman imperators, who led his golden imperium through a time of peace few have seen since. What you have done to him is what many of his foes sought to do, and yet he lived longer than any of them. Thus, it is he who still stands, much like the king for whom your father fights."

The aldorman sets the red pot closer to me. I grasp its handles and set it down at once—it stinks worse than Alfred's breath would if he had eaten too many apples and far too much honey.

"Are all the pots in your mansio befouled?" I say.

The aldorman laughs to himself. He takes up the pot and drinks from it, then offers it to me once more. I hide my nose beneath my linen undergown. I know not how he can abide such things.

"Your father drinks the same in the king's halls," he says. "I am told he finds his strength again after having taken a spear while he bore a shield against our western foes." My gown falls from my nose. "His sacrifice has won us a fleeting peace which the king seeks to make lasting."

My limbs come to life with the chill winds that sweep through our fields after the snow has melted. I take up the tall red pot and drink deeply of the burning ashes that swim within. I gasp until the fire in my breast softens into warmth.

"Have you read books that you know such words?" I say.

"Books, codices, parchments," says the aldorman. "I have read many things. I understand that you have done the same."

"Some. Not many."

"And have you also learned to write?"

"I have gone with mother's friend Isadora to gather oak apples for ink, but she would not show me how to use her writing feather."

"Your mother's friend is wise. Men look unkindly on things they do not understand."

I drink again from the red pot. The apples are not so bitter, now.

"Wood that splits itself," the aldorman says. "A belt that comes undone by no man's hand. A thane's body in a lake. How do these things come to be?"

I swallow the honey-water twice more and slide the pot over the table to the aldorman's hand. My body is on fire; my head spins; my throat retches without sound.

"Words are written," says the aldorman. "Words are spoken, within or without. Men fear a great many things, but they fear most of all that which they neither see nor hear. Those like you are followed by such men, or they are driven from their homelands as your friend Isadora must have been."

"You know her?" I say.

"The king knows her well and understands her better. He takes in those who would suffer at the hands of men who fear them." He sets a brown, wide-mouthed pot—the one in which my feet were washed—beside its tall red sister. "Do you know what the king does to those who harm his daughters?"

The aldorman grips the mouth of the brown pot and lifts his arm. Behind me, something shatters. My head swims with weary heaviness that keeps me from turning to see what has happened.

"He crushes them into nothingness," says the aldorman. "His thyle, who writes his histories, has not even the memory of a name to give to the strokes of her writing feather."

"What of your stone forefather?" I say.

"The name Marcus Aurelius is written in the heavens and on this earth," says the aldorman, "yet he who says he is king is not, and so our king would make them remember his name and deeds in another way. Most in these lands have forgotten the strength of the old imperium, nameless men such as those who brought you here and washed your feet. I have told them to leave you be. Likewise, I might speak to the king on your behalf and tell him how you suffer without your wounded father, who has fought well for him. He might be swayed to the thought of leaving you be for a time—until next year's harvest—if we were to find something within you that he does not like."

The aldorman sets his outstretched hand on the table. I give him mine without a thought.

"I will have my healer look over you," he says, "whereafter he will tell me of your sore sickness. We shall tell the king you must be permitted to stay at home until your illness has left you. Your mother might be the one who knows best when you are healthy again."

"Where is my mother?"

"She rests in a room. I understand she slept little yesternight."

"Does your healer look after her now? I would go to her and speak with her of this."

"My healer must be brought from his home south of here. My maid will help you bathe while you wait."

My thoughts sink down into my ribs, where they swim alongside my heart in the warmth of slow-flowing waters.

"I will see your healer," I say, "then my mother."

"I am off to fetch her," says the aldorman as he rises. "A warm bath stands ready for you; one of my maids will come and lead you hither. My name is Constantine, offspring of Marcus Aurelius, whose foes have been forgotten by history. The men you met at the lake, living and dead, are likewise forgotten." The aldorman takes the red pot by one handle as he leaves. "Thank you for your kindness, Ardelle. I will beg my horse's forgiveness on your behalf."

My head has become so light that I do not know I have walked anywhere until I am made to stand still amid white-grey walls brightened by sunlight that streams in through long gaps near the roof. The young woman who helps me take off my gowns wears the aldorman's dark blue with her sleeves tied above her elbows and her gown bundled beneath her belt so that her knees show. The golden hair that rests on her shoulders is honey; the flesh of her arms and legs is milk; her eyes are the river that flows not far beyond our fields.

"Why do you stare?" she asks.

"Are you the maid who helped my mother with her brown gown?" I say.

"Yes," she says.

"I ask myself what your name might be."

"Why do you not ask me? I am Winiburg. I have been told that you are called Ardelle. Step into the bath while I ready the bed."

"This bed you speak of is a stone with hard edges."

"I will set soft bedding on it while you soak yourself. Mind the stones—they are hot." She makes a sound. "I will have to wash your linen in the patio."

I step down into water above my shoulders whose warmth is somehow greater than that within me. The stone floor of the bath yields as well as any grass. I rest for a while with my eyes closed as I think on what a patio must look like. I open them to Winiburg, who lifts my wet hair and wrings the bathwater from it.

"We have not time to wash the blood from your head," she says. "Run your hands along your legs and feet to clean them for the healer. Your neck is filthy."

I wash myself while her fingers clean the flesh on my back and arms. She rests one hand on my shoulder as she digs her thumbs into the back of my neck. I set my fingers on hers. Her thumbs become still.

"Do you need something?" she says.

I shake my head. My hand stays where it is. Winiburg's face is beside mine. I turn to meet her eyes—she draws away as she breathes in through her nose.

"He must have given you wine," she says with a laugh. "Your face is red. Oh, there you are. Ardelle, the healer is ready for you. Come."

My body is as heavy as the stone against which it rests. Hands are beneath my arms; Winiburg has not the strength to lift me. She takes my right arm over her shoulders and rests her left hand on my hip. I am at once as light as any bird, sending water onto Winiburg's feet and wetting her gown where she holds me. When we reach the bed, she works a great cloth of white wool against the flesh of my back and arms and neck; on seeing that I do nothing to take the cloth from her, she dries my shoulders and belly and legs and feet until the healer clears his throat from beneath the hood of white wool that hides his face from me.

"Onto the bed," says Winiburg and hangs her wool over one shoulder.

"Where is my linen?" I say.

"Soaking in the patio's rainwater," says Winiburg. "You may wear it again when it has dried."

I have not yet lain down on the wool bedding when the healer takes my left arm and pulls on it as if he were trying to wrest it from my body. He does likewise with my right arm and with my legs. He looks at my teeth, searching for those in the back that have fallen out. He sets his hand on Winiburg's shoulder and whispers to her.

"The healer wishes to see whether you bear a child," Winiburg says without looking at me. "He will put a clove of garlic between your legs and wait until your flesh has fully dried, whereafter he will take in your breath. If it stinks of garlic, the king will know that the sore burning in your belly that keeps you from coming to him is not a child who hinders the paths within your body. Now, lie down, close your eyes, and breathe through your mouth."

The roof of grey stone becomes a starless night as I breathe in and out as Winiburg told me. After I have suffered through this, father might return to us and stay until next year's harvest. Longer, if I hide myself away as Alfred does and show the king that mother has none other to keep her. Having lain in stillness for some time, I open my eyes to see what the healer does and wish I had not: his manhood shows as I have seen of the scythe-men when they empty themselves of the day's water. I slide away from him, taking the wool bedding with me as I sit up. Winiburg stands in the room's opening bearing red and white gowns beneath which the end of a wooden stirring rod hides. She smiles at me; my heart quickens.

"You wished to see that I do not bear a child," I say to the healer. "What is this you do?"

The healer draws back his hood and shows me the aldorman's pear-nosed, sallow-cheeked face wet with sweat.

"I must draw the blood from between your legs else it will hide the garlic's stench," he says. "Should the king send his healers to do the same, I will tell them that I have lain with you but gave you no child. I will go with them and ask the king's forgiveness, whereafter he may send your father back to you at once."

"I am not his daughter, nor am I ready to have one of my own."

Winiburg sets one finger against her lips as she draws nearer to the aldorman with the stirring rod in her hand.

"Seventeen winters are enough to bear a child and the king knows this," says the aldorman. "We must show him that you have been faithful."

"Faithful to whom? How do you lie with a woman and not give her a child?"

Winiburg steps so softly behind him that he does not mark her or the gowns that fall from her arms or the wooden rod she wields. My fist strikes the aldorman's face before I know that my arm has stirred. He falls from the bed onto the floor as a hewn alder tree falls into a marsh. Winiburg's smiling face becomes even fairer as her loud laughter shows me teeth as white as the snowy linen she takes from the floor.

"I have long wished to see this," she says as she shakes with glee. "Your linen will take some time to dry. Wear these."

She hands me the red and white gowns and begins to help me into them—the aldorman looks as though he might stand. I flee through the bathing room's narrow opening and make my way to that great roofless patio where my yellow linen gown soaks in the rainwater pit. I find mother in a neighbouring room, wherein two blue-gowned women not half as fair as Winiburg knead the flesh of mother's arms and legs. Their eyes widen at the sight of me without my clothing.

"Daughter," mother says, "what on earth is wrong with you?"

"The aldorman," I say. "I know what you do with him."

Mother stands with greater haste than I have ever seen. She growls a curse in her tongue that sends the aldorman's women running. Winiburg is before me, slinging the red wool over her shoulder as she helps me into the white linen.

"Forgive me," Winiburg says.

"You knew of this?" says mother.

"Not as soon as I should have."

Winiburg takes the golden breastpins from her own shoulders, leaving her blue wool to hang down over her belt, and fastens my red wool to the white linen beneath it. She reaches into a leather bag on her belt.

"Take this shilling as a token of your forgiveness for me," she says. She sets the shilling on my palm and closes my fingers around it. "I will lie with the aldorman for you."

"Which you should have done before any of this," says mother. "Take me to the cart, daughter."

"Where?" I say. "Winiburg might show us."

"She is the aldorman's maid who serves him. She knows well enough what she does. I would have my daughter, who did not come here with her father as she should have, at least heed her mother and take her to the cart among the horses so we may leave this wretched mansio and never return. Where are the beads I gave you?"

"In the patio," says Winiburg and leaves with a kiss for my cheek.

Having taken mother's amber beads from my soaked and bloodied yellow linen, I help her to the wooden stalls. There, our wheatless cart is also without mother's green gown and the ox that bore her here, so I am left to pull its two handles with the strength of the lightning that runs through my arms and legs. Mother's sharp curses find no hooks within me; I tell her using every word I remember from Isadora's books how much I love her, and how from this day forth, I will only think of doing what she and father tell me to.

4

FLIGHT

As I haul mother back to our fields, my eyes mark the clay-bound sandstone beneath my feet so that I may know the way home without showing myself the worm-ridden earth that will one day lie beside the aldorman in his grave. Winiburg's red and white gowns end at my shins, having been woven for someone much shorter than I, but they are warm enough to keep her in my mind: she stands in the opening to the aldorman's mansio before a heap of hewn stone that was once the bathing room's bed, waving to me with a smile even as mother curses her.

"Take us from the path, Ardelle," mother says.

As soon as the earth is beneath my feet, striking hooves send me back to the path. The blue-clothed horseman who runs through the rain-soaked grass heeds the far-off groves of spreading ash trees better than the beings of flesh who would have made way for him had he but slowed his steps long enough to see it done. His horse leaves its thanks for our thoughtfulness from between its hind legs. I take mother's cart from the path to go around it.

"We once held our houses together using dung," says mother.

"The aldorman did say he was mindful of the old ways," I say.

"He is not the only one," says mother. "I lived in a house of rotting timber when I met your father. He was the one who took our cow droppings and closed the gaps against the night winds that froze my bones. Not long after that, you came to us."

"Do you hate Winiburg?" I say.

"The young woman?" says mother. "I would have forgotten her had you not told me her name. Why do you ask?"

"Will she come to our house again?"

"Only the aldorman knows whom he will send to us after today."

Her words take my feet back to dungless stones still wet with rain. I stop to gather my hair and hide it beneath my gowns should the clouds choose to shower us once more. Stamping hooves are beside us with such swiftness that I start away from mother's cart. Some among the horses' riders yell curses at me. How am I to know which of them wish me to make way? And where would I go when so many of them ride around me on both sides?

"Do not ask me whether you are to take their dung for our house," says mother when they have gone. "I will sleep in silence if my horse will let me."

It is not until I walk through the meadows before our fields that I understand whither they have gone: those same horses are bound to our harvest carts along with our oxen. Their riders stand among scythe-bearing men as they watch our swine run about the oak stump and into the wheatless furrows. One of them lowers his brow at me as I set down mother's cart.

"Take off that gown," he says. "Others will think ill of you
—and of us."

"Others think what they will of me whether I wear gowns
or not," I say.

Mother sets her hands on my shoulders as she stands from
her wooden bed.

"These carts were to have left this morning," she says. "The
aldorman gave her these gowns before she goes to see the
king."

"The aldorman would not have given her those to wear,"
says the horseman who walks towards us.

His eyes are shot with redness; his thick brown hair stands
on end; his breath drowns my nose in mead. His leggings
show no mark of having been made wet in his sleep, which I
take to mean he did not wear them. His fingers hold one of the
golden breastpins at my shoulders. Mother strikes his hand
away.

"You would rather drink than take the king's wheat to
him," says mother.

She sets her arms about my waist and leans against me.

"I would rather not be struck down as the aldorman was
by the men who will see your daughter in those gowns," says
the horseman.

"Struck down?" says mother. "What do you mean?"
Mother takes her arms from me and rests one hand on my
shoulder. "Ardelle, what does he mean?"

"Winiburg struck the aldorman with a stirring rod," I say.

Mother looks into my eyes, then at the men who stare with
arms folded, then at the dried blood above my forehead.

"Winiburg," she says.

Her frown sends my eyes to her feet. She turns away
from me.

"Take my hair in your fist where it becomes a braid," she
says.

I hold mother's woven strands of brown hair in limp fingers near the back of her head.

"You, who rode his horse around my cart without cursing my daughter," says mother. "Take your knife and shear my hair above my daughter's hand. I will give it to the aldorman to keep as a token of his forgiveness."

"Mother, you must not—"

"How many horses rode by us?" says mother in her tongue. "You do not know? Do you know how many times you told me you will do as I say from this day forth?"

The horseman stands before me with his unsheathed knife held beside his leg. I step back from mother with her braid still in my grasp. With three swift strokes, the horseman shears mother's braid from shortened hair that she smooths against the back of her head. Who is this that turns to look at me?

"Take twine from the house and bind the hair," she says. "While you are there, take off those gowns and wear whatever you find among my bedding. You will give the red and white gowns and breastpins and shillings to the horsemen along with my braid and whatever else the aldorman's maid left with you."

She begins to unfasten the brass pins from the shoulders of the brown gown Winiburg gave to her.

"Must I give them everything from Winiburg?" I say.

"Is she more worthy of your love than I?" says mother.

"Father and I said we would go to the king and not the aldorman," I say.

"And so your father is with the king but you are not," she says.

The top of her brown gown falls down over her grey linen waist-belt and hangs there lifelessly. Her eyes are the ends of long knives drawn from their sheathes. This is not my braid-less mother who speaks to me, but someone else. Someone who has forgotten her love for me.

My feet take me through our western fields beneath brooding white clouds that call my name in mother's tongue. I hasten through ankle-high grass to a grove of bushy chestnut trees, wherein I hide as I bind this thick braid of brown around my neck. Among carts no greater than the reddish-brown fruit on the ground all around me, mother stands amid men who ready horses and oxen as though they did not spend a thousand words telling her why they could not. I will go, then, to Isadora, who has more words than any of them, and tell her of what we did in the aldorman's mansio. She will tell mother and those men whether what I have done is right or not.

I weave through boughs of birch whose leaves hide me from the dwellings of men and the keen ears of playing children and the seeking eyes of the mothers who watch over them. It is in a small clearing beneath spreading chestnut trees that my toes and shins find a stone hidden among the bramble. The white runes carved into its grey body speak to me in a tongue that Isadora never taught me. I sit down before it with folded legs, take mother's beads from my belt bag, and string them between Winiburg's golden breastpins at my shoulders. Having done this, I set my hands on the runestone, close my eyes, and think on what Isadora would tell me of its meaning.

During those summers when my words became as hot as my burning face, father would come in from shearing tall grass for the king's horses and bring me to Isadora's house of stone. There, mother's friend, whom mother loved so much that she called Isadora her sister, sat me down among many dried cow hides she called parchment. She filled my summer days by teaching me to read the ink they bore and how best to use their words when I spoke to her—and only to her.

"Should you forget what I have told you and someone asks where you have learned these words," she said, "you must tell them that you have seen *codices*. They may think that you speak of the bodies of trees whereon young lovers carve the runes of their names."

One night, when the moon woke among the stars and I had read everything in Isadora's house, Isadora brought a candle to the table beside her bed along with bound sheafs bearing tall, flowery strokes. I sat for a time and whispered aloud the dark dreams written down in our tongue by the king's daughters. I was never to tell anyone that I had read them, not even mother and father, for if I did, they might think I had gone mad. Isadora told me little of the meaning of those dreams; her childlike answers as she blew the life from the candlelight made me laugh in the starless darkness of her stone house. In the morning, I woke to find the parchment sheets in ashes on the floor beside my reading candle.

Rustling leaves draw my eyes to green and yellow shapes stirring among the chestnut trees.

"We should talk to her," comes a whisper.

A woman wearing folded green-grey linen on her mouse-brown hair steps out from behind a tree. She bears a small clay pot in her hands. When I stand to greet her, she treads on her own brown gown and nearly falls over.

"What do you wish to talk to me about?" I say.

At once, men show themselves all around me bearing short knives and sticks and stones; behind me towers an ox of a man with a bushy red beard who rests a long, thick oak bough against his shoulder, as though he takes a spear to fish in the river.

"Ask her," says the ox-man.

The woman bearing the pot steps forwards.

"Have you come to take our children?" she says.

"I have not," I say.

"She is out during the day," says a stick-wielding man to my right. "I thought they only came at night."

"She must do something else, then," says the woman with the pot.

"I go to see the king," I say.

"She comes for the king's children," says the woman. She steps backwards as she searches the eyes of the men around her. "We should warn his thanes."

"If she comes for the king's children," says the ox-man, "there is little you could do to stop her, Sithebad."

"Do not tell her my name!" says Sithebad. "I have not told her yours!"

"You are right," he says with a deep laugh. "In the bushes I see one of those stones with markings. She may carve your name on it, now."

Sithebad grabs her gown with one hand and runs off, spilling water from her clay pot as she does. Four of her friends follow her. I am left with an ox and five men on all sides who step towards me as one would a snake that has not yet bared its fangs.

"I live not far from here," I say to them. "The aldorman has given me these gowns to wear to the house of my mother's friend, who will take me to the king."

"Then the aldorman's wisdom is beyond my ken," says a knife-man.

"I have heard of a maid who shattered a knife like yours and slew the aldorman's thane," says the ox-man. "Do you know of what I speak, brother?"

The ox's brother steps backwards without taking his eyes from me, as do his friends. One of them takes a stone from the leaves at his feet and hides behind a tree. Seeing this, the others do the same. Only the ox stands with me.

"Do you mean to see whether she breaks your stones before they strike her head?" he says. "You might find the answer by asking her. Is that what will happen, sister in red?"

My mouth opens, yet I will it shut, for I am mindful of Isadora's warning that I must not use her words with anyone but their keeper, and it is such words I would use to talk to these men who have no mind for them. In their stead, I use my feet, walking as slowly towards them as they did away from me. One of the men drops his stone along with his knife and flees into the trees. His friends soon follow him, leaving their weapons behind. The great ox lets his oak bough fall to the ground.

"Well done," he says and walks away.

I wait for a while to see whether the men will return; when they do not, I keep myself low to the ground until I have reached the river at the edge of the trees. I know not whether it is shallow enough to walk through, nor would I weigh myself down by soaking my red gown, nor would I bear Winiburg's gift above my head as I walk through the river's water and show stone-throwing men where I am. Must I leave it here?

Something strikes the nearby grass, then makes a sound as it goes beneath the water. Did it fall from the heavens, or was it from somewhere among—my eyes mark everything twice, now. The bones beside my left eye sting beneath my fingertips. I lie down in the reeds and there find a small stone. The smoke and stench of burning takes my back from the earth: those men have returned, one of whom bears bundled rushes and tree bark that falls in cinders from where he holds it at arm's length. Sithebad stands not far behind them, clutching her pot like she might a newborn child as the man readies himself to throw his burning bundle.

The winds that stir within my breast quench his fire and send him to the ground along with his friends. They find their feet in haste and yell curses as they flee into the oaks. Only Sithebad stays to take up her unbroken pot. She looks at me the way mother once did when I was so ill I could not stand from my bedding.

"I did not mean to ...," she says.

As I stand, she looks behind her and calls out. When her eyes meet mine again, they are those of a wounded fox. My back strikes the earth so hard that I cough up my own throat's water onto my gown. My nose is no longer straight; blood runs down onto my lips and chin; my shaking fingers take hardened shards of clay from my neck and ribs. When my breath is once again steady, I sit up. Bees swarm within my head. I creep to the river on hands and knees and there wash the blood from my face.

"She is still there!" calls a man.

I am in the river's water at once—it is far colder than any ice or snow. I am heavier than ten oxen, as are the rough and frosty breaths that threaten to leave me altogether as the water comes up to my waist and ribs. My feet find mud, sand, and stones as the water reaches my shoulders. Though I know not how to swim, I thrust myself towards the other bank. My soaked wool weighs me down so well that I can do nothing more than creep along the riverbed as my breast swells. When I feel as though I am about to burst, my outbreath sounds through the water, taking the aching from my lungs. I stroke mother's braid with my fingers, then make my way along smooth stones until they become sand, then moss, then grass. I haul myself out of the water, cough up the river's gift to my innards, and lie on my back in my drenched clothing until my heaving breaths slow. Above me flit many small red wights whose feather-like bodies are blessed with a weightlessness that sends them flying with the wind. Without warning, they flee: a hooded man in dark clothing stands within a longboat that drifts along the river though he wields no oar and no man rows his ship. He sets his long, thin black staff against the grass before my feet, bringing his boat to rest.

"You must give a gift," he says.

His words are the low, bellowing thunder that sounds before a mighty rain shower. I reach within my leather belt-bag, wherein I find mother's twine, iron rods for cleaning my fingernails and ears, and Winiburg's shilling. I set the gold on the boatman's bony fingers and sit down on the beam of timber at his shins. Grassy earth and reeds go by so swiftly that my eyes soon become weary from following them. The boatman strikes his staff against the side of his boat: there, in water whose mossy bed glows with the blood moon's wan light, floats a man's shirtless back. The boatman turns him over with his staff—worms writhe in the gaps between his yellow teeth; he wears a thin band of silver links on his neck; his belly bears snaking marks of reddish-blue ink above his waist.

"Those who drown sleep forever," says the boatman. "He was mine to take, yet another brought him here. Did your hand do this?"

"I only found him," I say. "And his body was in a lake, not a river."

"Tell me who sent him."

"I do not know."

"Your lies hinder my forgiveness. If you seek peace beyond, you must tell the truth."

He drops his staff into the river and grasps the top end of it before it leaves him. He lifts it from the water, hand over bone-fingered hand, drawing the thane's body with it. Far from where I sit, an ink-like snake strikes down from the darkness, rending the bough from a leafless oak tree and sending it to the ground. It has become wood to be burned on a hearth, made so by lightning from the cloudless midnight heavens. Lightning that breaks the golden buckle from a leather belt and leaves its edges in dust and ash. Lightning that has written itself on this man's flesh. It did not come from my fingers, nor from my thoughts, nor from any words I have spoken; and yet I would not have this boatman take mother or father to his unearthly abode, nor would I send myself to dream beneath the water beside the aldorman's thane.

"I sent him here," I say.

"As did you send yourself," says the boatman. "Until you offer your blood, you shall find no peace."

The boat comes to rest against the river bank. I alight and behold that faceless man until he has withdrawn into the darkness of night. Bright white stars show themselves among their red friends, who fall like feathers and dance about me as I make my way along the river. In time, darkness yields to bleakness: dull white clouds drift high above harvest grass that has begun to brown though winter will not be with us for some months; trees shed their worm-eaten leaves; a widening river foams with icy froth. I have become weary, and such watery cold does not make for a good bedside friend, but I lie down beside it nonetheless to rest my aching feet and still the thoughts brought to life by sweeping draughts of chill wind whose frosty fingers are somehow welcome on my flesh.

The red wights lie down beside me, warming me as they whirl about before my eyes like the little light from Isadora's bedside candle. One of them sets down to rest on my lips. I open my mouth to take in its weightless body—it floats away from me towards the river. I sit up at once and throw myself at it, swallowing the wight as I wrest handfuls of the river bank's grass from the ground and slide halfway down into the water. The wight smacks of a sickly sweetness that burns my ribs and threatens to hurl them from my mouth through lips wet with spit. I rest my forehead against the earth. My breast heaves, though I retch up nothing.

Hands are beneath my shoulders. The arms that take me are too weak to pull me from the water. I will my feet to take me up the river bank's slippery slope onto dry grass, where I rest against a gold-fastened gown of black wool.

"What in the world were you doing in that river?" asks Isadora. "And why do you wear a red gown?"

"The aldorman's maid gave it to me," I say. "Mother sent me to come and find you."

Isadora's brittle fingers feel along my cheekbone. I grunt when she squeezes my broken nose between her forefinger and thumb.

"I do not believe a word you have said," she says. "Red is worn by the king's daughters within their sanctuary, those whose dreams you have read. Never do they wear this hue where others can see it. It is a wonder that you were not— what is this bruise on your temple?"

"My what?"

"Here," says Isadora and sets her fingers against the bone beside my left eye.

"That hurts," I say.

"What hurts me is to see my sister's daughter like this. Come to my house and we will find you something else to wear. We will burn that red gown or cut it into tatters if the fire will not take it, and you will speak no word in opposition. Do you understand me?"

"Yes, Isadora."

"Thereafter, you will explain to me how you have come to know the aldorman so well that his maid gives you such *gifts*."

Isadora takes Winiburg's golden breastpins and mother's beads from me. I unfasten my belt and let the red gown fall to the ground. I place my hand in the crook of her arm and follow her fleeting steps as I shake with cold. The words that came to me so readily when I spoke to mother of all the ways in which I would heed her have left me. For Isadora, who keeps the king's laws and histories and the dreams of his daughters, there are no words I can think of that would tell her of anything other than how little I have learned from her.

5

ISADORA

Isadora stands a head shorter than I, yet she leads me by the hand to her house of stone hidden away amid shedding oak leaves and yellowing maple boughs. Where Isadora's shoes tread on the hard shells of fallen acorns nestled among soft leaves, I step aside to spare my bare feet. Within her house, Isadora closes her oaken door and bars it with a beam of the same, leaving only the dull glow of the hearth's ashen embers and the sunlight streaming in through the door's gaps to play on the long, thin golden hair clip that holds Isadora's black strands in a short tail.

"Rake away the ashes and breathe the hearth to life," she says.

While I clear the ashes with her iron striking flint, she takes up a cooking knife on the other side of the hearth, where her bedding lies, and begins to cut my red gown into tatters. I blow on the embers, thereby giving life to my aching head more than anything else. When Isadora looks up from her work, I hide my stinging, broken nose behind cupped fingers. Her sharp outbreath takes my hand from my face, whereafter I warm and dry myself before a slowly waking fire that takes its eventide meal of fallen oak leaves and the aldorman's blood wool in silence. Isadora feeds the hearth rough gown tatters, only to see them cough up black smoke without burning.

"You may now explain to me, child, how it is that you have come to know the aldorman so well."

"Have I done something wrong?" I ask.

"I will not have you answer me with questions of your own."

"I took mother to the aldorman to ask him to speak with the king and have him send father back from his battles."

"Branwen told me nothing of your father's participation in the king's battles."

"She has been … she lies with the aldorman—the aldorman's healer in our weaving house, yet father does not return. She did not wish anyone to know of this."

Isadora's knife rests on my red gown along with her palms. Her small brown eyes look as though they wish to harden, but her rounded cheeks and the soft lines of her jaw will brook no such unkindness. She sighs.

"Were your mother to hear you speak of her so …"

"May I have her beads?" I say.

"To take the place of the rope you wear around your neck?" she says.

Isadora's sharpened fingernails pick at mother's woven strands.

"Mother's braid bound with twine," I say. "She swore to give it to the aldorman when father came back to us, but now she sends it to the king."

Isadora takes up her knife and cuts into my red gown in earnest.

"Give me the hair," she says as the hearth's flames reach their greatest height.

I stand and step back towards the door. Isadora's eyes and eyebrows follow me.

"Why would your mother take her own hair, which she has so often told me is the wellspring of her strength, and give it to another?"

"Alfred, the boy from the neighbouring fields, said I split wood with lightning," I say. "The aldorman sent his thane to fetch me. When he grasped his knife hilt, his belt buckle fell to the ground without its belt. Later, I found him dead in the lake with reddish-blue snakes on his chest."

"Purple," says Isadora. She does not look up. "That is the name for that hue. You tell many tales today."

"Men came to me wielding knives when I sat before a runestone," I say. "They followed me to the river and threw stones at me. One of them, a maid named Sithebad, broke a clay pot against my face."

"How is it that you came to know her name?"

"Her friend spoke it."

"Should you see Sithebad again, you must show her the kindness she did not show you. Go on."

"I walked through the river and became so weary that I fell asleep on the other side. I dreamed of a dark man on a boat, who took the golden shilling the aldorman's maid Winiburg gave to me. He brought me to where the two rivers meet and showed me the thane's body floating there. He told me I had murdered him. I could not speak against this, so I said that I had done it. He said I would not know peace until I had given him my blood."

"Keep your mother's hair, then," Isadora says as she looks up. "Come here and sit next to me."

My shoulder rests against hers as she works her knife through the aldorman's gift with great strain.

"You should have gone to the king at once, not the aldorman," she says, "but you could not have known this, nor could your mother or father."

"Shall I write down my dreams and read them for you so you can burn them?"

"You will do no such thing. I will take you to the king's halls myself when the moon is high in the sky and men are asleep in their beds. We will reach the king before those men have risen with the sun."

Isadora sets her fingertips on my temple once more, then my nose.

"Will you see to these wounds now?" I ask.

"I know nothing of how to do so, though the king's healers may." Isadora shakes her head. "I should not have shown you those dreams. Those men who followed you fear the women who wrote them: the 'sisters in red' who come at night to steal children away from their mothers."

"The men in our fields told me to take off that red gown but would not tell me why," I say. "If they had told me—"

"If one man had told you of the meaning of that red gown, when next his friend's wife or child became ill, whom do you think they would blame?"

"Me?"

"You would lie beneath the earth before they did. They would go to the man who gave life to the unspoken thoughts of every other man there and set upon him with stones and knives and burning rushes."

Isadora cuts into the red gown once more.

"That is why it must be burned," I say.

"Yes," says Isadora, "but not while you are wearing it. Once you have dried, you may hide beneath my bedding and sleep. I will do the same when I have mastered this unyielding wool."

When my linen has dried, I lie down beneath Isadora's bedding and stare up at the straw-like threads of her roof. I should ask her whether she ever climbs on top of the thatch to take the fallen feathers of wayward birds who seek to help her with her writing. It is with one of those white-boned feathers that I would write of the dark boatman whose hidden face greets me as my eyes become heavy with sleep. In the day's waning light, Isadora's frown softens amid black smoke from the unburned shreds of my gown. She takes them from the embers with iron tongs and sets them in a small heap.

"Isadora," I whisper. "Do you think mother and father—"

"Still your tongue," whispers Isadora. "I will look to see whether anyone listens."

The oaken door opens slightly while Isadora is away, bathing the four angles of her stone walls in amber dusk. She makes little sound as she sets the wooden door beam in its iron arms and lies down beside me with her elbow against mine.

"Your father is alive," she whispers, "else the king would have sent someone to your fields. Your mother goes to him with your wheat."

"I should not have left her," I say.

"You should not have. There is nothing you can do now but go to her in the king's halls and ask her forgiveness."

Isadora takes the golden clip from her hair and the golden breastpin from her neck. She takes off her black gown and bundles it beneath our heads.

"Rest your eyes and words, now," she whispers.

When the darkness of night falls and sleep will not come to me, I can do little more than bury my face in Isadora's wool and listen to the fleeting sounds of flightless birds and acorn-seeking boars. For a long while thereafter, nothing more than Isadora's breaths fill the empty stillness. I set my forehead against her shoulder and find a fitful sleep harried by a man in dark clothing who comes to us from the river.

I wake to wan moonlight filtering in through the half-open

door. The bones of my head and face ache as Isadora lifts me from the ground. Wool weighs heavily on my shoulders. Isadora fastens what must be her bedding at my neck with her golden hair clip. I hold the folds of wool against my shaking body.

"I would give you my own gown were you small enough to wear it," she whispers.

"Whither do we go?" I say. "Is it far?"

Isadora sets her forefinger against her lips.

"We will walk south to the Roman road, then follow that west to the alder marshes near Durovernum, where we will hide until morning. The king's thanes are never far from his halls."

"His thanes?" I whisper. "Are his thanes like the aldorman's thane?"

"They stand above the aldorman in both might and wisdom," whispers Isadora. Her fingertips give greater life to the dull aching in my nose and cheeks. "He will look kindlier on us when we tell him that we go to the king to ask for his help. For now, you must keep your words to yourself. Take my arm below my shoulder and do not let go. If you need to rest or empty yourself of the night's water, pull on my elbow. If you are so careless as to lose me, you must wait in silence until I have found you again."

Isadora leads me into starlit darkness. I know not whither we go, only that my feet see better than my eyes and yet worse than Isadora's hands, for in straying even two steps from her side, I twice strike my head against the low-hanging boughs of trees. Thereafter, she holds my hand and helps me forget the scythe-shaped moon that hangs over my head and threatens to fall should we come to a river along which the boatman might meet us. Where we find the hardening earth of harvested fields, Isadora makes her way to their edges and bids us creep alongside them in the grass so none will know that we have been there.

When, at long length, Isadora's wool has warmed my body and my face is hardened against stinging by the night's chill winds, my feet find the welcoming stones of the path that will serve as our eyes until dawn's light greets us. Isadora hands me her leather shoes and asks me to bear them so that she may spare the ears of men who rise before the sun. Only her woollen hose shield her feet from the grit beneath them; when she becomes weary, I bid her walk on my right along the grass while my feet follow the stone path.

My belly sounds with hunger when the morning's first light shows itself. Isadora stops, hands me her woollen hose, and hies me into grass wet with water. I have no free hand to keep the bottom of Isadora's bedding from soaking. We walk until we have reached the thin bodies of tall alder trees whose meager boughs begin above our heads and do nothing to hide us from waking eyes. Isadora unfastens the wool bedding from my neck and sets it around my shoulders so that its water-drenched ends drip down onto the linen of my shins. She then asks me to hold her hair while she gathers it and binds it with her golden clip.

"Let us set the wool on one of these boughs," she whispers. "I would rather have them think you a grown child in your linen than otherwise."

"Otherwise?" I whisper.

Isadora sets her finger against my lips.

"Do not speak again until I tell you to," she whispers.

Where the sun rises from its bed having rested well, I have become tired with waiting. Beyond alder trees almost as slight as Isadora rises a swell of earth that meets stone walls thrice or four times as high as a man. One such man walks through the great opening in the eastern wall wearing a silver tunic and black leggings and a long sheath on his left hip. I dart back behind the alder tree and hold my back flat against it. Isadora frowns at me, stills my shaking shoulder with her hands, and holds her cheek against mine.

"Give me my hose and shoes," she whispers. "We will talk to him."

"We? Can you not talk to him yourself? He wears a sword."

"And an iron shirt as the king's thanes are wont to do. He must have come here to speak with those few who live within the stone walls to see how much of the king's wheat they have taken in on his behalf. Your mother may still be among them."

"Why did we not see her?"

"Men draw those carts swiftly when they wish to," whispers Isadora. "The sooner they do this, the sooner they eat deer and drink mead. Come."

"No," I say.

"Are you a child that you would not stand before this man yourself?"

I look down at my feet half-sunken in marshy water.

"I struck the aldorman when he wished to bed me," I say. Isadora sets her hands on my shoulders. "If I must go with you to this thane, you must hold my hand and tell him that I have not done this."

Isadora sighs and stares at me. She turns towards the stone path and offers the outstretched fingers of her hand. I take them as she lets fall the bottom of her black gown into the marsh water and walks with quick steps to where the black-clothed man draws near.

"Do you not want your hose and shoes?" I whisper.

"I will tell this man, thane or otherwise, that you are my mindless daughter who knows nothing of shoes or thanes or kings," she says. "Come, daughter. Heed your mother for once."

Isadora leads me to the stone path and waits there as her

friend walks with idle steps to where we stand as if we were not there. As he nears, his black tunic shows itself through the iron rings that hang from his shoulders; his belt bears a golden buckle that glows in the waking sun; between his arm and ribs rests an iron helm that will serve him well should the heavens send him a tree bough.

"Good morning," says Isadora. "I am glad to find the king's thane where I thought him to be."

"There is nothing of goodness or gladness in this morning if the king's thyle has strayed from her oaths," says the man. "Forgive me for blinding you with my belt buckle, child. I am Eldred."

"Branwen," I say.

"Your mother must have seen something of that fair raven in you that I do not," he says. "What brings you away from your house of stone, thyle?"

"My daughter," says Isadora.

The thane sets his helm on his head and folds his arms over his iron shirt. He draws himself upright to look down his nose at Isadora.

"She has become my daughter, I mean to say," says Isadora. "My sister died at the height of summer and left her to me."

I squeeze Isadora's hand harder than I should. Isadora clenches her teeth and narrows her eyes.

"She is not with her father," the thane says.

"Her father fights for the king in the west," says Isadora.

The thane nods, unfolds his arms, and steps towards me. I shrink from him, hiding myself behind Isadora though she is not tall enough to shield me.

"You have come to harm," says the thane. "I only wish to see what has been done."

Isadora takes my chin with her fingers and turns my eyes

to the grove of alder trees. The thane hums like a toad whose mouth has been bound shut.

"Your bruise is raw," he says. "Were you struck by something?"

I would look at Isadora, but she twists my head back to those thin boughs that shed green leaves between hanging red catkin tails.

"A young boy hunting hares threw a stone," I say.

The thane's fingers are on my bruise. I take Isadora's wrist from my jaw and step back. She grasps my forearm.

"Those hares must have been as tall as a man," says the thane. He stands over me. "As tall as two men if he drew blood from your hair. Did they stand on their hind legs in their grassy dales?"

"Come here, child," says Isadora. She takes my cheeks and draws the top of my head to her. "You did not tell me of this."

"It was a horse," I say.

"Horses and hares," says the thane. "Was it the horse's hoof that broke your nose or this boy who hunts his meals by throwing stones at clouds?"

"She struck her nose against a wall," says Isadora. "This was after I told her that her father had taken a spear to the ribs while holding a shield. I have come to ask the king to send her father back to her."

"What is your father's name?" says the thane.

"Gildewin," I say.

"I am sure Gildewin is a good king's man and that the king will send his steadfast men back to their wives and children before the snow falls. There are few who wish to fight when the weather becomes cold and the harvest has been taken in."

The thane steps away.

"What are we to do until then?" Isadora says.

"I do not wish to go to the aldorman again," I say.

Isadora lifts her eyebrows and widens her eyes.

"Are you with child?" she asks loud enough for the alder trees to hear.

"I told you I struck him before he could do anything," I say.

The thane bellows with laughter. His mirth comes to a swift end when Isadora steps forwards and opens her mouth.

"I have heard enough," he says with a wave of his hand.

"But she must—"

"The king and young Branwen's father are away at war, as they must be," says the thane. "The king's thyle and her daughter must likewise be within sight of the king's writings so that I may tell him I did not see them this morning."

"I did not wish the king to know that I had forsworn his laws in caring for my sister's child," says Isadora. "She has shown me how the heavens heed her will. There is none other who can bring her to him."

The thane sets his arms before his iron shirt once more and stares into the sun where it rises in the east. His eyes hold little of its light as he frowns at Isadora.

"I understand this," he says. "The king might as well, if I know his mind. What I do not understand is how a child bearing the name Branwen with a father named Gildewin comes to Durovernum the morning after we have greeted thirty carts of the king's wheat brought by a woman named Branwen whose husband Gildewin fights for the king and whose daughter has gone missing."

"I—"

"I will hear the truth from this child lest the king's thyle be found guilty of having borne or taken children," says the thane. "The king's daughters are forbidden such, and you know better than anyone else that you are named among them."

Isadora holds me in her arms. She will not look at me.

"A young boy said I called lightning from the heavens," I

say. "Men threw stones at me until I fled them through the river."

"Good," says the thane. "What is your name?"

"How is that good?" I say.

"Her name is Ardelle," says Isadora.

"Let it not be said that I have no kindness in my heart, Ardelle," says the thane. "I will take her to her mother while the king's *faithful* thyle goes before the queen and begs her forgiveness."

I look to Isadora. She brings my ear to her lips.

"The queen will forgive me," she whispers. "Her husband watches over those like you who are said to have harmed others. He knows they have done nothing. I know you have done nothing. You must forgive me for not believing what you said about your mother lying with the aldorman. I will tell the queen of what he wished to do to you."

In morning's waxing light, one star loses its hold within the heavens and falls. Where it lands, I do not know. The thane has followed it as well; he seeks its earthly glow in my eyes. I set my arm around Isadora's shoulders.

"I will speak to the queen on Isadora's behalf," I say. "I will tell her everything: that Isadora found me sleeping by the river and that I gave you my mother's name."

"You will?" says the thane with words that fall as if from a cliff.

"That is her way of asking," says Isadora.

"You may ask the queen, then," says the thane, "though she may stop listening when she learns you have gone against her husband's laws. Come. You will stay in a dwelling within the walls until the queen is ready to see you."

The thane leads us through a stone opening far taller than any man along half-hewn walls into the first timber house we see. Within, two men in brown wool and leather helms talk while two women in earthen gowns cook bread on a baking stone over the hearth.

"Men," says the thane, "you must watch over the king's woman and her friend until the queen sends for them."

A wind sweeps through the house, blowing the men and women out through its opening. Isadora lies down on the strewn hay bedding and closes her eyes. I sit beside her, setting her hose and shoes down against her legs.

"You slept little last night," she says.

"You watched me?"

"I see it in your eyes. Rest, now, so that they do not show the queen your weariness when we go to see her."

As I lie down, Isadora takes my head against her breast. She strokes my hair as mother did when I was a child.

"If you are a faithful daughter who heeds her mother," she says, "you must listen to me when we go before the queen; and you must do whatever the queen tells us must be done, even if she says things that you do not like."

"Should I use words from your parchments?"

"You may use such words with her, but know that she will not be swayed by them, for she knows them far better than you. You must promise me that you will do as your mother Isadora and the queen tell you."

"I promise."

"Sleep well. I will see that this bread does not burn."

Isadora's kiss on my bruised temple does not sting, but sends me off into a deep and dreamless sleep.

6

IMPRISONMENT

My dreamless sleep turns to mist as our dwelling's high-angled timber beams become a low-hanging sheet of grey-white stone. Sunlight spills through cracks and gaps onto the rough grit of a bed too hard and unyielding to be made of earth. When I sit up, the linen of my left shoulder drags against thick, flat, straight-edged stones that stand on top of each other and keep the roof from falling down on my head as I writhe against whatever it is that keeps my wrists bound. My bloodied head scrapes against rough stone, opening my wound anew and sending a small stream of blood down my cheeks and chin and onto my bare neck—mother's braid is missing. The leather string that might have held her amber beads now holds my ankles together so tightly that my toes have taken on a bluish hue. Before me in the dim light, a shape with fair and fleshy arms draws near. Rings of wavy brown hair fall to her shoulders; brown eyes sit above ruddy cheeks whose lines mark either side of her thick, rounded nose; broad lips rest above a wide jaw. She looks nothing like mother.

"I have been sent here to help you, Ardelle," she says.

"Were I not here, I would not need help," I say. "Whose friend are you that you know my name?"

"I am Annette," she says. "You and I are friends who sit beneath the floor of an old stone house. Men would light fires here to heat the rooms above."

"Friends sit together above the floor where they are warm rather than on fire."

"Those fires have long since died out. Men no longer come here, as they have no need for these stones."

"And yet I am here. Why must I listen to words when the silence of these useless stones will do?"

I spread my knees and draw them towards me, hoping to somehow break the leather binds around my ankles. Annette grasps my shins and holds my legs still.

"I have come to heal your wounds," she says.

"What hunter heals the wounds of a boar they are about to cook?"

Annette sits on my legs above my knees and brings her fingertips to rest on my broken nose. My tongue gathers water from my mouth to spit in her face—her forefinger is on my lips.

"Ardelle," she says. "What would your mother think if she saw you like this?"

"You are not my mother," I say.

Annette hums and shakes her head. Her hand returns to my nose.

"I have met few who bear a name like yours," she says as she looks over my face. "Who gave it to you? What does it mean?"

"My mother gave it to me. It means I am her daughter."

Annette tilts my head towards her lap and runs her fingers along my bloodied hair. She lifts my chin and rests the bones of her thumbs against my temples while she hums to herself.

Within my mind, the sea's waves kiss the sand below the white cliffs that father would tell me of to send me to sleep when I was restless. I close my eyes.

"My name was given to me by my sister from the lands beyond the southern sea," says Annette. "In her tongue, it means 'a little gift I have given you'. You may yet come to know her."

Annette's deep words sing the language of Isadora's parchments, flooding my limbs and breast with the soothing mist of unseen water. I no longer sit amid rough and faceless stone: I walk through tall stalks of wheat behind father as he returns from the river bearing a clay pot filled with water to be boiled for the next day's bread. Mother greets us when we reach the house's opening. She stands upright with no snake in her spine; her snowy teeth glow in the waning amber sunlight; her brown braid is long and thick. We eat together in silence around the hearth as dusk settles. Thereafter, I lie down between mother and father on the bedding and listen as mother tells me of how she met father in Powys, how he brought her all the way home by bearing her on his back, how mother stayed with me in her bedding those first four months after I was born. Annette's smiling face is before mine as though I have awoken from a dream.

"Must you be done?" I ask.

Annette slides herself backwards off my legs. I wrest my shoulders against my bound wrists.

"Will you free my hands so I can thank you?" I say.

Annette stops, meets my eyes, then looks to my bound, bluish feet.

"Mother has said you must stay this way," she says.

"Your mother?" I say. "Who is your mother that she leaves me in a hall so short and narrow that I am bound by being here?"

"The queen," says Annette.

"Annette, you said that we are friends. Can you not ask your mother to let your friend see Isadora? The king's thane said she is a 'thyle', the one who keeps the king's writings. After she has seen me, Isadora will speak to the queen about why I do not need to be bound."

"Mother speaks with a woman named Isadora now," says Annette. "I think she may let you see your friend when they are done talking."

"Isadora is my mother's friend. Her sister."

"Yes, I understand what you mean. I have five sisters who were not born of the same mother, yet the queen is mother to all of us. Branwen—is that your mother's name?"

"Yes. Let me see my mother."

"The queen might allow this, but you may wish to ask her rather than tell her."

Annette reaches for my hand. When she does not find it, she looks at my shins beneath my linen and pats them with her palm.

"I will speak to mother and ask her for you," she says.

She creeps on hands and knees towards a dim shaft of light. If I were to follow her, I would have to writhe along the ground as a worm does in the watery mud after a rain shower. I rest my shoulder against those misshapen stones that hold up the roof until Annette crawls back to me.

"My head feels much better," I say.

"You are welcome," says Annette. "The queen says you may speak to your mother before she returns home."

"How am I to go to her?" I say.

"You are not," Annette says. "Your mother will come to you."

"Down here? Has your mother no heart? What of Isadora?"

"Isadora may sit here with you in your mother's stead, but I do not think mother would let Isadora leave thereafter.

Isadora knows well what she has done. The queen is angry with her."

Mother's arms and back and legs are far thinner and weaker than Annette's. She would not fare well along this rough stone. Isadora can do nothing to the king—he would not keep her down here for long.

"Send Isadora," I say. "My mother must not know of this."

Annette leaves on hands and knees once more. I close my eyes and listen to my breaths for a time. They open again to the sound of grunting: a slight, wan-fleshed woman in undyed linen lifts her palms and knees slowly as she comes to me. Her black hair hangs halfway over her eyes and all around her shoulders. She looks over the leather around my ankles.

"Can you—"

"No," says Isadora. "The queen told me that I will be bound if I do anything more than look at your ruddy face. She has told me a great many things, more than I ever wished to hear. I would sit in silence for a time as I think on how the queen's daughter might like it if she were bound as you are and sat among the fires that once burned between these stone columns."

I have never heard Isadora talk of anyone this way, even when I read aloud to her of such things and worse from her parchments. When Isadora breaks her silence, she is as close to weeping as I have ever seen her.

"I am sorry for having done this to you," she says.

"The queen is the one who has done this," I say.

"She has done none of *this*," says Isadora with a tug on my leather ankle binds, "only said I was no longer her husband's thyle. Fifteen years of fidelity to the king so that he may strip me of everything and offer me a new house of stone whose roof stands too low even for oxen."

She hangs her head from limp shoulders.

"You are not bound," I say.

Isadora sits up and wipes her eyes with the back of her hand. Her brow has become dark; her jaw is grim. She takes the leather around my ankles between her thin fingers and pulls at it.

"I would be bound like you if I had struck the king's aldorman and run off," she says. "You left your own mother by herself. I think you must have left your brain somewhere on that stone path as well. Be thankful that the good king's men were there to watch over her where you did not."

"They did not even look at me when I left," I say.

"If other men had seen them chasing after you in your red gown, they would have thought they were out to murder one of those wretched sisters in red. Men who have only half a brain at best, and the half they do have thinks of nothing but the false tales they tell themselves. Your mother was to give that hair to the aldorman in sorrow for what you did. The queen knows of this. Now I am to stay down here unless the king's utterly faithful wife sees something in you that I do not."

"She will look kindly on me when she sees my wounds," I say.

"In this light, they do not look so sore," says Isadora.

She slides her finger beneath the leather on my ankles. My feet sting as though bees flutter about within them.

"You were told to leave those binds be," calls a woman.

Isadora sets herself behind one of those columns of thick, angled stones. Annette crawls to me and sits on top of my legs again.

"I do not need healing," I say.

Annette takes a deep breath and sets her hand on my throat. Isadora stirs onto her knees.

"Sit," yells Annette. Isadora does so, leaning against one palm while she stares at Annette. Annette's eyes come to rest on my chin. "If your mother does not tell the queen why she did not bring you to the king after men saw you call down the heavens, your mother will be bound even more tightly than you are, and it will be for the queen to choose whether she sits in a room like this or hangs from a tree."

Isadora grunts through her nose. I do not know what mother would look like hanging from a tree bough by her ankles. Annette leans her weight into me, sending my back on top of my bound wrists and my shoulders onto the stone. Her hand stays on my throat but does not tighten.

"This is how it will feel when your mother hangs by her neck from a tree," she says with shaking words.

Rushing wind blows through Annette's hair and sends her from my legs onto the stone, where she works the knuckles of her forefingers against her wet eyelids. Isadora holds her hand against her reddening, bloody cheek; her face and gown are caked with dust and grit. Annette hugs me and lifts me so that I sit upright.

"What I said is not true," she says. Tears take the dust from her eyes. "Mother told me to see whether the wind listens to you."

I spit in her face. She wipes it away with her blue gown.

"You are right to do so," she says.

"She is not," says Isadora. "Ardelle, you will ask this woman's forgiveness. Never again will you do that to anyone. What did I tell you of that maid Sithebad who broke your nose?"

"I must show her the kindness that she did not show me," I say.

"Look at her when you ask," says Isadora.

Annette lifts my chin with her hand.

"You are forgiven," she says.

"Annette," calls a woman from somewhere above. "We have felt it. Untie her binds quickly if you wish."

"Yes, mother," Annette answers.

Annette's thick fingers are not much better than Isadora's in sliding beneath the tight leather string on my ankles to find its knots. Isadora sits with both of her hands on her face. She is bent over so far forwards that her hair sweeps the dusty floor. Though her mouth stays closed, her groans hum within her throat.

"These binds do not hurt me," I say. "Will you heal Isadora before you leave?"

At once, Annette leaves my legs and takes Isadora's head in her hands. Isadora waves Annette's wrists away while Annette does her best to find Isadora's face with her fingertips. Her song begins thrice and comes to a stop each time.

"Annette," says a woman from the dim light beyond the many stone columns.

She speaks our new friend's name as lightly as the winds would take a feather from a bird and send it to the sea, yet Annette heeds her call with such readiness that the hard floor strikes against her hands and knees loud enough to be heard until she is out of sight. Isadora will not look at me.

"I told mother I would come and find you," I say.

"You did not," says Isadora.

"I am the one who brought us to this grave."

Isadora sighs through her nose with a half-frown.

"If I must trade one stone house for another," she says, "then so be it, but I will not have you sitting down here as if you are dead. Let me see your ankles."

Isadora picks at the tight knot that binds many winds of leather below my shins. When they do not yield, she bends over to bite at the string with her teeth.

"Ardelle." The woman who calls me is the same one who masters Annette. "Come here."

"How would you have me do that?" I call. "I am bound like a pig."

"Come here at once or I will bind your friend as well!"

"She sounds like a hound who barks the tongue of men," I say to Isadora.

"If you must use such words," she says as she sits up, "say them to me instead. The queen's daughter will not abide them well, nor will the queen when her daughter tells her what you have said. You will speak kind words to her whether or not she does the same to you. Go."

As a snake slithers, or a fish swims, or a worm wriggles on the hardening earth before winter, I set my legs and belly and face against the floor and writhe forwards, lifting my head only to keep it from striking against the stone columns and renewing my wounds. When the dim light begins to show me the narrow gap through which it shines, a shadow darkens it.

"Annette," says the woman. "Mother awaits us. Go below and see where your friend is."

The opening is only wide enough for Annette to squeeze through. How she has done this so many times, I do not know —I dread those places where I can not stretch my arms or legs as I will.

"She is almost here," calls Annette.

"Help her along, then, so we may leave before the sun falls."

Annette grasps one of my bound arms with both hands and pulls.

"You may drag me by the hair, if you wish," I say.

"You must stop talking like that," says Annette.

Where sunlight shone through the small gap in the stone roof, a black gown now stands. Unseen hands lift its folds to show me black leather shoes and black linen hose.

"She may say whatever she wishes to my feet," says their owner, "so long as she speaks her oath to them thereafter."

"I will speak aloud the oath," says Annette, "and you will do the same, Ardelle."

I would no sooner speak to this woman's shoes than I

would strike a horse's hind legs while staring at its hooves. I writhe forwards and set myself on one hip so that I may look up through the gap: a dark brown face framed by shoulder-length, tightly ringed black hair frowns down at me over a sheathed long knife.

"You are filthy," she says.

"And you are wretched," I say.

My left cheek strikes the stone floor once, twice, thrice. The bruise on my temple forgets Annette's healing. My head threatens to burst where it is held against the stone.

"Myrah," says Annette as one would speak to a child. "Take your foot from her. I will talk to her."

"And I will talk to mother," says the one named Myrah.

My head is no longer bound to the stone. Annette would lift me, but I do not let her. She sits before me so that I can see her from where I lie as she takes the two small golden breast-pins from her neck and leaves the fold of her woollen blue gown hanging.

"Listen to me, Ardelle," she says. "I once lived far north of here, beyond the river Humber along another river called the Aln."

"Those names mean as little to me as the one you call Myrah."

"And if my mother gave me a name, it has been lost to time. For twenty years I was bound to men who had slain our mothers and fathers and said we belonged to them. When we woke every day, we did nothing but what they told us."

Annette takes her arms from their woollen sleeves.

"One summer, when the weather began to cool, rain came to us for many days. It washed the paint from our fighting men's faces and kept them from bringing a reckoning to our bitter neighbours, who had slain five of their brothers and stolen twenty goats. Another ten among our flock fell ill and died in the grassy hills where they roamed. The men yelled at us and made us work even harder while it rained. A man named Wilfrith was one of the few who was kind to me—so kind was he that I came to love him and bore his child within me. I felt my son's feet against my belly. When he was hungry, Wilfrith found food for him. When he cried, I felt his sadness. But my son did not live long within me. I could not bear to look at him when he left me. After I buried him, I felt sorrow without end. The heavens showered us for weeks. The men somehow learned of what had happened within me. I heard them say that I had brought the rains that drowned our goats and flooded our fields. Then, one night, when Wilfrith was away, they set upon me with knives. Look here."

Annette bunches her linen undergown in her hands and lifts it above her neck. Her fleshy belly bears many light red lines like dried worms. The thickest and deepest of them lies beneath her left breast. Were my hands not bound, I would run my finger along one of her wounds to feel for myself what Sithebad's friends might have done to me—did Myrah not wear a knife on her belt?

"How old are you?" I say.

"Twenty-three," says Annette.

Annette's wounds are too raw and red to have lived for three years among five sisters who should have healed them a thousand times by now.

"They would have killed me had Wilfrith not stopped them," Annette says as her linen falls. "He brought me south on a stolen horse, far away from the hills that had been my home for so long. He did not wish them to ever find us, so he rode until we reached the southern sea. There, he found the sanctuary of Myrah's father. The king heard our tale and took us in after I healed some of his men who had seen battle. Now, he shields us from those who would wield knives and stones against us. In thanks for what he does, I have sworn an oath to him, and to his queen, and to their atheling, who will be queen when …"

"When my mother and father are dead," says Myrah.

Bare brown feet stand on the stone floor beneath the roof's opening.

"You will beg forgiveness for having called the owner of these feet wretched," she says. "Thereafter, you will speak your oath to them. When you have done this to my satisfaction, we will unbind you and bring you above, where you will greet your new mother."

Annette shoves her linen gown underneath her wool, thrusts her arms into blue sleeves, and fastens her golden breastpins at her left shoulder.

"What do you mean, 'my new mother'?" I say.

"When you speak your oath, the queen becomes your mother," says Annette.

My bitter breath forces itself through my nose before my mouth can open.

"You would have me forsake the mother who gave birth to me with mere words?" I say.

"My father's thane said your *mere words* made Isadora your mother until he drew the truth from you," says Myrah. "If you wish, you may stay below with your dear mother until my father returns. Father will not think well of you or of your mother when he learns how you lied to his thane and spoke curses to his daughter instead of an oath."

This is how it must be, then. I creep on my belly to Myrah's feet with my eyes closed. Bony flesh comes to rest against my lips and stays there for a time before withdrawing. I turn away from the stink of sweat; another foot greets my cheek. I offer it my lips until it leaves.

"Annette will speak the oath aloud," says Myrah. "You will do the same. Should you forget a word or misspeak, you will start from the beginning."

Annette's words float to me borne on the winds from some far-off hollow. I take them into my mind, write their runes onto the stone beneath my lips, and fill the carved lines with the croaking vomit of my own spoken oath.

"I, who stand alone, wrought by fire and earth yet now unyielding in winter's tide, bemoan my lost kin. I leave them without their daughter to become a spear hurled over the binding waves, landing at the feet of my king, he who lifts me from the frost-rimed grass, bears me unto the breast of his foes, and sends me to rest in tear-soaked blood. Beloved lord, in the mead halls I shall drink with you, beneath the welkin I shall sing of your deeds in battle, in the next life I shall lie beside your fallen brothers. I, kith of your birthright, your faithful daughter to the end of my days, swear this to you and to your queen, who shall *not* be my mother from this day, and to your atheling, who shall *never* be my sister."

Annette's weight is on me at once. She sets her hand on Myrah's feet.

"Leave her be," Annette says. "Tell your mother she spoke the oath."

"And tell her mother the one you call your sister wears a knife on her belt," I say.

Myrah comes below and takes her knife from its sheath. She slides it beneath the leather string around my ankles and frees them. Annette takes her weight from me. Myrah kneels beside my legs and stares at me as she hands her knife to Annette. At Myrah's neck, a golden, broad-winged bird holds together the fold of her black gown. My wrists are no longer bound to one another. Myrah takes her knife from Annette and sheathes it.

"We leave at once," says Myrah.

"And so you will leave Isadora here?" I say.

"You are the one who leaves her, *sister*."

Myrah's thin nose and amber-brown eyes bear hardness with greater earnestness than Isadora ever could.

"When we leave this stone," she says, "you will kiss your mother's ringed fingers and call her by that name as you have sworn. Then, we will go to the sanctuary, where you will meet your sisters. They will thereafter tell mother whether you should be allowed to speak to her on your friend's behalf."

I follow her through the gap in the stone floor's opening with hands and legs that are no longer bound, yet my eyes will not leave the black gown and black hair of this atheling who steps on my head and leaves Isadora in a hall of stone. When Annette offers me her arm, I keep mine at my side, ready to grasp Myrah's wrist should that knife of hers leave its sheath again for anything other than cutting her own gown into tatters and burning it.

7

SISTERS

A mouth of stone spits us out into a roofless yard whose yawning rainwater pit lies half-full. Myrah walks with quickening strides beside small, weed-ridden rooms to the lifeless patio's far end, where an opening in the wall has become home to a wooden cart filled with dead wheat stalks. She stands next to it and stares at Annette until we have reached her, whereafter she turns sideways and steps through the gap between the cart and the wall. Annette pats the chaff-strewn timber of the cart's bed with her thick fingers.

"Have I been harvested?" I say.

"You must stay hidden until we have reached the king's sanctuary far south of here," says Annette. "It would be better for you to think of yourself as shorn than to beckon others to come and take you from the earth."

"If we are kindred, you should at least be buried beside me."

"I must ride the horse that draws the cart," Annette says to my ear. "Myrah does not master horses, so she rides with her mother."

Myrah looks back at us from beyond the wheat cart as if she hears what Annette says.

"Listen well, child," Annette hums to herself.

When my arm has become weary of shielding my face from wheat heads and their bony stalks, I turn over onto my side and rest my forehead against the cart's oaken walls. Though my wounds bear well the shaking of the wheels against the stone path, I find no rest, only the unending lengths of my mother's unbraided hair. I search among the twine-crested waves for her beads until my limbs no longer hold me afloat—I sink helplessly into nothingness as the sweet smell of burning birch bark takes my breath from me.

"Ardelle, wake up. We are here."

Though Annette stands half a head shorter than I, she takes me from the cart with the strength of an ox. My half-sleeping legs follow her through the boughs of crowded birch trees to a broad door of oak set within a stone wall taller than ten men. From her belt Myrah takes an iron ring bearing several hook-toothed rods, one of which she slides through a narrow, width-wise slit in the door and pulls towards herself thrice. Annette takes it from her and wrests an unseen weight with both arms, then strikes the door open with her shoulder. We stand alone in a narrow, high-roofed hall.

"What of Myrah and her mother?" I ask.

"They do not come in through this door," says Annette. She shoves the door's beam through an iron hook bound to the stone wall. "You must bathe so your sisters do not smell the fields from which some of them came. If they deem you trustworthy, the queen may hear your words on Isadora's behalf."

Light comes to us through narrow, upright openings above our heads. Small, square stones of red and white under our feet form the likenesses of men. The bottoms of the walls are as green as grass, while the hueless trees that stand over them look akin to those stone columns between which Isadora now sits. Annette swings open an oaken door into a great room of white-grey stone and shuts it at once, setting a heavy beam of timber in wall-bound iron hooks to keep it closed. From there, she leads me into a smaller bathing room with a square pit whose water is warm to my feet. The floor, the walls, and the roof look as though they have been shaped from a single stone that begins and ends nowhere. Annette calls to me from the bath, where she sits without her gowns up to her shoulders in water. I turn away from her, let fall my linen, and step backwards into warm water that unfolds my arms and makes my shoulders slack.

"Does something weigh on your thoughts?" says Annette.

"In the aldorman's house … they heated the water with stones."

"We have fires beneath the floor here. Worry not that you might burn your feet. The men who made the stone path that brought us here came together to bathe in rooms much greater than this every day."

"Will Isadora be made to bathe?"

Annette looks towards the wall that shields the room's narrow opening from searching eyes.

"Myrah's mother has made her anger clear to Isadora," says Annette. "Keeping her bound would show her nothing further, nor would bathing wash away Isadora's misdeeds. I think she will at least be allowed a room in which she can stand. Soak your hair now, and I will comb it for you when you have washed it."

"Do we have time for this?" I say. "The aldorman's maid, Winiburg, said the same to me before the aldorman bid me lie on his stone bed so he could see whether I was ready for his child."

Annette lifts an eyebrow.

"That would explain much about why you behave so,"

says Annette. "When I bore my son, my mouth told me I needed to eat earth and grass." Annette shakes her head. "I will have Derwen augur your child, if you have one, but you are to tell none of this."

"Why not?"

"Your hair hangs down to your waist," says Annette as she runs her fingers through the length of it. "Shall I cut it for you?"

I stand up, sending water onto the stone floor beside the bath pit.

"I am clean," I say.

Annette rises from the bath water and hands me bundled cloth from a wooden table along the wall that hides the room's opening.

"You may keep your hair as it is," she says as she dries herself. "I only meant to say you might find shorter hair rests better beneath the linen we wear around our heads when we sing together."

No sooner have I worn my white gown than Annette grasps my wrist and walks swiftly in her linen through the great room that is neighbour to the bathing room. I nearly lose my footing more than once on the smooth stone that Annette calls marble. Shelves set into the walls bear more of the aldorman's painted, armless men. They watch over chairs and tables on which many parchments and bound books rest.

"Come, Ardelle," says Annette.

She leads me into a side room, whose oaken door she shuts at once. On a table opposite her stone bed lies a heap of many-hued clothing. The red wool she offers me brings my hand to the bruise on my temple.

"We only wear that within the sanctuary," she says with a smile. "Father will know where you have been if that red hue lightens in the sun."

"Or if I am dead," I say.

"Which you will not be if you stay within these walls. Your sisters may be willing to speak with you of their own—"

Footsteps and speech gather at Annette's door. Annette steps forwards to open it, yet it opens on its own: a stern woman in green with long, light brown hair and one arm stands in front of four others in blue, one of whom bears her friend on her back.

"Lift me up so I can see!" says the woman's friend.

"Do you ask your horse for arms? I am doing my best."

"Derwen," says Annette. "We must speak with you. Alone."

The one named Derwen takes the length of linen that hangs around her neck and gives it to the golden-haired woman borne by her friend.

"We will meet you in the hearth room," Derwen says and without another word shuts Annette's door behind her.

"She may be with child," whispers Annette.

Derwen takes my reddish fingers, turns them over, puts her thumb on my cheek, strokes my broken nose once, then places her hand on my belly and holds it there as she sings softly. It is then that my belly remembers I have not eaten in some time; its growling floods my arms and legs with burning needles. Derwen stares at me as she steps away.

"I feel nothing," she says. "If she is with child, we will hide it."

Derwen takes two breastpins each from her shoulder and waist. Annette helps Derwen take her arm from its woollen sleeve, whereafter Derwen gathers up her green gown and offers it to me.

"I will take your red gown, Annette," she says.

"Do you not have your own?" I say.

"I will wear yours so you do not have to."

I fasten Derwen's green gown at my neck with two of those small breastpins of gold inlaid with red gems and white shell.

Annette helps Derwen into a red gown that is somewhat too large for her; she fastens one breastpin at Derwen's waist and one at her shoulder.

"Derwen likes you," Annette says to my ear. "I think the queen will listen to you if you are kind to the others."

"You have bath water in your ears, Annette," says Derwen. "I think you should stay here in your room and empty your head."

"Someone must keep you from strangling Rosamond," says Annette. "Do not burden your newest sister with this obligation."

Derwen frowns and leaves the room with her gown's breastpins half undone.

"This is her way," Annette says. "Think nothing of it."

Annette leads me through two broad, white-grey-walled rooms of long oaken tables, high-backed chairs, and dead stone forefathers. In the third room against the wall furthest from the opening burns a bright reddish-blue fire within an iron bowl held above our heads by angled rods. It stands between two painted stone men whose armless shoulders rest on white columns; their brothers look down on us from small, round tables set along the walls and from narrow, square shelves carved into the stone that look as though they have always been there. In the middle of the room, facing the hearth's raised flames, Annette bids me sit down on a chair opposite a woman with golden, ringed hair resting halfway down the front fold of her red gown. Her forehead and cheeks shine with the amber hue of mother's beads. From behind us, a snowy-cheeked woman with wavy black hair bound into a tail walks arm in arm with her reddish-yellow-haired friend, whose face bears the sun's many kisses. They sit down in chairs beside one another facing me. Derwen walks by us in Annette's ill-fitting red gown and sits at a table not far from the hearth, where she takes up a bound sheaf of parchments and reads through them.

"Greetings, sisters, my name is Ardelle," says the woman with the golden hair rings. She sits on her legs where the others rest their feet on the floor. "And I am Florentina. Welcome, Ardelle."

"She has come here from her fields not long ago," says Annette. "You must forgive her for not knowing us as well as we know one another."

"Is that chair not hard against your ankles?" I say.

Beside Florentina, the wavy-haired woman holds her hand over her mouth and laughs through her nose.

"Your mother named you well, Ardelle," says Florentina. "My sister Rosamond does not share in your good fortune." She looks sideways at Rosamond, who takes her hand from her mouth and sits up straight. "When I was young, my feet became green, as did my ankles and shins. The king's healer cured me of this affliction by removing my legs at the knees. Thereafter, I asked myself whether I would ever be as gifted a healer as one who cures all ailments by simply removing the head from the body."

Florentina's words blow through me like the harvest winds before winter.

"Do you take your words from these parchments?" I say.

Derwen rises and throws her sheaf of parchments into the hearth fire. She stands before the bowl with her back to us and watches the flames wordlessly. Her four sitting sisters say nothing of what she has done, only watch as a wan woman taller than any of them wearing a long yellow-white braid comes into the room and, on seeing Derwen before the hearth, takes her roughly by the elbow and sits her down in a chair beside Florentina. She rests her hands on the back of Derwen's chair as she looks me over with hard blue eyes made no softer by the rough lines of her cheeks and chin.

"Luda," says Annette, "do not stare."

"Why did you burn those parchments?" I ask Derwen.

"We have read much," says Rosamond, "but we do not speak of it where others can hear."

The two great rooms behind us lie empty of anyone who might listen. They are as bright as the room in which we sit, though I know not where their light comes from.

"Might we speak of it now, then?" I say.

The woman bearing reddish-yellow hair who sits beside Rosamond looks through me with dim green eyes.

"How do you know of books?" she says.

"Maria," says Rosamond and sets her hand on her friend's wrist.

"Let Marigold ask," says Luda.

"You have two names?" I say.

"Father named me after the flowers which share my hair's colour," says Marigold.

"If she must be taught to speak, I should be the one to do so," says Florentina. "Luda's arms are weary from bearing me, Ardelle. Take me as bond-sister and I will teach you all you wish to know of colors, flowers, birds—"

"And where would you have her see these things?" says Luda.

"She has not yet sworn her oath to father," says Rosamond. "And do not talk to her of colours, Florentina, until you have learned to say the word correctly."

Florentina turns to Rosamond and frowns.

"Marigold asked her how she knows of books," says Annette.

"Isadora," I say. "My mother's sister who keeps the king's writings. Kept."

"Your mother is from Hispania?" says Florentina.

Rosamond hisses through her teeth.

"What?" says Florentina. "There is no harm in asking."

"What do you mean by sister?" asks Derwen.

"Annette said you are her sisters though you are not born of the same mother," I say. "Isadora is likewise my mother's sister. She has shown me the dreams you wrote down."

Derwen is on her feet so swiftly that her chair threatens to fall over onto the floor but for Marigold's steadying hand. Florentina lifts one eyebrow as Derwen runs out of the room. Luda sits down in Derwen's chair and stares at me. Rosamond shakes her head and looks at the floor. Marigold stands and walks with one hand held out before her. Annette rises to meet her, takes her wrist, and sets her down in the chair beside me. The fire that burns in the iron bowl gives life to smoke in the clouds of Marigold's eyes.

"I have dreamed of many things," she says. "Red stone paths to the sea, where men go to meet boats; great waves that flood onto the shore and wash away their sandy footsteps. Will you tell me of your dreams?"

"Maria," says Rosamond.

"Ardelle must be allowed to tell us of how she came here," says Annette. "Did we not do the same? Tell us of your dreams, Ardelle."

"I ran from men who threw stones and bore burning sticks," I say. "I swam through a river; on the other bank, I was met by a dark boatman, who showed me the body of a dead man. He had purple ..." Their faces are as still as Isadora's. "... purple snakes on his belly. I felt as though I must bear the burden of his death, so I told the boatman I was the one who had sent him there. Before I woke, the boatman said I would not know peace until I had given him my blood. That is when Isadora found me. She brought me to the king's halls."

"Where is Isadora now?" says Luda.

"Mother keeps her elsewhere until father comes," says Annette.

"Elsewhere," says Marigold.

"As if we would run off and free her," says Florentina.

"She should be kept," says Rosamond. "I think she is the blood you must give to your boatman."

"There is no need to meet dark thoughts with dark words," says Luda.

"Why are your words so unlike your fair face?" I say to Rosamond.

Florentina laughs. Rosamond lifts her head, sits up straight, and meets my eyes.

"Rosa," says Marigold, "we have only met her."

"Yes, *Rosa*," says Florentina, "why must you be as crude as your own dreams?"

"What does it matter that she has read our words?" says Luda. "She is one of us, is she not?"

"Mother felt Ardelle's wind," says Annette. "She may ask us whether she should hear Ardelle's words on Isadora's behalf."

"What of this place in your dreams?" says Marigold. "Was it dark like night, or did you see colours?"

"It became dark as I floated along the river, lit only by the fleeting red wights that hung in the—"

"Yes!" says Marigold. "That is my dream as well. Rosamond wrote it down for me, that is to say: towers of red bloodstone that reach high into the sky, great bridges between floating islands in the clouds …"

"I have not read of those," I say.

"I think those are the words that Derwen burned," says Rosamond.

"Oh," says Marigold. She hangs her head. "I wish she had not done that."

Derwen's red gown hangs before me, fastened with one small breastpin at her shoulder and waist where her sisters wear two. Before her right ear hangs a knotted braid among thick and sweeping strands of light brown hair that fall to her waist.

"How did you learn to read our writings?" she says.

"Isadora taught me."

"She should not have done that. Mother understands this even if Myrah does not."

Derwen takes the golden breastpins from my neck and sets them in Annette's lap.

"We do not wear them like that," she says. "That is for Myrah and her mother."

Luda takes one breastpin from the two on her waist, as does Florentina. Derwen bids me stand so she may fasten my gown at my shoulder and waist.

"Sit," she says in mother's tongue, and so I sit.

Rosamond makes a sound with her tongue as Derwen walks towards the wall where the men of stone watch over us.

"Do you consult the painted men for wisdom?" asks Rosamond.

"Tell me what you thought of Myrah when you met her," Derwen says to our forefathers on their stone shelves, "and I will tell you why I burned those words."

"Speak well of Myrah," Annette whispers.

"Shall I say that the snake who bore her fangs slithered well and hissed sweetly?" I whisper.

"You did not meet her at her best this morning," says Annette. "Derwen will tell Myrah what you say, and if Myrah does not like what you have said, when next you meet her, her mood will be no better."

"I wish I had never met her," I say. "I wish she had never made me come here and sit among those who neither need nor want me here."

Derwen turns to me.

"Then you may write down your thoughts of Myrah using the words that you have learned from your friend Isadora,"

she says. "We will read them aloud to one another and thereafter burn them so you may cleanse their evils and thus forget
them. If you have not enough words, take Florentina as your
bond-sister. She will speak for you a great many forgettable
words."

"You will sleep on the floor tonight," Florentina says with a
frown.

Derwen walks along the walls. Rosamond looks over her
fingers. Luda hangs one arm over the high back of the chair in
which she sits, so tall is she. Marigold's hand on mine is like
ice. I withdraw my fingers.

"Better than sleeping beneath a floor as Isadora does,"
I say.

"Ardelle," says Annette. "Be silent now. Let them think on
what they wish to do."

"What do you mean, 'beneath a floor'?" says Luda. "Is she
dead?"

"No," I say. The words that float through my blood in chill
stillness now flood forth from my breast. "The aldorman
wished to give me a child, but his maid Winiburg and I did
not let him. I ran from him with my mother's shorn hair to
Isadora, who took me to the king's halls. We woke bound
beneath the floor in a place where fires are kept to warm a
house."

"An aldorman lay with you?" says Luda.

"They kept you in a hypocaust?" says Florentina.

"Why would she cut her hair?" Derwen says to herself in
mother's tongue.

"Luda," says Rosamond, "would you be so kind as to tell
our dear friend Derwen that if her sisters are not permitted to
speak their languages that she must do likewise?"

"I will ask Myrah where she keeps your mother's braid,"
says Derwen.

"Forgive me, Ardelle," says Annette. "I did not know the

meaning of your hair when I asked whether you wished to shorten it."

"I will come with you when you ask her," I say to Derwen.

"You will do no such thing," says Annette.

"Did you not say she was wretched?" says Derwen.

"She told you this?" I say.

Derwen looks at the floor, carved of a single stone as the walls and roof have been. Luda takes her arm from the back of her chair.

"Did you say anything else to Myrah?" Luda says.

"Ardelle swore the oath to her," says Annette.

"To her feet," I say. "I meant none of it. I should have stayed in that *hypocaust* with Isadora so you would not have to sit here and bare your fangs at one another."

Florentina stares at her hands in her lap. Luda links her fingers and leans forwards with her elbows on her legs. Marigold sets her palm on my knee and stares at the door in the wall on our right.

"I will tell mother to hear your words," she says.

"No," says Rosamond.

"What?" I say.

"Myrah's father will not hear her words, nor will her mother," says Rosamond. "Maria does not see that which is not right before her eyes."

"Do you also call this man your father, *Marigold*?" I say. "Do you call Rosamond your friend when she tells you what you may and may not say? I think all of you would let Myrah's mother and father bind me beneath this floor and cook me like a pig so I may warm your feet in winter."

When I stand, the sisters sit up straight and look to the great room's opening. Derwen finds a chair and sits down in it beside Luda. Myrah comes before me, a head shorter than I am; her dark brown brow glows silver in the hearth's flames. She takes my hands. I sit down so she may not hold them, but she keeps them as she kneels upright and stares at my chin. The winged bird at her black gown's throat breathes fire into her cheeks.

"I am sorry for stepping on your head," she says. "My mother struck me once for each blow I gave you."

"She lies, Ardelle," says Rosamond. "Maria will tell you the same."

Marigold is silent. Derwen stares at her shoes. Annette turns away from me; Florentina and Luda look elsewhere when I meet their eyes.

"Will you tell your mother to let Isadora go free so she may take me home?" I say.

"Mother is angry with me," says Myrah. "I can make no promises."

"The others know I should not be here," I say.

"None of them should," says Myrah, "yet they have sworn themselves to father, and thus they are all much older than they would be otherwise. They speak of me as though I am a child when they think I do not listen. Derwen, most of all."

Derwen searches Myrah's flowing rings of black hair yet looks at her feet when Myrah turns her chin.

"I ask your forgiveness, now," says Myrah. "My mother awaits without. I will ask her to do what you say."

Myrah lets go my hands and looks into my eyes. Does her mother have eyes as brown as hers?

I look away.

"You are forgiven," I say.

"Thank you," she says.

Silence weighs down on us long after Myrah's footsteps have left us. Rosamond is the first to lift its yoke from her neck.

"You and Myrah are children," she says. "Both of you."

"Ardelle has learned what she knows from Isadora," says Derwen. "Do not lay this guilt at her feet."

"You are right, my darling sister," says Rosamond. "She does not even wear shoes."

"She is our kin for as long as she stays here," says Luda. "You can show her how best to wear shoes when she sleeps in your room tonight."

"I will show her how to wear hose as well," says Marigold.

She takes my elbow. Rosamond opens her mouth but says nothing. Thereafter, I hear little of what they say to each other, nor of the answers they give one another, for my mind and thoughts have left them to sit with Isadora and mother, wherever they may be. That night, when I make my home on the floor beneath Rosamond and Marigold's bedside table, only the moonlit darkness shows me that I am still among the living. It is when dreams begin to take me that the face of another comes to me: Myrah kneels beside me with my hands in hers and speaks of her sorrow over and over until at last her whispered words turn me away into the arms of sleep.

8

MYRAH

Myrah's grim face looms over me bearing a hardness that narrows her eyes and clenches her jaw. Her legs hold my arms against the floor; she sinks her meager weight into my ribs with such strength that my breath leaves me. With one hand, she closes my broken nose, sending aching waves through my cheeks and temples. With her other hand, she closes my throat. As I thrash beneath her, she spreads her lips wide and bares a row of stony white teeth like those squares in the floor of the hall whose door she unlocked for Annette.

"Tell me again that you have thought of me while I am not here," she says.

I mouth the words she wishes to hear, but she does not yield. Myrah leans over me and stills the fire within my breast by putting her lips to mine—

I sit up and strike my head so hard that the sleeping wound within my hair wakes and sends me back to the stone floor. My chest heaves as I gasp for draughts of the night's wind wafting in through narrow openings near the high roof. I free myself from beneath the table's wooden legs and am met almost at once by the raised stone on whose wool Rosamond and Marigold sleep. Nothing of the bedding comes to my fingers, only knees and feet—no, I must not wake them. They have room enough for themselves and no other. Rosamond was right to give me this floor: this bed, these chairs, this great house of stone are not mine. That is why I do not find sleep. I will go back to mother and sleep in her bed and stay within our house so that men who throw stones and bear burning rushes will never see me again.

The room's door does not yield to my hand, nor to my shoulder. My right hip finds a thick wooden beam that lies in the grasp of two hard, iron-like hooks on both sides of the door. I can not lift it. I shove against it until it jerks forwards with a loud scraping sound.

"Ardelle," comes a whisper.

"Rosamond?"

"Marigold. You may urinate in the pot behind the table when I am done."

"The stone hurts my back," I say. "My legs ache. I would walk for a time."

"The doors are bound with beams on both sides until morning."

"You do this to yourselves?"

"It is how father shields us from harm."

"The father who does not hear your words."

Marigold's gown glides against the smooth stone wall as her footsteps draw near. The soft breaths from her nose become a whisper.

"The woman who looked after me before I came to the sanctuary shut me in a room and gave me bread and water once a day," says Marigold. "When she learned that I make fire that does not die, she took me to other men and traded this fire for food, flax, wool, sometimes pigs and even sheep. One night, when my keeper had fallen asleep with her mead and left me unwatched, I fled her. I found the old Roman road and followed it to the sanctuary, where I showed Myrah's father my fire. He told me that I may live here and he would call me his daughter if I obeyed him in all things. Now, I keep the baths warm and, during winter, the floor beneath our feet. That he does not hear my oaths means little. I make him listen in other ways."

"You have no other whom you would call father," I say.

"You do," says Marigold. "You must wish to run away to him."

"If I wanted to leave I would have done so earlier."

"You may sleep on the bedding between us, if you wish, but you and I will have to sleep on our sides so Rosa does not fall onto the floor. When morning comes, I will tell her to braid your hair and set pins and flowers in it so men will not know who you are in your green gown. She will bring you to the door in the painted hall and leave you there."

"Will Rosamond listen to you? Will Derwen not know of this at once and tell Myrah?"

"You ran away in the night. Rosa talked to you while you walked but you would not listen. You will not have been the first to do this."

"Keep your bed for yourselves," I say. "I will rest by the door until morning so I do not wake you again by striking that table."

"As you say. Good night."

I set my head against the door where it meets the floor and breathe as Isadora taught me to when summer's heat became unbearable: take in the day's clouds through my nose, then send them back to the night stars from between my lips. It is not until the morning sun brightens the room that my eyes close and my thoughts end.

"Wake up."

Rosamond stands over me with her flowing black hair unbound, shaking my leg with her foot. I sit up and slide myself aside so that she and Marigold may shove the door's wooden beam from its iron housing. I set the beam upright where the white-grey walls meet and rest beside it. Rosamond takes a white comb from the table; she sits behind Marigold and strokes the comb's thin teeth through Marigold's thick reddish-yellow hair. Here and there, thin braids bearing red and white beads make themselves seen.

"Did you give her those braids, Rosamond?" I say.

Rosamond's eyes do not leave her friend's head.

"Florentina did," says Marigold.

"Your hair would be better washed without them," says Rosamond.

From without, the scraping of wood yields a sound against the floor and a slight shifting of our room's door. I rise and open it—Myrah's black woollen gown is the night sky; the silver on her fingers, the stars. Her frowning eyebrows send me back into the room. Rosamond sighs sharply through her nose as she shuts the door.

"Myrah will come for us when we take our morning bread," she says.

"Why do you eat in the morning?" I say. "Is there work to be done?"

"Given that you seem to understand nothing," says Rosamond, "it may be better for you to *do* nothing until you are told what is to be done. Florentina will take great glee in telling you the meaning of everything you do."

The fog that shrouds my thoughts and clouds my eyes lifts when I lie down on the bedding behind Rosamond to the sound of her grunted hum. In sleep, I find a stillness so abiding that any words Rosamond might offer in opposition drown themselves in a sea of welcome emptiness.

When next I wake, Myrah stands over me with her thick

black hair bound into a tail of white linen. The glow of her silver finger-rings hurts my eyes.

"You must eat with the others in the hearth room," she says.

"Hunger does not come to me until midday," I say with a yawn.

"I did not ask for your thoughts. I am telling you what is to be done."

Myrah takes my left arm below the shoulder and pulls on it, but my weary limbs will not leave their house of wool. Myrah takes the bedding from me and throws it onto the floor before the table. When she takes my elbow, I sit up, but my legs have no mind to lift me.

"Stand up," she says.

She kneels on the bed and puts her arms around me below my shoulders. When she stands, my spine makes a loud sound. She brings her face to mine; I set my hands on her shoulders and rise with her. She shoves me away.

"What on earth is wrong with you?" she says. "Go to the hearth room. Now."

I follow her into the room wherein that smokeless fire ever burns within its tall iron bowl, wholly unseen by the six red, long-sleeved gowns sitting close beside one another at a round table of alder laden with crusted bread rounds, wooden bowls of milk, palm-length eggs, and large clumps of yellow-white cheese. I take a chair from beside the wall and sit down far enough from the sisters in red that I may hear them without showing them that I listen.

"I have seen her gown," says Rosamond. "It is brown."

"Why brown?" says Luda.

"That idiot smith boiled the madder in the dye bath," says Rosamond.

"After you told him to do so?" says Florentina.

"No," says Marigold. "Only one man does what Rosa tells him."

Loud laughter bursts forth among them.

"Shut your mouth, Maria," says Rosamond as she grins.

She strikes her friend's wrist with little weight behind her blow. Annette looks around to see who laughs with her, though she knows well who does, and falls silent when she sees me. I look over my toes to see whether yesterday's bath has done anything to clean them. Myrah returns from within the neighbouring bedroom wearing shoes of blackened leather. She stops and stares at me.

"Do you know nothing at all?" she says. "Do your eyes and mind not tell you, if nothing else, to do what everyone else does?"

Here again is the slithering snake that sent me from my bed. Annette sets her arm around the back of her chair and leans towards me as if to say something. Better to step on the asp's head than take its fangs.

"I did not sleep well," I say. "My head feels like an ox stepped on it. A loud, braying ox."

Myrah stares at me with narrowing eyes. She walks to the table and waves her hands swiftly away from herself. The women rise and set their chairs closer to one another, leaving a gap in which Myrah stands. She takes from each of them some small share of their food and sets it before her. I blink once and she is at my side, bidding me rise from my chair, which she then hauls to the empty spot at the table and drops onto the marble floor. As soon as I am sat down, Myrah shoves my elbows onto the table with one knee on the back of my chair.

Red-sleeved hands grasp one another's fingers softly. Annette on my left offers me hers, as does Florentina on my right. They close their eyes; Derwen speaks to the stone roof far above us.

"Our father who watches over us, we thank you for the

bread you have given us this day, and for your walls which shield us from the evils without. We ask that you forgive us when we are guilty, and we shall forgive those who know not what they do. May your strength be ours in times of weakness."

Florentina wets her hardened bread with milk and bites into it. I have no hunger for the egg or cheese before me, but take from Annette the tall greenish cup of ale-water she offers me, drinking until I have reached the tops of the pear-headed snakes that creep up the glass from the bottom. Florentina, whose gleaming blue eyes have not left me all this while, drinks the rest, whereafter she leans over to me.

"If you can not eat," she whispers, "take the food to my room and leave it on the table beneath an upturned bowl beside my hair rods."

I gather my food into Florentina's emptied milk bowl.

"Stay seated until we have eaten," says Derwen.

"Have we not shared our food with Florentina every day?" says Luda. "If she falls ill before midday from not having eaten or drunk when she needs it, I will tell mother while she is still here that Myrah forbade Ardelle from helping her."

Derwen sits up straight, eyes her bowl of milk, and nods her head towards the bedroom door set in the wall to our right.

"Leave everything as you find it," she says.

Within, I set Florentina's bowl of food on her table beside several thin brass rods as warm as the floor. Beside them are iron tongs, a white comb like Rosamond's with teeth above and below its handle, and—

"Ardelle," calls Florentina.

At the table, the sisters face Myrah, whose hands rest on the high back of my chair. I turn it around and sit before her, yet she does not step away. My knees are against her black wool, so near to me does she stand. She stares at me with a child's grim frown that I can not help but meet with laughter. Myrah's words do not come to her until Luda asks her what she wishes to say.

"Father rode his horse along the stone paths all night long so that he may take the oath of his newest, mirth-hearted daughter," Myrah says.

"What do you mean by 'daughter'?" I say.

"We will sing together before our midday meal," says Myrah. "As Ardelle has taken her bread somewhere other than her belly and does not have a room of her own, she may await us in the bathing room."

"What am I to do in the bathing room?" I say.

"*Wairth hrains,*" Florentina says to herself, as if the truth of her words were enough to make me understand them.

"Will you teach me your tongue?" I say to her.

"No, she will not," says Myrah.

Though Myrah is as slight as Florentina, when Myrah straightens a length of Florentina's golden, ringed hair between her middle finger and forefinger, Florentina shrinks from her.

"If father hears that you have spoken that Gothic tongue of yours," says Myrah, "I will have to tell him that you fell asleep at the bread table and dreamed that you were a child in Emerita Augusta. The more words I must use to allay his fears, the shorter he may ask you to cut your hair to better rest beneath your head linen."

Florentina clenches her hands into fists that shake beneath her cheeks.

"I have said nothing," she says. "I will say nothing."

Myrah kisses Florentina on the temple and leaves. Florentina holds her hands flat against the table and breathes heavily through her nose.

"Take a bath," Annette says to my ear, "or Myrah will cut your hair."

My flesh still sore with sleep does not take the heated water well. How did men carve these rooms from only one smooth stone? Myrah looks into the bathing room from behind the wall that is meant to shield those who bathe from being looked at by those who are not bathing.

"Good," she says.

When she has left, I gather my hair before me and sink into the water up to my shoulders. As I rest against the bath's stone wall, fingers knead life into my back and shoulders—Winiburg's fingers, her smiling face, her arms as soft as our morning's milk—when from within my waist and hips arises an aching that brings my knees to my breast. Is this the memory of what the aldorman has done? I should cleanse the unbidden sight of his wild wolf-eyes and writhing worm-lips from my mind. Myrah brings him to me in this bath, that ill-tempered wretch whose dark brown cheeks aglow with the hearth's fire only worsens the gnawing below my belly. I stand at once, dry myself with linen from the small table near the bath, clothe myself in white and green gowns, and set myself down at the end of the room's narrow, hall-shielded opening, where I may look out at those who walk by but do not bathe.

Yet as I sit, my legs will not lie still, and so I take them into the great room, wherein I walk along the wall beside painted men who stare at one another over long tables of oak and alder. They tell me, in their wisdom, not to leave their side, nor am I to open any of the bound books over which they watch, nor am I to follow loud laughter through Rosamond and Marigold's great room into the hearth room, where Myrah and her sisters bear tables and chairs and set them beside the walls, thus stripping the room of its usefulness. I sit on a chair near the opening with my hands clutching the wooden seat while my hair dries in the lap of my gown. I meet Myrah's eyes; her legs meet mine.

"Do you not have knees of your own?" I say.

"Yours would not shake with cold if you had stayed in the warm bath as you were told," says Myrah.

"She awaits me," says Derwen as she comes beside Myrah. "I told her I would explain to her what needs to be done."

"And what you meant by the word 'daughter'," I say.

Myrah's ringed hair sways as she shakes her head.

"You have no brain," she says and walks away.

Derwen sits down next to me and leans over her legs.

"You do not yet have shoes," she says.

"I have no need of shoes," I say. "I will not stay long. Myrah will not need to tell me what else I do not have."

"Be kind to her and she will leave you be," says Derwen.

"Sing to the snake and it will not bite you."

Derwen takes off her shoes and sets them below her chair. At her behest, I help her untie the linen bands above her knees that hold up her hose. Derwen's sisters come to us, leaving the room empty of all but two chairs in its middle that face the great room's opening. Luda sets Florentina down on the wooden seat to my left before sitting on the floor with the others.

"Why are your shoes and hose beneath your chair?" Annette asks Derwen.

"Ardelle does not yet have shoes," Derwen says.

Marigold begins to take off her shoes. Seeing this, Rosamond does the same. The others do likewise. When they have bared their feet, Florentina shows me the woollen socks she wears to keep her legs warm.

"What do you think father will do when he sees us like this?" she says.

"He will see that Myrah has not given Ardelle shoes," says Derwen, "nor has she been given a gown long enough to hide her shins. Father will tell Myrah to smile when she speaks kindly to one he will call his daughter."

A tall, sturdy man strides into the room bearing snow-white hair on his head and on his weathered face. His tunic, leggings, and shoes are as black as Myrah's gown, as is the long length of wool he wears around his shoulders bound along his left neck bone with a leather string. The golden rings on his fingers glisten as they rest against the iron helm cradled under his arm. Long, swift steps take him to the left chair in the middle of the room. As he sits, Derwen and her sisters rise and stand in a row with Luda bearing Florentina at its head and Annette at its tail.

A woman then walks through the opening, half a head shorter than the man, wearing a gold-fastened black gown that glides over the marble as she walks. Her thick, midnight hair is bound in a tail of white linen like Myrah's; her silvery dark brown cheeks and forehead shine as Myrah's do in the hearth's billowing flames. She sits down in the chair on the right as though she is a feather falling from a bird; when she has landed, Myrah stands beside her with a hand for her shoulder. Myrah looks at me with a frown, lifting her chin and eyebrows. I fold my arms; she looks away.

When the man smiles, Luda and the others walk to him as if he had spoken. He takes from each of them a kneeling kiss on his ringed fingers—Florentina does so from Luda's back— whereafter they rise, only to bend forwards and take a kiss from Myrah's mother on their cheek. It is when Myrah stares at me over Annette's shoulder that I find myself standing before this seated king and queen of stone whose unblinking eyes find nothing but my unbending knees.

"Father," says Luda. "Florentina will whisper the oath to Ardelle's ear. She has not had time to learn it by heart."

"Good," says this man they call father. His words are deep and rich. "By speaking this oath, you choose to bear a burden for the greater good, as do we all."

Florentina breathes this morning's cheese and eggs onto my neck.

"I, who stand alone, wrought by fire—"

"Where is my mother?" I say. "And what have you done with Isadora?"

"There is nothing to fear," says Myrah's mother with words almost as deep as her husband's. "Your mother—"

"Do I shake with fear now? Is that what you see?"

"Your mother fares well at home," says the queen.

"Does Isadora fare well in a hypocaust?"

They do not speak.

"Set her free and I will speak your words," I say.

The king turns his head slightly towards Myrah, who steps forwards so he can see her though he does not look at her.

"Did she or did she not speak the oath to you, daughter?" he says.

"She did," says Myrah.

"I only did so thinking to ask you to free Isadora once my wrists and ankles were no longer bound," I say. "But I could not, for you hid yourself from me."

Luda steps away from me. Myrah's mother stares at me. Myrah's father rises and holds his hands behind his back as though he looks out at the sea from where he stands astride towering cliffs.

"This hangs over you as your hair hangs over this marble from the old imperium," he says. "The stone of this sanctuary is made from hundreds of shards brought here from afar. My daughter Derwen shaped them into seamless wholeness. Before her, my daughter Florentina lived among the misshapen, unbound stones as she healed my men with unmatched vigor and showed me, through her deeds, the worthiness of a life devoted to restoring men who had fallen from greatness. And thus, I began the great and worthy undertaking of rebuilding that Roman imperium in lands that have forgotten its wisdom. These fifteen years we have striven with little success to make men remember the strength we once wielded: our rain blesses the wheat, our earth yields its fullest harvest, our fire offers warmth without end during the longest winters. I could not have foreseen that we would one day be made whole by one who calls upon the heavens themselves. Therefore, I ask you: Isadora, whom you name friend, and who is sister to your mother, and whom I once called thyle when she kept my words well—what would you have of her?"

"Her freedom," I say.

"Beloved daughter, I would make it so."

My blood and flesh are fire. The painted men on both sides of the raised iron bowl threaten to fall over as a gale of wind quenches the reddish-blue flames to embers, thus darkening the room. When the fire comes to life anew, our stone forefathers give their thanks by bowing their foreheads so low to the ground that they break their noses. Myrah's father beholds me with a broad smile that does not hide the gaps between his marble teeth.

"With such strength," he says, "we shall restore the imperium to its greatest glory and make whole the broken hearts of men set adrift among the ruins of their forefathers' sunken ships."

"I have no need of men or ships," I say, "only my mother and father and Isadora. *Restore* them and I will leave you to the *glory* of your imperium."

"There is nothing that happens within these walls that I do not know about," he says. "Your sisters keep no secrets from each other, nor would they hide anything from me. Those you call mother and father rest within their home; they send their love to you as you begin your new life among us. I would tell you now what your mother told my wife ere she left. I only ask that as you listen, you spare our forefathers from further harm."

"They are stone."

"Then let your heart be made of the same. Seventeen

winters ago, your father served his king well against the men of the west in battle along the great river Tamesis. He took a spear in his ribs and would have gone to the next life had his king not found for him among the slain women of their foes a daughter too young for words. You brought him mirth as his wounds healed. His king returned him to his home, where he was given land on which to grow wheat and oxen to plow his fields. As he awaited the return of warmer weather, his king found for him a wife who had come from Deva Victrix, the old city of the Roman *legiones*, in search of a child of her own, as she could bear none herself. They met one another and fell in love; and they accepted the daughter they had been given as their own. At her father's side, she helped him harvest hay and wheat and rye. At her mother's side, she spun linen and wool to be woven on their loom and ground wheat for their bread. You are the daughter I gave to Gildewin so long ago, and now that you have shown them the strength of your gifts, they have sent you here to bless their king with the same devotion they have shown you these many years."

I should send all of these stone men to the floor and Myrah's sisters along with them, for none of them have done so much as open their mouths.

"Anyone who thinks I will believe a tale like that may throw himself from the cliffs into the sea," I say.

Behind me come the whispered words in mother's tongue that I would use to curse this man who tells wicked lies yet still sleeps well at night.

"Derwen," says the queen. "What is this you say?"

"Nothing," says Derwen.

"She says that all of us have our own wretched histories," says Annette, "and that few, if any, who do not abide within these walls have ever believed them."

The king nods his head as if Annette has told him that I

will worship his footsteps and lick clean his shoes with my tongue.

"You have sworn an oath to my atheling," says the king. "Your oath to me must therefore withhold nothing: all of your hatred and suffering must be bound up in the words you speak to me. It may be that you yell them at me. It may be that you weep as you let bitterness fall from your lips. Your sisters have done the same: they have left behind noble homes, old tongues, great houses and halls, the freedom to walk beneath clouds and tree boughs whenever they wish, the faces of those with whom they shared their lives from their first memories. Those memories must be enough, now, for when men come to those who raised you and ask whether Ardelle is their daughter, that young woman who wears red gowns and steals children from their mothers at night to drink of their blood, they shall tell those men you are not their daughter, and it shall be the truth; and those men will not thrash and burn your crops to the ground, and set fire to the timber of your house, and take the hides from your cows and oxen while they still live, and hang the beaten and burned bodies of your mother and father from the alder trees near the stone walls of Durovernum for all to see. For she who was once their daughter will have spared them from such bitterness that death becomes a blessing."

My words are vomit. How evil are his lies that he makes himself believe them?

"One of my faithful daughters," says the king, "if she sees in you what my wife sees beneath those bruises and behind those thorned words, may speak an oath on your behalf. Her spoken oath along with yours will send Isadora to live with Gildewin and Branwen for the rest of her days; and to your father, who has lost his foot in battle, I shall send my aldorman Constantine. He shall oversee my fields; his men shall plow and sow and harvest what Gildewin can no longer; and they shall bring to me my yield while Isadora and Branwen grind wheat for their daily bread. Who among you, then, will speak her oath for Ardelle?"

"I will," says Florentina.

"This will not make her your bond-sister," says Myrah.

"Nor will it take the stench of dung from father's words," says Florentina.

Myrah leaves her mother and stands beside me with her arm on my elbow. I close my eyes. My fingers grasp at something that is not there—mother's ankle as her burned body hangs from a tree. Fingers close around my palm and bring me to my knees against the hard marble.

"I, who stand alone, wrought by fire and earth ..." Myrah whispers.

Her words are lost amid the stone columns of the hypocaust from which Isadora walks free. When I have spoken all that is to be said, I remember that I am to set my lips to the golden snake on this man's leathery hands and stand to take the kiss of Myrah's mother on my cheek.

"I am your father, Athelbert," says the king. "You are my daughter, who obeys me faithfully in all things."

Myrah's elbow draws a grunt from my ribs.

"Father," I croak.

My words are the mud in which a pig bathes.

"I am Ziri, queen to your king," says Myrah's mother. "You are my daughter, who obeys me faithfully in all things."

"Mother," I whisper.

The pig washes itself in the river where men shit.

"I am Myrah, atheling to your king and queen, daughter to your mother and father, sister to you and your kindred."

"Sister."

The pig hides beneath the earth from misty rain, frightened by the thought of being cleansed of the filth that has become like unto its own flesh.

"Let it be so," come the deep and bellowing words of a man who speaks and waits for no answer.

I sit with the broken stone men on the floor until the room is empty but for the hearth's flames that stand watch over their shattered bodies. A black gown lifts itself from the black shoes it hides.

"Shall I take them off as the others have?" Myrah says.

I shake my head. Myrah kneels down beside me and searches within my eyes for something the hearth's fires do not show her. Her face nears mine, slowly, as her eyes look to my forehead, my eyebrows, my nose—what does she seek that she does not have? Her lips come to rest where my cheek meets my mouth. When my lips wake, hers are gone. Still she stares at me, blinking as she draws away. My eyes follow her unsteady steps through the great room's opening. By the time my legs find their strength again, Myrah is gone from the great room next to Rosamond and Marigold's bedroom, nor is she in the great room next to Annette's bedroom. The others, if I found them, might tell me to bathe myself again. They would not be wrong.

I sit down in the heated water and let my heavy legs rest against the stone floor of the bath. As the water flows over them, they float apart. Behind the wall that hides the bath, someone looks in—someone who is not Myrah. No, here is Winiburg, sitting opposite me, her wet white linen taking from me all other thoughts. The aching returns to my hips; I meet it with my hand, then my fingers. Myrah's kiss will not leave my mind—I must not let Winiburg leave my mind—until my fingertips and Myrah's lips have stilled the many thoughts I have of her.

II

SANCTUARY

9

EVENSONG

Marigold's hearth fire in its raised iron bowl dries my hair where it hangs over the high back of a chair. The stone men who ward the hearth stand upright once more bearing misshapen faces that somehow bear no mark of having been broken. My eyelids hide them from me, leaving Myrah and Winiburg to stand in their stead—my fingers will not work their black and blue gowns from my mind. Bleariness gives way to red and white in Derwen's arm. She stands with her knees and shins far enough from mine that Myrah might learn well from her how to do this.

"Father will stay for our evening song before he leaves us again," says Derwen. "We are to give thanks at the runestone in the day's last light."

"Thanks for what?" I say. "Men with knives? Women with clay pots?"

"For not being dead."

Red wool and white linen fall into my lap. Four small golden breastpins nestle within their folds. A length of undyed linen hides them.

115

"I need my gown," says Derwen.

I stand, sending her gift to the floor in a heap. Her green wool and breastpins, however, I offer to her from my arms. Derwen's sisters come to us from the bathing room wearing gowns as red as hers; only Annette is without her wool.

"Will you sing with us this evening?" says Annette. "None will harm us within these walls."

I turn from them with folded arms and stare back at the painted men whose misshapen faces glare at me without naming the wrongdoings of which I am guilty.

"Myrah's fingers have straightened my hair," says Florentina. "I need my hair rods, Ardelle. Ardelle, did you hear me? Take me to my room."

"Why do you ask me?" I say.

"I offered to swear an oath for your dear Isadora," she says. "Luda's arms are weary. I think you should at least bear me to my room in thanks for what I have done."

"It was Myrah who spoke," I say, "not you."

Florentina growls like a cat who has been asked to share the mouse it has caught. When I turn to her, her face bears no mark of having been angered.

"Was Rosamond right, then?" I say. "Was Myrah lying when she asked my forgiveness?"

Annette frowns at Rosamond. Rosamond takes Marigold's elbow and draws her friend closer to her.

"Myrah's mother does not strike her," bellows Annette.

She looks to the emptiness of the two great rooms behind us, as if she listens for fleeing footsteps. Derwen gathers her gifts from the floor with Annette's help and holds them in her arm as one might a newborn child.

"We walked with mother and father to bid them farewell," says Derwen. "It was Myrah who left her own mother to come back to the hearth room, claiming that she had forgotten something. What did she forget?"

My lips twitch. Florentina lifts one eyebrow. I let my arms fall to my sides.

"She forgot to tell me that I am to shed the aldorman's white linen," I say. "I will take Florentina to her bedroom and there do so in peace. When Myrah has learned that Florentina's horse can do nothing for her, my dear old mother Florentina will tell Myrah's mother to send me home."

"Ha!" says Florentina with a grin. "Whose mother am I?"

Florentina's arms are around my neck, choking the life from me.

"Set your arms under her legs and hold your hands together at your waist," says Luda. "You may need to lean forwards until Florentina learns how not to strangle you."

"Come, horse," Florentina says. I walk on legs that bend more than they should. "To my hair rods. First, we must heal these wounds of yours that Annette has forgotten about."

"I had yet to do it," calls Annette. "Myrah bid me do otherwise."

"Myrah, Myrah, Myrah," Florentina says to my ear. "I will help you and you will help me and thereafter, if my hair is as fair as it was before Myrah threatened it so wickedly, you will sleep on a bed that is not a floor."

In Florentina's room, I set her down on a chair and rest on the thick woollen bedding that hides the raised stone beneath it. Marigold comes to us with one hand sliding along the door and wall and down onto the table, where she sits in a chair beside Florentina.

"We have only two chairs, Ardelle," says Florentina, "so you will have to stand. Take my head cloth and hold it at the bottom of each rod. Marigold and I will do the rest."

As I do so, Florentina winds thick lengths of golden hair that run halfway down her back around brass rods that come to life with Marigold's warmth. Where Marigold's hands and arms work without tiring, my legs have become numb by the time Florentina has given her hair the long, winding rings that had never left it. She looks over each strand as one would a hen's egg that might hatch at any time. With a nod of her head, she claps her hands together.

"Here," says Derwen. She throws her gift of red and white onto the bedding from the room's opening. "I will take your aldorman's linen."

Marigold rises from her chair and leaves on the elbow of Rosamond, who has come to meet her. I turn away from Derwen, let fall my linen, throw it behind me without looking, and take Derwen's white gown. It rests much softer against my arms. Derwen takes the aldorman's linen into her fist, strides into the hearth room, and sends it aloft into the hearth fire, where it burns with light grey smoke.

"Sit," says Florentina.

She pats the wooden seat beside her. I have only sat down when Florentina's fingertips on my temples send all the water of the sea rushing through limbs that did not know they had need of healing until the butterfly chill of winter's frosted kisses soothed their flesh and bone into stillness. When my eyes remember the gift of sight, Florentina's high-cheeked smile meets them.

"Now, wear your red gown for your dear old mother," she says.

My arms slide into the red wool's sleeves. Florentina fastens two breastpins at my waist and two at my neck with fingers that must have done so every day for ten years or more. A yawn leaves my mouth; my eyes become heavy. Florentina bids me lie down on thick bedding whose woollen folds warm me so well in my gowns that I might walk out into the sea's coldest water and yet feel nothing of its chill.

When I wake, the stone roof that hides in the shadows of the setting sun's glow must be as tall as seven men—eight if they are short. Florentina crawls onto the bed with her hair shrouded in linen and feels along the unbroken bone of my nose.

"I have never heard a song so fair," I say.

"You are welcome," says Florentina. "In Emerita, I healed some men so well that they wished to wed me. You, however, have only to bear me to the runestone and back. Set your hair down the back of your gown so we do not have to hide so much of it."

Derwen sits down beside her and helps her wind the linen around my head until I am bald. I bear Florentina's slight weight somewhat better now that she does not take the breath from my lungs with her forearms. Behind me, her sisters follow us through the great rooms in a row with Annette once again at its tail.

"Why is Annette last?" I say.

"She is the youngest," says Florentina. "Well, you are, but you bear all thirty-two of my years on your back as hard as this stone floor. And still you have no shoes. Oh, Myrah, how thoughtless of you. No, not over there, Ardelle. That door is locked. Straight through the open door to the hallway where it goes left and right. No more talk from you, now."

Though I know not whither we go, Florentina's whispered words lead us through winding halls whose marble becomes rough stone that stings the bottoms of my feet. Light comes to us through narrow openings, darkened at times by spear-bearing men in iron shirts and helms who talk to one another with laughing words as they wander among flower-edged hedges. When their eyes meet mine, I look away and stride forwards, striking my forehead against the stone wall of an unlit hall whose roof begins at my waist and leads into noth-ingness. I set Florentina down and crawl in the dark along stone that makes my elbows and knees ache through the thick-ness of my red wool. When my hands find the wood of a door, fingernails dig into my neck.

"When we return," Florentina whispers, "you will crawl while I rest on your back so your sister Luda does not have to do this for you. Now, take me up and open the door."

The small, iron-bound door opens into a great grove of high-boughed oak trees, whose thick bodies wear gowns of tall hedges and browning harvest grass. The heavens bear dark grey tuft-clouds that smell of rain. The others take off their shoes and hose and leave them beside the sanctuary's hard walls. Derwen taps her foot against the browning grass.

"Had you shoes and hose," she says to me, "this is where you would leave them."

She leads us through thickly clustered oak boughs to a clearing in which the king stands with his back to us before a runestone taller than he. His wife stands to his right, and his daughter to her right. They, like we, wear no shoes. Should this mean something to me?

Derwen stands three steps behind the king. Luda is not far behind her. Marigold and Rosamond stand to one side with arms linked. Annette is beside me. We abide in silence for a time.

"Derwen?" says the queen and turns to her.

Derwen looks at her feet. A soft song greets the clouds— they are Rosamond's words.

"Set me down!" Florentina hisses into my ear.

I do so, and she sets her palms against the grass; her words float away along with those of her sisters to the heavens, whose dark grey clouds bestow soft showers on our head linen. Where Annette knows only every third word, I know nothing, and so I stand as still as any of the painted men until I am told what to do.

When our gowns can hold no more of the heavens' water, the sisters still sing. I search among the thick-nested boughs for an opening through which I might leave while they worship the sound of their own words. What I find are stone walls whose tops reach almost as high as the leaf-shedding oak boughs. At length, our song comes to an end. I bend down to take up Florentina, but she does not climb onto my back. The king faces us, as do his wife and daughter. I sit down on the wet grass and hang my head, for I have never heard him open his mouth for anything less than a thousand words.

"Your unending devotion has brought our foes to the mead halls, where we talk of the peace found in your song and which you have so faithfully held in your hearts even as you stand here before us." Arms lift me to my feet. "In keeping yourselves from the sight of men, you have worked your gifts upon our northern and western brothers without calling forth that timeless fear of the unknown, which would otherwise bring them together against us with renewed strength. We are the keepers of the old ways, and it is the steadfast keeping of those worthy traditions that will lead our kingdom to witness the dawning of an endless night, a rebirth in which we seek to sow the seeds of forgotten truths in the minds of men that they may grow into understanding. You have come from near and far to live together with your sisters, whose thoughts, words, hearts, and lives are so unlike your own. So, too, must the many men of these lands live with one another, bound by laws whose abiding truths bring order to our grasping incomprehension, lest we make friends of one another only when we have awoken together in the next life. And thus, I must ask you …" His chest heaves. "… to keep yourselves hidden from sight for a month as we seek to make peace with those who have borne spears against us."

My legs lose their strength. Luda comes to me and grasps her wiry forearms around my waist.

"Will you be faithful?" says the queen.

"We will," Luda says, as do her sisters.

"Ardelle," says this man who calls himself king. "This burden weighs greatest upon you. Your sisters know this. Your suffering wakens within them bitter memories best left in ashes. What I ask of you now is that you share in their willing sacrifice by remaining hidden away."

"You would have one day among you become thirty?" I say. "Am I to feel free in this grove of trees met on all sides by tall stone walls? Am I to believe that it was not my mother who gave me to my father, but you who plucked me from the clouds and brought me to rest on earth for my father to find among your slain foes?"

"I will give whatever words you wish to your mother and father myself," says Myrah. "You may watch as I write them down."

"And if I do not sit and watch you smear dung on parchments to be brought to those you say are not my mother and father?"

In the falling rain, a slight stirring of Derwen's head yields a chin no longer softened by song.

"You will die," she says to the ground beside her feet.

"Then when I die locked away in one of these stone rooms," I say, "you are to bury me near this lifeless runestone so flowers may grow from my rotting flesh."

"And thus the bitterness of our words is equal to that which the heavens give us now," says Myrah's father. "Let us find peace within these walls once more."

The words that Derwen and the others speak as one are lost to the misty wind that stings our faces. Florentina's wet gowns make her heavy on my back, even more so when she rests her weight on me as I creep through the lightless, low-roofed, rough-floored stone hall on my knees and elbows. When at last we have made our wordless way through dim and winding halls into the bright light of the first of the great rooms, Florentina wrests my head to the right with one hand.

"We bathe after our evening song," she says.

"Then bathe," I say.

Florentina's arms free themselves from my throat when I sit down in the bath's water. She sits on the stone floor and stares at me as her sisters take off their gowns and I free my hair from its soaked linen. Some of them stop before stepping into the bath.

"What is wrong with you?" says Rosamond. "Must you be told to take off your gowns before bathing?"

"I was asked to wear this gown," I say. "And so I shall."

"If you do not wish to bathe," says Annette, "take off your gowns for Marigold to dry and wait in my room. You are among friends, here."

I stand from the bath, leaving my soaked red wool and breastpins on the floor, and walk in my wet linen to Annette's bedroom, where I sit in a pool of my own chilly thoughts. When the shaking wetness of my arms and legs becomes greater than all else, I wring the water from my linen onto the great room's floor and leave it there to dry. A sounding at the door sends me beneath the bedding. Myrah steps in and leaves blue and white gowns on the table without looking at what she does.

"I will take your words while you wear these," she says and shuts the door.

I dry myself with the rough woollen bedding, working reddish life into my flesh. Thereafter, I wear Myrah's gowns and fasten a breastpin at each sleeveless blue shoulder as mother has done for me so many times. Without warning, Myrah walks into the room as if I am not there. She would send me onto the bedding did I not step to one side and stand against the wall. The table takes her parchment, pot of ink, and writing feather. She sits in Annette's chair with her back to me. I lie down on the bed facing the marble wall. Should she think to look at me, she will find only Winiburg's blue gown.

"Will you not watch as I write your words to Gildewin and Branwen?" Myrah says. "You may learn from doing so."

"Would you teach me anew the names of my father and mother? I will speak to them myself tomorrow. You may write whatever you wish. Good night."

The darkness behind my eyelids weighs heavy with the great stone the aldorman's drunken harvest-men sent to one another in my dream. The bedding beside me shifts: silver earrings shine from on high, where they overlook the night sea of Myrah's gown. I withdraw my eyes to the wintry, wind-blown stillness of Derwen's marble wall.

"I will take you to that door," Myrah says, "the one Annette opened for you when we came here. Beyond that, I can not go with you."

Fingers stroke my bruised temple. I throw off my woollen bedding and sit before the door on the edge of the bed's raised stone.

"The wound on your head is almost gone," says Myrah.

"When I slept on the floor in Rosamond's room," I say, "you sat on my ribs and took the breath from my throat with your hands."

"Shall I ask forgiveness for your dreams?"

"I would ask that you stay out of them. When I woke, I struck my head against Marigold's table and woke her as well."

"You must have spoken with her. She has had none but her sisters with whom to speak. I need someone to talk to as well."

"You have six sisters."

"Derwen does not speak to me," says Myrah. "I know Florentina's thoughts before she does. Rosamond tells me only what I wish to hear. Marigold's dreams are much the same from one night to the next. When I speak to Luda, she listens but says nothing. Annette only ever asks me to allow her to leave with her man. He is the same one who brought her here to keep her from harm."

"Why has she not left, then? Why must she ask you?"

"Others have died for doing the same," says Myrah. "She knows this. She thinks I can help her, but I can not. And I do not wish to see this happen to you even if you hate my father and mother."

"Did your mother tell you to come in here?" I say.

"She did. She also told me I will go with her to your fields bearing your words. I will be the one to read them aloud, whatever they may be."

She stands as if to take her chair at the writing table, but sits down beside me with her gown resting against mine. I look away from her—lips find my neck behind my ear and are gone before I turn to her. My heart beats itself into my ribs; my blood quickens with dusk's heat. I should strike her on her mother's behalf. Myrah shifts herself away from me. Why do I not stand and leave this bedroom at once?

"Marigold told me of your dream," she says. "A man on a boat."

"I have many dreams."

"Tell me of your dark boatman, and I will tell you something of my own darkness."

"You said you would beg your mother on my behalf, and yet I am still here."

"I am to live here among your sisters at the sanctuary without mother's wisdom to tell me how to do so and without father's strength to keep his watchmen away from me," Myrah says. "The watchmen come to me and tell me how fair I must look without my gowns. Do you know what father says to me when I tell him of this? He says I am to answer them as an atheling would. I know not what that means. Neither does mother, but she looks on his words as if they are the rain that comes down from the clouds."

"Are they the spear-men I saw through the gaps in the wall when we went to the runestone?"

"Their spears are meant to keep others from harming us. Like your father does."

My heavy outbreath sinks along with my shoulders. Myrah's hand stirs as if to set itself around them, but rests on her knee instead.

"Like my father *did*," I say. "And yet the boatman in my dreams still wishes to take him. He said I must give him my blood, else I will never know peace."

"Your many dreams each bear some small shard of truth," Myrah says. "I ask that you forgive me for having choked you. I have never wished to do so, but I will not tell you that you lie."

"You are forgiven," I say.

"Now come and watch your dark dreams take shape once more." Myrah sits at the table and dips the writing feather's sharpened bone into the ink pot. "You are not the first of your kindred to have fled this sanctuary. You would also not be the first to lie beneath the earth for having done so. It is thus that you were kept bound in that hypocaust: mother knew what would befall you if you left us. She wished to show you the truth of this. But you do not listen, and I can not make you listen. Give me your words, then, ghost, and I shall listen to them. Tell your mother and father of your love for them, or tell them of your hatred for the king and his daughter, or tell them that you will see them soon; and I shall speak these words to them when those words are all that they have left of you."

Mother and father's names come to life on the parchment, written in the high-stroked letters found in Isadora's books.

"Will you also read these words to Isadora?" I say.

"To Isadora and to your sisters, whether you call them that or not. I will offer your bitter words to the hearth, where they will rest among their kindred ashes."

With halting words I tell Myrah of my love for my mother and father and Isadora, of how I think of them every day, of how I dream of them within these stone walls, and of how I wish one day to be together with them again. The telling draws forth a burning ache from within my heart made lighter by Myrah's thick and willowy strokes; and by her lissome fingers, which will one day be kin to mine when I write my own tidings of love and tales of wistful dreams.

10

INQUISITIONS

Mother would often tell me, while I sat beside her bedding and kneaded her palms with my thumbs, that the days become shorter as we become wiser; and that our greatest wisdom, when our children are old enough to bear their own children, lies in so filling those days that their shortened length rekindles our own childhood. I would like to ask mother how wise she has become—welcoming father's yew bough on the backs of my legs as I do so—without her mindless daughter there to hinder her. For two days, I sit in Florentina's bedroom wearing Myrah's blue gown and listen to the sisters in the hearth room as they speak of nothing at all using words that would have me believe otherwise, until at last on the morning of the third day, Myrah comes to me with tidings from my mother.

"Be good," she says.

"My mother said nothing more than that?" I say. "Who wrote those words?"

"I did," says Myrah. "Branwen does not write. Have you eaten nothing these two days?"

Myrah lifts my bread round from Florentina's table, spilling bits of crumbled cheese.

"Your sisters say you would not come out of your room for anything," she says. "When you slept at night, they wondered whether you still lived."

"What did you write on my father's behalf?" I say.

"Your father wishes you well," says Myrah. "Isadora is with them. She helps your mother weave wool for winter."

"Could she not have written down her own thoughts?"

"No," says Myrah and sits down in a chair beside my bed.

"How is father's leg?" I say.

"The aldorman looks after them. You need not—"

"I asked of his leg."

"His leg was hewn at the shin. There is nothing more to be said."

"Show me their words."

Myrah shows me the parchment, where she has written their few thoughts in letters much smaller than my words to them. She sets it down on the table beside my morning meal, which has now become Florentina's.

"When you have made your peace, you may burn it in the hearth's fire," she says. She taps my foot with the bottom of her black leather shoe. "The tanner makes your shoes. Will you wear hose?"

"I have learned how not to fall down on your marble floors," I say.

"Well done," says Myrah. "Isadora told me you found great happiness in reading your sisters' words, and yet here you sit having learned nothing from what they might say to you themselves."

"They are not my—"

"Yes, yes, they are not your sisters. You do not wish to talk. I understand this. I thought you might like to listen for a while."

For the next seven days while we are hidden away, Myrah comes to speak with me when the sun's light begins to wane and the sisters have not yet sung. We sit alone in the room I share with Florentina and Derwen, at first in chairs at the table where Myrah's sisters can hear us from the great room, then later on the bedding opposite one another with the door shut as our talks lengthen into eventide. I follow her speech as well as I am able—she tells me of her mother and father as though they live in the tales sung by drunken men in mead halls, yet the words that bring them to life are unlike any I have read in Isadora's books. And unlike Isadora, Myrah tells me of their meaning and even bids me use them in tales of my own, meeting them with smiles and laughter that tell me nothing of whether what I have said is wise or meaningless.

Myrah's mother, she says, hails from a place once called Mauretania Tingitana along the northern coast of sun-blessed lands whose hills stand taller than the cliffs along the sea. When the old imperium left, she was sent eastward by men who told her she had forgotten who she was. In cold and craggy lands she met men and women alike who wore tall hats and long leggings and wielded bent bows on horseback. Among them rode Myrah's father, who had come from afar seeking a wife whose mind had not forgotten the old Roman ways. On the night he met Myrah's mother, Myrah came into being, and since that day, Ziri has been a faithful wife to her husband and a loving mother to her daughter.

"Their women fight alongside their men?" I say.

"They do," says Myrah. "They are also buried in barrows with their weapons as the men are. You may use horses to flee, but you must never take up a spear."

"Annette said you have not learned to ride horses."

"I have learned to sit on their backs without being thrown. Have I done well?"

When, on that seventh day, Myrah has said all she wishes

to, Florentina asks me for the seventh time whether I will wear a red gown and bear her without to the hearth's fire. Raised eyebrows and half-smiles greet me as I come to stand with the sisters in red amid brightly lit, high-roofed marble walls whose column-bound stone watchmen meet our eyes from all sides. The broken-nosed men beside the raised iron bowl stare at the hue of my red gown as though their hearth does not bear the same. Florentina bites at my ear, which I take to mean she has something to say to me.

"Myrah talks with everyone when they first come here," she says, "but I have not seen her talk at such great length with any of the others. How is it that you have learned so many words from reading our dreams?"

"I learned most of them from reading yours," I say. "You write more than anyone else."

Florentina takes off my head linen and drops it on the floor.

"We do not wear these in the sanctuary," she says.

"But you wear yours," I say.

"You talk too much. Did your friend's books speak of anything other than our dreams?"

"I would not know which are your dreams and which are something else."

"It may be that Myrah seeks to find this out from you," she whispers. "Withhold from her some of what you know and she may like you better."

"Or it may be that she wishes to have someone around who has not heard all of her tales."

"Her tales are few and send me to sleep when the sun is still overhead," whispers Florentina. "Myrah wishes to know a great many things that are of little use to her. In you, she may have found a kindred spirit."

"Why do you—"

"Be silent now. Rosamond sings."

Myrah does not talk with me thereafter, but comes to my bedroom the next evening with no tales of her own. She asks instead about my cheeks and nose hued red and why they are lighter today than yesterday; she asks why I wear my hose and new shoes when we sing and never elsewhere; she asks why I unweave Florentina's braids after our song.

"That is the way of things," I say.

Myrah smiles and draws nearer to me. The door swings open.

"Why did you not come when I called you?" asks Derwen.

Where storm clouds on the foreheads of others might darken the whites of their eyes, thunder lies in wait behind Derwen's words.

"We were talking," I say. "I did not hear you."

"Nor did Myrah, who has more than once heard things whispered in neighbouring rooms," says Derwen.

Myrah only smiles and stares at me.

"Have you two nothing to say?" says Derwen. "Why is it that we sing without you while Florentina sits on the ground?"

Myrah blinks at me and lifts her eyebrows.

"Florentina told me she thought Myrah and I were kindred spirits," I say.

"So you would lay the guilt for this in Florentina's lap?" says Derwen as she swings the door wide. "Florentina! Ardelle is ready to bear you now."

"I must first use my—"

"She is coming," yells Derwen.

My legs have not yet straightened when Derwen grasps my left arm beneath my shoulder and walks me into the hearth room. There, Florentina sits not on the floor, but on a chair beside one of its empty kin. Opposite her sits Annette, who sews woollen thread through the sleeves of a brown tunic too broad for her. Derwen tells me to sit down; my legs are on the wooden seat before the words have left her lips. My hair hangs over my knees like the weighted boughs of a willow tree. I start along with Florentina when our bedroom door slams shut. Luda comes to us from the neighbouring great room and stares at the oaken door with her arms folded.

Florentina talks with Annette for a time, telling her of the woodland animals who live near the sanctuary and, though they fright readily at the sight of men, fight among themselves as wretchedly as do those from whom they run. Between thread stitches, Annette asks Florentina to explain how it is that cats and mice are able to speak to each other without the latter being eaten. Florentina's answer drowns in the waves of yelling that flood into the hearth room when Myrah opens our bedroom door. Derwen falls silent; the door closes itself.

"Why is Derwen angry?" I say.

"You may go and ask her if you wish," says Florentina.

I rise from my chair. A hand pulls on my gown.

"I did not mean that you should go and ask her," Florentina says.

"Those were the words you used," says Annette.

Florentina whispers a curse in Latin and asks me to take her up so she can choke me with her forearms. Within our bedroom, Derwen and Myrah face one another on both sides of a table amid a field of battle where once mighty chairs lie overthrown.

"Let me talk alone with Myrah for a time as you have done these seven days," says Derwen.

"Florentina makes ready for your song," I say.

"Yes, Derwen, the song you have not been singing," says Florentina. "Did you keep your words to yourself for seven days so you could yell them at Myrah?"

Myrah folds her arms and stares at Derwen. Derwen gathers her long, light brown hair and shoves half of it under her gown before setting her head linen around her neck.

"We wear shoes and hose," she says to me as she leaves our bedroom barefoot.

Myrah does not follow her. I set myself down on the bedding with my back to Florentina so that she may braid my hair.

"Why are you here?" Florentina says.

The door closes. Fingers weave my thick strands of hair with a deftness I have not felt from them. A hand on my chin keeps me from turning my head.

"I have not yet fastened your hair with pins," says Rosamond.

"When did you come in?" I ask.

"Yes, Rosamond, why *are* you here?" Florentina says.

"Myrah asked me to help you so that she has many sisters behind whom she may hide when I lead us in song once again," says Rosamond. "You have been here long enough to know that we sing in the evening. Father depends on Derwen to uphold his traditions when he is away. You might ask Myrah to hereafter talk with you after our midday meal. You might also meet with Derwen after we have sung and seek her forgiveness in the tongue you share with her."

"Not Latin," whispers Florentina. "She will take your head off if you speak it to her."

"Ardelle's Latin sounds as though the words have been washed with a dirty sponge," says Rosamond. "Thus, I have counselled Ardelle to speak Derwen's tongue to show Derwen the earnestness of what she says. Come, now."

Dread floods my breast as I stand in my red and white gowns and head linen and woollen hose and brown leather shoes bearing Florentina at the head of a row which I have learned takes us from oldest to youngest. Derwen stands before the hearth's raised iron bowl.

"Marigold, come here and give our song your strength," she says.

Marigold walks by each of us, running her fingertips along our left shoulders, until she reaches Derwen's pinned gown sleeve. Derwen grasps one of the iron rods that hold up the hearth's bowl.

"Ardelle," says Derwen, "set your hand on my right shoulder."

Luda takes Florentina from my back and stands so close behind me that I must step forwards lest her bending knees strike my legs hard enough to send me to the floor. I set my hand on Derwen's right shoulder as softly as a mouse might walk over a shallow stream on the tail of a sleeping cat.

"You must sing whatever you know," she says to me.

The words of our song have become well enough known to me that I forget few of them. Where my words are but a fleeting hum, Luda yells her song to the stone roof far above our heads loud enough that it should splinter the legs of chairs and split the hearth room's three broad oaken tables. Derwen breaks her own halting song to tell me I must do the same as my sisters, but I can not, for the life that should come from within my throat has fled in fear down into my breast.

As Derwen takes up her song again in earnest, so, too, does Marigold's fire burn brighter, flooding my breast and limbs with a warmth that goes far beyond that of our bathing water. My mouth becomes dry, my lips cracked; my head stings with blinding lightness. When Derwen is at last still, my red gown is so wet with sweat at my neck and below my arms that I throw off its breastpins and let it fall to the floor. Derwen takes me by the wrist and walks me to the other end of the room while her sisters stand and stare. Myrah frowns without looking as she walks by us through the room's opening.

"Why do you not ready yourself for our song when the sun goes down?" Derwen says. "You have all day to spend talking with Myrah, and yet you choose to do so when evening draws near."

"I choose nothing," I say. "She does as she wishes, and you have done nothing to stop it. Which one of us do you hate more?"

"From your speech, I might think that you have as little need of this sanctuary as Myrah …" Derwen looks towards the opening in the wall. "… yet neither of you has left!"

In the next room, a woman grunts as heavy table legs shift against the hard floor. Derwen follows the sound of hastening footsteps into the neighbouring room, where she sits down at a long alder table from which she takes up an open book. Seeing this, her red-gowned sisters gather chairs and sit with one another in silence. Rosamond comes to me where I stand hidden beside the opening.

"Ask Derwen's forgiveness so that we may sleep in peace this evening," she whispers. "She may be of a mind to do so if you ask her to teach you to write."

Rosamond sets her hands against my back and leans into me. No sooner have I walked through the opening than I behold hardened green eyes that gleam like a wary snake's scales. I step back but am met by Rosamond's hand where she hides from Derwen on the other side of the wall.

"Go away," says Derwen.

The snake settles down into dusk's shadows as the great room's light seems to dim though Marigold's fire burns as brightly as ever. Derwen's frown should burn the letters of her book into ashes. I take one step towards her, then another, then three more until I stand on the other side of her table.

"Guragun tanc," I say. Let us make peace.

She lifts her book as if to throw it at me.

"Rosamond said you will teach me to write," I say.

Derwen drops the book on the table.

"Myrah spends more than enough time with you to teach you that," she says.

She rests her arm on the alder wood's dark brown marks like to the sea's waves coming to shore.

"Leave me be now," she says in our tongue, and so I do.

In the hearth room, the sisters sit in stillness.

"How did she take your words?" says Rosamond.

"She almost threw a book at me," I say.

"She must like you," Rosamond says, "else your forehead would bear her book's mark."

"She threw our bedroom chairs at the floor instead of at Myrah—does that mean Derwen likes her?"

Florentina's mild laughter warms her cheeks with blood. Rosamond stills her own mirth when she sees that Florentina shares it.

"Derwen is twice as old as Myrah," Florentina says. "More than anything, Myrah's childish ways vex her."

"Is she really so childish as you say?"

"Did she not step on your head? Ah, you are but a year older than she; you would not know. Come, let us sit with our sisters and wait for our dear old mother to calm herself before she goes to the bathing room with us to soak her head."

When Derwen has become too weary to yell any further, she sits with us in the warm bath water and listens as her sisters spend their breath speaking of all the men they might wed were they not bound within these walls. A young woman —or is that a boy?—calls from the great room. As one, the sisters rise from the water and dry themselves, wearing only their linen as they bear their red gowns to their rooms. When they return, they sit down facing the narrow opening that leads to the rough stone halls where men with spears watched over us from among the hedges. Why does the oaken door in Annette's hall of painted floor stones bear a lock while this room's door does not?

"Do we wait for something?" I ask Florentina.

Annette and Luda rise to meet the young boy in brown

who enters. He stops at the opening and stares at my red gown, then that of Derwen, who walks along the wall furthest from the opening. She turns and yells at him without breaking her slow stride; he flees out of sight. Not long after Derwen has likewise left, a frowning man in dark brown steps in. He takes Annette's hand to his breast and her words in his ear before leaving. Thereafter, the boy looks into the room from where he hides with one hand gripping the stone wall. When Annette waves him towards her, he leaps out and walks before eight men in many-hued, knee-length tunics; their thin leather belts bear sturdy brass buckles and knife sheaths that hang empty. One black-haired man in green lifts Florentina from her chair and sits down with her facing him in his lap. Their lips become so tightly bound that they forget for a time that they still have need of breathing. When I have leaned far enough away from them, Florentina's man takes her up in his arms and walks off into the neighbouring great room.

Rosamond and Marigold take the blue-sleeved arms of men who hide their faces from me as they walk by. Annette holds a man as wide as an ox cart with a bushy black beard and strewn straw hair. He wears a broad brown tunic with woollen stitches in its sleeves. They kiss one another as I have seen mother and father do when they think I sleep. Luda sets her arms around a hairless man who is somehow taller than she. They do not kiss, nor do they hold hands as they follow Annette into their bedroom. The young boy and his watchman set a beam of timber in the iron hooks on both sides of their door, then go to do the same to Rosamond and Marigold's room. I am thus left alone with three men who stare at me as a cat does brown mice trapped outside stone-stopped burrows while their yellow sisters hide in hedgerows.

"My name is Edward," says a dark-haired man in blue with a shadow for a beard. "I watch over many fields far north of here, where the weather is cooler."

"I am Oswald," says a brown-haired man in red-hemmed yellow who looks as though he could be a younger brother to Isadora. "I have been told of your knowledge of reading and writing."

"Who told you of this?" I say.

"Gerahard," says a crag-jawed, broken-nosed man in brown darkened to black by dung. His head and cheeks are shaven so well that some of the skin must have been taken with the hair. His tunic ends at his elbows, whereafter his undyed undershirt's sleeves rest bound around his wrists by sinewy leather strings. "I will have you in this life or the next."

I take a step back as his friends laugh. I can not flee this man and hope to live.

"What am I to do with such words?" I say.

The one called Gerahard straightens himself. His lips and cheeks strain under the burden of a smile.

"We have given you our names," he says. "What is yours?"

"Ardelle."

"Ardelle," says Gerahard. "One who is keen. For you, I shall be a mighty spear who rends the heart of any who would do you harm; at your side, I will be a hound who comforts you."

I step away from the hound who comes to bite at my heels. Gerahard's friends draw near to me.

"You could tell me of what you do in your fields," says the one named Edward.

"We could sit for a time and talk of the many words you must have read," says Oswald.

In creeping backwards, I am met by the watchman who stands within the great room's opening. He strides around me and takes the chair on whose back Oswald rests his hands. The young boy stands to one side and stares at us.

"The master comes to shut them in their rooms," says Gerahard. "I will sit with you, if you like, with my hands bound in my lap as I tell you tales of what I have seen and done in Francia, the birth land of your sister Rosamond. You may find some satisfaction in the listening."

"I would leave you with a gift," says Edward as he reaches into a leather bag that hangs from his belt.

"You would buy her," says Gerahard.

"That is not the way of things," says Edward.

"I would tell you of my family, Ardelle," says Oswald, "and learn of yours. There are many things we might share with each other."

"Your words are the shield that hides the spear," says Gerahard.

"I know not what to say to you," I say. "I would not have one of you glad while the others are saddened."

"You have given her a fright, Oswald," says Gerahard. "You and I come from the fields, Ardelle, as does your sister Rosamond, who lives in these halls with you. We are friends to waiting; we are true to those on whom we wait. If fortune is my muse, we will meet again. In your absence, I will think of you often, even if you have no thoughts for me."

My legs weaken; I sit down on the chair beside me. The words I speak next are not my own.

"My lord, I would not—"

Gerahard's laughter sounds throughout the great rooms.

"I am her lord, men," he says. "See how worthless your shillings and books have become. I shall have you, Ardelle, in this life or the next, in body or in spirit."

The watchman walks with Gerahard to the opening that leads to the halls, then stares at the others as he clutches a spear that is not there.

"He means to win you after he has left," says Oswald.

I set my palms against my knees and drive my heels into the marble until I stand upright.

"I am not to be won," I say.

Edward looks to his friend, then reaches again for the leather bag on his belt.

"I would not place myself in your thoughts unwanted as that man in black does," he says. "I would leave you instead with a token of friendship."

Edward offers my palm a golden shilling bearing the likeness of a man. Beneath his neck and shoulders lie the carved runes of his name.

"Theodosius," I say.

"A great man," says Edward. "I hope one day to be as great as he."

When you give the dark boatman this shilling and he takes you to the life beyond, you will be the king's equal in having become nothing.

"Do you bear a spear for him?" I say.

"Gerahard is right," says Oswald. "You are keen."

"You will not see us but when you go to the runestone," says Edward. "The king does not allow us within these walls unless we have great need."

"As you do now?"

"Will you not choose one of us with whom to spend the evening?" says Edward.

"To talk and nothing more, if that be your wish," says Oswald. "Thereafter, you may walk freely through the halls and in the oak groves, though you should not wear that red gown when you do so. We will watch over you."

"Have you a mother and father nearby?" says Edward. "Frankish traders send their ships here often. What does your mother wish for?"

"Now I think you do buy her, brother," says Oswald with a laugh.

As they have done with the others. That is how we are sisters. Shall I ask Derwen to sleep on the floor beneath our table while one of these brothers talks to me until he has given me the child the aldorman did not? Here, my lord, is the boat-man, who has come to take your blood from me. Do not ask me why, for there is no answer to be found in this waking world that does not stink of death.

I set the shilling in Edward's hand and close his fingers around it. His eyes also close when I set my lips against his. His friend Oswald's sadness quickly leaves his face when I give him the same kiss. They smile, and therefore I shall not die.

I run from the room between book-strewn tables whose unneeded candles burn with Marigold's reddish-blue light. In the bright-walled hearth room, Florentina and her man have forgotten how to breathe as they do their best to suck the life from one another's lungs through their mouths. Within my bedroom, my arms are beset with a sudden strength that lightens the door's heavy wooden beam as I slide it through the wall-bound iron hooks. I set my shoulder against the oak and steady my breath in dusk's moonless glow.

"You did not take a man?" asks Derwen from the bedding.

"That watchman Gerahard said he would have me in this life or the next," I say.

"Good," she says. "You know who they are. Come here." I lie down beside her on the wool. Her words become a whisper. "Some men are like bees who use honeyed words to bring you to them so they may sting you. Others are like the great birds in the northern mountains who drive you away with their wings and screeching calls. When you have left, they swoop down on you and bear you back to their nests."

"So I should not talk with Myrah?"

"You may talk with Myrah if she asks it of you, but you must know that she only seeks to satisfy herself. Her friendship is as fleeting as the waves when they come to shore."

"Will she be angry at what the others have done?"

"Those men care little for father's prohibition against

bearing children, nor do they remember that Myrah is his daughter when she tells them she does not wish to lie with them. When she comes to let us out of our rooms tomorrow morning, she will see that we have taken no men, all of us, and have thus been faithful to her father, all of us. When next they come to you, let those humming bees fly freely without angering them and they will not sting you." She turns away from me. "I have burned your mother and father's words for you. They were Myrah's words as much as anyone else's. Good night."

Derwen's gown rises and falls in the waxing moonlight as sleep takes her. She has bid me a good night, but as her sisters in their rooms sit and talk and lie with their men, I can think of nothing good that will come of such. Even as the stars begin to play on the marble roof overhead, I find no night forthcoming but for that darkness I make for myself by resting an upturned forearm on sleepless eyelids.

1 1

DESIRE

Darkness yields to soft morning light through the narrow slits far above our heads. Our rest is made unquiet by the scraping of iron against wood that drops onto the floor on the other side of the door with all the weight of a dead ox. Though I am still weary, I bring myself to my feet and help Derwen lift the door's inner beam from its rusting hooks. I have not yet set the timber down when the heavy, iron-bound oak swings open, nearly striking me as I step aside.

"Come," says Myrah.

We follow her, in the hearth's bright light, to the long, waist-height table emptied of its floor-strewn parchments. Florentina lies beneath it with her hands held flat against the spreading hem of her red gown on the hard marble floor.

"You know in whose room she is to sleep," says Myrah, "yet all of you are guilty. What do you have to say for yourselves?"

Derwen stands to one side, drawing Myrah's eyes away from the rest of us. Luda comes to me holding her long white-gold braid in her fist.

"Take up Florentina," she whispers.

She gives me a light shove between my shoulders. I walk past Myrah's stony glare to where Florentina sleeps with her eyes open. I kneel before her with my back to her and await her arms around my neck. They do not come.

"Florentina," I whisper over my shoulder. "I will bear you now."

"Go away," she rasps.

I turn around, kneel with my ankles to one side, and lift Florentina by her waist and shoulders. Her arms hang at her sides; her hair sweeps the floor. When Derwen kneels down beside me, Florentina comes to life at once. She climbs onto my back and throws her arms around my neck. Derwen makes her light enough for me that I may stand with her and grasp my wrists at my waist with my forearms under Florentina's legs. She rests her head on my shoulder and at once becomes heavy with sleep.

"Ardelle, why does Florentina not sleep in your bedroom?" says Myrah.

She stares at me as well as any of her father's men of stone. I am your daughter now, Marcus Aurelius. I will keep your secret.

"Even you, Ardelle?" she says. "Forget those thirty days father spoke of at our runestone. They have become seven, now, but may seem to you like seventy, for you must stay bound within your locked rooms while father talks of peace with the northmen. He has allayed the wrath of our western brothers without your help; let us now see whether you think those not of our kith worthy of the same friendship."

Rosamond's sigh wakes Florentina long enough for Florentina to whisper a curse.

"Why here?" I say. "If we are not to be seen, why would you not send us elsewhere?"

"Do you expect an answer where you give none?" says

Myrah. "We take our morning meal in our rooms. Keep your doors open."

Myrah strides swiftly to the hearth room's opening. She stops in the gap in the wall twice as tall as she is and faces us, squeezing the fingers of her left hand as if they were snakes threatening to strike.

"It is the king who tells you to do this," she yells. Her throat cracks beneath the weight of her father's words. "If he must come here to tell you of them himself, they will weigh much heavier on you."

Luda hugs Marigold with her nose in Marigold's uncombed hair and beaded braids. She sets one hand on Rosamond's shoulder and smiles at her as Annette kisses Rosamond's cheek. Annette comes to me and does the same, then takes Florentina's hand in her palm and pats it twice.

"You may be the one to teach Ardelle to write," Annette says.

"If there is nothing else in the world to be done," yawns Florentina.

We leave one another for our bedrooms neighbouring the three great rooms. Florentina settles onto our bedding as Derwen shuts the door on someone who was about to walk in. She opens it in haste to the boy from yesternight, who bears a tray of bread and cheese to our table; it does not rest well on top of Florentina's hair rods. Myrah follows him bearing the same; she clears the table onto the floor and unburdens herself. Two thick-armed men bring us a waist-high clay pot filled with water, then return with another waterless pot around whose neck stretched linen has been fastened. Three thin, flat wiping stones rest on top of the cloth. They take our old sitting pot as they leave, coughing and shaking their heads as they do. There, Myrah tells us, is where we shall sit for the next seven days when our food and water are ready to leave us. She says nothing of whether the winds through the narrow openings near the roof will be enough to quell the stench, nor what we are to do if one of us bleeds.

The door shuts. Derwen frowns at the wooden beam that rests at the foot of the walls.

"Is she angry about last night?" I whisper.

"She knows nothing," Derwen breathes. "She will know nothing."

Without forewarning, the door opens once more.

"Derwen," says Myrah. "Come here."

I sit at the foot of the bedding with only Florentina's breaths to mark the length of my waiting. A yell from without startles her into sitting, followed by loud blows that threaten to beat down the oaken door. Derwen's fist nearly strikes my cheek when I come to meet the sisters gathering in the hearth room. Derwen lifts her fingers towards my face before withdrawing them.

"Myrah tells me I must bind the marble to the doors so we can not leave," she says with softer words. "I have told her she is mad."

"Can we not set the beams in their hooks as we do at night?" says Luda.

"Those who will see these doors must not be made to think that anyone lies waiting behind them," says Myrah.

"Why, then, do we not go elsewhere?" I say.

"Yes, Ardelle," says Myrah, "why do you not go elsewhere after having said so many times that you wished nothing more than to go back to my father's fields overseen by your good friend the aldorman?"

"Shut your mouth," says Derwen.

"What did you say to me?" says Myrah.

"*Mundus stercoris!*" yells Florentina from our bedroom.

Myrah holds Florentina's eyes while the rest of us hold our mouths shut. Florentina hides beneath her bedding like a butterfly before its birth. Myrah faces me and, with the bottom of her foot, swings the door shut as if it does so on its own.

"You have been told many times not to speak your tongues," says Myrah.

"You speak your mother's tongue with her," says Marigold.

"Does my fire warm the floor and the bath waters?" Myrah says. "Does my earth hold these walls together? Do my waters heal father's men? Does my wind upend our painted fore-fathers?"

Marigold says nothing. Myrah meets my eyes.

"Why did I find Florentina beneath a table this morning?" she says. "Anyone could have come and taken her."

"There is no lock on the door that keeps *anyone* from the great rooms," I say.

"None is needed," says Myrah. "The watchmen must be able to reach you unhindered should they have need of such."

Derwen looks away from me, as do the others.

"Ardelle," says Myrah, "tell Derwen to bind the doors to the stone when her sisters have gone to their rooms and I will forget what has happened here."

"Ardelle owns your ears," says Derwen, "not mine."

"Tell Derwen," says Myrah with heated words, "in the tongue that the two of you share, to bind her sisters in their rooms as father has said, else I shall also be kept in a bedroom of my choosing. This, father has also said."

Derwen's face floods with more redness than I have ever seen on mine in the lake's water.

"Do I lie now, Rosamond?" Myrah says. Rosamond looks at her feet to spare herself the knives in Myrah's eyes. "Would you care to find mother and ask her of the verity of father's words and see whether she does not strike your head from your shoulders?"

Is this the same Myrah who spoke to me so kindly in our

bedroom about men in far-off lands and the tongues they speak and the clothing they wear?

"Florentina has often wished to use her room to heat rings into her hair before we sing in the evening," I say. "She felt she could not while you and I talked. She slept beneath a table in the hearth room last night to show us her anger."

Myrah lifts one eyebrow as she looks from my feet to my eyes.

"That seems unlike Florentina," she says as though she hums to herself.

Myrah faces each of her sisters in turn; they will not meet her stare. She looks at me from the sides of her eyes.

"You and I will go for a walk," she says. "While we are away, the rest of you will sit beneath Florentina's table and think on what you have done."

Rosamond leads Marigold beneath the long table where we might have taken our morning meal did the great golden bird on Myrah's neck not wake with fire in its breast. Annette sits beside them while Luda must lie down so she does not have to sit bent over her long legs. Derwen stands as still as our stone forefathers and stares at Myrah.

"Come," says Myrah and walks towards the hearth room's opening.

Derwen frowns at her, sits herself down beneath the table away from her sisters, and sends me after Myrah with a wave of her hand.

Myrah's short yet swift strides take me first to the bathing room, where she bids me leave my red gown. When we reach the last great room's door-hidden hall, she takes me left through winding stone so narrow in places that we must make ourselves flat against the wall and step sideways in the sun's light streaming in from somewhere above. When the hall widens once more, we have come to a small, dimly lit room, wherein Myrah asks me to help her shove the door's iron beam to one side.

"Why does no such iron beam keep the door to the great rooms?" I say.

"Derwen shaped this sanctuary's stone and set the doors," she says as we shove against the iron. "She did not want to feel trapped within, so that door has no beams, though father wanted them as you do."

When the heavy beam has yielded and its door has opened, she takes me by the forearm beneath a cloudless sky to a waist-high wall over which we climb. The wind chills me through my linen gown; the memory of mother's warm bedding and the smell of her birch-scraped hair rushes over me and holds me where I stand. Behind us, a watchman steps through the door's opening and looks out towards the sea, where soft water foams against sand watched over by large swathes of bushy trees. Myrah pulls on my arm—we make our way down a steep slope of clumped green grass, amid which dark-leafed plants take in the last of the harvest's sun. Though she does not need to, Myrah takes my hand. I hold hers as lightly as I would a summer butterfly: within cupped palms one may behold them, for a time, until one is overtaken by a yearning to set them free as they should be.

"Come, Ardelle," says Myrah as she returns my hand to me.

Blackbirds take flight as we near a grove of birch trees at the bottom of the hill.

"Did you not warn me against leaving?" I say.

"Yes," says Myrah, "and now I will show you the truth of this. If you wish to leave, without your red gown, you may follow the old Roman road north to Durovernum and head east from there."

Myrah stands with her hands held before her black gown.

In silence, on a mild harvest day, in the sun's best light, she is as fair as I have ever seen her.

"I will think on this while you show me whatever it is you would have me see," I say.

"Come," she says.

Through many boughs of birch, elm, and oak trees, we make our way to a clearing amid unfallen leaves so thick that none may see us from without. Myrah walks with her hands held behind her around four waist-high, straight-angled stones as long as men made of the same marble found within our sanctuary.

"You have seen our painted forefathers," she says. "Do you know what these unpainted stones might be?"

"Small rooms in which our forefathers are bound as we are," I say.

"They are, as you say, the homes of those who have come before us," says Myrah. "Here lie your slain kindred who wandered from the sanctuary: Domitia, Hypatia, Julia, Laurentius."

"What names are these? Was Laurentius a man?"

"He was but a boy—all else who have come to father have been women. Whether men are slain more readily before they reach him, I do not know, nor do I wish to know. Father gave him that name after he died. His name was Hugo, from Rosamond's homeland."

"Francia," I say.

Myrah stands on the other side of the stone graves and lets her arms hang at her sides.

"So she has told you of this," she says. "You should know of him. You had a brother, for a time, not more than ten summers old, who came to father when only Florentina and Derwen lived at the sanctuary, so father tells me. Derwen took to him and loved him more than any other. They were not often away from one another. Yet one summer's day, he wandered to the sea where those white cliffs loom in search of flowers. To him, there was no greater bliss than to sit in Derwen's lap and take her kisses on his cheek. When the sun began to set, he had not returned. The watchmen found him nowhere within the sanctuary, nor in the fields ringed by those stone walls. When the sun was almost gone, they found his body at last where it had been broken on the sharp stones at the foot of the cliffs. Derwen was heartbroken. She said nothing when father bade her bind him within this stone grave, nor did she say anything to Florentina until Luda came to them some months later. Luda told me, when … she told me not long before you came that Derwen only stayed among the living at Luda's behest. You see how Luda watches over her even now."

Myrah walks between the stone graves and stands before me.

"She can not watch over everyone," she says. "Nor can father watch over any of you if you wander away from those walls."

I step back from her hardening words.

"Did Hugo fall, or was he made to fall?" I say.

"Nobody knows," says Myrah. "That is what hurts Derwen most of all. I would not have her bury another of her siblings in a stone grave such as these."

"You spoke to your siblings this morning as if that sanctuary would be their grave," I say. "You, the one who wears the keys to their doors on her belt and sleeps elsewhere. If you had lived among them for a time, I think you would be kinder to them."

Myrah narrows her eyes.

"I first came to the sanctuary after this winter's snow melted," she says. "I am seven years younger than Annette, who is twenty-three; and she is but a child to Florentina and Derwen, who are ten years her better. How do you think they see me,

Ardelle? I have heard them moan to one another about how father wishes them to heed the crying of a newborn."

"Then why do they fear you?" I say.

"They do not fear me," says Myrah. "They hate me. I am not one of them, yet they must call me sister. Do you not see how well they welcome you though you have been with them but a fortnight?"

She steps forwards, standing near enough to me that her shoes are almost on my feet. When I step back from her, she grabs for my forearm but misses, yet it is enough to hold me in place.

"You must have also seen what I have done to welcome you," she says. "Shoes, hose, a blue gown when you did not want the red, speaking with you every evening to make you forget what have you given up, taking you from the sanctuary so you may go back to your mother and father if the burden is too great for you to bear. If you do not believe what I have told you of Hugo, you may ask Derwen of it and hear the truth from her lips."

The leather of Myrah's shoes rests against my toes, beside them. When she looks up at me, her nose is almost on mine. Were I to bend down and lean forwards …

"I think Derwen may have told you of things she has never told me," Myrah says.

"Did you not stand like this with Derwen?" I say.

"We talked in her bedroom, nothing more." Myrah's hand pulls my neck towards her. "Is there something else we should have done?"

Fingers come to rest on my hip. The blood within my legs quickens. Myrah's nose is on mine. I am on fire with summer's heat though it has left us; winter's winds blow through me though they are not yet here; my heart thaws and melts into my waist.

"Your face reddens," Myrah says. "More than I have seen it

do. And you look at me in a way the others do not. What happened last night to make this so?"

My lips reach for hers. Myrah stops me with her hands beneath my shoulders.

"What happened?" she says.

Her lips float so close to mine that I forget who I am and where I stand.

"They took some of the watchmen to their beds last night," I say. "Derwen and I wished to have nothing to do with this. We kept Florentina and her man from our room."

"How selfish you were," she says, and with one hand on my shoulder kisses my lips for as long as butterflies rest on the palms of hands that have opened to the heavens.

"Father does not allow your sisters to bear children," she whispers to my ear. "That you and those like you suffer is enough. He will not have you bring more suffering into this world. He will not have another Hugo. He talks with the king of those northmen to see whether they can not be made to think the same."

"What of our own men?" I say. "They are the ones who would come into that sanctuary before any other."

"Father will tell them that you and your sisters are the ones who have won peace for them. The watchmen will love you for it."

Myrah laughs to herself as she takes my wrists. Her humming brings my fingertips to her waist and shoulder. The wind that was cold to my flesh now sweeps through my limbs and linen as it would the feathered wings of a bird high above the seaside cliffs.

"Are they so readily swayed?" I say.

She lifts her eyebrows and tilts her head slightly to one side in answer.

"Why can we not stay elsewhere while your father does this?" I half-whisper.

"Do not ask," she says and takes her hands from my wrists. "He has kept your sisters from harm for many years."

Myrah takes my right hand from her shoulder and holds it at her side.

"I would have the same of you if you are willing to do what must be done," she says. "Come, now. I need your help in making the others see the truth of this."

She leads me by the hand from the clearing towards thick-leafed trees.

"Swear to me that you will tell me, and only me, of such things from now on," she says to the oaks.

"I do not know—"

"Swear this and I will tell father that I must be bound in a room with you, where we may talk without hindrance. We shall thus make the days much shorter. When I know of what your sisters keep from me, I will not have to speak so ill before them as you say I did this morning."

"I swear."

Myrah squeezes my hand and leads me through shrouded boughs whose grasping leaves and rough bark I trade for the flesh of her palm on mine, the sound of her leather shoes against the twigs and acorns underfoot, and her thicketed rings of hair hued as the mistle thrushes who greet us at the edge of the grove before flying off to meet their kindred in the treetops overlooking the sea.

1 2

PLEAS

One of the many keys on Myrah's belt ring slides the sanctuary door's iron beam open from without. Within the sanctuary, those narrow, winding, dimly lit halls bring us at last to the welcome light of the three great rooms and their tables laden with books, Florentina's board games, unlit candles, parchments, and half-empty water cups. In the hearth room, only one table now sits in the middle of the otherwise empty floor; its chairs bear the sisters in red, who have sent the long oaken table's lesser siblings to stand beside the bodiless men of stone.

"Am I not worthy of your love that you do not heed me?" Myrah says.

Derwen sits with her forearm on the table and taps her fingers against it as she stares at Rosamond. The raised hearth bowl's bluish-red fire wreaths Myrah's head like the bushy boughs of her hidden grove. The sisters meet her wordless glare as I wear my red gown and fasten its golden breastpins. Luda breaks the silence with an answer for Myrah that has no need of her eyes.

156

"What brings you back to us, Ardelle?" Luda says.

"Not what," says Rosamond. "Who."

"I told you we do not eat at this table today," says Myrah.

"Nor do we eat on the floor," says Marigold.

"But it is there that Florentina should sleep?" says Myrah.

"Florentina has been here since you were a child," says Luda. "I will see to it that she is still here when you leave us."

Myrah meets my eyes and nods her head at a chair standing against the wall beside my bedroom's opening. I bring it to the sisters, though I know not which of them will take me beside them. None of them, it seems, for they do not slide their chairs away from one another. I sit behind Luda and Annette far enough away from them that my breath will not tell their necks I am there. When Myrah steps behind Derwen and sets her hands down on Derwen's shoulders, Derwen looks up at me as if I have yelled at her. The hearth's purple-hued flames bestow on Myrah's thinly ringed hair a shroud of writhing snakes.

"I am to stay with you in your rooms," she says. "We will not have time to write down all the ways in which you hate me, so let us make it known to one another while we are still allowed to speak."

"You might stay with Rosamond," says Florentina with a yawn. "She knows well the worthlessness of seeking the love of others when the face in the lake is without match."

"Would it not then be better for Myrah to stay in a room by herself?" says Rosamond.

"Have you made yourself atheling in my absence?" says Myrah.

"What did you and Ardelle speak of in your *absence*?" says Florentina.

"Myrah has made Ardelle atheling with the earth still on her feet and a face that matches our red gowns," says Rosamond.

I look down at my legs so my sigh does not give unwanted life to the brown rings of Annette's hair.

"We talked of where I might stay while you are hidden away so that you do not feel you must talk to each other like this," I say.

"Stay with your mother, then," Luda says over her shoulder.

"Ardelle shows a willingness to be helpful that the rest of you might learn from," says Myrah.

"You did not ask us to go for a walk with you," says Marigold.

"She did not *tell* us we were going for a walk with her," says Rosamond.

"I tell you now that I will stay in a room with Ardelle so she does not have to see your grim faces," says Myrah.

"The rooms will have little lighting with their doors closed," says Annette.

"And thus did Myrah's looking glass wallow in darkness," says Rosamond.

"Ardelle," says Derwen. "Bear Florentina to Luda's room so she may sleep. When she wakes, her strong-armed friend will tell her how having lived in the sanctuary since Myrah clutched at her mother's gowns hast lost its meaning."

"Should she not be allowed to keep her room?" I say.

"Ardelle found her brain when she went with you, Myrah," says Rosamond. "I hope you will not let it go to waste."

"Florentina may keep her beloved room if she so wishes," says Myrah. "Your sister Ardelle is welcome to spend many long days among those who do not even set aside their chairs to make room for her at a table long enough for twice as many. To your rooms, now, where you are to wait for Derwen to shut you in."

Marigold slides backwards in her chair, but Rosamond's

hands stop her. Derwen's fingers become a fist against the table. Luda slings her braid before her shoulder and grasps it in both hands. Annette clenches the red wool resting on her legs. Myrah meets my eyes, looks off into the neighbouring great rooms wherein their bedrooms await, and stares at me once more.

"Ardelle," she says.

"Yes?" I say.

Rosamond laughs to herself.

"Show the others where their rooms are," Myrah says.

I set my chair against the wall beside one of the painted stone watchmen and walk towards the great room's opening. I am alone in doing so. I might ask Myrah what to do did the gathered sisters not now stare at me. Myrah's narrowing eyes quickly soften into a smile as I near her.

"Should we not go into the rooms?" I ask her.

The sisters look away from Myrah as she beholds each of them. Her brow furrows; she breathes out sharply through her nose.

"We should," says Myrah, "but we do not. I shall talk to father and see if he can not shorten our seven days together."

Myrah's hardened eyes look through me as though I am one of the stone men staring back at her. Her shoes sound against the marble floor as she walks off.

"Father will lengthen our stay," says Derwen when Myrah has gone. "That is his way."

"And now it has become Myrah's way," says Luda.

"Would this have happened if we had sat beneath the table?" I say.

"You could have sat with us," says Rosamond. "Yet here you stand."

"You know Ardelle speaks the truth, Derwen," says Luda. "We heeded you in taking these chairs. Now we will heed

Myrah and be made to think this is her father's will whether it is or not."

"I have made Myrah see that my sisters are worthy of much better than what her childishness would have them believe," says Derwen. "I know that you would do the same for your sisters, Luda." Derwen searches my eyes. "I hope you come to understand this, Ardelle."

No words fill the silence thereafter, not least of which Florentina's, whose speech is as a child running through a meadow of pillowy white flower seeds without a care for where her feet land. Mother once told me, when I brought her some of the golden flowers that bear those seeds, not to pick them again lest I wet myself in my sleep. When Myrah returns, her look is that of one who would not willingly wake at night to help Florentina to the sitting pot.

"Father tells me there are now eight of us," she says. "He will spend as many days drinking mead with our foes in these halls."

Luda stands, shoves her chair against the table, and leans her palms into its high back. Rosamond sighs. Marigold sets her hand on Rosamond's shoulder. Derwen stares at me with the guilt of one who has brought life to evils by speaking of them.

"Father has asked us to make ready the sanctuary for the northmen," Myrah says.

"The northmen," Annette says to herself.

"How many times must you be told not to speak of your histories?" says Myrah.

"We will be together for eight days," says Annette. "Do you think we should say nothing?"

"Yes," says Myrah, "for those same men search the fields and meadows and trees for women who walk alone. Need I tell you what they do to those they find? You will fill your sitting pots so that their stench tells the men you have died in those rooms."

"And when we are dead," says Annette, "we will have time without end to think on whether it was northern men or western men or our own southern men who killed us."

"Have the watchmen fill the pots," says Derwen. "They may die in our stead."

Rosamond strikes Derwen's shoulder with the back of her hand.

"Rosamond," says Myrah. "Have you something to tell me?"

"Nothing," she says. "Derwen does not listen to you. That is all."

Myrah holds her hands before her waist and draws herself up to her full height. She stands only a head taller than Annette, who sits in a chair.

"The blue hue in the hearth's fire must be made yellow," says Myrah.

"Father said it was not to be quenched for anything," says Marigold.

"He will still have use of you when your fire does not burn," says Myrah.

"It is not that," says Marigold. "He spoke until my ears bled of the old Roman imperium and how they kept a fire burning at all times. I do not think he would have told you to do this."

"So now you know my father better than I do?" says Myrah. "You need not quell the fire, only alter its hue."

"How am I to do that?"

"Why do you ask me? I only know that it is to be done."

"Shall I learn to urinate in blue because you ask it?" says Marigold.

"What?" says Myrah. Her face hardens. "Have you learned to speak so from Ardelle?"

Myrah takes Marigold by the arm beneath the shoulder and lifts her from her chair. Rosamond stands at once.

"Sit down," yells Myrah, and so Rosamond does.

Luda walks away through the great room's opening. Derwen stares at Myrah but does nothing. Myrah's lips bare snowy teeth. Annette's eyes flee to her clenched fists against her legs.

"Myrah," I say.

The embers in her eyes bid me bring them to life and see whether I do not burn. She nods her head towards the raised iron bowl.

"Blow the fires into stillness," she says.

"I do not know how," I say.

Myrah lets go Marigold's arm, strides to the iron hearth bowl, and shoves against its sturdy rods. With the third thrust, the bowl falls to the marble floor with a loud sound, spilling its ashen wood and purple flames onto the marble floor, where they burn as if nothing at all had happened.

"Kill the flames," she says.

"No," I say and come to stand between her and the table where her sisters sit.

Footsteps leave us: Rosamond runs hand in hand with Marigold into the neighbouring great room. The sound of heavy wood striking against iron marks the first of their eight days in hiding. Myrah's eyes are wide, like those of a child who does not understand what goes on.

"Will you speak to Maria for me?" she says.

"She does not know how to do what you ask," says Annette.

"Ardelle does," Myrah says. "She understands what our time together today means to me. And she must know that after eight days, when father has made peace with those men and they have left us, we may walk together in the meadows and fields again. All of us."

I hold my hands behind my back so Myrah can not reach for them.

"I will tell you whatever you do not know," she says, "or whatever you wish to know after you have talked to Maria and bid her come to the hearth room to still the fire."

"The same fire that burns at our feet at your behest," I say.

Myrah's jaw becomes hard. Her thin-lipped smile does little to soften it.

"I only wished to have Marigold do what must be done," says Myrah.

Her words are soft, like a child who tells her mother that she has broken a water pot. I shall be her mother, then.

"Men I do not know came after me with burning rushes," I say. "And now one who calls herself our sister would do the same. You do not understand that which lies within us, for if you did, you would not have taken Marigold's arm and threatened her with that fire. Was it your knife that opened anew the wounds Annette took three years ago?"

Annette's hands now rest on the table. Myrah becomes silent.

"Isadora told me I must show kindness to the maid who broke my nose with her clay pot," I say, "yet I still do not understand her wisdom. I think it would be better for me and for those you call your sisters to die in these rooms as your father wishes than to be buried in those stone graves you showed me."

Myrah's eyes begin to glisten.

"Why did you take her there?" says Derwen.

A tear runs down Myrah's cheek, followed by another.

"Ardelle," says Myrah, "I beg you to talk to Maria and ask her to come to the fire so that her sisters do not hate me for making her do something she does not like but which must nonetheless be done."

"Would you have her use this fire to dry your tears?" says Derwen.

"Shall I fetch her cloth from the bathing room?" says Annette.

"That cloth is for bathing," says Florentina with her eyes closed, "not for false weeping."

"Ardelle," says Myrah. "That is what I spoke of. This is how they talk to me when mother and father are not here. Will you not do something?"

"Florentina," I say. Her eyes open. Three heads turn to her at once. "If I take you as my … what was it, bond-sister? If I do this, will you tell the others to—"

"It is done," says Florentina. "You are not queen, my darling atheling-sister, but I will tell the others to behave themselves as if you were, and you, in thanks for our kindness, will go soak your head in the bath water before staying with Luda and Annette in their room, where you may learn how to be silent."

"Florentina," says Annette, "Ardelle does not know what she says."

"Must you speak our thoughts aloud?" says Florentina. "She has done it. Look at me, atheling. Your father promised me anything when I first came here, any one thing I might ask for and have. I have not asked for it until now. If he is here, you may tell him of this before Derwen shuts us in."

"So that is the way of things," says Derwen.

Myrah wipes her cheeks with the back of her hand.

"Derwen, you may bind Annette and Luda's door when I have brought my things thither," she says. "Thereafter, Ardelle will see to the fire."

Myrah leaves through the great room's opening, as does Annette. Florentina waves me to her and bids me take her up. Derwen's song comes to us from the neighbouring great room as I set Florentina down in a chair beside me.

"On the ground," says Florentina, "like we did when we sang at the runestone."

I help Florentina to the marble floor, against which she flattens one hand. The other she sets on my back as Derwen's song comes to us from further away—she binds Myrah's door.

"Set both your hands against the marble and be still," Florentina says.

A song from the sea washes over me with warm waves; I turn my face away from bluish fire that swells to twice its height and threatens to burn up the thin strands of hair hanging from my sweaty brow. The great rooms dim to darkness, leaving only the shadowy light of the sun through our bedroom's narrow openings beneath its roof to guide us to the table that bears our bread and cheese for the next eight days. Derwen sings to our door, then shows me with one shoulder how it does not yield though the iron hooks are without their wooden beams. She sits down on a chair beside Florentina, who eats a round of bread so quickly that her food needs little chewing.

"Can men see us from above?" I say.

"No, but they can hear us," says Derwen.

She hands me a round of meaty bread.

"I am not hungry," I say as I sit down on the bedding.

"Eat with your bond-sister," she says, "else you will lose the strength to bear Florentina wherever she wishes to go; and your mind will be so clouded by thoughts of eating that you will readily yield to Myrah when she seeks to take Florentina away from you."

"Would Myrah do so?" I say.

"She threatens," says Florentina, "nothing more."

"That you have not seen otherwise does not mean she will not do what she says she will," says Derwen.

"Would she have burned Marigold?" I say.

"Why should Marigold fear her own fire?" says Florentina as she takes a handful of chalk-like cheese.

"Does her fire not burn like any other?"

Florentina sets down the small mound of cheese she was about to swallow.

"I can not heal myself," she says, "nor can Derwen make whole her own broken bones, nor does Marigold's fire burn her. Did you not know this?"

"How was I to know it?"

"If you do not know what you have asked me, then what Myrah said may be true. You do not understand the oath you have sworn to me."

"What oath?"

"She does not even know that she has sworn an oath," Florentina says to herself and lets crumbled cheese fall into her mouth.

"As she knew not what she did when Myrah took her to the grove," says Derwen. "She must have talked to you of Hugo, Ardelle, else she would not have taken you there. I only hope that your lack of understanding does not lead you to an early grave as it did him."

13

───────

SECRETS

We abide in silence in our dimly sunlit bedroom, saying nothing lest the men who have gathered in the hearth room hear us over the few words they speak. At eventide, when the darkness of dusk settles over us, we hide ourselves from harvest's chill beneath great lengths of wool as we listen to the lifting of many heavy things. I sleep little, for Derwen, Florentina, and I must lie on our sides almost on top of one another beneath bedding only wide enough for two.

We wake to a morning meal of hardened cheese crumbs and crusted bread made soft by water from the drinking pot. Striking against our door sends Florentina from her chair so quickly that I must drop my food and take her waist so she does not fall onto the hard edge of the bed's raised stone. Derwen eats as though nothing happens; after seven more blows, some mightier than others, the door has not yielded. At Florentina's wordless behest, I watch the door as I chew what is left of my unsoftened bread round. Florentina watches the wall behind me with her back against mine.

It is not until the third day, when the men are at their loudest, that Florentina whispers into my ear: she bleeds, yet neither Myrah nor her watchmen have given us linen beyond that which hides the sitting pot's stench. Derwen takes the hem of my undergown to where two hard edges of our stone bed meet and begins to tear it until the talking in the hearth room stops. Thereafter, we must withstand whatever stench comes from the sitting pot—Florentina rests on its bundled linen with her forehead against the stone walls. I would wash the reddened cloth with some of our drinking water, but Derwen says the sound would make the men stop talking again and we would not have enough water for eight days, so we set the bloody linen within the open-mouthed sitting pot.

On the fourth day, we have become weary enough of our small room and the yelling men in the hearth room that we begin to draw letters on our palms and forearms to speak with one another. Derwen's high cheek bones seem to fall as she tells of her homeland in Powys near a great town of stone called Deva Victrix. When I ask of her childhood, her face is too tired to harden; she shakes her head and closes her eyes. They open again when I ask how she lost her left arm.

Ask your friend Myrah, she writes. *She will tell you everything you wish to know about me for whatever you are willing to give her.*

Florentina sits close beside me, as close as she can without sitting in my lap, and takes my hand from Derwen's fingers. She begins to write the tale of her own childhood, of which she had only told me that she lost her legs below the knees, and which her short-nailed finger now writes on the palm of my hand at length:

Before she had become a woman, she learned of her healing in the popular baths of Emerita Augusta when the warmth of the water around her brought life and wellness to her ailing family: her mother's breaths were no longer strained, her mother's brother stood up straight, and her father found his manhood with her mother again. They sought to keep this secret among themselves, but others felt the vitality of Florentina's water and offered her mother and father wealth and goods in trade for their daughter's ministrations. As her family's standing rose, so too did the standing of those who called on her, until at last she came to serve the town's episcopus, a great aldorman named Masona who gave them land and titles.

Thereafter, war broke out between the king of Hispania and those he had angered by giving their land and titles to his sons. Masona called on Florentina to heal the king's many fighting men, but she could not save all of them—twelve aldormen died among them. She worked without rest for so long that she became weak with hunger; her thirst took her words away; her feet grew green. When the king's men stopped returning to him in great numbers, he accused Florentina of helping his foes against him. The king threatened to kill Florentina and her family if she did not atone by healing more of his men. Masona saw Florentina's greening legs and told her that she suffered for having sinned against their god; thus, she was beyond the help of even her episcopus. He bound her and hewed off her green legs, sending her into a deep sleep. When she woke, she learned that her father had given Masona his family's wealth to send Florentina away on a ship to Francia.

After many days at sea, she reached the sands of Francia, where the ship's greedy owner traded her to spear-bearing men for gold. They brought her to their king, a man named Chilperic who had been wed to the daughter of a former king of Hispania but had slain her so he could take a serving maid as his wife. He was of a mind to likewise kill Florentina, who served the king of Hispania, but on hearing the tale of her childhood, saw in her his beloved Fredegund, and so instead held her in a small room no greater than this bedroom of ours.

One day, Florentina learned that she was to be sent north

over the sea to the sons of the Cantiaci in trade for men and spears against Chilperic's eastern foes. When she came here, she was welcomed by Myrah's father, who called on her from time to time to heal his men but otherwise left her in peace.

That was almost sixteen years ago, Florentina writes. Myrah's father keeps me from harm, but these walls have become little better than those of that man Chilperic.

Did you speak your oath to Myrah's father willingly? I ask.

As willingly as anyone who would otherwise be taken out to sea and left in the water, she writes. They would have done the same to you.

Derwen closes her eyes and nods.

Before Myrah took me to the grove, she said I could leave if I wished to, I write. Would they have come after me?

Derwen takes Florentina's hand and writes so quickly that Florentina shakes her head. She and Derwen then whisper to one another softly enough that I do not hear what they say. After a time, Florentina brings my ear to her chin.

"How did Myrah behave when she took you to the graves?" she whispers.

I look within the lines of my open palms for an answer.

"Did she draw near to you?" Derwen whispers to our laps.

Florentina blows a breath of bread and cheese at the hair beside Derwen's forehead.

Tell us what Myrah told you, Derwen writes on my leg. We will ward you against her.

It is not as grim as Derwen says, writes Florentina. I have seldom seen Myrah so glad, nor have I ever seen her weep. You must have said something to her.

I open my mouth but stop myself from speaking. I know not whose hand I should take, so I write on my own.

Myrah told me not to say anything about what we did in the grove.

We keep no secrets from one another, writes Florentina. *Tell your bond-sister what Myrah said. I will teach you Latin.*

Derwen sighs soundlessly. I await her frown, but her eyebrows have long since bowed down to men who do not shut their mouths even after the sun's light no longer fills our room.

I told her of how Alfred wanted a kiss from me, I write. *Myrah wished to do the same, but I would not let her.* Derwen's eyebrows climb her forehead. *I gave Alfred his kiss thinking to make him go away. He asked to lie in the hay with me. I called my father, who came in from the fields shirtless. He ran after Alfred swinging his scythe to frighten him away. Alfred yelled the life-breath out of himself, wet himself, and did not come back.*

Florentina smiles and at once hides her mouth behind her hand.

Do you still think of your Alfred sometimes? she writes.

He is not mine, I write. *I gave him back to his father.*

Good, writes Derwen.

On the sixth day, we have only six rounds of bread left, enough for two days. Derwen tells me that we must set aside some of it for Florentina, who is to eat whenever she is hungry lest she fall ill and her legs become green again. I would fill my belly with as much water as I can to soften my hunger, but our drinking water fills only a fourth of the pot; and Derwen says we must go hungry and somewhat thirsty this day and the next while Florentina softens her bread with our water.

On the seventh day, my breast is fire and my throat is ash. Florentina no longer teaches me Latin words, for I have no thought of anything but eating. Florentina hides what bread we have left beneath the trays. Derwen lies with one ear against the bedding and her hand on her other ear so she can not hear the men who eat in the hearth room from dawn to dusk to dawn.

On the eighth day, I take heart as we await the striking on

the door that will tell Derwen we are to be freed. As the sun's light waxes, so does our mood. As the sun's light wanes, my hunger sends me lower and lower until I have been made kin to the stone floor. When night falls, Florentina gives to each of us half a bread round, keeping the last one for herself. It is not nearly enough, but it masters my hunger well enough that I sleep until morning.

On the ninth day, the sitting pot's stink fills the room though the narrow openings near the roof give us wind at times.

On the tenth day, Florentina eats the last half of her bread round, and thus we are without food. Hunger makes the chill harvest wind even colder. I rest my knees against my ribs beneath wool bedding not broad enough for three. Thick water runs from between my lips onto the marble beside our stone bed. If I were a horse, I would eat the woollen sleeves of my gown. We empty our drinking pot of the last of the water. Derwen says that if the men without do not leave tomorrow, she will unbind our door and kill them all.

On the eleventh day, I wake to Florentina's hair rings on my chin where she hides herself from the cold against me. Derwen stands beside our door with her hand against the marble wall. She breathes loudly through her nose; her cheeks are red with blood. She shakes as much as Florentina does until, without warning, our door sounds with many loud blows. Derwen sings for a time, then shoves open the door with her shoulder.

I bear Florentina on my bent back and legs of dragging stone through amber dimness to a long table bearing brass-bowled wax-lights and laden with more food than I have ever seen at once: drinking horns carved of bone, soft bread rounds, cheese, boiled eggs, apples, smoked hen, dried fish, and cups of ale-water, mead, and even milk. Florentina and I have little thought for anything else but eating, nor do her sisters, who sit down and take into their mouths whatever they find before them. Even Myrah, who looks as if she has been half-asleep these eleven days, bites off a fish's head without seeing what she has done.

When our bellies are full and our throats are wet and our blood has once again quickened, Derwen speaks words of thanks for the food we have eaten. Myrah sets her chair down behind mine. I set myself closer to Florentina so that Myrah may sit beside us; Derwen turns to me, setting her legs between us.

"We may all go into the meadows together," says Myrah. "Father has said so."

Myrah's lips find my cheek, as do many eyes. She goes to Marigold, whose cheek she likewise kisses, before taking Marigold's hand and bidding her follow.

"I bring Marigold below to light the fires so that we may abide winter's frost in warmth," she says.

Not long after they have left, the floor becomes so warm beneath my feet that I leave my chair and sit down on the hard floor. I help Florentina onto the marble while Derwen and Annette and Luda sit or lie as they will. Only Rosamond, whose flesh is ice and snow, stays at the table. Myrah returns to Rosamond with Marigold, then comes to Derwen bearing a small comb of white bone with long teeth on both sides of its handle.

"Let us be friends again," Myrah says and leaves the comb in Derwen's lap.

Myrah takes a candle from its brass bowl and bends down behind the table. I stand to see what she does: there, in the middle of the room, between this long table and another, rests a ring of stones around wood-strewn ash. Myrah holds the candle's light against the end of a mead-stirring stick, whose flame she uses to work reddish life into sleeping embers.

"Good morning, daughters," says a man whose deep words ring hollow in my ears.

"Good morning, father," says Myrah.

None of Myrah's sisters rise to greet their father. His wan face takes little warmth from the hearth's reddish-brown glow.

"You are weary," says Myrah's father. "So weary that you can not speak, yet you shall take heart at what your devotion has won for us. Eight days have come and gone, one for each of you, and another for your mother, and another for your father. Now, on this eleventh day, we have won a lasting peace with those who were once our foes. Those western men will serve their own king who keeps his halls far from the men of the east; and the northmen will live among us for a time with the understanding that we shall not do those things which make men fearful of us. Thus you may, from this day, spend what time you will beneath the sun no further than the great groves of oak trees. No longer will you be kept shut in your rooms at night, but you must heed the watchmen who look after you so that you may keep these freedoms. Come, daughters, away from this room to feel the grass beneath your feet, the fair scent of morning's white flowers, the rough kiss of tree bark on your fingers, and even the lake's frosty waters should you wish to bathe therein. Annette, you may ride a horse today if they will bear the weather. The one place you must no longer visit is the grove clearing, for that is forbidden, and I have admonished your atheling-sister for having misused it."

"Father," says Rosamond, "are we to wear these gowns?"

"Take heart," says the king. "The waning harvest sun will not lighten your rich reds."

When Myrah's father has left, Rosamond meets Myrah's grim glare with her own face of stone.

"Is that your father, or was he slain in battle and another lives in his body?" Rosamond says.

"Take me up, horse," says Florentina. "Follow our atheling-sister who will be queen after Rosamond has murdered her mother and father with words."

Florentina's wrists choke me until I stand and set my forearms under her legs. Marigold takes Rosamond by the arm and lifts her from her chair. Derwen, Annette, and Luda are slow in leaving the marble's warmth.

"Come," says Myrah.

She leads us by candlelight to the third great room. There, she feels among her keys for the one that unlocks the door to Annette's hall of painted floor stones. Their hues go unseen in darkness that bids us make our way forwards with our hands. Annette asks Luda to help her shove the iron beam from the hooks bound to the stone wall, and at once the world becomes bright with the sun's light through the half-emptied boughs of oak trees shrouding a bed of fallen green leaves. No sooner have we left their thick limbs than the wind's chill finds its way into our woollen gowns and sends us from one another in search of warmth. Florentina does not wish to go far—she asks me to set her down amid a small grove of oak trees to the northwest, where we may hide from wind and rain showers should they come to us. Myrah follows us, as does Derwen. Derwen sits down with Florentina and speaks to her using more words than I have ever heard from her. A hand pulls on my arm.

"She stays with me, my darling atheling," says Florentina.

Myrah lifts me to my feet as if my legs were nothing.

"Your queen has need of Ardelle for a time," Myrah says. "We will not be gone long, or even gone at all."

Myrah's hand leads me away from Derwen until Florentina's laughing words become lost in the wind. Myrah stands with her back to them so they can not see how her hands take mine.

"I thought of you often in my room," she says. "Do you remember what we did in that forbidden grove?"

"What did you—"

"What did *you* do those eleven days? Did Florentina teach you Latin? Did she talk of her man? Did Derwen speak of me?"

"We spoke of many things, yes."

"Rosamond talked of her time in Francia," says Myrah. "She watched over noble children and learned from their mothers and fathers how to behave oneself. Has she learned well?"

"I thought you were to stay with Annette and Luda," I say.

"I showed Rosamond how to live in peace with those who are unlike her," says Myrah. "We shall all have to do the same from this day. Did you know that Rosamond sought to become close to Florentina before Marigold lived with us? Florentina saw through Rosamond as though she looked to the muddied bottom of an otherwise clear lake."

"Florentina said her aldorman gave her mother and father land and titles," I say.

"So she did," says Myrah. "And of what did you tell her in return? Of me? Your mother and father? Isadora?"

Derwen walks to one side where she can better see what Myrah does. Myrah follows my eyes and lets fall my hands.

"We spoke little thereafter," I say. "Florentina bled on the sitting pot's cloth and would like fresh linen for the stench."

Myrah blinks twice and stares at me.

"Can you not wash the linen with some of the bath water?" says Myrah.

"Florentina does not wish to use it again," I say. "She says … she says she feels something within her."

Myrah draws back from me.

"Is she with child?" she says.

"If she knew, everyone else would know as well."

"She must not be with child. Mother and father will … be unhappy with me for allowing this. That is why I needed you to stand with me, Ardelle. You were to show the others that they need not keep their secrets from me. Here."

Myrah takes a white comb from her leather belt bag.

"Derwen did not want it," she says. "It is yours. From me. If Florentina bears a child, we will hide it."

"What would your father do if he knew?" I say.

"He will never know," Myrah says.

She sets the comb in my palm, closes my fingers around it, and leaves me with a kiss for my knuckles. As soon as I come to sit beside Florentina and Derwen, their talk ends.

"Did Myrah bring you elsewhere to kiss you where we could not see?" says Florentina. "What would young Alfred think?"

"I made Myrah leave by telling her you think you are with child," I say.

Florentina sends her laughter to the clouds. Derwen smiles. I have never seen this fairness in her face. It leaves when I show her Myrah's comb.

"Keep it," she says. "It is made from the teeth of whales who swim not far from the shore in a kingdom called Gweneda. They are such strong swimmers that their teeth give women children."

When I drop the comb on the ground beside Florentina's red gown, she takes it up in haste and throws it into my lap.

"You will have a child before I do," she says with a laugh.

For three days we rest beneath the cloudless heavens when we are not eating or sleeping. Florentina tells me that the trees have grown eyes but will say nothing further of her meaning. On the fourth day, the bathing room has grown a door that does not swing on its hinges, nor does it open to any key. After our morning meal, we step out into snow that reaches the bottoms of my shins. Myrah bids us bathe in it if we wish, and so I do behind a thick oak tree, where none but Florentina should see me. It is then that I learn of the northmen and their eyes hidden behind the trees.

"What on earth are you doing?" says Rosamond as I lift my gowns to wash my legs.

"Myrah said we should," I say.

Rosamond shakes her head as she walks away.

"Bathe quickly," says Florentina from where she sits in the snow. "We go back within when you have done."

"To do what?" I say.

"To warm my legs. They become ice in this weather. See how your reddening hands do the same."

Thereafter, where I would have spent my days wandering in the cold so that I might better warm myself by the hearth's fire, I sit instead in the glow of candlelight moving stones about on Florentina's game board while she teaches me Latin in words made too soft to be overheard. Rosamond takes Florentina's place at times, for neither she nor I can win against Florentina—only Luda is her match—yet Rosamond takes great mirth in besting me.

"Why Latin?" she says to Florentina one day when I have begun to win. "Why not teach her that thorny Gothic tongue of yours instead?"

"So she can tell me what you say when I am not there," says Florentina.

"Vici," says Rosamond and shows me that I have lost after being made to think otherwise.

Our sanctuary takes on a chill through the bedroom openings that drives Rosamond to forego her chair for the warmth of Marigold's fire beneath the floor. Even Myrah comes among us to play against Florentina, and it is thus that Florentina's face becomes, for a time, as red as my hands after she loses.

"Again," says Florentina.

"Tomorrow," says Myrah as she stands.

"Luda, tell her to play again," says Florentina.

"You are the one who has made her queen," says Luda.

"Ardelle," says Florentina. "Tell her."

Warm hands come to rest on my shoulders.

"Tomorrow," I say, and Myrah's hands leave me.

"Unfaithful," says Florentina.

Later that day, we learn that the northmen have found Derwen singing to herself at our runestone. Myrah's father takes us to the sea and shows us among the rough and craggy rocks far below how our runestone rests in shattered shards almost too small for my eyes to find. I would ask him which of us this should have been did Florentina's shaking arms not choke the speech from my throat.

"I did this," Myrah says. "I knew of it but did not stop her."

"Then we shall see to it that you live among them so you are better able to do so," says her father.

That night, Derwen sings to Florentina's belly and tells her that she feels nothing within.

"Shall I make a show of weeping?" says Florentina.

"Keep your tears," I say. "I will leave Myrah's comb beneath your bedding. You may yet bear a son."

"Ha!" says Florentina.

The following morning, when Derwen and Florentina still sleep, I rise from the heated stone long enough to stretch my legs and find on the table among Florentina's hair rods a leather string of amber beads along with a small parchment sheet bearing flowery letters.

I wish for nothing more than your well-being. Your mother's beads may help you keep this better than my comb. —Myrah

That day, we are made to listen to the sounds of striking and the bellowing of men who grunt as much as they talk to one another. Our books and parchments and ink and writing feathers have gone missing, as have Annette's waxed thread and sewing needles. Florentina keeps her hair rods by hiding them beneath her bedding for our backs to find should the men be so kind as to let us sleep in peace this evening. Myrah hies into our candlelit hearth room for her game with Florentina.

"How are we to play with such sound?" says Florentina.

"I will stay in my room until the men leave," says Myrah. "I have a board of my own. Your sisters may walk blood into their legs by telling me of your move; I will send my answer back with them."

"I see what you do," says Florentina. "You wish to keep yourself from me so I can *not* see what you do. Go, then. I will have Luda tell you of my first move."

What Myrah does not see is how Luda helps Florentina when Myrah has begun to win. Rosamond comes to sit beside them on the floor and offers her own wisdom. Florentina listens well, nodding along even as she tells Rosamond how wrong she is.

"There," says Florentina and moves a dark stone. "Horse, ride off to Myrah and tell her of this while Luda rests her legs."

"Myrah's room is right, left, then right again," says Luda. "Do not look at the men or talk to them and they will leave you be."

"If she were as tall as a horse like you, they might do the same," says Florentina.

Her laughter sends me through winding halls to where sweat-soaked, shirtless men frown as they work. They swing sharp and blunt hammers in clouded light that streams through the wall's rough-edged gaps. As I near Myrah's door, I mark without wishing to a bald man whose sweat runs down into the neck of his dark brown tunic. He turns to his friend and shows me his bent nose—I hasten into Myrah's room without first sounding against her door. She sits in a chair before her game board wearing a nest of woollen bedding while she reads from a sheaf of parchment by candle light. Her dim room of dark grey stone is otherwise bare—has she made ready to take her things elsewhere?

"Have we become so close that you need not sound at my door?" she says.

"That man, Gerahard," I say. "He came to us that night when the others took the watchmen to their rooms. He said he would own me in body or in spirit. I do not think he saw me."

Myrah sets down her parchment.

"He will do no such thing," she says. "If I must, I will show him that I have done it in his stead so that he has no need of it."

"What?"

"Gerahard comes to us from a kingdom that is neighbour to our trading friends on the other side of the sea. His king also wishes to be friends with father."

"And his king shows his friendship by sending men to break your father's walls?"

"Father makes a show of goodwill to our southern friends, against whom no such walls are needed, and to the many northern aldormen who fight among themselves for a share of father's blessings."

"Do you mean land? Titles? Oxen?"

"Children," says Myrah. "Father has not yet told them they may have no such thing. None of your sisters are with child, so Derwen tells me. You and your bond-sister Florentina must have had a good laugh after you told me the tale of her child. Did Derwen laugh with you?"

"She almost smiled," I say.

Myrah's smile leaves her as she stands.

"Whom do you think Derwen loves best?" she says.

"Derwen told me little of herself even when we were bound in our rooms those many days," I say. "She loves Hugo, I think, though he is gone."

Myrah's shoes come up against my feet.

"Me," she says as her face nears mine. "Derwen loves me best."

I step back from Myrah. She steps with me.

"Why else would she sit at the runestone?" says Myrah. "Father forbade her from sitting alone in a room with me after our talks became something other than talking. She is old enough to be your mother, father told me. Mother said the same, but her words were not her own. Do you know why? No, you do not. Father thinks I would run away with her. Mother knows I would never do this."

"Florentina said that after she left Emerita, her king fought against his own son," I say.

"Yes, father knows your histories better than any other," says Myrah. "It is history he loves best when thinking on what is to be done. He loves it so much that his daughters may one day find themselves forgotten among the unwritten words of his histories. But I, I can not forget you. And that is the greatest secret of all: you are in my thoughts more than any other even where I do not wish you to be."

"Am I in your thoughts when I do not do your bidding?"

Myrah shakes her head and takes my shoulders.

"Listen to me, and listen to me well: do not believe my father's lies."

"Why does your father lie?"

"He tells me what he thinks I wish to hear. And so, too, would I have you tell Florentina that she is your bond-sister, whatever she wishes to hear. Call my father your father though you know you do not feel this. Do this, and I will see that you live with your mother and father once more."

"I should not have to win this by doing what you ask of me."

Myrah nods to herself. She bows her head and rests her forehead against my neck bone.

"You will live with them, whatever you do," she says. "I will make this happen. And when I do, if I should call on you to shield me from my foes, whomever they may be, I hope you might be thankful enough to give me what I ask of you."

"Who would harm you?"

"None, if you stay close to me."

Myrah sets her arms around me so tightly that there is nothing between us. She looks into my eyes for an answer to something she has not asked and finds it in my lips. Her breath bears unto mine the winds that blow through the sand along far-off seas. My breast swells with the warmth of their gales. I am elsewhere when Myrah's lips leave mine. The candle's light shows me only Myrah's face, fairer by far than Winiburg's ever was.

"I will," I say.

"Good," she says. "Now, go and tell Florentina that she has won. Tell her that I am so angry about having lost that she must wait until tomorrow to play again."

Before I can answer, she turns me around and shoves me forwards through her door, which then shuts behind me. None of the men's sweaty faces or grunting strikes against the stone find a resting place within my mind. I do not know that Florentina awaits my words until she strikes me on the knee with the half-burnt mead-stirring stick she must have taken from the hearth.

"Did you lose your way that you were gone so long?" says Florentina.

"She looks as though she has fallen in love with one of the men," says Rosamond.

"And I was of a mind to send her to Myrah more often," says Florentina. "So, Ardelle, what is your beloved queen's move?"

"She sets the game board upside down," I say. "She does not want to play again until tomorrow."

"I did not think I had won so soon," says Florentina.

"I think her father must have yelled at her again for allowing Derwen to sit beside the runestone," says Rosamond.

"Rosa," says Marigold as she sits down beside her friend. "Do not speak so."

"Rosamond shows her wisdom this once," says Derwen. "Do not dwell on what can not be, Ardelle, for such idle thoughts lead only to suffering."

14

BETRAYAL

When winter's tidings send frosty winds into our sanctuary, Myrah comes bearing the gift of an iron beam for the door of the third great room. As Derwen searches for the best place to set the wall hooks, the door opens with a mighty shove, bringing us two watchmen whose smiles are less than mirthful. They bid Myrah give them the key-ring from her belt.

"My father did not tell me to give you my keys," she says.

"Nor did he tell you to give this door a beam," says one of the watchmen.

"We must see that you sleep in your bedrooms behind closed doors," says his friend. "Our northern friends might otherwise think you ask them to come to you at night where *none* are allowed to do so."

Myrah lets the iron beam fall to the floor with a loud sound that bears her answer well enough.

That night, Derwen stands on a chair as she sings stones into the narrow wall-gaps below our bedroom's roof, where-after she does the same for her sisters' rooms. Marigold takes two candles for each bedroom and hues their wicks with her fire. They, along with our bedding and gapless walls, keep us warm until morning, when those same two watchmen await us in the hearth room.

"The weather has somehow warmed during the night," says the tallest of them to Myrah. "Your father says you and your sisters are to spend the day asking the sun why this is so."

Myrah blinks thrice, then waves her hand towards herself to hasten our flight from our watchmen's glaring eyes into Annette's stone halls, whose tree-like columns stand hidden in darkness. We step out into life-giving wind beneath an unclouded sun whose warmth Florentina greets by lifting the breastpins at my neck and breathing in deeply.

"You smell like fish," she says. "Pike, I think. We will not cook you, though."

Myrah leads us down a hill of green grass that awaits the return of winter's frosty bedding. Butterflies hued white, black, red, and yellow flutter up from among green-stemmed flowers bearing brown buds that look like sleeping spiders. One such butterfly bearing the red hue of Luda's wool lands on her shoulder as she walks.

"Myrah," says Luda. "I will take Ardelle to swim at the lake."

"The lake is beyond the trees," says Myrah.

"Father said I could," says Luda.

"Father is not here," says Myrah.

"Yet the watchmen know what he says," says Luda.

"And who will watch you, then?" says Myrah. "The northmen?"

"Yes," says Luda. "They will find it enough to watch us from afar."

"Let us swim, my dear queen," says Florentina.

"Is this the same dear queen who now lives in my little bedroom?" says Rosamond.

"Our bedroom," says Marigold.

"The same queen who sits on your sitting pot," says Florentina.

Myrah sighs.

"Florentina," she says, "do not stay at the lake so long that the men feel they need to swim alongside your bullheaded sister."

"They could not catch her in the water even if they wished to," says Florentina.

When we have reached the northern grove of trees that bind us to our sanctuary, Luda waves her winged friend away and sheds her red wool, whereafter she also takes off her linen and sets it around Florentina's neck before handing me her hose and shoes.

"Are you not mindful that the northmen watch you?" I say.

"They know where we are, even now," says Luda. "They will not stop us from bathing."

She leads us between thick trees over a bed of dried leaves and hardened acorns that make me wish for my shoes. Though the lake is small enough that it might find shade beneath the boughs of summer oaks, the water brings chills to my flesh before I have set foot in it. Luda dives into it from its low bank, misting my feet with icy water. I set Florentina down on the grass beside Luda's shoes and make myself as bare as our bullheaded sister; Luda smiles at me from where her spreading arms allow her to float. My foot freezes when I set it in the water—Luda grabs my ankle and wrests me into a world of ice. I thrust my head above the water and gasp for breath even as my feet find the lake's bottom.

"Shall I have Ardelle hold you, Florentina?" says Luda.

"I would rather drive a nail through my forehead," says Florentina.

"As you wish," says Luda. "Wait while I warm the water, Ardelle."

She sings light and lithe words in her tongue, of which I understand only half. My gasping gives way to steady breaths; my flesh softens. As my breast warms, I send myself up and down with the tips of my toes against the lake bed. Luda swims away from me on her back. The lake's mossy bed becomes too deep for my feet to reach. Luda treads the water as if her legs stretch to the lake's bottom.

"Your hands are not so red, now," she says. "Come to me with your arms and legs."

I thrash my arms and swing my legs until I have no more breath and my limbs are weary.

"Good," Luda says as I hold myself up with my hands on her shoulders. "Now, swim back to Florentina and rest for a while."

When I reach Florentina, I am dead; and Florentina tells me how glad she is to see me so. Luda swims around the lake as well as any fish, whereafter she comes to me and holds my belly aloft while my arms and legs do what I have seen of her. When my body aches, she bids me swim out to the middle of the lake once more and back to her. My lungs heave with fire when I return to her; though I am as heavy as stone, she lifts me onto the lake's grassy bank and swims while I dry myself in my linen. When the wind has cooled my water-warmed flesh, I wear my red wool once again. Luda dries herself without her clothing until Florentina takes the linen from around her own neck and throws it at Luda's back.

"Clothe yourself, you brute."

Luda wears her white linen and squeezes the water from her long braid.

"How did you learn to make the water warm?" I ask her.

"Water does not learn wetness," Luda says. "Florentina did

not learn how to breathe. I do not learn how to send blood through my body."

"Is there nothing more than that?" I say.

"Our devotion hardens our strength during times such as when we were bound in our rooms," says Luda. "You must learn to abide suffering willingly, for this will make you stronger; and it may be that when next you sing, the wind will hear you better."

Myrah's black gown leads four red and three brown in a slow walk to where we sit among grass up to our shoulders. When she comes before me, she does me the kindness of not standing on my feet.

"Ardelle," she says, "as you are the one who told me of the bargain your sisters made with their men …" Myrah looks at Rosamond. "… they now ask that we all become good friends with them so their minds do not dwell on what you have done at the lake beyond the trees."

"You think I am the one who made the others do this?" says Rosamond.

"It was not a bargain," says Annette.

"Nor was it a secret for long," says Marigold.

Luda shoves my shoulder. Florentina rests her head against my back.

"We will no longer bathe at the lake," I say.

"That much is clear," says the one among the men who wears no beard, "but you were not to have done so at all."

"Am I to lie with one of you?" I say.

"No," says Derwen.

"I am," says Myrah.

Derwen frowns at her.

"Would your father allow this?" I say.

"Father says I am old enough to seek my own king," says Myrah. "Am I not allowed to do the same as the rest of you?"

"You may do as you wish, dear queen," says Rosamond.

"Ardelle?" says Myrah.

"If that is your wish," I say.

"What is *your* wish?" Myrah says.

Derwen's eyes flit from me to Myrah until they come to rest on her own feet.

"Take your king," I say.

"He will not be my king," says Myrah, "but I will do as you say." She turns to the men. "I will meet you in the third great room this evening. Any who comes to my room before then will find himself bedless."

When the men are gone from our sight, Myrah bends down, kisses me on the lips, and walks away. Derwen starts away from my eyes as though they were blades. Rosamond, Marigold, and Annette follow her swift footsteps.

"So that is how Myrah bade you tell her what we did," says Florentina.

"She would have learned even if Ardelle did not tell her," says Luda.

"Yet we have learned that Ardelle tells her," says Florentina.

I bring my knees to my forehead and look down at this gown bearing the same hue as the one Winiburg gave me. I never should have left mother.

"Wilfrith is as large as an ox cart," says Florentina as she pats my back with her palm. "They would have found him whether Annette hid him or not."

I lift my head to find them smiling at one another.

"What of your man, Luda?" I say. "Would they also find your hairless giant?"

Luda and her long braid fall over laughing into knee-high grass. Florentina crawls over to her and pushes her fingertips into Luda's arm beneath her shoulder as children might do to one another when their mothers are nowhere to be seen.

"Tell her," says Florentina, "or I shall never stop."

"Brant," says Luda. "His name is Brant. He is my brother. He has come here to watch over me."

Luda sits up; when Florentina does the same, Luda shoves her shoulder so hard that she falls down. Florentina sits up once more. Luda looks at her with narrowed eyes. Florentina raises a fist with clenched lips. Luda waves her hand at Florentina and looks away.

"Do you think nothing of what Myrah said of me?" I say.

"Oh, yes," says Florentina. "We hate you."

"We do?" says Luda.

"We *will* have to live with her forever," says Florentina. "That is why Luda teaches you how not to drown."

"*You* will have to live with her forever," says Luda. "When I return to Geatland four years from now, I will bear a son by a man known to me. There are some who may still wait for me."

"Not the aldorman," says Florentina.

"Must I tell her?" Luda says.

"Would you have me tell it?" says Florentina.

"My aldorman had a son of fifteen who was weak of breath and heart and did not know how to swim," says Luda. "When, after winter, the icy waters had melted well enough, I took him out further than I should have in teaching him. He did not bear the cold well, and, as I watched him, he sank below the unsoftened ice. I thought he would come back as you did, Ardelle; when he did not, I went below to find him but could not see him in the darkly clouded water. I swam further down, thinking that I saw an arm or a leg. It was then that my lungs began to swell and I sought to go above again. When I found my breath, I gasped so heavily that I could not sing. I had not thought to warm the water before I taught him—I did not think one who lived amid snow and ice would be mastered by them so swiftly. I dared not go beneath once more for fear of becoming like him. The fire within my breast turned to retching filth as I told his father of what had happened. His wise men found me guilty: not of murder, but of weakness, the same which had taken his son below. Thus, instead of killing me, he bid me sail the southern seas to Jutum and from there along the winding shore to live among whomever would take me. After some months, I came to the bitter stone walls of our sanctuary. It was there that I knew I should spend my fifteen years for what I had done. Myrah's father watched with a broad smile as I sang to the swelling sea, whereafter he took me as his own daughter. I have since come to know that he thinks of me as no such thing, as has Florentina, as have the others but for Myrah."

"I know of this as well," I say.

"You know of Myrah," says Florentina.

"Did you also know that there are some who wish to give us children thinking they might wield that which is within us for themselves?" Luda says.

"I think some such men watch over us," I say. "An aldorman may have asked them to do so."

"You have learned well this day," says Florentina.

What I do not wish to learn well is whether those men do likewise with Myrah thinking to wield her father's strength.

On the following morning, when I sit with Florentina in the grass near the sanctuary and thus far from the trees beyond which we must not go, Annette comes to us on a horse leading another of its kindred. Among us, she finds none who wish to learn: Luda masters horses better than Annette; Rosamond will not be seen riding a steed; Marigold becomes sick on anything that sways like a ship; some horses listen to Derwen's arm, while others do not, and she does not wish to learn of this horse's mood by being thrown from it. As I stand before Annette's four-legged friend, he shakes his head and neighs, as if to warn me that his skull is harder than mine.

"He has chosen you," says Annette.

I begin by holding the horse's bridle and walking about

with him, bidding him go left and right and bringing him to a stop. I speak kind words until he becomes friendly enough to allow me to climb onto his back, only to slide from his body when he starts. Annette calls to him by making a sound with her tongue.

"How am I to ride that which does not want to be ridden?" I say.

"Show him that you master yourself and he will trust you well enough to yield to your will within his bounds," she says. "He is not unlike our watchman friends."

I swing my leg over my steed's back once more and take the leather straps. I make Annette's sound with my tongue and, with the help of one leg or the other held against his back, walk him around Florentina's meadow thrice. Florentina claps her hands when I return the riding straps to their master.

"You have learned how not to fall off a horse," she says. "Rest, now, and see whether you do as well tomorrow when I ride you through the meadow."

Three days after Myrah had left us, she returns with cooler winds and hardened eyes that lead us down to the sea to bathe while her beloved watchmen watch over what we do from the cliffs high above us. She does not look at me, nor I at her, most of all not when she takes off her gowns and leaves them on the sand beside her shoes and hose. I keep my eyes from her rich brown shoulders and her waist fleshy from eating honey with every meal and the thin rings of black hair she washes in short lengths. The blast of water that wets the side of my face must be Florentina's way of telling me to hasten my bathing and return to her on the sand where she dries herself.

"Up the hill," Myrah bellows as she wades to the shore. "All of you."

My linen clings to my undried flesh as I bear Florentina up the mild swell to where our watchmen await. Myrah's father stands among them in his dark clothing with his hands held at his sides clutching the hilts of knives that are not there.

"Our northern friends," he says, "have seen how we abide in peace among them. We shall thus eat of our harvest, which their women will serve to us in thanks for your abiding friendship and kindness. They will send for you when the sanctuary stands ready."

After the king and his men have left, Myrah comes to stand beside Florentina and look out into the oak trees as I do.

"Have you taught Ardelle any more Latin?" she asks.

"Nothing," says Florentina. "I told her that the men might overhear us. Or your father, who would be more severe. Or you, who would be the worst of all."

"So you have taught her Gothic that I might not understand you."

"Do you speak your mother's tongue with the birds in these trees? Leave us be and go back to your northern friends."

"They are not my friends," says Myrah and walks away with hasty strides.

While we wait, Florentina tells me a tale of her woodland animal friends: on summer's longest day, a family of red squirrels banded together with a brotherhood of sleepy-eyed mice against the goshawks and foxes who hunted them. The mice were at first in good spirits, but they came to loathe being kept at the edges of the great gatherings where the squirrels chose a leader from among their own kind. When the mice made their worries known, the squirrels did not heed them; and thus, in their wisdom, the mice broke away from the squirrels and sought out the foxes, who readily agreed to unity in opposition against such evil misdeeds. The foxes invited the mice to sit with them for their midday meal. The mice spoke words of thanks for the food they had been given, whereafter they were eaten.

"I will kill any fox I see," Derwen says to our shoulders.

Myrah comes to us clothed in her black gown and leads us through Annette's painted halls to where her dear father and mother await their obedient mice. In the hearth room stands a single long table with a candle burning before each of its ten chairs. Myrah sits down to the left of her father; on his right sits Myrah's mother in a gown as black as her daughter's bearing a golden hawk at her throat.

"Be seated," she says.

I take my seat furthest from the king beside Annette, the youngest of us before I came here.

"Come and sit beside me," Florentina whispers loudly enough for all to hear.

I stand and take up my chair. Myrah's mother raises her eyebrows.

"Myrah," she says, "have your sisters forgotten everything they learned from you?"

"My dearest Ziri," says the king, "let us not forget that such things take time. Let us also not forget that we must be mindful of those old ways which show us what is right." He stands. "One of you has forgotten those ways. One of you has been unfaithful. I have long known this but have said nothing until now when it weighs upon us most heavily."

The back of my chair slides from the grasp of my hands; its legs strike the floor.

"Myrah said I may take Ardelle as my bond-sister," Florentina says.

"Bond-sister," says Myrah's mother.

"Of this we did not know until now," says Myrah's father with a look for his daughter.

"You said we could bathe in the lake," says Luda.

"We allowed the hearth's fire to die," says Annette.

"Was this not father's will?" says Marigold.

"Yes, it was, Maria," says Rosamond. "Anyone who blames

you may go beneath the floor and make the fires there burn however they wish."

"Daughters," says Myrah's mother, "your father does not speak to you so. Will you not show him the same kindness?"

"What kindness?" says Marigold. "Father will blame our woes on whatever misdeeds he finds among us. We will be made to suffer far beyond ten days while he thinks on how to draw the wretchedness from those who only leave his halls when he wishes them to."

"I have earned your bitter words," says the king. "I have kept secrets from you. And now, I shall withhold my own bitter words from you as I ask you of the secret you have kept from me: who among you is with child?"

We look at one another with widened eyes. I stare at Annette. She shakes her head.

"You have taken men whose children you may not bear and thus made them suffer," says the king. "You have further made our northern friends suffer by leading them to think they may do the same. Your atheling-sister, Myrah, has taken this burden from them. This, she has learned from all of you. She has done what you did without her mother's blessing."

"Nor have I blessed anyone who sits at this table," says Myrah's mother. "You know this, yet you show your atheling otherwise. I will have you abide this winter in faithfulness, with Myrah among you, as I think on what is to become of you."

"You may bring the maids to us, now," says Myrah's father.

Myrah leaves through the hearth room's opening and returns with ten women in brown bearing wooden trays laden with bread, fish, eggs, carrots, and smoked meat. The maid nearest Derwen sets her tray down on the table; her short knife gleams in the hearth's fire as she draws it from her belt sheath. She smiles when Derwen meets her eyes—Derwen sends her chair to the floor with her legs and strikes the maid's nose with her fist, sending blood down her lips and chin. Two of her friends drop their trays onto the floor and unsheathe their knives; the others step backwards or flee the room, some of them throwing down their trays as they run. Marigold takes a wooden tray from the floor and holds it out before her—it burns with deep purple flames that brighten the hearth room's marble walls into snowy whiteness. Rosamond hides behind her. The maids who bear no knives flee the sight of Marigold's fire. Derwen's bloody-faced foe takes Derwen by the hair and thrusts her knife into Derwen's arm, drawing a yell from her. Derwen strikes the maid's face again, sending her to the floor, whither Derwen also sinks. Luda goes to them and sets herself between them as they wrestle. Annette speaks weightless words to the two knife-wielding maids. Myrah's father stands with his hands held behind his back and smiles as if nothing at all happens. His wife stands beside him with one arm on his shoulder. Myrah steps out from behind her mother's gowns and goes to Derwen where she holds her hand over her knife wound.

"You can do nothing to help her, daughter," says the king.

Myrah steps onto the bench, walks on top of the table, drops down, and shoves Annette aside.

"Kill me," she growls at the knife-wielding maids.

A draught of wind stills the candles and dims the hearth's fire to ashes, leaving only Marigold's tray burning. I lift my chair and hold it over my head to frighten the maid nearest me. The wood has become so light in my hands that the chair breaks itself against her head and shoulders and comes to rest on top of her where she lies with unblinking eyes on the marble floor. Her friend drops her knife and rushes towards the hearth room's opening. I take her weapon and with two swift steps have her hair in my fingers. I seek her arm—as her friend did to Derwen—but find instead the thin flesh of her neck. Her life-water bleeds out onto my fingers and down to my elbow. Luda throws me against the wall and holds me there; she squeezes my wrist until the knife falls from it.

"Florentina," says Myrah, "come out from beneath that table and heal our *friends*."

The maid whose neck wets her brown gown runs through the room's opening on unsteady legs. Florentina crawls to the young woman whose head bleeds from the chair that struck her—her eyes are clouded glass. Florentina's song breathes enough life into her that she finds her feet once more. Thereafter, I bring Florentina to Annette; together, they soothe Derwen and the maid whose knife she still wields.

"Drop it," says Luda, and so Derwen does.

"Thus was our misunderstanding born," says Myrah's father. "I shall tell the northern aldormen of how we mistook your cutting knives for long knives, for your men have never worn weapons in our halls. Come now, dear friends, and take me to your wise men that we might forgive one another and seek their wisdom on how best to heal our friendship."

The serving maid whose head is still bloodied from the chair stares at me until Ziri takes her shoulder and walks with her beside her husband. Her friend spits on Derwen's feet before following them through the hearth room's opening. Myrah's mother looks back and waves Myrah towards her. Myrah clenches her fists at her sides. Ziri speaks to her husband, then comes to us.

"What you have done here today is of little help to your father," she says to Myrah. "You must hereafter behave yourself as a queen does lest you earn a king who seeks strength over truth."

"I do not like the northmen," says Myrah.

"Then your king need not be one of them," says Ziri. "Your father has many good men he would willingly give you. If you wish to be a queen, you must learn when to yield. I will take your keys."

Myrah takes her iron key-ring from her belt and hands it to her mother.

"Learn well from what your atheling has done," Ziri says to us.

When her mother has gone, Myrah grasps the long end of the table and upends it, sending candles, trays, and food onto the floor. Before she leaves, she walks by me, though she need not do so.

"Remember what you promised me," she whispers and follows in her mother's footsteps.

15

BATTLE

For the next eight days, the third great room's oaken door stays shut without a beam to hold it, nor does Myrah unlock the painted halls for us, yet we find each morning that the hearth room's long table has been laden with more food than we can eat, having been left for us by shadowy hands and faces in the dimness of the floor hearth's soft embers. On the ninth morning, when I still sleep, mother sets my old green and yellow gowns onto my legs and rests her hand on top of them. I reach for the golden bird on her neck that glows in Marigold's candlelight; Myrah meets my hand with an apple as yellow as the linen on my legs. I have no hunger, yet my belly does not heed my mood—I still its unwanted growling with honeyed flesh.

"Your mother sent these to you," Myrah says. "She would want you to wear them on a day like today when the sun and the moon are most brotherly in the heavens."

"Where one is seen, the other is not," I say. "How is this brotherly?"

"It is not. Father does battle with the northmen, who have

no love for his brotherhood. I wished to spare you this, but you would not leave."

"I need no sparing," I say. "And had I been murdered on my walk home, I would have left altogether."

"I would have sent men with you," says Myrah. "That man who shut the sanctuary's door behind us. His brothers. They would have watched your fields until your face left the memory of those who wish you ill."

"So you say."

"Or until serving maids had forgotten your face, at least."

"Or yours."

"My words, you mean to say. And that is all they were: words, nothing more."

"Nothing more. Annette says the same, but her words to me in the hypocaust were not nothing."

"The northmen are of the same mind as you," says Myrah. "They do not forgive."

"What is there to forgive?" I say. "It was done willingly."

"As do Derwen and Luda *willingly* go to help my father in battle. Do you think they may tell him otherwise? The others will heal the men he brings to them. Their own sisters, should they be among them."

"As they healed Annette's wounds?"

"Annette opened them anew at mother's behest when she learned of you from the aldorman. Father did not yet know of you. There, you have her secret."

"And what of Marigold?"

"You did not hear this from me: father brought her to our wounded foes, once. I was there as well to learn the truth of such things. The memory of burning flesh never leaves one's nose."

I set my half-eaten apple down on the bedding.

"What does he want of me?"

"To help your sisters frighten our foes," says Myrah.

I run my fingers along mother's beads around my neck. Myrah sets her hand on my shoulder.

"Luda wears a wolf's tooth from her brother on a woven strand of Florentina's hair," she says.

"You cut it?"

"Florentina did. Luda keeps that token with her should they not see each other again."

The door swings open. Derwen's shoulder-fastened over-gown is as green as the one that rests on the red wool in my lap. She drops a white comb with teeth on both sides into Myrah's lap—when did she steal this from me?

"We will see each other again," says Derwen.

"So we shall," says Myrah.

At once, she is on her feet and shuts Derwen from the room. She sits back down so close to me that her breath warms my neck.

"The aldorman Constantine and his men watch over Derwen and Luda today." The hair on my neck stands up straight. I take my shoulder from hers. "He will keep them from harm. Luda's brother brings horses should they need to flee."

"Whither would they flee?" I say. "The northmen know where we abide."

"And thus they would come to us—to me—with hatred in their hearts rather than love." Myrah sets her hand on mine. "Give us your strength."

"What strength?"

"I know not what is in your heart, but the ice on father's heart will melt if he learns that I have brought you to him."

"Marigold's fire did not melt it."

"Forget my father, then." Myrah grasps my hand. "Help me. I think of you. Often. And I would have you in my thoughts as one above all others who helps me when I need it."

Her winding, writhing words send me to my feet. I throw the green and yellow gowns against the wall.

"You can find the truth of your thoughts for me well enough when I am at home where I should be," I say. "I do not live to seek your happiness."

My golden breastpins strike against the wall and land on the table among Florentina's hair rods. Myrah turns her head away as I send my bundled red wool and white linen flying with my feet. The bone that binds my green wool to my yellow linen at my shoulders looks as though it could have been taken from Myrah's comb.

"Leave your shoes so those who watch you walk will not wonder who you are," Myrah says. "And keep your mother's beads hidden as well lest our foes think you openly ward against them."

"You might have worn them so the northmen would not have followed you to the lake where we swam."

"They would not have helped me," she says. "I lay on my belly as your sisters told me they did so I would not take a child."

"Did you like it as they did?"

"It *hurt*," she says as she stands. "They took from me and gave me nothing in return. For this, they do not forgive me." Myrah takes up my half-eaten apple. "Such is my life."

She bites into the yellow flesh, chewing loudly as she shoves open the bedroom door. Myrah's sisters do not await us in the hearth room, nor in the hall whose floor stones look like painted flowers, but beneath a clouded grey sky at the foot of the eastern hill among Florentina's beloved red poppies that have begun to wither. Marigold's namesake flowers, whose leaves have withstood the early gift of snow, still hang heavy with sleep. Derwen takes my arm as we walk to the eastern trees.

"If the northmen overtake you and do not kill you," she

says, "you must give them the name Bertha and tell them a tale like the one you have heard from Annette: you were taken from northern lands before your earliest memory and have lived among southern men all your life. You have learned their ways but have always felt an inner longing whose meaning you did not understand."

"Will they believe this?" I say.

"You could tell them you are a sister in red come to take their children," Luda says over her shoulder.

"They may see in you their lost kindred and take you to live among them rather than sending you beneath the earth," says Derwen.

When we reach our blue-gowned sisters, Marigold is alone in coming to me. She hugs me and sets her cheek against mine.

"Derwen and Luda have done this before," she says. "They have always returned."

"Do the others not share your kind thoughts?" I say.

"They would not have your last memory of them be one of sadness."

Florentina waves to me from Rosamond's back until Myrah stills her hand. Myrah balls her own hands into fists at her sides. Derwen and Luda each take one of my arms and walk with me into the thick-boughed, leafless oaks that once shielded us from what lies beyond. Two hundred steps bring us to their thin-bodied birch brothers. Within them stands a tall, bald, shaven man clothed in the same brown tunic and leggings as Luda, though he wears shoes where none of us do. A thick leather strap over his right shoulder holds a fist-length black sword hilt against his left hip; its lower handle bears an iron ring to which two glass-beaded strings are tied. The end of his maple sheath reaches below his knees as he walks to us.

"My brother, Brant," says Luda. "Brant, this is Ardelle, my sister."

"Your sister?" he says to me.

"I am today," I say.

"Then I would have you be wholly unlike your sister," he half-whispers with a smile. "Walk softly and say nothing."

Luda shoves his shoulder. Two horses whose bridles have been bound to tree boughs step with their hooves as Brant takes their straps. We follow him through the thicket for so long that Derwen and Luda let go my arms to make their way between the trees. On our right, the sea comes ever closer yet shows us nothing of the sand that leads to it. Where the trees open up into harvested fields, Brant brings us to a stop.

"How shall we do this, Brant?" whispers Luda.

"Do what?" I whisper.

"Many ships lie berthed on the shore far north of here," Brant whispers to me. "This is where they might watch for us."

"She does not need to know this," whispers Derwen.

"I will take the horses around the fields," whispers Brant. "You must wait here until I am out of sight, then go far from one another and walk through the rows as if they are yours. When you reach the trees again, wait for me to find you."

Before Brant has left our sight, Luda walks away from the sea, bidding Derwen go towards it. Luda is not long gone and I have taken only ten steps when Derwen runs back to me and takes my hand.

"Come," she says.

We walk together through hewn and stunted stalks as if our husbands had done this to the wheat and rye not long ago and we have come to look at how the earth makes its winter bed. Derwen stops within sight of a thick grove of trees whose leaves are like needles and drops my hand to take up one of their fallen boughs bearing hard red berries. Luda runs to us with swift strides and leads Derwen by the hair into the trees where Brant awaits us. He frowns as he takes his sister's fingers from between Derwen's long brown strands of hair.

"Yew does not grow here," Derwen whispers. "They know we have come. They need not watch."

Luda wrests the yew bough from Derwen's hand.

"You behave as a child who still shits in her gowns and hold Ardelle's hand as if she were no better," she says.

Brant strikes Luda's shoulder with the back of his hand.

"Beyond this grove is the ridge where they will lie," he whispers.

Brant ties his steeds' bridles to two of the thickest oaks lest the horses make themselves heard. Where the ground becomes rough and craggy, we are met by a man in dark brown whose like-hued hair is bound into a tail by a golden clasp, and whose shoulder-belt bears a sheathed sword like Brant's. The smile on his thin lips brings to mind the strong drink that stank of rotten apples and tasted of vomit and took me to a bathing room, where I did not become clean even with the help of the aldorman's maid.

"Ardelle," whispers the aldorman. "I am glad that we meet again as friends."

"Friends?" I whisper.

"He and his men will stand between you and the northmen who might come up the ridge," whispers Luda.

I look down at the yellow and green gowns which have been washed of the blood that once made them filthy.

"Have you been a good friend to my mother?" I say.

"Speak softly," he whispers. "I have been faithful to the queen, yes."

"Branwen," I half-whisper. "Did you give her a child?"

"I know of no child that Branwen has borne but you," he whispers with clipped words, "nor of any but you that she will have lost if you do not speak softly. Let us be friends, now."

He comes to me and sets his arms around my back,

drawing me against his bony ribs and into the overly sweet stench of his bare neck. I shove him away.

"I do not need your friendship," I whisper.

"Had I given Branwen another child, I do not think she could have kept it," he says to himself. "Yet here she has kept a child long enough to grow into a woman who burdens me with her own life though she cares nothing for whether I live or die. This burden I give to you as well, Brant." The aldorman sets his hand on Brant's strapless shoulder. "We lie in wait in those trees to the west, where we have sight of the hill that leads down to the sea. Watch us well and we shall tell you when the women are to look over the ridge."

Brant claps the aldorman on his left shoulder.

"Should any of them come to us," Brant whispers, "I will send them back below twice as swiftly."

The aldorman smiles, as does Brant, and they cup one another again on the shoulder ere the aldorman and his hard leather shoes walk away without treading on the sturdy seeds that lie scattered over the unhardened earth.

"I will go down to the water now," Luda whispers and walks back through the trees.

"Why does she leave us so readily?" I whisper to Derwen.

"She must stand near the water to call on it." Derwen holds my arm beneath my shoulder. "Ardelle. If you see the aldorman's men rush out from the trees, you must run to the horses and ride away whether I am with you or not."

"You would have me leave you?" I whisper.

"Luda and I know that we may die at any time," she whispers. "But you, you must live today even if we do not. Be silent, now, and think on how you will be kinder to those northmen than you were to the aldorman should your life be in their hands."

The soft harvest wind blows through our hair where we lie

on the ground, I on my belly and Derwen on her back. I rest my forehead against the grassy earth and think for a time on what Derwen must see of the sun's light through the tree boughs overhead. Mother often wondered that I would stay in the house in the evening and dream of what went on in the waning light of dusk—I had only to step out and see for myself.

A hand strikes the back of my legs. Derwen crawls forwards. I follow her well enough until we reach the stone of the ridge, where my elbows and knees sting with aching that dulls at the cliff's edge. Below, great gatherings of men stand facing each other on a field not far from the sand of the sea. Those on the left are three times as many, as are the horses in the rear bearing men in iron shirts and helms. Under midday's harvest sun shrouded by lifeless grey clouds, these men wield dull swords and long knives and sharp-edged spear heads on shafts as tall as their bearers and half again. I back away; my morning meal of half an apple finds the ground beside me. I grasp the beads Myrah gave to me from my mother.

"Why do you hate Myrah?" I whisper.

Derwen blinks twice and looks away, then draws herself so near to me that the ribs beneath her left shoulder rest against my arm.

"I would have you and Myrah live to be as old as I," she whispers. "She has learned much from her father's books and words, but they teach her nothing of the ways of men who would bury her before her father does."

"She said she watched Marigold burn her father's wounded foes," I whisper.

"Such only teaches you how to empty your belly," whispers Derwen.

"What of that yew branch?" I whisper. "Will they not come up here?"

"Father does battle as the men of his old imperium did: on open fields beneath the heavens. He does not hide among trees, nor does he beset his foes without warning, nor does he shrink from them when they overwhelm him."

I look to the trees on our left whither the aldorman went to his men hiding amid the oaks. I should ask Derwen what she means by this—a great bellowing from below brings me back to the ridge. The men on the left speak as one and beat their spears against wooden shields painted red, white, black, and grey. From among them strides a shirtless man in short leggings, who stands on one foot as he hurls a long spear at the raised shields of the men on the right. The shield that takes the spear's blade breaks in half and sends its bearer to the ground, drawing a roar from the men on the left. The fallen man then stands and, lifted onto the shoulders of his friends, calls out his answer, as do his brothers. The spear-throwing man returns weaponless.

"Wait until they fight one another," whispers Derwen. "Then we sing."

"Where is Luda?" I whisper.

"Worry not for her, for she knows well what she does, nor for Brant, who has come here to watch over her."

My eyes only leave Derwen when, on the field below, two great walls of shields come into being. From both sides, men hurl spears at the darkening clouds overhead. Their weapons fall among their foes; some strike shields, while others plant themselves within the earth to be used again. Only a handful find the breasts of men. The shield-bearing men on the right stand close together, while those on the left drift away from one another. Without warning, the horsemen in the left rear rush forwards between their shield-men and drive their steeds straight at the opposing hedge of rounded shields that have been set on the ground. Another row forms on top of those at men's waists; some hold their shields before their faces. On the right, fifteen or twenty shoeless men drop their spears and hie away along the sand. They do not heed the men in iron shirts who call after them waving swords.

"Why do they send their horses to die beneath them?" says Derwen.

"Do we sing now?" I say.

Neither she nor I find any answer as the horses break through shields and throw men to the ground. Bladed iron takes the legs of upright horses so they can no longer run, and the legs of those who lie on the ground so they can not stand again, and the innards from those who can not stand so that their breathing stops. Long knives find the hearts of men whose life-breath was not choked from them beneath their steeds; swords take the heads of those who creep on hands and knees; spears break the spines of those who run away. Of their thirty horses, only three return over the field alongside five riders. Misty rain begins to fall from black clouds that threaten to bring night while the sun still hangs in the sky.

"Sing," says Derwen. "They will come together now."

I know not what I am to sing, nor to whom, nor where I should look as I do so, for I would not watch these men do such things to one another even as my eyes forbid me from looking away. Derwen sets her palm against the rough stone of the ridge and sings wordlessly as the men on the left set a long wall of shields together and walk forwards. Bellowed words from a white-haired horseman on the right—Myrah's father? —send ten men wearing iron shirts and forty or fifty spear-men in brown running into a hail of spears from the left that fells five of them. The iron-shirted men climb the opposing wall of shields, swinging their swords at the shield-bearers, while their friends behind them thrust their spears between the gaps. Men behind the shields fall, as do those before the shields without their shins and feet.

A call from the few horsemen on the left sends the shield-men forwards without heed for the fighting among them. The five iron-helmed men who still stand take twenty spear-bearers beyond the shields on the right; those who lie wounded on the field are slain as the northmen come upon them. The strides of the shield-men lengthen and become swifter. They no longer hold their shields close together, but spread them such that they stretch from the shore almost to the foot of our ridge. They move forwards quickly, now, and threaten to form a ring around the tightly clustered boards opposite them. I shrink away from Derwen, for I will not sing with her if we are to kill all of these men—

A great shaking of the earth hinders the steps of many men at once, taking from them their shields and weapons and throwing them onto their backs. My ankles sting, as though they bear the full weight of this stony ridge. I stand to soothe the aching—a sharp tug on my rain-misted hair brings me back down to the earth. Derwen sets her hand on my cheek and strikes me weakly.

"Do not let them see you," she says. "*That* is how I lost my arm."

Brant runs towards us from among the trees bearing a shield on his forearm. He darts before us—a hurled spear strikes mightily against the iron in the middle of his shield and falls over the ridge. As Derwen hastens away from the cliff's edge behind Brant, I follow, as does the spear-man, who draws a long knife from his belt sheath. He meets Brant, striking down at his shield, but Brant steps to one side as if he will fall, sending the man forwards onto his knees. Brant breaks the man's head open with a blow from his shield. Another man comes up the hill and, on seeing his fallen friend, runs towards Brant with a reddened face.

"Away from the ridge," says Derwen, "lest Brant be seen by more of them."

Brant's foe throws his spear with such strength against Brant's shield that Brant drops it and shakes his arm. The man is almost upon Brant when Brant thrusts his foot into the man's chest, taking the breath from him. Brant grips his sword hilt with both hands and swings his blade through the man's neck. The man's head and body drop to the ground at Brant's feet. My lungs heave with the stink of rotting apples though I have nothing left in my belly.

Brant turns to us as if to say something—from the northern trees near the ridge rush tens of men bearing spears and shields and knives, led from the rear by the aldorman on his horse. They are met by as many of our foes who storm up the hill beside the ridge. Derwen flees towards the western trees with strides I can not match, yet the three spears that strike into the wet earth before me are my betters: my shins strike against their shafts, and I fall to the ground with them. The men who now run alongside Brant and his raised shield throw twice as many spears at Derwen before they are set upon by the aldorman's men. Half of their weapons fall short of the oak grove; two of them land on either side of Derwen; the sixth strikes into her leg and fells her not far from the trees. I rush to meet her. I can not wrest the spear from her leg; it has driven itself into the bone.

"Go to the horses!" yells a sword-wielding man who may as well be on the other side of the sea.

I stand but do not move.

"Retec ad ir cefelou!" Derwen says.

My arms take the spear from her leg at once. Derwen falls silent; her eyes close. My shoulders spin around before my waist does and I am thrust to the ground—was that a fist? Blood runs onto my lips and chin. I crawl backwards on my palms and feet. A weaponless man stands over Derwen, yet Brant is only a few steps from him wielding his sword, sending the man running from him into the trees. Brant takes up Derwen's bloodied spear and hurls it into the body of the young birch tree behind which our foe throws himself; the tree body splinters and falls over where the spear struck it. Another spear-man comes towards us. He looks at Derwen where she lies still, then at me where I rise to my feet several steps from her, then at the trees where his friend takes Brant's spear from the cleft birch's body. Brant hastens backwards with his shield held towards the trees and his sword held up against the raised spear before him.

The man in the trees plants his heel and throws his spear towards Derwen. With one swift step, I stand between her and death. The spear-man's eyes go wide. His weapon strikes into my gown below my ribs and burns into my heart but for a short while ere the aching leaves me, as does the spear and its haft and its bearer. Brant has likewise left me, as has Derwen, whose body I would seek did the sea's waves not call to me with such soothing words that I might walk below and abide nearer to their song.

Men who lie on the ground sit up as if they have awoken from a sleep of many years. One man bears a reddening wound on his neck from below his right jaw to above his left shoulder. He turns away from the shore long enough to smile at me.

"Your friend has strong sword arms," he says to the sea.

I kneel beside him and set my fingertips against the cleft that should keep his throat from speaking. He grunts at my strokes along his raw flesh but does not shrink from them. His skin bears the chill of the harvest wind that no longer blows beneath a grey and cloudless sky. From below comes the sound of laughter. I rise and look down from the ridge: many men sit and stand with one another as horses wander between them unheeded. One of the men waves to me, as do his friends as they call to me. I have no thoughts against their beckoning, nor any thoughts at all, and so I walk along the ridge towards the hill that I might meet with them.

The men who rest at the foot of the hill bear red blade

strokes that have rent their wool; their faces and legs are dark blue with bruises. Some of them look over their spears and long knives as one might a dead bird; others hand a round shield to one another as if it were a tray bearing a midday meal. One among them strikes his knuckles against its leather-banded wood and nods. His friends laugh as he sets it on the ground.

"This must be it, then," says a grinning man with hair above his lips. He looks to me. "Are you one of the southern king's women in red?"

From the clouds fall red feathers so light that their fluttering brings to mind the wights I saw when I dreamed beside the river not far from Isadora's house. When I look again at the men, they await my answer in silence. Whether they see the wights as I do, their eyes do not tell me. Derwen said I must tell them a tale such as Annette's lest they bury me here.

"I am Bertha," I say, "born in the north and taken by southern men. I have come here to return with you to the lands of my birth."

My words meet hoarse laughter from men whose greying flesh looks no warmer than the wan heavens.

"You have come too late, then," says one. "No, we have done this to ourselves."

Where their ships rest berthed on the shore, the clouds no longer soak them with misting rain. It may be that this is where Luda hides herself, though I wonder whether she needs to do so if these men do not even heed the low-bellied horses who walk among them bearing wretched wounds that do nothing to hinder their hoof steps.

"How did your ships bear these horses?" I say.

"They did not," says a bearded man. "Those are the long-boats of our friends. They stole your king's horses while he and his men slept. Their ships fetched us where we waited on the river Tamesis. Your battle-hardened steeds stood ready on the sand for our king and his aldormen. Good horses, they are."

I walk by one such horse on my way to the ships; when I set my hand on his dun neck, he starts and sets off into the sea. He, like I, stares out at the dark shape standing in a boat on the far-off waves. Fifty steps bring me to boats whose long and curving boards rest on the edges of one another. The dark boatman's ship, however, must have been carved from a single great oak tree. Its timber begins and ends nowhere, much as the marble rooms of our sanctuary.

Behind me on the sand, the men come forwards as one. They walk with heavy steps to where I stand before their friends' longboats. The boatman holds up a hand of bone as white as Myrah's comb. Their footsteps stop. My feet become stone. As many faces as the steps that brought me here stare at my gowns with mournful eyes, as did my sisters who did not wish to speak to me before I left them. Though Luda is nowhere to be seen, she must hide somewhere in the water whither these men wish to go. She would not have me leave them on their own.

"Give to me your blood," says the boatman.

My hands are lifeless; my fingertips take no heat from my cheeks.

"I have only myself to give," I say.

My feet do not stir, though I will them to tread the timber of his boat alongside these men.

"I suffer lies and theft," he says. "If you have not blood, I will take a token. Then, these men may come."

I run my hand along mother's beads where they rest on my neck. I did not send these men here. These words the boatman speaks are not for me and my sisters, for we have done nothing, nor has my mother anything to do with this.

"I have no token for you," I say.

"When your own blood ripens," he says, "these waters shall take it."

With those clouded words, the dark longboat leaves the shore, rowed into swelling mists by an unseen hand. I walk through the hanging heads of woeful men whose faces, along with my feet, run wet with blood that falls from the heavens like rain. It flows unhindered until, among the timber of shields and the iron of weapons, I lie down beside a closed-eyed horse whose belly has been rent from neck to tail.

Where rain drops no longer fall, those red wights have taken their place; one of them floats not far above my nose. It flees my hands and thus does as it will, for the flesh of my back has become like to the earth. I watch for a time as it goes where it wishes before settling on my lips, as did Luda's butterfly friend on her shoulder in the meadow not far from our sanctuary. As quickly as her winged friend left her, I lift my head with open mouth and swallow the wight. I turn my chin to one side and heave with clenched teeth as my throat burns with a sickly sweetness that threatens to send my innards through my nose. When the fire within my breast is gone, the warmth of sleep takes me and lets me rest for a time.

I sit on the earthen floor of our house at mother's knee. Father comes in from having shorn wheat in the fields to eat of mother's baked bread. Our happiness is made even greater when Myrah comes to us in a bone-fastened green gown bearing a basket of golden apples and tells mother that she wishes to live in peace with us for the rest of our days.

FREEDOM

The heavens are once again blue; their clouds are white like Isadora's writing feather; the wind bears the stink of rotting flesh. The wights that float not far from my face take shape into a sweat-laden, thin-lipped, long-nosed face belonging to the aldorman. He takes me against his bony breast. The stench of burning wood lives in his thicket of brown hair still bound by that golden clasp.

"That gold would look better in Luda's hair," I say.

"Then she shall have it," he says.

The aldorman takes his arms from me long enough to close my fingers around his hair binding.

"You and your sisters have won much for us this day," he says.

"Where have they gone?" I say. "Are they dead?"

The aldorman waves. The many men with spears who stand about us walk away but for one.

"I lost half my men on that ridge," he says. "I did not see your sisters among them, nor do they lie here. For that, we may be thankful. Gerahard, have you seen Ardelle's sisters?"

A man who wears a shirt of silvery, linked rings takes off the iron helm that hides his broken nose. His head bears only a rough shadow of hair, as do his craggy cheeks. His eyes, on seeing me, lose their hardness.

"Aldorman," he says. "I have not. I think they must have gone back with Brant. I will ask Athelbert of what he knows."

"Who?" I say.

"The king," says the aldorman.

"How does Gerahard know of Brant?"

"Gerahard is here on behalf of his king in Francia, who wishes to trade with us as much as his neighbouring kingdom does. The Frankish king knows that we are strong and have little need of … words such as these for which you have no mind. He is here to protect you, as am I, as is your king—here he is."

"Cyneric," says Myrah's father from his saddled white horse. "It is done. You and Gerahard may gather our wounded and bring them to my sanctuary."

Myrah's father steps down from his horse, takes off his helm, and bends one knee before me where I sit. He grasps my shoulders with bloodied hands. His hair is as white as his horse's tail.

"I know not what you have done," he says, "nor whether you have done anything at all. I know only that you and your sisters have brought us peace with these northern men and shown them the truth of the old Roman ways."

The men whose eyes and bellies have been opened to the heavens have no breath to tell me of whether this is true. Black birds glide along the wind far overhead, telling us of how they will care for these fallen men after we have left.

"Did I do this?" I say.

"They did this to themselves by coming here," says Myrah's father. "Where we sought a reckoning for the theft of our horses, we have taken the lands of that northern king,

Sledda, along with his fighting men. We go now to talk with them of what you have done to bring men together this day; and I shall have them spread word of the good you have done here, as will our men do among those who once hunted you. It is strength such as yours that shaped the wisdom of our forefathers, and you are the ones who will tell us of the path that returns us to their greatness."

"Good. My path takes me home."

"So it does. I would be wrong to ask that you stay within the brittle walls of my sanctuary hereafter. Know that I take great sorrow in having kept you there. Rest well at home this winter and think on whether I might be worthy of your strength when the snow has melted. I shall send Myrah to see you then and take your answer. Whatever you would have of your king, your atheling will make it so."

I grasp mother's beads.

"I had a dream," I say. "Myrah came to live with us."

Myrah's father takes one of mother's beads between his thumb and forefinger.

"Give her my love when next you meet her in your dreams," he says.

"Give it to her yourself," I say. "Make her dreams real."

"I will," he says, "as will you, even if when she comes to you some months from now, she tells you of her king." He stands. "Cyneric, come here. Take Ardelle home on my horse and thereafter leave her be."

The king's horse takes me on his hard leather saddle and heeds my bridle well. The aldorman leads me up the hill to where dead men lie with half-open eyes that stare through me as the king's stone forefathers did. Constantine's welcome silence makes the aching in my legs and backbone no more bearable as we thread through trees and the hafts of lifeless spears that stand between their living kindred. The hardening earth of harvested rows and frosting grass beneath my horse's hooves stir within me a longing for mother, who in my mind stands from her bedding to take me in her arms; and father, in whose lap I sit and play with the hair of his beard as if I were a child; and Isadora, whom I hold for as long as she will bear it.

The sun hangs low in the west when I slide down from the wooden saddle and stand on legs of stone from which my gown has nonetheless drawn sweat. Mother's quern rests beside the leaning door to our home, as do father's oxen and swine within their wood-ringed yards not far from it. The aldorman meets my eyes before speaking to clouds that have become amber against the setting sun.

"As the king has bid me, you shall not see me," he says. "Know that I thank you for what you have done and will think well of you even if you are not of a mind to do the same for me."

So long have I been away—more than a month—that I strike the leaning door to my own house as I call to mother and father. Stirring within brings a bloodless woman in brown wool with unbound black hair to me. She takes my wrists, pulls me to her, and slides the door into place against the chilling wind. Isadora feels my forehead and cheeks with the back of her hand. Her face has become fleshy; her fingers are thicker than I remember. Mother's braid hangs to her knees as she stands from her bedding and kisses me. Father sits on a wooden bench with his arms outstretched, taking me onto his lap when I come to him. His beard smells of the bread mother cooks over the hearth. Isadora offers me a meaty round as she chews on one of her own beside mother, who does the same. I bite into ground oats baked to hardness made soft by warm milk, a gift from Harold's cows kept near the hearth in a cooking pot that hides father's linen-wrapped, footless shin. I set my ill-eaten bread round near the hearth's embers and hold my belly with my arms.

"I saw men do that to each other," I say.

Father sets down his water pot and takes up two lengths of carved oak. Thick handles rest beneath his shoulders when he stands.

"I still walk well enough," he says with a smile. "When the snow has come and gone, we will walk along the river together."

Three days later, winter's frost falls in earnest. It hardens into a low-sweeping hand that keeps our house's door shut so well that father and Isadora and I must shove against it together to fetch mother's thread and sewing needles from the weaving house. I hold mother's thread on my fingers while she stitches waxed linen through the neck and hem of my undergown, or wool through her bedding, or leather through Isadora's shoes where the binding strings have broken. Father smokes whiting-fish brought by the aldorman's anglers and cooks the fox meat their spears find from time to time. Isadora is ever at our side, talking with mother and father of what they did in winter when they themselves were children. When Isadora's words become frost before her mouth, she goes out into the snow to gather wood for our hearth.

In the evenings, when mother and father lie together for a time, Isadora listens with closed eyes as I speak of the sanctuary. After many such nights, I have spoken as much as I wish to thereof, and I tell father of those things I saw on the field where men slew one another, and of the faces of men whose rent bellies and bloodied limbs still live in my dreams. Father leaves his bench to sit beside me and hold my hand, nodding at my wretched words. Mother's arms around my waist as I sit in her lap make my linen rough against my flesh, somehow; she rests her arm instead on my shoulders while I tell father of how horses ran through men and fell on top of them, squeezing blood from their throats that stank worse than the filth in their leggings when I sat among their lifeless bodies.

I wake one morning to empty myself of the night's heavy

water, having done so twice yesternight and thrice yesterday, and find that the door yields unwillingly to snow that meets my knees. So heavenly is this unbroken sea of white clouds that I wade through it, leaving footsteps for the wind to fill with ground snow from winter's quern. I find among the nearby trees those old, frost-boughed oaks beneath which foxes hide from the eyeless, ashen men who hunt them with broken spears. I empty my innards onto the tree bark, then hie back into the house lest I draw the bitter glares of ice-hearted men.

A sounding at the door calls Isadora, who bears her half-eaten bread between her teeth.

"A young woman says she has come to ask your daughter's forgiveness, Gildewin," says Isadora. "Harold sent her."

Father's frown meets mine.

"Let her come within and tell us of Harold's wisdom," he says.

A young woman whose face hides under a brown hood kneels before me where I sit with my emptied belly on mother's bedding. She takes the wool from her head; on her grassy brown hair she wears greenish-grey linen. Father eyes her as he drinks from his clay pot.

"Sithebad," I say. She lifts her chin. Her blue eyes widen. "You broke my nose."

Father empties his pot onto the earth all at once. Sithebad starts.

"I was wrong to do so," she says. "I should have hidden myself from those men after the harvest. I went with them, fearing what they would do to me in their drunkenness if we did not do it to you first."

"I did not smell mead on them," I say.

"Child," says Isadora, "think of that young woman who threatened you in the hypocaust. What would have befallen her if she did not do what she did?"

"Only Myrah's mother knows that," I say.

"Did you not live with Annette in that sanctuary?" says Isadora. "She must have had kinder words for you."

"She only went there to flee from men who hated her," I say to Sithebad. She looks at her lap. "Someone told Sithebad she must come here, else she would not have."

"You are forgiven, Sithebad," says father. "Battle has hardened my daughter."

"Might we ask why you have come here in such snow?" says mother. "You may tell us the truth. We will not speak of it with others."

Sithebad's shoulders slacken; her neck becomes limp. In the lap of her brown woollen gown, she runs the nail of her right hand's forefinger against her left hand's thumbnail.

"Mother says I am ready to wed," she says. "Ardelle's friend Alfred is to be my husband." I sit up straight, sending fire through my spine. "His father says we should be good friends to our neighbours."

Father's sharp outbreath sounds like laughter, yet his face shows otherwise.

"And what is it that Harold needs from us now?" he says.

"He only wishes to live in peace," says Sithebad.

"Good," says father. "Harold will no longer come to me every day asking where his son's 'wife' has gone. Here she is."

"His wife?" I say.

"How is young Alfred?" says mother. "I did not know he had grown into a man."

"This is his fifteenth winter," says Sithebad. "He grows taller every day."

"As he should," says mother. "Ardelle is eighteen this winter and has long since grown tall. Do you know of any young men who are yet unwed?"

"I am wed to death," I say.

Father's hands rest on his knees. Isadora stares at me with

unblinking eyes. Mother holds her own hand—my fingers sit clenched on my legs.

"I will leave now," says Sithebad as she stands.

"The king's daughter sent me to battle," I say. I take the aldorman's golden hair clasp from the bag on my leather belt beside mother's bedding. "If you wish to know of forgiveness, bring her this token of what she has wrought. Tell her to come here herself and show us what forgiveness means."

Sithebad holds the clasp in both hands though she needs only one to do so.

"I know nothing of the king or his daughter," she says.

"Nor should you," says father. "Keep your Alfred. We will keep Ardelle where she belongs."

Father sets his emptied water pot beside him on the bench. Mother gathers four bread rounds and shoves them into a linen bag.

"Share this bread with your husband," says mother. Sithebad sets the golden clasp among the bread rounds and ties the linen shut. "And with his father, from whose fields it comes."

"Thank you," Sithebad says to my feet.

She walks out into the snow with her linen bag held beneath her woollen gown to shield her hands from the icy wind.

"Did Myrah teach you to speak so?" Isadora says to me.

"Her grim words are born of darkness," says father. "The same that has taken my foot has taken her mind. Winter will do much to make her forget these memories, as must our words also do, Isadora."

"I am no keeper of words, Gildewin," says Isadora. "I saw something in Ardelle when she came back to us that my hands could not have felt in her flesh. But I will do as you say and still my speech so as not to draw it from her."

That evening, after we have taken our meal of meat and

bread, I lie down on mother's bedding to rest my eyes. Mournful words from somewhere among the snow drifts draw me without to bare earth that has become soft again beneath my feet. Ashen men lead me along the old stone path to the sea, where at the bottom of a ridgeless hill they ask me with unspoken words to take them to the beyond. I wade out into the waves and they follow, yet where the icy water meets my waist, my legs do not listen, nor will the darkly clothed man who stands over them in his longboat take them hither. The men walk beside me, then beyond me, hiding their faces from me as the moon guides them into the depths. The last of them turns to me: he wears mother's eyes and nose and lips.

My forehead is wet with sweat. My breath shakes. Mother holds the back of her hand against my cheek.

"They walked with me into the sea," I tell her.

"That is where they met their end," says father from his bench.

"Gildewin," says mother.

"I see them fighting when I sleep," says father. "They do not leave me. And now, my daughter."

I eat little for many days, taking only a few bites of what mother and Isadora offer me when my belly growls. One morning, when warming weather has melted the river's bedding into icy shards, I empty myself of filth for the first time since winter came to us. I wash my legs with freezing water and set myself down before Isadora, who asks me to eat from the meat of our eldest swine. While I eat, her hand finds the flesh beneath my ribs, as does her ear.

"Branwen, she is with child."

Father stands unmindful of his missing foot and almost falls. Mother sets aside my pig's meat and listens to my breathing.

"You have grown into a woman," she says.

"And I would like to meet the boy who has grown into a man," says father.

"I have been with no man," I say.

"Was it one of the king's men in his halls?" says father. "I might have words with our king."

"You would do as well to speak to his halls," says Isadora.

"She will tell us of her child's father when she is ready," says mother.

Father takes his walking sticks and shoves aside the door. Frosty wind blows through his hair and beard.

"I think I may see what Harold knows of my daughter's child," he says.

Father returns with the westering sun and throws his walking sticks to the ground beneath his bench. Snow falls from his beard as he sets himself before the hearth to warm hands that have become redder than mine.

"Our wise friend Harold has gone to the aldorman as he so often does," says father. "In his wisdom, he takes his son and his son's wife with him. Soon enough we will know of our child, and of their children, and of how many carts of wheat Harold will ask of us to feed their hungry mouths, and of how many cows the aldorman sends Harold in trade for his fields."

Over the next month, I eat as much hare meat as father will give me. When, one day, the meat is gone and father's throwing spears have hunted the hares into hiding, a striking at the door nearly sends our cooking stone laden with mashed fish from mother's legs. Isadora greets a bearded man in brown bearing a basket. She turns away from his black-gowned friend, who wears a golden bird at her throat and golden earrings with a blue gem hanging from each loop.

"We have brought you a basket of red squirrels," says Myrah.

Her black-ringed hair has grown even longer—so long that she wears it bound in a long golden hair clasp like Luda's. My child thrusts itself against my belly at the quickening of the life-blood that keeps it. The man's arms are around me. I lean away from him. He laughs.

"You do not know me now that I leave my hair unshaven," he says.

The sea's blue waves float within his eyes beneath yellow-brown hair that looks nothing like his brown-flecked red beard. He smells of the wolf's hair on the neck and sleeve-ends of his tunic.

"Brant," he says.

My shoulders soften. I set my hands against his back and hold his rough-haired cheek against mine.

"Where are Derwen and Luda?" I say.

"Their greatest foe has become finding ways to keep their hands from lying idle while they wait for winter's breath to warm," says Brant.

"Is her child yours, then, that you hold her so close?" says father.

Brant leaves my arms and steps towards the door. Myrah sets herself down beside me and fills our house with light laughter.

"I stood watch on the ridge where she and Derwen looked out over the battlefield," Brant says. "We were set upon by many men. I thought Ardelle lost, but I am happy to be mistaken. Our foes knelt before the aldorman and his king not long after Ardelle took one of their spears in her breast and hid herself away."

Mother crawls from her bedding in haste, pulls the neck of my linen gown away from my shoulder bones, and feels with her hand down the middle of my ribs until, below where they meet, she finds with her fingertips the softened scar as long as her palm where a spear-head once made its fleeting home. Mother's worried frown draws Isadora to her side. Father waves Brant over to the bench to sit beside him so they may clap one another's shoulders. Isadora's hardening stare becomes stone when Myrah takes my hand and sets her fingers between mine.

"I must tell you something," she says. Her breath gives my neck warmth that floods down into my limbs. "My father knows of your child. Do you remember when he said that one of us had been unfaithful? He believes that this was a fore-telling bestowed on him by the same god who now calls him to the imperium in the far southeast where men still follow the old Roman ways in earnest."

"So your father has gone mad," Isadora says.

Mother offers Isadora her arm. Father and Brant have stopped talking. Myrah leans her shoulder against mine.

"Come to the sanctuary and tell him not to leave," she whispers.

"How am I to do that?" I say.

"I have come to talk of this with you," she says. "It may take many days. I will lie beside you at night while you think on this."

Mother and Isadora stare at us from the other side of the hearth. I take my shoulder from Myrah's. She squeezes my hand and draws me back to her.

"What of Derwen?" I say.

"She has learned to play Latrones well enough for Florenti-na's liking when Luda tires of their game," says Myrah.

I turn to speak to her so none other will hear. When she faces me, I must lean backwards to find her ear.

"Have you not done this with Derwen?" I whisper. "Was she not able to tell your father to stay?"

"Derwen keeps herself from me," says Myrah, "and I from her, and both of us from my father. He spends his days thinking without end on what is to be done. Only mother may speak to him when he is so, and only then to ask whether his thoughts are truths or half-truths. This is how she asks."

Myrah kisses me. Her eyes close where mine do not. Father looks to mother. Mother lifts her eyebrows. Father runs his fingernails through his beard.

"So, Brant," he says. "If you are staying for a time, you might help me find the hares that have been hiding from me before we gather wood for the hearth."

Brant stands without a word and waits as father finds his walking sticks.

"Brant," I say, "you might also take some of those squirrels to Alfred and Sithebad in the neighbouring fields. They were wed not long ago."

"What happiness they must have found," Myrah says.

Brant takes half the squirrels from the basket and sets them beside the stones of the hearth. Father leaves his cutting knife unsheathed beside them and follows Brant to the door.

"Send them in before you leave," says Myrah.

"Them?" says Isadora.

Not long after Brant and father have gone, a wan-faced, soft-nosed woman with wavy black hair bound into a tail walks wordlessly into the house wearing a long wooden sheath on her belt. She leads her friend, whose cheeks have been kissed by the sun, to father's bench. Within her thick hair hang thin braids whose red and white beads come together with soft sounds as she takes parchment and a writing feather from her friend's belt-sheath.

"Rosamond and Marigold have come to take down your memory of the battle," says Myrah.

"Is it wise to wear that red hue?" says mother.

"Men no longer fear our gowns," says Rosamond. "Some of them have begun to wear red themselves to show their love for us. I shall write of how Ardelle and her sisters made this so."

"Your sisters?" says mother.

"The king calls us his daughters," I say.

"He has many words," says Isadora.

Marigold sets her hand on my belly. Rosamond is beside us with a kiss for my cheek before kneeling at father's bench.

"Shall we begin, Maria?" she says.

Marigold takes a clay pot from her belt bag, removes the linen that binds its lid, and sets the open-mouthed pot next to Rosamond's writing feather.

"Are you his thyle, now?" says Isadora.

"Ask the one who wears the king's black," says Rosamond. "Tell us of the battle, Ardelle. Leave nothing out."

There is nothing to be said that I have not told father or witnessed in my dreams a thousand times and more, yet I speak of it well enough for Rosamond's ink to fill five sheets.

"What else?" says Rosamond.

I come to her, take the writing feather from her ink-hued fingertips, and write in my own rough letters of the slain men the boatman would not take when I did not yield to him my mother's beads. Rosamond reads my words, as does Myrah, who then tells Marigold of them.

"So they may never go to those wonderful kingdoms we see in our dreams," Marigold says.

"I see no such things in my dreams," I say.

"You would do well to stay away from water hereafter," says Rosamond.

She sets the sheets on the hearth's embers, where they blacken into ashes.

"You wrote all those words to burn them?" says mother.

"Shall we give them greater warmth?" says Rosamond.

Marigold sets her hand on the glowing embers. The reddish yellow brightens into a bluish red that gives light to the shadows in which Isadora hides and warms mother well enough that she sheds her woollen bedding.

"Better not to ask, dear sister," says Isadora.

That night, we sleep in our linen without need for anything

else. I lie beside mother with my eyes closed and wait for the steady breath of her sleep to calm me so I may stand before the boatman in my dreams without dread in my heart. Someone comes to me—Brant? Isadora?

"Lie with me," Myrah whispers.

"What do you do, king's daughter?" mother says with weary words.

"I talk to Ardelle," says Myrah.

"Then talk where Ardelle's mother and father can hear," says mother. "Who is the father of her child?"

"I do not know," says Myrah.

"You do not know, or you do not want to know?" says father from beside mother.

"I … I have asked my father many times," Myrah says. "If he knows, he will not tell me. I think he would lay bare his heart if Ardelle stood before him in his halls."

"I saw how you kissed my daughter," says mother. "Have you also come here to lay bare your heart to her?"

Myrah says nothing. I open my eyes. She sits before me with a frown for her own hands.

"What would you have me say?" Myrah says.

"That you will take my daughter's child as yours," says father. "Show your own father what it means to be a father."

"If he wishes to play games with us," says mother, "we will give back to him his fourth of our fields and he may work it himself."

"Then send your daughter to him," says Myrah. "She may tell him that when he took her as his daughter, his words were true."

"What in the world does that mean?" says father.

He lifts his back from the ground with one hand. I sit upright to shield him from the sight of Myrah. He lies down again and draws closer to mother. I turn away from them and set my forehead against Myrah's. Her breath smells of honey and berries. She sets her hands on my arms below my shoulders.

"Tell him this," says Myrah, "and he will stay."

"Else you will leave?" I say.

"Else my heart will leave me," she says.

Her glowing brown cheeks grow wet with tears. These unseen threads that hang between us flow red with the blood of the men Myrah's father has slain. And now, as Marigold said he would, he blames us for what he has done. Myrah's warm breaths turn to frost on my ice-rimed lips even as the sun's hand strokes snow from the waking grass. I take my forehead from hers.

"If your father will not stay for his own daughter," I say, "he is not a father. Nor are you. What you gave me in the grove among our kindred, what you have shown my mother and father today, I have felt this. Whether it might have ever become something, I do not know, but I know that it must be nothing more than words to be burned into ashes, for you only give me this when you need something from me."

Myrah holds her lips together as her hands fall from my arms. The gleam of Marigold's fire in her amber-brown eyes glides down her cheeks and throws itself from her chin into the bottomless depths of her lap's black gown.

"Then let today's kiss be our last," she says. She straightens her back, stands, and looks down at me from atop those white cliffs. "I must ask your forgiveness for having thought you any better than Derwen."

She beds down not far from Rosamond and Marigold with the blackened bottoms of her hose hiding her eyes from me. Would Rosamond tell me her tears are false? Let her sleep and dream of happier things. I will forgive Myrah in the morning if night's darkness has not taken me and thrust me before the faceless boatman to suffer his wordless reckoning once more.

Myrah makes ready to leave with the sun's first light. She

will take none of mother's bread rounds, leaving Brant to thank mother in Myrah's stead as he fills his leather horse-bag with rough rye bread.

"I will feed that to your horse before I eat it myself," Myrah says.

Brant takes me and my child from the earth into his arms.

"I hope that when we see one another again," he says, "we will not have forgotten the memory of today's happiness."

Myrah looks about my house though nothing within it is hers, nor has she left anything here. Marigold quenches her fire in our hearth. Father stirs yellowish-red life into it with one of his walking sticks. This is the boatman's staff that brought his boat to shore yesternight to there look down on me until I withered beneath his eyeless glare.

"Should I have given the boatman my beads?" I say to Myrah. She stands in silence with her arms folded and her back to me. Brant lifts an eyebrow. "Myrah. Should I have—"

"You have no thoughts of your own," Myrah says to the timber walls. "This I have long known, yet *this* is what you choose to say to me after I told you that I would take your child as my own. Take your mother's beads and throw them into the sea that those men might still find peace, else you could have gone with them so that you would not have to send that maid Sithebad to ask *me* whether *you* should forgive *her*. From this day, keep your kisses for your child and your child's father and those you love, *sister*. I shall do the same for the king I must now take."

Myrah takes the aldorman's golden clasp from her hair and throws it into the hearth's fire. Somewhere deep within me, a great wound opens.

III

THE HIDDEN WORLD

BURDENS

Warm winds blow winter's frost from the grass on which mother and Isadora and I walk every morning for as long as my legs and mother's back will allow it. The sun does not yet shine with summer's warmth, yet the aching in my growing belly and weakening spine makes me heavy with weariness even after falling asleep before the sun lies down and waking after it rises. Where father kept his evenings for kneading the flesh of mother's back, he now comes in from the fields during the day to do the same for me while I eat everything mother cooks for me.

My morning walks with mother and Isadora come to an end when summer's heat brings shirtless men to scythe tall grass for horses. I spend my days sweating in my linen while I sit upright against a bundle of hay so I do not have to gasp for breath against the weight of my child on my lungs. Only the night's cooling winds soothe me to sleep—and there, in my dreams, the boatman awaits me on the sea, or on the lake, or on the river not far from our house; and with an outstretched, bony finger, returns me to a waking world wherein the moon is still as high in the heavens as it was when I bedded down. My legs begin to ache, as though the boatman's hands grasp my swelling ankles and do their best to pull them sideways from my waist. He chokes me as I eat mother's bread and thereafter leaves me with the gift of fire within my heart that only dims when I have drunk the honey-sweetened milk Isadora brings from the aldorman's cows, which were once Harold's.

In the middle of summer, when the sun burns hotter than I have ever felt it, the boatman threatens to take my child from me, but it will not yield to him. For a day and a night, the claws of his lifeless fingers dig themselves into the flesh of my waist and legs until at last, on the following morning, he leaves me to dream of Florentina coming to us and giving me the healing mists of water on which the boatman finds no berth. I wake instead to Myrah's fair face hardened into ashen stone beneath flowing rings of black hair.

"Come with me to the aldorman's mansio," she says. "Our sisters give their blessings to men and women who have come from near and far. Florentina can help you."

"She goes nowhere," says mother. "Her child comes soon."

"The aldorman wishes to ask her forgiveness for what he did to her," says Myrah. "He will do so before her gathered sisters."

"I have no other children," says mother.

"Have they forgiven him on my behalf?" I say.

"They are at least willing to hear his words," says Myrah. "He will thereafter tell you of the father of your child."

Father comes in from the fields in a linen shirt soaked with sweat at the back and neck. Mother waves a wide, thin board back and forth to cool him but soon hands it to Isadora to do the same lest mother's spine send her to her bedding.

"The aldorman should have sent you with the name of my

child's father," I say. "You could ask my forgiveness on his behalf."

"He would not tell me," Myrah says. "And unlike you, he wishes to ask your forgiveness himself while he stands before you."

"Is this what our king has sent you here to do?" father says.

"Our king is gone," says Myrah, "as is my mother."

"And so a child comes here to tell us—" begins Isadora.

"To shut your mouth and listen," says Myrah. "My father's men and the men of the north have chosen me to be their queen. Those little kings fight among themselves as if they do not have to ask me to wed them. Their mother Ardelle might come to the mansio and tell me which of them behaves himself best."

"Brant," I say.

"Neither he nor his sister will wed any of us," says Myrah. "Three years from now, Luda will ask me to let her go back to her snow and oxen so she and her brother may find a husband and a wife from among their own. What should I tell her?"

"That she has waited three years to ask you of things for which you have no answer," I say. "And that you are wise for having waited only three months to ask me."

"Your bond-sister asks for you," says Myrah.

"First the aldorman, now Florentina," I say.

"You may speak with her yourself if you do not believe me," says Myrah.

"Bring them here," I say, "the aldorman and your sisters—"

"Our sisters."

"—and have him say whatever is to be said before my mother and father."

"My father told him to stay away from these fields," says Myrah. "The aldorman is faithful to his king, as he is to the king's daughter. Would you like to know how faithful to me he might become?"

Mother stands and strikes Myrah weakly with the back of her hand. Father takes mother's arms, holds them behind her back, and sits down on the ground with her. Mother is not wrong, nor does she look like my mother. Myrah looks too much like herself as she stares at me.

"She is nine months with child and you speak to her so," mother says from the earth.

"Come to the mansio," Myrah says to me, "or men will fear you. While you are gone, your mother and father will keep my fourth of these fields and Isadora, who serves them faithfully. I will send you back to them before you give birth to your child."

"*Your* fourth of our fields?" says mother.

"You can not know this," says father.

"Derwen can," says Myrah.

"Would you have me believe that one who keeps herself from you also asks for me?" I say. "If you had been at that battle, your words would be far kinder."

"The serving maids you struck with chairs and knives will be there as well," says Myrah. Mother makes a sound. "Show them your child. They and their husbands will know that you do not come to them at night wearing bloodied gowns to steal their children, for you have your own."

"And when am I to do this?" I say.

"Now," says Myrah

She offers me her hand as though I will not wrest her arm from her body. When I do not take it, she lifts me beneath my shoulders but has not the strength to bear my child. She sits down with me in silence while mother and father stare at her. In the narrow gap between our leaning door and the house's timber, Florentina sits wearing long, winding golden rings that hang almost to the lap of her red gown.

"Are you coming, bond-sister?" she says as she rests against the opening's frame. "We will return you before the day's end. Tomorrow at the latest."

"What does she mean by 'bond-sister'?" says Isadora.

I lift myself to my aching feet.

"She means I will be back before night falls," I say.

Myrah's arms do little for me; they find better use in taking Florentina onto her back and walking with slow, heavy steps through the house's opening, sending the leaning door sliding down onto the ground. Without, a stone-faced woman with a long white-yellow braid wearing a brown tunic and brown leggings waits on the saddled back of a bridled horse hitched to a wooden cart. On seeing me, Luda leaves her mare and heaves me onto the cart, where I sit down in a thick heap of grassy fodder. Florentina sits beside me with her fingers spread out over the red gown on her lap.

"You answered my call," she says. "You are wiser than you look."

I do not wave to mother and father and Isadora in the house's opening, for I will not be long gone from them. When the cart starts and shakes life into our limbs, Florentina takes my chin and searches my face. Whatever it is she seeks, she finds it.

"Close your eyes so you are not blinded by the falling droppings of passing birds," she says.

Her song breathes soothing mist into my throat, strength into my spine, weightlessness into my belly, and stillness into my legs. The burning in my heart softens into cooling ashes. Florentina rests her hand on my knee.

"You should do the same for Myrah," I say.

Florentina's laugh rises to the tufted white clouds above.

"Myrah has sworn not to bear a child until you have chosen her king," she says.

As we ride, Florentina says nothing, leaving the calls of

clustered birds who fly overhead to tell us of the kings and
kingdoms of summer hares and foxes. Feathery green leaves
from ash trees on both sides of the old stone path float to us
where we sit. Florentina takes one in her hand; the heavens do
her the further kindness of sending a white gift hurtling to the
shaking cart's timber before the lap of her gown. She curses to
herself in Latin as she takes great handfuls of hay from behind
my back and spreads them over the cart's wooden beams.

"Had those birds lent their hue to my gown," she says, "I
would find their brothers by the sea and wipe away this milky
mash with their fluttering wings."

"And what would Myrah do to you for speaking Latin?"
I say.

"She would answer me in Latin with words that sound like
she reads from a book," says Florentina. "My queen, whom I
called such before anyone else did, gives greater weight to the
evils she sees and hears for herself rather than those within her
absent father's mind. She is weary of hearing men lie about
the misdeeds of others, as if by doing so they could win her
love. Good morning, queen."

Myrah rides beside us on a steed as black as her gown. His
long, sleepy strides send him ahead of us so swiftly that
Luda's mare looks as though she has stopped to eat grass.
Myrah's eyes mark nothing but the stone path.

"Myrah's lips drew the secret of our watchmen from you,
and here you sit, the only one of us with child," Florentina
says.

"Do you wish one for yourself?" I say.

"Myrah does, but her spine has no wish to bear it for so
long," says Florentina. "You might share your child with her if
Constantine does not know who the father is."

"Why would he not know?" I say.

"You may ask him and see whether he answers," says
Florentina. "Only Myrah knows his mind, and her under-

standing is not much better than that of the aldorman himself."

In the fields beyond the stone path, thickly growing grass slowly gives way to scattered swathes of sandy earth. Women in dark blue gowns bearing large clay pots walk alongside us through a wide, tree-ridged meadow of light purple flowers. They stand still and stare as Luda's horse takes us from them.

"Their eyes still bleed at the sight of this hue," says Florentina. "They need only soak their heads in the sea to cleanse it from their thoughts."

Smoke rises from the aldorman's house of stone. A great many men and women in earthen clothing stand gathered near the wooden stalls where the horses are kept. On seeing us, they take their whispered words with them behind the mansio where we can not overhear them. Luda lifts Florentina from the cart and follows them, leaving two women in blue and white gowns to stand over me as a hunter would a wounded deer. They climb up onto the strewn hay in their leather shoes, unaware that one of Florentina's winged friends has left them a gift somewhere beneath it. They take me beneath my shoulders, lift me to my swollen feet, and lead me towards the stone mansio away from where all the others have gone.

"Come, Ardelle," says the round-faced maid on my left.

"Have we met?" I say to her.

The women look at each other.

"Fetch Myrah for me," I say to her red-cheeked friend.

"Who is Myrah?" says her friend.

"You know who I am, but you do not know the queen?"

The maids stand and stare, as if winter's bitterest winds had blown through the mansio and frozen every living thing into frosty stillness.

"I am she," says Myrah from behind us. "Ardelle will ask your forgiveness later. Leave us."

At the sight of her, the maids run to where the others have gone.

"Does the aldorman heed you so well?" I say.

"Why do you ask?" she says with a frown.

"I would like to know that the aldorman does not take me to a room as he did when last I came here," I say.

Myrah folds her arms in front of her black gown held together at the throat by that great, winged bird of gleaming gold.

"You have grown so heavy with child that there is nothing further Constantine could do to you," she says. "I shall tell him, however, that the maid Ardelle wishes the master of this mansio not to come into his own rooms while she is here. In thanks for his sympathy and understanding, she will show him kindness when she eats in the same long house that he does. Thus, our men and the men of the north will know that her growing child and its mother abide among them in lasting peace, which we go to do now."

Myrah leads me by the wrist behind the mansio to where a house as long as she said it would be belches black smoke from two openings in the roof's thatch. Within, two hearths burn brightly between long tables and long benches that seat one hundred of Myrah's friends as they take in the aldorman's many words, which he must have learned from Myrah's father. When the last of his endless words have thrown themselves from the white cliffs into the silence of the sea, the gathered men and women stand beside their benches in rows and wait to kneel before either Florentina or Annette and take the blessing of song through a hand on their head. When all have been so blessed, they talk to one another about how wonderful they have been made to feel while maids in blue gowns bring in trays and pots of freshly cooked fish and boiled hare that wake my child from her sleep and send her growing fingernails into the flesh of my belly.

I sit down before one such tray, unmindful of the standing woman who frowns at me for having taken her seat, and eat of the fish though it burns my fingers and mouth. A man in clothing bearing the hue of rotting blueberries comes to me and takes the tray from me. He hands it to a maid, who looks at him with raised eyebrows.

"Has anyone ever told you how lovely your red cheeks are?" the man says.

My child thrusts its foot at him through the flesh of my belly, drawing from me a grunt that makes my ribs ache.

"Has anyone ever told you to eat shit?" I say.

A thin woman with ringed brown hair like Annette's is between us at once with her hands on his shoulders. She kisses him on the lips and whispers words to him that send him to Rosamond. Rosamond takes his kiss on her cheek with laughing eyes that harden into a glare at Annette over the man's shoulder.

"If your child is hungry," Annette says, "tell one of us, and we will fetch bread for you."

"Are you not hungry?" I say. "Your bony cheeks have lost much of their flesh."

"I have given it to yours," she says and smiles as she takes the flesh of my face between her thumb and forefinger.

"Where is Wilfrith?" I say. "Did he see what you did?"

"No, and neither did you. This secret you *will* keep."

Annette sets her hand on my belly and sits me down on the bench near the head of the long house, where her sisters stand and talk. She fetches the tray of fish from the serving maid and sets it before me, then sits beside me with her back to the table as I eat. Long, brown-sleeved arms set themselves around my shoulders.

"The aldorman eats with us," Luda says with a mouth full of food.

She leaves my cheek with a kiss whose bread crumbs I

wipe away with my fingertips. Rosamond's fish tray-stealing friend sits down opposite me, as does a fair-faced woman with flesh as white as the milk from the aldorman's cows. Where her fair hair shines gold in the hearth's fire, the aldorman's bound brown strands are the smoke that floats up into the thatch. The woman kisses the aldorman's thin lips with the fullness of hers, as though they have long been wed.

Winiburg. So this is what has become of you.

I have lost my hunger, but my child has not, and so it eats through my mouth. Derwen sits down beside me in green where her sisters wear red and, instead of greeting me as everyone else has done, bows her head. All those gathered in the long house do the same but for the aldorman, whose mother must never have taught him how not to stare. Myrah stands beside me and speaks a mere thousand words that would leave her father wondering whether he had not taught her better.

"Let it be so," Myrah says and sits down to the same tray of half-eaten fish as my child and I.

"What brings you here?" Derwen says to my ear.

"My mother gave Myrah the back of her hand," I say.

I have never heard Derwen laugh. Myrah's eyebrows say the same.

"Was I wise to tell the aldorman to ask another to wed him?" Myrah says.

Winiburg's blue eyes will not let my fingers take any more fish. The aldorman blinks at Myrah before biting into the flesh of his hare.

"Winiburg," I say. "What did you say when the aldorman asked you to become his wife?"

The aldorman sets his hand to his mouth as he coughs.

"How do you know my name?" Winiburg says.

Something strikes against my swollen foot beneath the table—Myrah's leather shoe.

"Does it make you glad to be the mother of his children?"
I say.

To this, Winiburg says nothing. The aldorman sets down his leg of boiled hare and washes his fingers in a wooden bowl of water. I take his cup of milk and drink all of it.

"Winiburg would yell at me for asking her to bear my children before we are wed," he says. "I would see the wisdom of her words, for she is far too young to speak anything other than the bare truth."

"Yet I have come here to hear *your* wisdom as you have asked," I say.

"I believe it was your sister Maria who bid you come here," says the aldorman. "That you have fulfilled her wishes speaks to your kindheartedness."

"It is true," Myrah whispers into my ear as she takes my fish-wet fingers. "Marigold began yelling at the wives of men in Latin, telling them that a slain spear-man speaks through her. It was only when the aldorman said he would find the father of your child that she stopped. She stays in a room by herself until we meet with him." Myrah sits upright and clears her throat. "When we have eaten of our meal, she will sit with us as the aldorman speaks of what weighs on Ardelle's mind."

The others eat as though Myrah says nothing. I have given my child as much food as I can bear, yet it asks for more. Derwen stills the shaking of my leg with her hand on my knee. I would like nothing more than to leave this long house and walk out to the sea to stand in stillness beneath the cliffs. There, the scattered shards of our runestone still lie in their rocky grave above the earth. A thin, short, bloodless arm sticks out from beneath them. Hugo?

I start awake and take my head from Derwen's shoulder. She listens as our sisters talk to mothers and fathers of the children we ourselves might one day have. Myrah meets my sleepy eyes and taps her fingers on the aldorman's hand over the table.

"Let us go now before Ardelle falls asleep again," she says.

Myrah and Derwen lead me from the long house through the mansio's many rooms into that large, roofless hall called a patio, whose rainwater pit lies half full. A side room near the mansio's northern end is home to a long table, ten high-backed chairs, and painted marble men who stare down at us from shelves carved into the walls that keep them. When I am long gone, they will still stand here, those kings and thanes and aldormen of their golden imperium of stone.

Rosamond sets her hand on my shoulder as she walks by. Derwen stands to give Marigold the chair on my left. Myrah sits on my right.

"Do you not sit with Rosamond?" I whisper to Marigold.

"I am glad to see you and your child as well," she says as she feels along the flesh where my lap once lay.

"Were I a mother or even a queen," says Florentina, "I might ask our dear Myrah to give me her chair as Derwen has done for Marigold so I may sit beside my bond-sister."

"She is bound to her child, Florentina," says Myrah.

"So she has become your mother as well," says Florentina. "I see."

"Does Derwen say it is a son or a daughter?" asks Marigold.

"She will know soon enough," says Derwen.

The aldorman's dark blue tunic and leggings become almost as black as Myrah's gown where he stands in the shadows left behind by the sunlight streaming in from the patio. A shade of hair rests above his lips; his chin is so well shaven that it still bears reddish knife marks. He stands behind his chair on the other side of the table and rests his gold-ringed fingers on its wooden backing.

"You must forgive me—forgive us—for asking you to come

here, Ardelle," he says. "I swore to Theodosius that I would leave you be. However, I have something to say that all of you must hear: I have yet been unfaithful to your father."

"Myrah's father," says Marigold. The warm floor soothes my aching feet. Marigold's fires must burn below. "The king said the same to us once when he thought one of us bore a child, but we did not."

"Are you with child, aldorman?" asks Florentina.

"Constantine," says Myrah, "explain to Florentina how you have been unfaithful."

"I *am* with child, my dear Florentina," says the aldorman. "It lives within Ardelle."

Florentina's smile leaves her. Derwen glares at the aldorman. Marigold breathes out through her nose. Rosamond looks over her fingernails. Annette and Luda turn to one another but say nothing. As for me, I come to stand behind a woman in green and yellow gowns heavy with child and look over her shoulder as her eyes fall to her lap, where her fingers link themselves into snakes that writhe against one another to see which of them will choke the other to death first. Somewhere in the patio, a man gives a long speech in which he asks forgiveness for having set the snakes on her legs. He uses so many words that Myrah's father would smile at his wisdom.

"You think of my thane whose body you found in that lake," says the aldorman. The woman's child wakes; her brow becomes sweaty. "His wife and children want for nothing, nor shall our child."

"Did you not also find Ardelle's body on the battlefield?" says Marigold.

The aldorman closes his eyes and nods.

"I lost half my men defending Ardelle," he says. "I was not in my right mind."

"And yet Ardelle did not lie with the thane's body," says Marigold.

"*Maria*," says Rosamond. "What is wrong with you?"

"If you do not like what I say, Rosa, you may write it down and burn it as we did Ardelle's dream of the boatman. He would not take the slain men beyond the hidden world. He laid the guilt for this at Ardelle's feet."

"So do not lay it at the feet of men who should know nothing of what we do," says Derwen. "You fill their hearts with dread and their minds with evil thoughts of us."

"Constantine does the same to us," says Marigold. "Ardelle did not kill your thane, aldorman. You left a body in the lake for her to find. You lied to her then, and you lie to us now."

The aldorman steps back from the table. He looks over Marigold's thick yellow-red hair for a time, then holds his own hands behind his back and sweeps his shoe along the hard floor. Myrah sets her hand on the yellow sleeve of the woman to her left, whose hair of like hue rests beneath the neck of her undergown. I set my hand on the woman's left shoulder; she takes it.

"You often tell Rosamond not to speak for you, Maria," Myrah says. "Let Ardelle now speak for herself."

"I am not here," says the woman, "nor was I on that field of battle. My child is not yours, aldorman. Marigold's words speak the truth as well as any of ours."

"Do you feel ill, Ardelle?" says Annette.

"Illness abides within this room whether I am here or not," says the woman. "I did not need to come here, nor did Myrah need to fetch me. The aldorman may say my child is his if he wishes. I will give birth to it at home with my mother and father and Isadora, who will care for it. If the aldorman wishes to help us, he may do so by leaving us be as he said he would."

With those words, the woman leaves into the patio. I am a ghost who floats beside her; together, we lie down in the same room where mother once awaited me while the aldorman's healer did nothing to heal me. Derwen takes my hand—she sets it on the floor as soon as Annette begins to sing to me with her fingertips stroking the sweat from my forehead.

"I dreamed of Hugo," I say to the stone roof. "The unseen hand that sent him below belongs to none."

"Is this the same hand that brought you here?" says Derwen.

"No," I say. "That was a horse-drawn cart and the summer wind."

"For a long while, I thought myself the one who had slain Hugo," says Derwen. "After some years, I became the hand of Myrah's father and forgot myself. Let Florentina and Annette now help you do the same."

Luda sets Florentina down beside me. Her hand and song become one with Annette's. Within my belly, my child becomes still. My breathing slows; my limbs become lighter; I float with my thoughts as freely as the wights in my dreams. With one hand against the roof, I look down at a ruddy-cheeked woman who rests in peace among her six sisters. I leave the aldorman's mansio and glide along the stone path to the fields where mother and father await. Father, with his two feet beneath him, sets a scythe haft in my right hand and takes me by the left. Mother stands in our house's opening and watches as father leads me into waving rows of wheat far from the sea and its rocky shore. When my own daughter is born, I will do the same with her, and she will come to know this as the wellspring of her mother's unending love.

18

PROPOSAL

Winter's sun hangs in a cloudless blue sky as Luda and I lope amid freshly fallen snow. Through an endless sea of white runs a river whose cold water slakes our thirst so well that our throats ache for having done so. We lie down in knee-high drifts to wash clean our reddening skin. Luda sweeps her arms and legs through the frost, leaving the memory of where she has been until the wind blows the shadow of her twisting braid and long legs and wiry arms into the sea's abiding stillness.

Shaking chills take my limbs from the warmth of the mansio bedroom's stone floor. Hands take my shoulders and legs and drag them along the marble until my head finds woollen bedding. I rest in a room of many grey and brown stones whose walls house nothing but a table bearing candles that burn with reddish-blue fire. Not far from them, two women of flesh and blood speak to one another. I should be glad of this: with no body to weigh me down, I am free to float on my back without gasping for breath under the burden of my child.

"When will you wed?" says the woman in green with golden breastpins—Derwen.

"Whether this is before or after we have won, I do not know."

The woman who answers wears gold-fastened black on her arms, golden rings on her fingers, and blue gems on her golden earrings—Myrah.

"Of what do you speak?" I say.

"I wish Myrah happiness in wedding," says Derwen. "Did you sleep well?"

"Did you dream of me?" says Myrah.

Derwen frowns at Myrah's smile.

"Happiness in wedding whom?" I say.

"I see," says Derwen and stands. "You may speak to one another without me, then."

Her green gown becomes smaller as she walks through the patio. She sits down beside the rainwater pit and washes her face from it.

"Why does she not wear red with the others?" I say.

"Your sisters ask the same of you," says Myrah.

"Is that what you have come here to tell me?" I say.

"I have come here to sit with you," she says.

"After nine months," I say.

"Four of which winter's bitterest cold took from us," says Myrah. "Did I not come to you when winter left us?"

"I do not remember."

"Nor do I. We left you be as father bid us. Constantine did the same."

"And will he do the same?"

"I have made it clear to him that his mansio is yours while you are here, my dear king."

My body's weight returns to me. My lungs lie heavy with child.

"I think your father's battle will never leave me," I say.

"We did not burn the bodies of the dead, this time," Myrah says. "They rest beneath the earth. Let us think well of them while I speak to you of what must be done."

What must be done and nothing more. My throat clenches. I close my eyes and breathe deeply through my nose. I choke on my own words, for I know that once spoken, they will become far greater than nothing.

"Did Derwen come here to bless your wedding?" I say.

"She did, though I shall not do so for some time," Myrah says. "Whom would you have me wed?"

"Me," I say without a thought for what I have said.

Myrah's eyebrows find the rings of her hair above her forehead.

"If that is your wish, we may live here in the mansio together," she says. "I will need to leave often to speak with my wise men and at times to gather fighting men from their fields."

"And where would my mother and father and Isadora live?" I say.

"The mansio has many rooms," says Myrah. "They may each take one of their own. Their oxen might even wash themselves in the rainwater pit as Derwen does."

"Mother and father would not need two rooms," I say.

"Nor would you and I," says Myrah.

I sit up onto my elbows. Myrah lifts me so that I may rest my back against the wall.

"And Constantine?" I say.

"He would sleep in whichever bed is warmest," says Myrah. She unfolds her legs and stretches them out before her. Her shoes rest beside my feet. "Do you mean what you say about living here with me?"

My child wakes from its fitful sleep and runs its fingernails along the flesh of my belly.

"We can talk of men who wield bows on horseback when

you find time to come to my house," I say. "Tell the aldorman … tell your king that he did well in keeping Brant from being overtaken."

An arm sets itself around my waist. Myrah's hand rests on my right hip.

"Is Constantine the king you have chosen for me?" she says.

"I saw no man I liked today," I say.

"Nor did I," says Myrah and rests her head on my shoulder.

I should not, but I set my head against hers. We sit like that for a while.

"In the days of the Roman imperium," Myrah says, "men on horseback would ride along the stone paths all day. At night, they would sleep in these rooms."

"And?"

Myrah takes my shoulders from the wall with both arms and lies down beside me.

"They did not lie alone in their beds," she says.

Her left hand goes beneath my child and there gathers wool to lift it above my shins. I grasp her fingers to keep them still. She brings her lips to mine. Her breath gives me the honeyed wheat bread she ate in the long house and the ale of which she drank. It is this that makes her do what she does. My child knows this as well and tells me of it with her foot before I become short of breath. I set my hand on the bones of Myrah's neck to keep her from me.

"I have nothing for you," I say.

"I ask nothing," she says.

Dark red drops of blood-amber somewhere deep within her eyes tell me otherwise.

"Not nothing," I say.

"I only want what you have," she says with her hand on my belly.

"And the same kind of father?"

"Not the same kind. The same."

I take the weight of her hand from my daughter so my child and I may breathe without hindrance. Myrah sets her fingers on my warming forehead. The chill of her palm is welcome; the hand that bears it, less so.

"I told you the truth of Constantine," she says. "He asked me to wed him. I told him to ask another who knows nothing of what he has done to you." Myrah's hand lies on the woollen flesh of my daughter's womb. "He then asked Winiburg. She would not wed him either, for she would have struck him herself had you not done so after he brought you to his healer's bed."

"He has no healer," I say.

"Which is why he asks me for mine," Myrah says. "You and Winiburg have brought him low enough to kneel before me and offer me the strength of his fighting men. They are the same whose brothers died for you and Derwen and Brant on the ridge near the sea. Derwen thanks the aldorman for her life and gives us her blessing. Constantine wishes to know without asking you whether your heart softens into kindness as Derwen's has."

"He opened the ribs and heads of men with a blade that also rent horses from neck to tail and left them to rot beneath a sun darkened by black birds who hunger for their innards. And after this he somehow becomes hard enough between his legs to thrust himself between mine and give me a child. In which world, this or the next, does my heart soften into kindness for such a man?"

"A world in which you see that one who leaves slain men to suffer on the shore where they died is still beloved by many," says Myrah. "Derwen is among those who do so. She sees the good in you, and in Constantine."

"Then her wisdom is beyond my ken," I say.

"Your blessing is but a mere spoken word—"

"As is speaking against it. You would lie with me as the aldorman did and thereafter ask forgiveness for having lain with someone other than your king."

"Constantine has said that we may do this."

"And so he would heed us no more than a swine does the hens who come to pick seeds from the rain-soaked earth that clings to his hooves and hind legs."

My breath comes out through my mouth and nose, hindered by the snot that pools in the back of my throat. I lift my head into Myrah's lap to send this filth swimming back down through my heart and into my waist to be emptied onto the mansio's stone floor when my child is born.

"I am not the one to whom you speak," I say. "You speak to someone who lives in your mind. Someone who tells you that whatever you say is true and whatever you wish is yours. Someone who is not here with her head in your lap."

Myrah leans over me to set her lips against mine. I turn away so that she finds only my cheek. She takes my left hand; I wrest it from her icy fingers and shove it beneath my right arm for warmth. With her fingertips, she kneads the flesh of my left shoulder where it meets my neck.

"I will sit and listen to whatever you wish to say to me for as long as you wish to speak," she says. "You are right to be angry. You are right to hate me. Tell me of what weighs on your heart and mind and I will do whatever I can to lift those burdens from you."

I lie in silence while Myrah softens my neck with her thumb and fingertips. When she turns me onto my side to work her fingers into the flesh of both shoulders at once, I close my eyes and let her do this. I have nothing to say to her that will not later come out of her mouth and make men do things I would never have asked of them myself. When her fingers lie still beneath my shoulders, my thoughts lie with them.

"It is not Marigold's fire that burns below," she says. "She will not do this for Constantine's mansio."

"He should not ask her to," I say. "Nor should you."

"Though she has sworn an oath to me along with her sisters."

"She does not give you her blessing. Mere words, as you said."

"I would thus be unwise to ask an oath of you. You are bound to your child, now. I have had to yell at Florentina more than once."

"For speaking Latin?"

"For speaking as though she owns you. I asked her to think on whether she would ever speak of her child the way she speaks of you."

"Would you see her become a mother?"

"Not yet. There are things to be done first. I know Annette and Luda wish for children. Marigold wants the same. We spoke of this at length when I was bound in a room with her."

"When you bound yourself in her room. How did you talk?"

"We wrote on one another's palms with our fingers. Marigold would have two boys; Rosamond needs no children of her own. Constantine wishes to help make their dreams come true."

Mother's beads no longer show within Myrah's eyes, only smooth river stones made dull by loam and weeds and grime. I set my fingertips against the amber around my neck. Myrah's fingers do the same; I close my eyes.

"Father has gone," she says. "The northmen now ask Constantine for help against their foes."

"The same who killed half his men?"

"And yet he made them kneel. They fear their northern

neighbours, men who live in the fens and call themselves the sons of the wolf. These wolves threaten war against their southern neighbours if Sledda's men do not clear a path for them to come here and strike against me. The wolves think I made my father flee by winning the love of the sisters in red and turning them against him."

"Who knows their thoughts so well? You?"

"The northmen. They still battle us on their knees with words. I would let our sisters have their children so we could show the wolves that we have no need to steal from them, but the sons of the wolf speak of their queen of old who still lives within their memory after hundreds of winters. They call her Boudica. She fought against father's Romans and killed many of them, even those who had knelt before her. She killed so many that the Roman *legiones* banded together in earnest and drove her away by slaughtering her men, their wives, their children, their horses and oxen. The wolves fear I will bring her to them and seek a reckoning among them for having allowed their queen to meet her end in a way that speaks ill of her strength and spirit."

"What men would believe such things?"

"Fearful men can be made to believe a great many things."

I open my eyes and turn to her. Myrah's thin nose seems to widen slightly where it nears her false smile.

"Women can be made fearful by showing them what is not there," I say. "They can be made to come to a mansio."

"Where they take fear from men by showing them peace."

"And having done so, they return home."

Myrah clenches the wool of my green gown in her fingers.

"Will you not live here with me?" she says.

"Live here in peace with your king," I say.

"I will take that as your blessing."

"It is no such thing, but you may believe whatever you will."

"And when the wolves come to show us what they believe, will you still withhold your love from me?"

I sit up. The stone of the mansio's walls seems to shake softly. Myrah sits on the backs of her legs before me and takes my hands.

"When they come to bind me within these walls, bring the stone down on their heads," she says. "Whether I live or die means nothing to them."

"Am I to murder at your behest?" I say. "Would you have me find the bodies of men among the stone while others look on and talk of the evils that have befallen them by my hand?"

"Even if you did kill Constantine's thane, he must have been a wretched man who had earned his death."

"How would you know this?"

"After your child has been born," says Myrah, "I will wait for you in this mansio. The wolves will come for me. The northmen may be with them. When they come, I would have you do for me what you did for my father. Make them kneel before you as I do now. Whether you do this or not, I will tell Constantine that you and I share a bed when he has no need of me."

"Did you say the same to Derwen?" I ask.

"I have told you of how she kept herself from me. Do you not believe me?"

"You, who kept yourself from me."

"Do I do so now?"

"You should."

I take Myrah's neck and hold her mouth against mine until she can not breathe. Myrah strikes at my back and arms with her hands; I yield and allow her to draw away from me.

"Thank you," she says between gasps.

"I have done nothing," I say. "My child wishes to go home and see her mother's mother and father."

"I hope to one day know the same happiness," says Myrah.

The mansio shakes mightily, bringing the table beside the wall down onto the floor where my ankles would have lain had I not taken them away in haste. Myrah's widened eyes meet mine—this is not my doing. My legs are thrust apart from one another; they threaten to come off my body. A dark hand seeks to reach into me and take my child from me. Never at home did I feel its grip so tightly. It will squeeze the life from me if I do not harden myself against it.

"What is this?" says Myrah.

"The boatman," I say. "He has done this before. I will bear it."

"I will fetch Florentina," she says.

In making ready to leave, Myrah almost walks into Derwen. Derwen lifts my gowns and looks beneath them.

"I see the head," she says. "Myrah, stay with her while I fetch Florentina."

"Can you not help her?" says Myrah.

"Florentina will not believe you when you tell her Ardelle's child comes so soon after you brought her to the mansio," says Derwen. "I will drag her by her hair so we do not need to use words to bring her here."

A dull aching besets my spine. Myrah's wrist on my neck and the bones of her fingers become nothing as waves of burning water flood through my waist and hips and empty themselves into mist beneath the lap of my dry gown.

"I will stay here with you," says Myrah. "I will not leave."

My eyelids grow heavy with the weight of my burdens as they swell once more in my waist. Let Myrah say whatever she wishes. She may walk away from this mansio if she so chooses. To stay here is to share in the boatman's grim mirth as he seeks to wrest my heart from my breast. If that thane was as wretched as Myrah says, then let her also be wed to death and take for herself more of my suffering than any should have to bear.

19

DAUGHTER

Derwen comes back to us clutching bundled cloth rather than Florentina's hair. Rosamond follows her, clinging to Annette's gowns the way a young boy might follow after a snake that slithers through soft earth made wet by fresh rain. Rosamond rests her slender fingers on my unborn child, while Annette's knuckled alder twigs find my sweaty forehead. Myrah waves Derwen's green-gowned legs away from her cheek.

"Florentina does not come," says Derwen as she steps back. "Constantine's head is wounded. He has need of her."

"What happened?" says Rosamond.

"You did not feel it?" says Annette.

"We felt it," says Myrah. "Constantine more so than we, it seems."

Myrah's eyes search mine.

"Go to him, if you wish," I say. "I will bear it."

Myrah takes my hair from beneath the neck of my linen. She lifts my head into her lap with my yellow strands spread out over her legs and onto the stone floor like straw. Derwen sets her bundle of cloth under my head.

"All this stone for bedding and a table," she says.

"We will find better use for it," says Myrah. "Now, do the same with your words and hands so Ardelle's child does not hate you for keeping her from her mother."

Derwen kneels and sets her hand on my belly but does not sing with Annette and Rosamond. The aching in my sides ebbs into the slow-flowing calm of a summer stream's water, though my hips still suffer in the unyielding grip of unseen, bony hands. Rosamond looks up.

"*That* is what happened," she says.

The aldorman walks through the room's opening and falls onto his knees clutching bloodied linen against his head. Rosamond, Annette, and Derwen stare at him, as if by doing so they could keep his life-water from running down into the neck of his tunic.

"One of you, help him," Myrah growls.

They stare at one another while Constantine groans words in a tongue that none of us speak. Florentina drags herself into the room by her forearms, one before the other, her red gown following after her. Derwen stands and walks to her with bowed legs. When she bends down to take up Florentina, Florentina waves Derwen's hands away. She sits up next to Constantine's wounded head and brings her nose up to her eyes at the sight of what lies beneath his reddened head linen. She shows us the ridges of her palm bearing smeared blood.

"Where is Luda?" says Derwen.

"Am I her keeper?" says Florentina. "She goes to fetch some maid the aldorman wished to give the blessing of life when Ardelle's child is born. He should have given himself the same. Speaking will make it no better, Cyneric. Lie still."

The aldorman does as Florentina wishes so well that he neither speaks nor stirs thereafter. The blood-soaked linen falls from his hand; his head has been cleft above his right temple. Amid his hair writhe green worms fat with blood. Fingers hide my eyes.

"You had nothing to do with that," says Myrah.

A wave of stinging, hot water floods through my belly and into my waist, where it empties itself into mist beneath my dry gowns. It leaves behind a row of stones beneath my spine that neither shifting nor shaking will set free.

"Heed your breaths," says Derwen. "When your child calls to you, still her cries by blowing the morning's mist out through your lips."

"Where would I find this mist?" I say. "The sea?"

"You are a bird," says Rosamond. "Take in the clouds through your nose and send them back to the heavens through your mouth as slowly as the winter winds blow snow from the tops of frosted hills."

"Where did you learn of this?" says Annette.

"I learned how to calm my friend's mother when she would have otherwise murdered her own daughter," says Rosamond.

"I like you better when you do not talk," says Florentina. "I will do what I can to soothe your aldorman's aching, Myrah. Derwen will help me instead of sitting there like a frog on a water-leaf."

I take Myrah's fingers from my eyes. Florentina's hand keeps the aldorman's brain from leaving his skull as she sings, so wide has the gap therein become. Did this stone roof not hide the heavens, black birds might swoop down from the clouds to await their meal. The aldorman's hand stirs and strikes his leather belt bag twice before falling limp against the stone. Derwen opens it and lets hang a brown, braided horse's tail between her fingers. Mother's braid. Derwen sets it in my left hand. Rushing water swells in my breast and throws itself with foaming waves against the bones in my waist. My breaths are but a spoken whisper amid the bellowing tides; my legs burn like a swarm of stinging bees.

"Why do I sing?" says Florentina. "I do as little for him as Derwen does for Ardelle."

"I do not think I should be here," says a woman.

She hides behind Luda's leggings. Her brown hair sweeps back from the middle of her forehead, bound into a tail by a clasp of dull brass.

"Sit down beside Ardelle, Sithebad," says Luda. "Rest your hand and eyes on her child and think of what your son will look like when you bring him into this world."

Sithebad kneels, closes her eyes, and feels along the wool of my gown with dry, shaking fingers for a place where the hands of others do not lie. Myrah steadies Sithebad's wan hand with the warmth of her palm.

"I have seen this before," says Florentina. "In Emerita Augusta, the king's aldorman Masona once asked me to heal his thane whose head took his horse's hooves after he fell from it. He did not believe me when I told him his thane was beyond healing."

I look up and meet Myrah's eyes. She lifts her eyebrows. Sithebad stares at me. What am I to tell her?

"I did as he bid me," says Florentina. "His thane learned to walk and look at birds as they flew between the clouds. When asked of kings and kingdoms, he had nothing to say, so men stopped asking him."

"His king thought you guilty of this," I say.

"And here I am," says Florentina, "doing the same for Myrah."

My child calls to me by digging her fingernails into the flesh of my belly. My legs lie flat and angled against the bedding, and yet, as my daughter comes to my hips, she would have the bones of my waist spread even further from one another though they would do no such thing without breaking. Annette and Rosamond sit on the back of the same horse that draws my child from between my legs. You should not have asked me to do this, daughter, lest your mother leave this world before she has seen your face.

"Should I leave?" says Sithebad. "I should leave. I did not mean to make Ardelle speak like that."

"You did nothing," says Derwen. "It is always like this. It will be the same for you."

"I will also wish for death?" says Sithebad.

"Take his head from my lap, Derwen," says Florentina. "Make your hands more useful than your words."

"Sing together, you two," says Myrah. "Let others hear you, if you must."

"We would do more for Ardelle, I think," says Florentina.

"Never again will I watch men break each other's heads open," I say. "Sing to him. Constantine. Whatever he calls himself. And whatever men might call him when he wakes and walks and talks again. Give him peace. I will bear this suffering so I do not have to see his bloodied head in my dreams every night."

Myrah takes my hand from the floor and kisses the back of it. Derwen sits beside Florentina and sets her hand on the aldorman's bloody head wound. They sing together, at first with words soft enough that they drown in my child's calls through my throat, then with strength that draws the eyes of the men and women who stand gathered in the patio. Derwen's words swell to yelling. Annette moves from my side to my legs.

"It comes now," says Annette. "Send your child into my hands."

My child takes Rosamond and Annette's song with an asp's fangs for the flesh beneath their many fingers. On that night when my sisters took their men, any of them could have had a child if they wished, yet I understand now why they did not, for they would lie here as I do, writhing against that from which they can not free themselves: it is within them.

"Again," says Annette.

My daughter's thrusts rend the flesh of my belly as well as any blade. I strain with what little might I have left, yet my child will not come now, nor on the second breath, nor on any of the following breaths. The stink from beneath my gowns tells me that I have emptied myself of nothing but the day's meal.

"Once more," says Myrah.

Waves of aching fire rush through my body. A long, loud, sharp yell deafens me for a time. It is not until the room is once more still and Derwen's face is above mine that my open mouth and raw throat tell me that I am the one who has yelled. Sithebad's hand leaves my belly. The little braid beside Derwen's ear hangs its red bead onto my cheek as she looks into my eyes for something she can not find.

The world goes white. Emptiness creeps into my flesh and limbs, where it washes away the aching from my belly, then from my legs, and my hands, and my head. The room comes into being, dimmer in hue and half-misshapen. On my right, Annette's knife rests on the floor. On my left is the bundled linen Derwen set behind my head. From beneath my gowns comes no sound, nor does my daughter rest within my belly any longer. She is nowhere in this room, nor in the patio, nor anywhere within my sight. Only her afterbirth lies between my legs; and this I clean from the stone with the linen on which my head lay.

He has taken her from me as he said he would. How does the boatman's hand reach so far from the sea? I would not give him Constantine to go and lie in the river with his thane. And so I am left to wonder, as I weep with none to see me, whether my daughter does the same.

Stirring limbs wake me from my thoughts and dry my face.

There, on the linen Derwen had bundled and set beneath my head, lies a newborn girl as pale as Rosamond with hair as black as Myrah's. I take her up into my arms and rest her head and body and little hands against me, mindful of the hard bone at my shoulders that holds my gowns together. Her life-cord has been cut from her belly; she bears neither blood nor afterbirth on her flesh—these things mean nothing. She is mine. How she has come here, I do not know, nor do I wish to know. Her shrill cries bid me set her on the bedding so I may take off my rough green gown and its linen sister. Thereafter, my wailing daughter rests against my flesh with nothing between us. My thin yellow gown is her only shield against a cold that is not there.

We lie together like that, I with my mind empty of all but my child, and she, searching with her eyes and mouth for the mother who holds her. Those floating red wights come down to meet us once more, and though my daughter sees only the flesh of my breast, the wights' glow stills her cries and slows her breaths. I reach for one that I might show it to her—it hies away to its kindred, who flutter about as though a soft wind blows through the room. As they flit about, the blue of my daughter's eyes leaves me; she drifts off into sleep. I would dream with her, but I have no mind for it, for there is nothing dearer to me in this world than the child who sleeps in my arms, and whose head is so small that my fingers hold the whole of it, and to whom I will give all of my love and the days of my life that she might grow to be as old as her mother.

When next my daughter's cries take me from unkind dreams, the wights have left our room. My child works her lips against my flesh: she needs milk, and so I shall give it to her. I take my daughter in both arms and slide backwards to the stone wall where I may rest against it. Her lips find the tip of my breast, and though she has no teeth, her sharp sucking tells me how full with milk I have become. Yet she draws none of it from me, so that when I take my breast from her mouth, she asks me with weak mewing why I will not feed her. I squeeze with my fingers to see for myself the milk my daughter seeks, but neither she nor I can find it. I set her upright and stroke her little head while I think of what is to be done. Mother said she could not teach me this, for it must be learned by doing.

I let her lie against me once more and—I know not how—her mouth latches onto my breast and draws my milk into her belly with loud in-breaths that send fire through my ribs. With each sharp and searing wave that washes over me, I breathe the clouds in through my nose and send them to the stone roof above us. One hundred times I have done this when my daughter turns her head away from her milk to look up at me with eyes as blue as the sea.

I set her chin on my shoulder and strike my hand against her back lightly as mother taught me. After some time, wind comes up from her lungs with a belch that leaves a milky white mash running down my shoulder—a flying bird's gift one might hide beneath many handfuls of hay. Is my child ill? Has she swallowed something where I did not see her?

I set her down beside me and take up the linen to wipe myself clean. As I do so, my daughter begins to cough and choke. I throw aside the linen and take her up again, setting her chin onto my shoulder and striking her back with greater strength until nothing more comes up from her lungs. We sit like that until her steady breaths bring her to sleep in peace. She must be cold and in need of something to warm her as she dreams. I swathe her in my yellow linen so that only her face shows, leaving the rough green wool and its hard bone fastenings amid the bedding, where I may rest my head when I am weary.

With linen in hand, my legs bear my lightened belly to the room's opening and I must stop—whatever still lies within me wishes to come out through my legs. I crawl on hands and knees over unforgiving stone to where the patio's rain-water pit lies half full and take from it summer's gift, washing the filth from the unfolded linen until it bears only the mark of having been soaked with water. I wring the wetness from it and take it back to the room, where it dries while I watch my daughter's sleeping breaths until my own eyes close.

I wake to aching in my belly—must I give birth to something else? In haste, I trade dried cloth for my sleeping daughter's yellow linen so she is not without the warmth of her swaddling for long. Gnawing turns to growling that sends me in search of something to eat. The broken skin on my knees and elbows will not let me creep along the floor to the cooking room, so I must walk with my hunger until, after twice resting, I find on a table near the ashen hearth many soft bread rounds and a pot of ale-water. I eat and drink before walking back to our room, resting only once for a short time as I think on whether my daughter might have woken and now stirs within her swaddling in search of her mother's arms. No, she still sleeps, and when she wakes, her mother's milk will give to her what her mother has eaten.

I know not how many days our sleep has taken from us, for the darkness of night does not come to us, nor do I know how many times I have given my daughter her milk. It is on one such day or night when I have fed her and drawn milky breaths from her lungs that she begins to call out and will not stop though her mother holds her and speaks kind words. I would sing to her, but the third word of my song is drowned out by a shrill cry that stings within my ears—and then she is silent. Those red wights float above us, again, some fluttering as butterflies do, others sweeping back and forth as though they were falling feathers. I turn my daughter around in my lap and lift her chin so she may see them. They do not come to greet her, but the sight of them is enough to hold her eyes and still my own thoughts.

In the room's wide opening, I meet the yellowed eyes of an ashen-faced woman whose pale and hueless flesh rots beneath her dusty brown wool. She wears a folded square of linen on hair that breaks off like brittle hay as she turns away from me.

"Sithebad?" I say.

The boatman shows me Sithebad's face after he did not take my daughter, for this is not his dream, but mine. And in this dream of mine, Constantine's head was not wounded so greatly that he could not be healed, nor did Sithebad die, nor do I leave my daughter by herself in search of a queen whose need for me is a dream I might have had in another life. The sea is east of here, far enough away that the boatman can not come for us if we stay away from rivers. If we are to stay here in this hidden world, then we shall abide here until the wights have become friendly to our grasping fingers and my daughter is old enough to take one of them in her mouth as well as her mother does. When that time has come, my daughter will wake to my arms and I to hers; and others will see that I have become a loving mother whose kind words and soft hands show them how they might do the same.

My daughter has not slept long when the wights float down before my lips, as if they wish to bid me take myself from my child. I hold her in my arms and speak to her with soothing words that should wake her, but she only hums. Her dreams must be fair; these wights will have to come again some other day. I would not have my daughter's dreams darkened by their mindless play, so I take my left arm from its linen sleeve and lower the neck of my gown. She takes my breast deep within her mouth as she has learned and drinks her milk without waking. I have thus made my daughter's dreams sweeter, and I have taught her to take her milk so well that we may rest in equal peace.

With every waking day, my daughter grows. She learns to smile at the sight of her mother's teeth. Her head and eyes follow the wights when they make themselves seen. Soon enough, she reaches for them with her short fingers. I offer her my own fingers instead, which she grips as she stares at those floating feathers. As I watch her play with my lengthening fingernails, I wonder how long it will be before winter's bitter breaths dry my hands and make them as red as the wights.

The cooking rooms are home to great mounds of bread and meat left over from gatherings whose meaning I once knew but have forgotten. The two bread rounds I take whenever I wake fill me for so long that my daughter has taken her milk thrice before I am in need of food again. The bread should harden but does not, and so I become wary of the undried fish and unsmoked hare, which still smack of having been hunted not long ago. Though I crave them, I will not take their meat lest my milk make my daughter ill and she learns to hate it.

The hay in the wooden horse stalls beside the mansio becomes home to the filth from my daughter's linen swaddling. Though I do not see the rain that fills the patio's pit, fresh water awaits me every time I come to wash clean my daughter's linen swaddling. Not long thereafter, the rainwater becomes snow that does not melt and does not chill my flesh as I bathe myself with it, nor does my daughter cry out at its frosty kisses on her own unreddened skin. As if I had called on them, the grey, ashen men from the battlefield stand before my mind's eyes. Are they as unmindful of winter's breaths as my daughter and I? What do they do now? I shake them from my head. I must not think on anything but my daughter, who lives and breathes and needs none other than her mother, nor do I need any other but her.

My child learns to turn over from her belly onto her back. I let my hair hang down over her so that she may grasp at its strands and take them into her mouth. She would take the beads from my neck as well, but she may not have them. I can not tell her why, for she does not yet know my words, nor do I remember why I wear them. Soon enough, she sits up with the help of my hand on her back, and when she does, she begins to speak without saying anything at all. We thus understand nothing of what the other says, yet what she says to me is all I wish to hear.

In time, my daughter learns to sit up by herself. She moves herself along the stone floor by thrusting her legs, taking the wool of the bedding with her. She sends herself from the bedding so often that I tire of having to sit in the room's opening and stop her from leaving. When she learns how to use her hands and knees, I become twice as weary from keeping her flesh unbruised on the hard stone of the floor.

I wake one day or night or morning or evening from a dreamless sleep to find my daughter gone—there, in the patio, she plays amid a great mound of the snow with which we bathe ourselves.

"Ma ma ma ma," she says to me.

I smile as I take my daughter, who has thus given me a name—what shall I call her? Why have I had no thought for this? How soon after I was born did my own mother give me my name?

"Come, child," I say. "Let us see whether this stone house does not keep better clothing for us. We might also find a name for you."

Near our small bedroom is a larger room with a long table, ten chairs, and stone men who stand in silence on shelves carved into the walls. The letters written below them in angled strokes would make strong names for their sons. One opening leads to a room with a stone bed and an empty pit; another, to the cooking rooms; a third I find at the other end of the long table where the walls meet. At the end of its long, narrow hall stands an unlocked door, which my daughter shoves open with her little hands.

"Did you do that by yourself?" I say to her.

A great bed of feathers rests to our left, kept from the ground by four wooden legs. Tables along the walls bear gowns, tunics, and leggings of all lengths and hues. My daughter reaches for them; I set her down so she may take all of them from the tables onto the floor and swim in a sea of blues and browns and greens. She finds for herself undyed linen, and for her mother white linen, blue wool, and two brass breastpins. I would swear to anyone who listened that I once knew someone who wore the same, though why my heart longs for her I could not tell them, for I do not know myself.

I close the door and set its wooden beam in the iron wall hooks. I may sleep in peace knowing that when my daughter wakes, she plays without wandering until her mother has rested well. Did I ever play with my mother's clothing?

"What do you think of the name Branwen?" I say to my daughter. "And her mother's name … what is her mother's name? My father's name is Gildewin, but that is not a name for you. His mother's name is … was … Mildred."

"Ma," she says.

My daughter has hidden herself beneath white sheets and seeks a way out. I lift the cloth from her head and sit down with her.

"Mildred," I say. I take the beads from my neck and set them around hers. "Wear her strength and let it bear you when you are weak."

My daughter makes no answer. My beads have found their way into her mouth.

From then on, we sleep on feather-filled linen behind a closed door whose wooden beam is well above Mildred's head. When she learns to stand beside walls and tables, she brings me from my dreams by striking her little hands against the door's timber and calling my name. Thus, we go out into the mansio, where she searches the rooms for things to look at and put in her mouth. I call her by the name that I have given her, and she, after she has heard it often enough, looks at me when I say it. Her thin black hair becomes thick and wavy; her eyes deepen into a rich blue that shows me the boatman's dark shape at times. That I see in her eyes what I once saw in … Myrah. Her name was Myrah, and her brown eyes bore drops of blood-red amber like the yellow beads around my daughter's neck.

"Ma ma ma," says Mildred with an outstretched forefinger.

The red wights have come to us again. Mildred follows them into the patio, her mother not far behind her, and through many small rooms into a sea of snow whose sweeping waves stand so tall that Mildred loses herself among them. I take her up onto my shoulders and there hold her hands as she gives wordless names to everything she sees. When I was a child, I ran through such snow up to my ankles and thought on what it would be like to live in a world where grass was snow and the sea was ice.

I set Mildred down and sit with her as she runs her hands through hardened snow that becomes soft when she swings her arms against it. She stops when a red feather floats down into her hand and rests there, unstirring, even as my daughter closes her fingers around it.

"Is it time for us to go?" I say.

I look about and find many wights floating above me, teasing me with their childish fluttering. I stand to take one as my daughter has done, but they flee my grasping hands, as do they take flight from the words that rush at them from my throat. Mildred offered them her hand without thought or wish or will and they came to her. She knows nothing of what she does.

I open her fingers and wave the wight away. Mildred forgets what she has seen and sets her palm into the snow before her, leaving her little hand behind for the wind to hide when she and I have gone.

"Not yet," I say to her. "When you grow old enough to understand what you do, you may take one of those wights, and I will follow you wherever it leads us. But not now."

Until then, you may play in snow that is not cold and run along stone that will not hurt you and grasp at wights that will not take you from a mother who lives for nothing else but to watch over you and keep you for as long as you will let her.

CONSTANTINE

My heart aches with a longing that does not leave me until I take Mildred into my lap and keep here there while she does her best to flee her mother in search of white hares and foxes that none other sees. Her cries and reaching fingers will not let me keep her from what she seeks, nor will I let her forget her mother's hands even when the mansio is no longer within our sight. Where the white drifts become the slow-flowing water of a narrow river, my daughter's play comes to an end. She throws herself against me to make my arms weary enough to set her down, but I will not. Instead, I blow wind through my lips against the flesh of her cheek and neck and work my fingers under her arms until she laughs once more and we have found the mansio amid this sea of blinding nothingness.

The wooden horse stalls west of the mansio house neither horses nor stalls, for the wind has blown their timber into a great, snow-frosted heap. Now, I will have to find another place to leave Mildred's filth, as will I have to search for my bread within the cooking rooms, whose many pots lie overturned beside legless tables and misshapen meat-hooks rent from hewn beams. The long-tabled room's wall shelves are empty of their stone men; within our bedroom, the great swathes of clothing on which Mildred plays have been taken from the floor and bundled on top of our bedding. Not far from them sits a man wearing gold-trimmed dark blue before a table. He holds a writing feather above a thick sheaf of inkless parchment. Behind his chair on the floor lie the bloodied shards of one of the stone men. If his head bleeds, he does not show it.

"You have awoken," says the aldorman. "Have your dreams been peaceful?"

"I have had none," I say.

"Mine have been sweet since you left us," he says.

Mildred thrusts herself against me until my arms yield. She runs to the aldorman's shin and pulls on the wool of his leggings—he lifts her onto his lap. Mildred takes a golden clasp from his long brown hair and bites into it with the few teeth she has grown. The aldorman smiles at her with thin, bloodless lips beneath eyes made even narrower by the strength of Mildred's grip on his brown strands of hair. Mildred's laughter brightens our grey-white room though no candles burn here. The aldorman laughs with her and sets his forehead against hers.

"What is her name?" he says.

"Mildred," I say. "The name of my father's mother."

"That was my mother's name as well," he says. "I have only ever met her in my dreams."

From among the feathers of my daughter's linen bedding I take my mother's braid and tie it around my neck with twine.

"I would not keep that from you," says the aldorman, "nor would I keep your daughter from you, for she is not mine."

"Whose, then?" I say. "You brought me to your mansio to tell me that you lay with me while I slept on that field."

"I … I have but a fleeting memory of that man's face." Constantine looks down at the table for a time before shaking his head. "His name does not come to me. I have lain with many women, yet none of them have borne me a child. One bore a child who died before it was born. Another died with her child while giving birth. The others … I thought that if I were to lie with you, or the one who had borne you, or even one who is like you, your strength would give me the son I have so long wished for myself. But it was not to be. Will you not let me bear your daughter for a while? Only for a while."

Without another word, he stands and leaves still bearing Mildred in his arms. I must half-run to match his swift strides through the rooms of his mansio. Without, the knee-high snow drifts that greet our shins do little to slow his steps. The red wights follow us far overhead, watching over me as I walk little better than a newborn ox whose limbs still sleep beneath the bedding of its mother's afterbirth. Mildred reaches for the wights with short, grasping fingers that she waves towards herself, but the wights do not heed her. Constantine's eyes follow her; whether he marks the wights or not, his face does not tell me.

"Would you go up among the clouds to see who lives there?" he says to Mildred.

I follow his path through a sweeping sea of snow beyond his roofless long house and from there towards the sea. The wights take flight along a gale of snowy wind that neither stings my face nor chills my flesh. My daughter calls out to me with outstretched arms.

"I am here, Mildred," I say. "I am behind you."

"Your mother follows us to the sea," Constantine yells over a rush of wind. "There, we might see whether those white cliffs still stand among so much snow."

"Are your arms not weary?" I say. "I will take my daughter for you."

"She is no burden to me, my dear," says the aldorman. "We shall only stand there on the shore, or the ice if winter has been so kind to us. This much snow I have never seen in my life. Which of these great seas is fairer, do you think?"

My legs bear me with unearthly swiftness to Constantine's arms. I wrest my daughter from his fingers and hold her head against my shoulders. Her breaths warm my heart well enough to melt the frost that has made it heavy.

"Would you not rather go to a lake and there look on the water?" I say.

Constantine laughs into wind that would sweep my hair from my back did it not rest beneath the neck of my gowns with the help of mother's twine-bound braid.

"That man you found was not my thane," Constantine says to the snow. "He died in battle. His wife and children lived well thereafter. My smith drew snakes on his belly with ink; my men took his tunic and left him in the lake for you to find. I feel as though someone had once told you this. Do you know of whom I speak?"

"Shall I vomit her name into the snow?" I say.

"The wind would hide it soon enough," he says. "You wear the gowns of that man's daughter. She sat with the young maid Sithebad when she gave birth. Sithebad did not live, but her son will have a mother. Ah, yes, Winiburg. Why do these names live in a sea of clouds within my mind?"

My footsteps stamp the snow into hardened, bitter ice.

"I tell you these things that you might forgive me as Winiburg has," he says.

"I am not worthy of her kindness," I say. "Why do you lie to me now?"

"So that you might forgive me in full as our queen has done. Your sister did the same after she smashed a stone into shards against my skull and thrust a long knife into my heart. She said your name when she did so. That is no lie, Ardelle."

Constantine grasps his tunic at the waist and draws it up over the bones of his neck. On his flesh, beneath where his ribs meet, rests a fat, reddened worm the length of my forefinger. The spear wound in my own breast is but a hueless memory. Constantine walks towards the sea, and so I follow him, if only to see whether the boatman will not come for him so long as I am here. He stops among the snow drifts where they yield to a sea made white by frost-rimed ice.

"Where does the water hide?" he says to the heavens. "This bedding bears the same hue as those cliffs from which the northern spear-men would have thrown you had they overcome you." He turns to me. "Shall we walk south until we reach the ridge overlooking our battlefield? I shall throw myself from it in asking your forgiveness."

Constantine sits on horseback among men with long spears and knives and leather helms. They rush out from amid trees and set upon the men who bear me bound to an iron rod on their shoulders. When they have slain each other to the man, none are left to free me from the sight or stench of their rotting bodies.

"Is it true that you lost half your men on that hill?" I say.

"They lie with their spears and shields beneath the earth, where they may see the sun when it rises over the sea," he says. "How many of them there were, I can not tell you."

"I should thank you, then," I say. "That ridge is nothing like the cliffs near our sanctuary."

"As you say. I would have done anything for you in that battle, even if it meant that I myself would have gone to that hidden world of which your sister spoke. Let us now go south along the shore and see whether we can not look upon that ridge once more with kinder eyes."

I follow him beside the sea, where winter's frost-breathed kisses lie thick upon the water—so broad and far do the icy sheets stretch that I know not where the snow meets the heavens.

"What might lie beyond all that ice?" Constantine says.

He takes a step, but only one. He looks down at the snow in which his foot has left its mark.

"When you came to me," he says, "I wished to write of my life so that I would not forget, but my thoughts fled me as if they belonged to someone else. Whose steps are these?"

"Yours," I say.

"If you say so," he says and smiles. "Will you not come with me and make my footsteps yours?"

I know now where the sea meets the heavens: at a dark shape in a far-off boat like those berthed on the shore near that field of battle. I should hie away from here with my daughter —whither does the aldorman go?

"Take one of those wights in your mouth and walk among the living once more," I say.

"What am I now, if not alive?" he says with a laugh. "I will take flight with these snowflakes and ride along the wind."

The shattering of brittle ice turns Constantine to the boatman. Two dark eyes beneath that black woollen hood clutch my throat and draw the breath from my breast. I must walk to him and take his bitter kiss if I wish to breathe again.

"Ma!" says Mildred.

Constantine nears with slow steps and takes my daughter from me. I am beset by a gnawing cold that weighs down my neck beneath a yoke of heavy ice and drags me to Constantine's feet. I lift my leaden arms to free my daughter from his stony grip.

"Never have I felt such peace," he says.

The icy ground gives way to a watery chill that clenches shut my throat and weighs on my woollen gown, as though a tree had fallen down on top of me. My arms thrash; my legs seek something on which to stand; I sink into nothingness.

Neither burning birch bark nor mother's waves of brown hair would warm the bone-deep cold that floods through my body where it had never done so before.

Where is Mildred? Where is my daughter? There is nothing of her small body within these dark and frosted waters. I will go above, somehow, and find my breath again before I … whose face is this? The aldorman? No, it is the son of Luda's aldorman, who drowned when Luda would not go deeper into the water to find him. I will die—does one die in this place?—even as I swim into the depths and find with my hand that wretched ice as thick as a man is tall. How did the boatman break through it as though it were nothing? Here, at its bottom, I come to Constantine: his eyes are closed, his lips blue, his flesh white. Has my daughter left his arms? Where is she? If I can not have her, I will lie here in this watery grave forever.

On my bare foot are the unwelcome lips of a fish. I reach down to take it from my toes—they are little fingers. I grasp their thin wrist and bring Mildred's closed eyes to mine. I would kiss her did she not look so unlike herself. I hold her with one forearm; my other hand claws at the craggy ice face with fingernails that have grown long. Something hard rests against my back—the boatman's staff lifts us from the water and onto the ice. I choke on water that rushes from my retching breast as I strike my coughing daughter's back. A dark, hooded shape looks down on us from where he stands in his long ship of black timber, whose beams begin and end nowhere.

"Give to me your kin," he says.

"I have nothing for you," I say.

The boatman's staff slides from his hand into the water, stopped from falling by the grip of his bony fingers. He fishes below for whatever it is he might find thereunder. I hie away with my daughter. We will return to the mansio and abide there, even if it means I must suffer through this boatman's nightmares once more.

My legs become nothing. I fall to the snow. Mildred holds my gown with both hands and calls my name.

I lie unmoving on a grim field of horse-stamped ivy leaves that have not yet begun to flower. A bloodless sun made wan to match the greying heavens hides behind billowing black clouds whose tufted fingers reach down amid the grasping hands of spear-bearing men and lift me to my feet. The men bind my hands behind me so tightly that when they take me from the ground, face down, hanging by my arms and fettered ankles from a thick iron rod, I beg for the aching of my wrists in place of the unforgiving fire that burns within my shoulders.

As they bear me, the spear-men bid me look on a woman clothed in red who lies dead. The soft flesh of her face yields to the hardness of her fleshless cheekbones and lipless teeth. One spear, by itself, has somehow rent her thigh from hip to knee and shattered the bone within. From beneath her ribs sticks the haft of another spear thrust so far through her body that its sharpened head has split her spine in half. I turn away, but the spear-men hold my head so that I must look at her until I have emptied my eyes and belly.

Thereafter, the men walk with springing steps that lift me towards the heavens and send my binds against the iron bar when I fall, worsening the strain against my shoulders so unbearably that I cry out for them to stop. The men only laugh to themselves and tell me that I will soon rest with my brother before them on the ground: Brant lies on his belly with his skull broken open and eyes too wide to be his.

And there, at the ridge overlooking the field of battle, the men hold my iron bar so close to the edge that my head spins as though I fall. Where my body would land rest shapes as grey and white as any of the walls in our sanctuary by the sea.

They call out to me with throaty, broken words that can not come from the mouths of men. They are but broken-boned bodies that still stir, though blood no longer flows through the reddish-grey flesh that falls like bird dung from their faces and ribs and shins.

The men face one another, take my iron bearing-rod from their shoulders into both hands, and swing me back and forth. I beg them to stop, but they will not, for I am to fall among their brothers and rot alongside them for having left them there. With the third swing, I am aloft and falling. My thoughts seek a handhold but find none; they flee the grassy earth that rushes up to meet us.

"Ma ma," says Mildred.

Her fingers squeeze my cheeks. Beyond her, the boatman shows me the end of his staff. He sets it back into the water and waves towards himself with bone-white fingers.

No, I will not come to you. There is no mother in this world who leaves her child in search of death.

I take Mildred back to the snowy shore and there lay her on her back as she plays with my long hair. My hands will not rip it from my head, so I must take my blue woollen gown still weighted down by the sea's water and heap it on top of Mildred so that she can not stand. I wrest my hair from her grip and offer her instead my mother's braid. I hold my hands over my ears so I do not hear her calling to me as I run out onto the ice towards the boatman, yelling with all my might to drown the unspoken words that bid me step onto his boat. I drop from the broken ice into water through which I now swim freely in my linen, yet it still floods me with its chill as swiftly as though I had never left it.

I find the aldorman, Constantine, beneath that cliff of ice, sleeping in his wool made so heavy that my aching lungs would burst before I took his tunic from him. I strain mightily in dragging him by the wrist up the icy cliff beneath the water, awaiting the boatman's staff to again help us, but it does not come. My lungs no longer hold my life within me; my breath streams forth into the frosted water as it did when I crept along the river's bottom in flight from Sithebad and her friends.

The fire within my breast lifts Constantine's heavy wool and heaves him above the water—my deadened arms will not take him up any further. It is the boatman's staff thrust into his spine that sends water-vomit from his mouth and his arms from his sides to the shelf of unbroken ice before us. My breath comes back to me, as does my strength unburdened by soaked wool. I lift myself and my linen onto the thick ice and crawl to my daughter, who has made a game out of hiding under the length of my blue gown. She has won her game and thus her mother's arms.

"You took me from a wondrous dream," Constantine says as he leaves the water. "Myrah and I were wed in a meadow of golden buttercups on a fair summer's day. You and Mildred were there. Do you know that maid Sithebad? She was there as well, along with the son she and Alfred gave to us in thanks for having brought him back from the king's battles. We ate in our long house with a great gathering of men and women who blessed us with their kind words."

Constantine stands, takes mother's braid from Mildred, and holds it out to the boatman. Mother's twine-bound hair, once her strength, now makes its home within the folds of the boatman's dark clothing.

"I shall take this token," he says, "but for this man only."

"Did Myrah's father wed you to his daughter?" I ask Constantine.

"No," he says, "it was you who made us whole."

Constantine's brown leather shoes wet with the sea's frosty gift make my bare feet seem closer kin to the ice on which they stand.

"My dreams are not so kind as yours," I say.

Constantine sets his hand on the head of the boat. His lips send frosty mist into the wind.

"Your dreams may yet be made real," he says. "I will live with mine from this day. For this, I thank you."

He takes my hand in his as he strokes Mildred's back. His lips find her cheek before she shies from him. He then comes to me, but I can not bring myself to share with him a kiss that bears the mark of truthlessness. He steps away.

"I have wished for many things," he says. "I have none of them now, yet I want for nothing. May you one day find this peace which you have also given me."

Constantine sits down on a narrow wooden beam within the boat, as though he takes a chair at the table in his bedroom. Behind him, the boatman's staff drifts through water bearing those many shards of broken ice. They float away from us slowly, wordlessly, without need for haste or speech or thought. I hold Mildred close against me and step back from the shore to ward myself against those old fears which are no longer there, for they leave with the man whom I have borne for so long bound within my heart. I hold the aldorman's eyes in mine until he is gone into the mists, whither, as he has wished me, I must one day also go.

SITHEBAD

Five thousand, five hundred steps lead from the shore to the mansio in which the aldorman no longer lives. They did not seem so many when we walked to the sea, yet I did not mark them then, nor did Constantine ever burn so brightly within my mind. It is only now that I have taken him from his house of stone and from the great stretches of winter's white ash that my footsteps bear any hint of sore sickness for having done this. He lay with me while I slept, or he did not. He was my father's child, then he was not. I would shear my own hair and bind the braided strands with twine if that were enough to keep him from my thoughts as I follow our path back to the stone walls that shield us from the sea's bitter depths.

The bloodied shards of stone are gone from the floor beside the wall when I sit down in Constantine's chair. My daughter has climbed onto my legs and asks me, with her hand on my lips, why I would speak to her of a man who is only alive to me when he is no longer among the living. I set Mildred down on the floor and bid her find something worthy of her fingers wherever she wishes to wander. She does not leave the bedroom's walls, nor does she walk through the room's opening into the hallway to see what once lay behind the door that is no longer there—where has it gone? Mildred stands beside the table and reaches for the small clay ink pot. I set it on the wall shelf behind me where she can not stand tall enough to take it. My legs are what she wishes, and so I shall give them to her in trade for her nose.

"I have your nose," I say to her and show her my thumb between my first two fingers.

Her laughter banishes all other thoughts while I run after her throughout the mansio, threatening to take her nose away anew. When she has need of it again to smell the hardening cheese in the cooking rooms, I give it to her and show her by wrinkling my face that she should not have asked her mother to give it back to her.

When my daughter has become weary, she rests on feathered bedding while my head hangs heavy beneath a yoke of thoughts too dark for the aldorman's empty parchment sheets. How might I write of them using kind, flowery words to make them seem as though they are not someone's else curses whispered into my ear? I have read such words, elsewhere, but those who wrote them are as far above me as black birds in flight through greying clouds at which I stare as though I could break their tufts apart with my eyes.

My wandering mind meets instead with a golden-haired woman's gleeful description of how the aldorman bends his knees on the sitting pot and the hue of the wiping stones he uses. My belly growls in sympathy though I warn it against doing such; hunger gnaws within me even as I dwell on things that should have driven the thought of food furthest from my mind. My weary legs bring me to the cooking rooms—cooking *room*, for all but one have been emptied. I take two unhardened bread rounds from the seven that lie on a legless table among water pots, one of which I bear to my room and set beside the bedding for Mildred to find when she wakes before I do.

Thereafter, on every seventh waking morning, the wights come to us to play for a time, as do my thoughts of Constantine, who tells me of his life as he watches Mildred and her red-hued friends. They brighten the greyness with mindless play that draws gleeful laughter from Mildred as she walks after them with her hands held aloft. When I do the same, they flee as swiftly as Mildred and I would run from the boatman were he to show himself in this mansio. Thereafter, Constantine falls silent and I set his writing feather down below the ink of the few words he has given me.

After the wights have left us for the seventh time, I wake before my daughter to take snow from the rainwater pit with which to wash my linen. I would not look twice at the wall of the room in which I gave birth to her did its stones not lie strewn about on the floor. The neighbouring room has been emptied of its chairs and table, as has been the cooking room of its iron cooking pots, as have all of the rooms overlooking the patio. So long as these outer walls stand, however, I shall write down what little I can of Constantine, even if what I write is nothing more than lies I tell myself to drive bitter memories from a mind that finds little rest even when I dream. It is not until Mildred sleeps that I tell her of what I have written of Constantine so that my words will have left her when she wakes:

Before the world became dull and lifeless, there was a aldorman named Cyneric who lived in a house of stone near the sea. One day, not long after the last of the snow had melted, he saw a young maid named Sithebad bearing a clay pot to the lake to fill it with water. Taken by her fairness and the wan flesh of her bare feet as she walked, he rode to her on his horse and asked her to wed him. She said she could not, for she had given her heart to Alfred, a boy from the neighbouring fields. Cyneric wished her well and went back to his house of stone.

Summer came and with it came war. Cyneric, the king's aldorman, called on Sithebad's father and Sithebad's husband, Alfred, to fight for the king. At night, when Sithebad's mother slept soundly, Cyneric came to Sithebad's house and hied away with her to the weaving house, where he told Sithebad of his undying love for her. Sithebad wished to have a son so earnestly that she lay with the aldorman. Thereafter, she told him the truth of what she did: Alfred had lain with her many times but had given her no children. Sithebad loved Alfred so much that she was willing to bear the aldorman's child and lie to Alfred, telling him that he had at last given his faithful wife a son. The aldorman left, his heart broken and his tears bitter with the salt of the sea.

The next day, the aldorman went to the king's sisters in red and asked them to set a curse on Sithebad's husband so he would not come back from war. Little did Cyneric know that the sisters in red saw through his wickedness and set their curse on Sithebad instead. Not long thereafter, Sithebad's child came sooner than it should and the two of them died as she bore a clay pot to fetch water from the lake. There, the aldorman found her body and wept for three days and three nights. He gathered his weapons and his iron shirt and rode off to battle in the far north, where he sent his horse alone into one hundred men and slew twenty of them before he himself was slain. His dying words, as he took a spear beneath the meeting of his ribs, told of his sorrow for having given Sithebad a child whose father he could never be.

My daughter is awake and has set the aldorman's chair against the wall. She has climbed up onto it to wash her hands using ink from the clay pot on the wall shelf. I grasp her wrists to keep her from seeing whether this thick black water is anything like her mother's milk.

"No, my dear," I say. "You will not like it."

"Mine. Me, me, mine."

I take her to the rainwater pit and there wash her hands with snow, but there is not enough of it to clean all of the ink from fingers she puts in her mouth as willingly as anything else she finds in this mansio. I take her out among what should be sweeping drifts of snow but have become nothing more than patches of snowy white amid waking grass. Mildred likes what she sees so well that I need not wash her hands for her; she wipes them clean with every small mound she finds until what little snow is left lies crumbled on the earth.

I follow Mildred as she wanders along the mansio's west wall, where the snow melts into the earth as if the wooden horse stalls had never been there. She goes behind the house to where the great hall's thatch should yield nothing to wintry winds. It does not, for the snowless ground there is without its long house but for the sunken rings wherein the hearth's stones would have kept fire from spreading to the tables and benches and walls—is this what befell the men here?

I would have seen them here, those who were dear to me. My heart stirs at the sight of their faces within my mind, yet they flee my thoughts as quickly as they come to me. Sithebad. She is here. Was here. I saw her in our bedroom's opening not long after Mildred was born. I should take these words I have written to where she must have gone—to where she lived with Alfred—and read them aloud to make them truth before burning them. When I think of her, I will think of what I have written, and thus forget the filth that slides from my mind down through my throat and into my breast.

I take Mildred from where she plays among leafless ash trees and lift her into my arms as I make a game of running back to the mansio. I will fetch for us fresh gowns and linen—I have no mind to wash what we wear—and take a basket of that bread which is always in the cooking room even when tables and chairs and cooking pots are not.

Yet there is nothing of the mansio here. This is where it should stand. Have I lost my way? We have spent so many days here that I should know at once where it is. Only a stone wall to keep oxen from wandering runs along the old path, though I have seen neither oxen nor deer nor foxes nor hares these many days or months. Mildred shows me with her fore-finger the clay pot of ink on the earthen floor of what was once our bedroom among the shin-high stone walls of our roofless mansio. In what was the cooking room lie half-eaten bread rounds that might be food for ants and flies were the weather any warmer. I take three or four of them, as many as my arms can bear—

I throw the bread to the ground. There is no mansio here. Let us leave behind the memory of those who lived here and what they did to one another. Let this be a great forgetting, even if my hunger tells me otherwise, for if I find nothing to eat in Sithebad's house, then I shall eat nothing; and my daughter may take her mother's milk.

My feet ache from the old path's stones long before I reach Sithebad's fields. In my mind, Isadora walks beside me. She rests her pale, long-nailed fingers in the crook of my arm and tells me of the words I might use in speaking kindly to my memories of Sithebad. Silence takes her as we come to Harold's many rows of barley and oats now waking from their bed of frost to a colourless sun that keeps the blood from my cheeks. Between the stalks blossom many heads of black-grass that have often made Harold's rye bread smack of horse dung, for in his haste to drink harvest mead, he had always planted well before we slaughter oxen for winter's meat.

"You should not think such things," says Isadora as we near Sithebad's house. "Had the king given them his wheat and rye to grow, your father would have been the one asking Harold whether you might wed his son."

"Are you dead that I remember you?" I say to her.

"Do you wish to make me so with your words?" she says with a frown. "Go and speak to Sithebad, who took your place among the living, as if she had never left us."

I step down onto the sunken floor of Sithebad's house, thinking to find pots standing near timber walls and clothing hanging from hooks and the hearth's embers resting beneath cold ashes. The pots lie in shards, tattered linen hangs from wooden beams beneath what little is left of the thatch overhead, and the hearth's stones lie scattered by the same wind that must have taken most of the roof.

"Ardelle," the shadows rasp.

I hold Mildred close to me and step back towards the opening. Behind the great iron cooking pot stands an ashen-faced woman whose hair is the tall grass horses eat in summer, hidden by a square of linen folded into three edges. Her lips are cracked and bleeding; her reddened eyes are ringed by blood-fattened worms that have burrowed beneath her flesh; her feet are as earthen as the ground on which they stand.

"Sithebad," I say.

Unlike those slain men, her bones still bear her flesh, bound to it by brown clothing that holds itself together better than anything else her ribs and limbs wear.

"*Child*," Isadora says to my ear. "She is still with us."

"As are you," I say. "And I have a child of my own, now."

"So you do," says Isadora.

"You speak to those who are not there," says Sithebad. "Have you gone mad?"

"You may speak whatever ills of me you wish," I say. "I have earned your words."

"I speak only the truth," whispers Sithebad. "I went to the

sea. The dark man would not take me onto his boat. He spoke your name. Is that your daughter?"

Sithebad nears, sending Mildred up onto my shoulder. A backward step would take us through the opening, yet I must not leave.

"I am held down by a great yoke that weighs heavier on me than anything else I have ever felt," says Sithebad. "The heavens do not even show me a moon to tell me how long the days are."

"Have you seen those red feathers floating about?" I ask. "They might tell you."

Sithebad's eyes search mine.

"You *have* gone mad," she says. Thick water flies from whatever is left of her mouth onto my cheek, where it burns my flesh. "Sister in red. Do not speak to me of the hue worn by those who sent me here."

I lift my woollen gown to my face and wipe it dry. The blue wool has become purple where it bears Sithebad's anger.

"I did not send you here," I say. "Myrah also had her hand on my belly when I gave birth, and I have not seen her here."

"Your queen sent me here? What have I ever done to her to earn this? It was when *you* sent me to her to ask for *your* forgiveness that she yelled at me and threw a chair and struck me with the back of her hand."

"She did no such thing."

"Says the *dead* woman who was not there. If you will not believe me, you may take your daughter and drown yourselves in the sea."

"Forgive me, then, for having sent you here," I say.

"And after I forgive you," she says, "I will still be here without Alfred. Where is the father of your child?"

"I do not know."

"So you are a half-wit *and* a whore."

Sithebad sits down on the backs of her legs. She stares for a time before bowing her head and closing her eyes.

"After you died," she says to the ground, "I heard men calling to me from afar. Their words were soft at first. I lay with Alfred every night. I thought his child would still their speech, but they became louder. They told me I should lie with them instead. When the aldorman gave Alfred a spear and shield and took him away to fight against some northern foe I have never seen, the men started yelling at me as if they lived in my head. They cursed me day and night, even in my dreams. After three days of this, I could take it no longer. I bound stones within my gowns and walked out into the river. But I have only traded one aching for another." She lifts her head and glares at me. "What am I to do now?"

"The boatman would not take the aldorman," I say. "The one who sent your husband to fight. He went beneath the water and stayed there, dreaming of his wife. He has found peace."

"You murdered him," Sithebad says. She stands upright on earth-darkened feet bearing an unseen weight. "This is what you do here. Let me at least hold your daughter as I would my own while we walk to the river. You will find stones for me."

From somewhere beneath her brown wool, Sithebad offers blackened fingers whose flesh falls away like ash. Mildred climbs onto my back. She cries out when Sithebad's hands take her wrists from my neck—it is Sithebad who cries out. She starts back and holds her reddened palms out before her as she weeps.

"Your child's flesh is fire," she says. "I can not even have this?"

"I ..."

"I hate you," Sithebad says. Tears run down her cheeks and into the bleeding cracks of her lips. "Take me to that lake where your dead man lies. You may think of him when you murder me."

I hide Mildred from bitter eyes that burn holes into the wool on my back as we follow the old stone path through fields of wheat and barley until we have reached the swaying green reeds along the lake wherein I found that thane so long ago. Sithebad kneels and looks at herself in the water: young, fair, soft of cheek. Mouse-brown hair falls to her shoulders beneath her head linen. The wights show themselves to us not far above the lake's still waters.

"Red," says Mildred and reaches for them from my arms.

"Have you learned to speak so soon?" I say to her. "Do you see them, Sithebad? The red feathers."

Sithebad shakes her head without looking up.

"I was with those men who came after you," she says. "They said they would burn you, hew your arms and legs from your body, break open your head with a stone so you could not stand again and show them your wrath. I did none of that, but I spoke no word against them for fear they would do the same to me." She meets my eyes. "Is this what I have earned?"

"No," I say. "You have earned a child whose flesh and blood are yours."

"That I shall never have."

"You may, in your dreams. I would have held your child—"

"*She is still here,*" whispers Isadora.

"I will hold your child in my arms when you come to see me in my fields, and you will hold Mildred in yours when I come to your house to help you with the bread-making."

Sithebad bows her head.

"If you wish my forgiveness," she says, "you must first ask it of the man you drowned."

"I did not—I know not how I would do this."

"You do not know where your dead friend lies? I will watch over your daughter for you and take you from beneath the water when you have been forgiven."

"I will not leave her alone," I say.

"I should speak to your unseen friend instead," says Sithebad. "She will not lie to me."

Sithebad throws herself into the lake's water, leaving only her feet among the reeds. I set Mildred down and bid her look at the wights dancing above the grassy field while I do my best not to empty my belly of whatever is left of yesternight's bread. My cheeks are hot; my breaths are too many; I hold my linen sleeves for warmth against the chills that take me. Thrashing from within the water brings Sithebad to rest beside us.

"I can not do this again," she says and lifts herself up onto her knees.

Her ashen flesh has become fair; her pale face bears a hint of redness; her eyes no longer look as though she has never slept.

"You must do this for me," Sithebad says. "If you have not the strength to drown yourself, let me dream of Alfred and our son."

And how would I do this? I would close my eyes as I grasp Sithebad's shoulders and shove her forwards into the water with all the strength my vomit-weakened arms can give her. She would thrash about beneath me, threatening to send me from her back; I would bend my knees and drop myself onto her. She might push up with her arms to throw me off, but I would lift myself and drop down on top of her once, twice, three times. Those spear-men who bound me to an iron rod in my dreams would laugh at her with yellowed teeth. Sithebad would turn to face me beneath the water and beg for her breath. I would choke the words from her throat with my left hand and shove her head against the lake bed with my right.

After a time, she would no longer stir, but I would not yield lest she wake and come after me for what I have done.

"Red gone," says Mildred as she waves a bundle of uprooted reeds in each hand.

"So they are," I say.

Sithebad looks at herself for a long while in the water. She takes from amid the reeds a rough stone shaped like her fist and holds it out before her. A loud sound sends blood running into the water. Sithebad sways on her knees with the bloodied stone in her hand. I hide Mildred's eyes with my palm. Sithebad strikes herself again and falls forwards into the lake so that only her legs still show. I turn away from her and hold Mildred in my arms—I must keep myself from singing my words to her lest she fright at them—until her eyes find a yellow flower her hands wish to pick. As she does this, I hie to the water and take Sithebad by the gown at her shoulders, dragging her down until her feet are hidden beneath the water. I can not keep myself from feeling along Sithebad's face—her head is whole, her hair thick and unbroken, the flesh of her cheeks and lips full and soft, her eyelids closed and still.

Mildred takes the leaves from her flower one by one. I send myself beneath the water and there look on Sithebad for the last time. She is free from her burdens, now, resting in stillness on the lake's mossy bedding. We will leave her to dream of the son and husband and fields and friends she would have had in another life. I hope that, even if only in her dreams, I may be among those friends.

"Those sound much more like your mother's words," Isadora says.

I creep along the ground in my water-weighted wool until I reach the edge of the reeds, where, in a meadow of yellow, white, red, and purple flowers, Mildred holds a marigold stem between her few teeth as she waves flowers in both hands.

When she sees me, she drops them and holds out her hands to me.

"Go," she says.

I set her in my lap and look into the lake's water. What did I write of Constantine? I take the sheaf of parchments from my leather belt bag, unfold the soaked bookfell as well as I am able, and tear the ink-blotted sheets until they have become small enough that the wind will take them when they dry. As for my daughter and I, the wind takes us along the edge of the lake to a runestone hidden among the reeds not much taller than Mildred. There, at its bottom, beneath the tall grass, in runes so small one must strain to read them, have been written words I might have read of myself had Isadora not found me: here lies the grave of Sithebad the maid, who often came to this lake to look at herself and dream of what might become of her life.

REUNION

My feet find the rough, lime-bound stones of the old path. If mother were here, she would have me come to our house myself to see what has happened while I have been away—I have no wish to see her in this place. Those dancing red wights come to Mildred's fingers once more. She holds out her clenched hand bearing one of them.

"Go," she says to me.

"Go?" I say.

"Mmm."

Though she has but few words, Mildred has grown old enough to speak and make her wishes known. In her wisdom, my child tells me that I am to leave behind my endless unkind thoughts by becoming like these wights and fleeing whatever weighs us down. I open my mouth and show my daughter with my finger where on my tongue she should set her friend. Her little fingers flee my biting teeth; I smile at her laughter even as my wight rests in icy bitterness against the roof of my mouth. Mildred takes another wight for herself and does as her mother has shown her. Her closed eyes and thinned lips and wrinkled cheeks tell me of the sickly sweetness she has swallowed. My throat and breast and ribs and belly warm with the fire of overly sweet mashed apples I once drank in someone's house of stone.

With Mildred in my arms, I sit down on the grass beside the path and wait in silence as the grey heavens flood with the sea's hue. I lose my blue woollen gown to sweating that wets Mildred's linen at her neck and beneath her arms.

"Sun," she says.

I know not where she has found this word, for we have had no need of it until now. I fold my useless woollen gown around Mildred and set her against my back, thus bearing her while my weary arms rest. My cheeks become warm to my fingertips, yet I have no linen with which to hide my face from Mildred's sun. Let us hasten, then, to the fields which I have not seen for so long, whose keepers my daughter has not yet met.

Mildred rests her head between my shoulders as we walk beside thick rows of green-stalked wheat heads waving softly in the wind. Amid the tall grass stand men in brown leggings, sweeping scythes along the ground to harvest the year's first, roughest hay to be fed to sheep who have no mind for summer's fairer fodder. One of them lets his scythe fall to the ground and stands upright to better stare at us as we walk by. I will let him look as he works, then, and when he is done looking and working, he may fill his belly with mead. I will look away when he runs naked around the harvested fields; and I will tell him, if he asks, that my daughter has no need for a father.

My steps quicken in taking us from the stone path. I must find where the little river is narrowest before the boatman comes to us—here the water is shallow enough for us to run through. I catch Mildred before she can send herself from my arms into the stream. In another life, I might grin as I watch her make waves with her hands and soak her linen against the sun's warmth. In this life, my feet curse the twigs and nettle beneath them as I thread through closely clustered oak trees on the other side of the river. That Mildred has not told me of the "boat" stills my fears only when the trees give way to our short-stalked rye and wheat fields, which themselves give way to nothing but earth and grass. Where our house should stand lies only rounded, sunken earth beneath a bed of drying leaves ringed by stones. There is nothing here to tell us of our weaving house, or of the wooden walls that house our pigs and oxen, or of our iron cooking pot, or of our stone quern for grinding wheat.

"Isadora," I say, "where have you gone?"

"To whom do you speak?"

A young man in brown little older than Alfred stares at me from amid shortened wheat stalks that still stand taller than he. He bears no scythe, no hair on his face, and no look of kindness in his eyes.

"Do you know where the man and two women who live here might be?" I say.

"None live here," he says. "I watch over the fields until they are ready for harvest."

"Only one man? I saw many elsewhere harvesting hay."

"And they will come here to do the same some months from now when these stalks stand much taller. Those are the aldorman's wishes."

"Aldorman? Does he live in a mansio near the eastern sea?"

"What is a mansio? I do not know where he lives."

He walks away from me and takes up the wooden haft of a scythe with more strength than he needs. I back away from him.

"Do you know anything of who lived here?" I say.

"If they did not leave, they are dead," he says. "My aldorman says a black death has come from over the southern sea and taken many men and women."

"Those dead you speak of would have been my mother and father and my mother's sister," I say.

"If this is so, why do you only now come to look for them? Where is your husband?"

"Where are *your* wife and children?"

"I have neither wife nor child, so the aldorman has chosen me to stand watch over these fields. If your face were fairer, I might abide your outlandish words well enough to take you from here. Where do you come from?"

"Did you not hear me tell you my mother and father live here?"

"So you say. Everyone else bearing a child has gone north away from the sea, yet you do not."

He wields his scythe in both hands and hardens his child-like face. My feet heed his words before my thoughts tell them to.

"Stay away from water," he calls after me.

I know not whither I should take Mildred. Our sanctuary on the sea? The king's tall stone walls not far from the marshes where alder trees grow? Along the northern shore? None of these would help us hide from water. Isadora's house is north-west from here, though it lies beyond the wide river where the boatman might await me, knowing that I flee from what his hand has wrought. Mother and father may be with Isadora in that little house of hers, or she will know where they have gone, or she will have left behind something for me to find that tells me where they are.

I lengthen my stride, thinking as I walk on how to reach the other side of a river too deep to stand in bearing my daughter on my back. As we near the groves wherein I sat before a runestone, Mildred's words take me from my wandering thoughts: she has thrice asked her mother for milk, and thrice I did not answer. I sit down among tall grass away from watchful eyes and give my daughter her milk while my own belly growls that I have given it nothing this day—why must we eat so often?

When Mildred has drunk her belly to fullness, I strike lightly against her back with my fingertips to call forth the milk that sticks to her lungs. A neighing horse lifts her head from my shoulder; I hide her in my arms and lie down flat against the ground, listening with one ear to hooves that tread the earth not far from us. They linger for a time, as if its rider searches for us. I am a mother who gives her child milk; he has nothing to fear from us. The horse's hooves leave us, yet I lie still with my hand over my daughter's mouth until the wind has blown through our tall grass unhindered twenty or thirty times.

I sit up as slowly as a flower blooms into brightness over a long summer's day. Neither horse nor rider stare down at us. I set my daughter in her blue wool against my back and half-run bent over at the waist to where the river flows wide and deep. I can not go through it here. I must follow it as it winds west until it becomes narrow enough to walk through—the boatman is here. He has sent his horseman. I wade into the water up to my shoulders with Mildred's head against my neck and there tread the mossy bottom while I sweep my arms before me as Luda taught me. On the other bank, my legs weigh heavy beneath Mildred in her soaked wool, yet I can not stop to take her from my back until we have reached Isadora's house of stone still hidden among high-boughed oak trees that will not shed their thorny acorns beneath our feet for many months.

I close the door and find within the house a hearth whose

embers have cooled into ashes without the iron rod that once stirred them to life so they could burn my red gown. In the shadows along the walls lies Isadora's wooden box, wherein she once kept inked parchments before burning them. Beneath it I find a thin, flat stone bearing dim runes I can not read until I have opened the house's iron-bound oaken door and given light to the sharp-angled strokes that bear my name: In memory of Ardelle. Faithful sister, beloved daughter.

"Ardelle?"

In the opening stands a bearded man wearing a shoulder-belted sword on his hip and dark brown clothing held together at his waist by brass-fastened leather.

"I am Bertha," I say. "This is my child. We will leave."

"Bertha," says the man with a smile. "That is the name Derwen told you to use if the northmen brought us low. I am Brant, Luda's brother. I think when last you saw me, I had not so much hair."

"Brant, yes," I say as I stand. "Much less hair."

I take him into my arms. The dried fish and hearth smoke on his wolf's hair tunic brings water to my mouth and longing to my heart. Mildred frights at his arm around my shoulders where her head should rest. My whispered words do little to lighten her mood. Brant gives me back to her and steps to one side to better look at her. She hides her face in my linen.

"Mildred shies from those she does not know," I say. "Everyone but her mother."

"She looks much older than these ten months you have been away," says Brant.

"We knew nothing of night or day in that hidden world," I say. Brant nods as if he knows this well. "What is this black death of which the men here speak? Why do they say we are to flee north?"

"I know not why death comes to us here more than elsewhere," he says, "but what they say is true: you and Mildred must leave now. We may speak as we ride."

I set my hand on his shoulder before he turns away from me. I must know.

"Is that where my mother and father have gone?" I say. "Isadora?"

"Derwen may have taken them to Powys," he says. "Myrah bid me come here after the snow melted to take them north, but they were not here. Luda came after me and asked me on Myrah's behalf to wait for you. Come, we must ride away from here."

I tighten Mildred's wool around my ribs and fasten its breastpins anew. Brant takes us up onto his horse and sets off along the stone path at a slow run that shakes Mildred's laughter from her. Scattered groves of wide-stretching oak boughs wave to us as we ride south towards the sun to meet the old path. When fear and dread have left me and I am of a mind to sit in silence as my daughter does, I speak to Brant's ear over his horse's hooves striking against the stones.

"Have they gone to Powys?" I say.

"I do not know," Brant says to the wind. "From the way Luda sits and eats and speaks, I think she may know, but she tells me nothing, not even that she does not know. And if she will not tell her own brother, she must have sworn an oath to someone."

"Myrah?"

Brant slows his horse for a time.

"Myrah's father sent her a letter telling her that her mother had died from that black death of which the men here spoke to you," he says. "He warned Myrah away from the shore so death would not come to her over the sea. That is why you see none but the men who keep the fields. We have rid ourselves of houses and halls so that when death comes for us, it will not know where to find us. Constantine is not with you as Myrah had hoped. It must have found him."

"Why would she think that I could bring him back to her?" I say.

"Myrah thinks her wise men seek to choose a king who will take her place rather than a king who will wed her. The sons of the wolf in the far north worship Derwen as their queen come back to them from among the dead to lead them once again. While Derwen was there, the men cared nothing for Myrah, but now Derwen has left them, and they can not find her. They have sent many men in search of her. Myrah fears they will come to hate her and her sisters for having driven Derwen away."

"Others would make Derwen flee before any of us did," I say.

"You will have to speak of it with your sisters some days from now," he says. "We go north through Londinium, right at Camelodonum, and left at Venta. You should read the stones for me. I have never needed those Roman letters."

What good would they do me? Do they tell me where mother and father are? No, they only tell me where Myrah is and that I am to go to her before any other. I let my forehead fall against Brant's back.

"Take me to Powys," I say.

Brant's horse slows to a stop. He slides down from its bare back and holds its leather mouth straps in one hand while he takes my fingers with the other.

"Death has taken so many that any who are still alive hide from it," he says. "I do not know where else your mother and father might have gone. If they were dead, we would have found them. They did not come to Myrah."

"They might have gone to Hispania, where Isadora was born," I say.

"It is the southern sea that brought death to us," says

Brant. "They would not have sought it out. Come north with me to where we live in peace with the wolves and make Luda tell you where Derwen has gone. The sight of your child may stir something within her heart, or you may pull on her braid until she tells you, or you may ask Florentina to speak until Luda becomes weary and yields the truth to her."

And as she does this, Myrah sits ever nearer to me until our legs rest against each other. She draws me close to her with one hand on my neck and kisses my cheeks, my chin, my lips and tells me sweet lies that sit bitterly within my belly even as my heart aches with a longing that does not die.

I slide down from the horse, letting Brant take me with his hands under my shoulders, and stand with bowed head while I look at the earth beneath my fingernails.

"If you can not take me to Powys," I say, "I will walk there myself. I walked to my fields from the sea."

"You would walk for many days before you came to Powys," says Brant. "Those who hide in houses and elsewhere may think you the hand of death to walk so freely among them bearing a child. They might send you back to him."

The bones in my cheeks ache. I can not look at Brant.

"You will not take me?" I say.

"I will not stand between you and your wish for death, if that is what you want, nor will I hasten you to meet it."

I have not enough tears to wash the earth from my unclean hands. Brant stills Mildred with his hand on her back while her mother shakes with weeping. When my eyes have emptied themselves of all else but the gift of sight, Mildred and I climb back onto Brant's horse and sit in silence as we ride along the old stone path that leads us north to Myrah and her sisters.

The next day brings us west through marshes whose water might bear boats as well as the northern sea not far from the stone path. Where the fields and groves give way to broken stone walls and crumbled towers, we are given the gift of a great river from which Mildred and I hide our faces so the boatman will not know who we are. Thereafter, Brant takes us north through wide, flat grasslands that keep us away from the eastern sea. The old stone waymarkers still bear the names Brant spoke of; their angled letters are not the flowery strokes of Florentina or Rosamond, but they tell us well enough where Myrah and our sisters await us.

At the end of the third day, we have eaten all of the bread from Brant's leather bags. I give Mildred her milk as eventide's cooling wind dries our sweat while Brant hunts hares. The heat has driven Mildred to sleep so often during the day that I wonder whether she will find rest this night. Brant returns in dusk's dimmest light with two leather-strung hares hanging from his neck. Mildred's milky breaths are so soft that even sleep seems to have fled her; she will not wake to my shaking fingers.

"Brant," I whisper. "I can not wake her. Has the ..."

Brant feels her fleshy arms and legs with his fingers; he leans forwards with his ear to her lips.

"She sleeps well," he says. "If the black sickness had taken your daughter, her face would be hot with nightmares."

"Have you seen this?" I say.

"If I had seen it, I would be among the bodies from whom the sickness must be burned away," says Brant.

"Might we ride with greater swiftness tomorrow? I would not have her fall ill."

"I will wake you before the sun."

When the sun first shows itself on the morrow, we must wait for its light so that I may read the stone way marker that tells us of the place called Venta. We follow the leftmost path and ride it as swiftly as Brant's horse will take us. The sun is high overhead when we near many houses of timber close together on a raised bed of earth and stone not far from flooded marshes. Brant's horse slows and neighs. He alights to meet the tall, braided woman in brown running to him from the meadow almost as swiftly as his horse brought us here. They take each other's arms and laugh. As I slide down from the steed's back, Luda eyes me wordlessly.

"Where are my mother and father?" I say.

"Why would I know?" says Luda.

"Brant says you know but will not tell him," I say.

Luda frowns at Brant and shoves his shoulder.

"Brant misunderstood me," she says to him.

"If you knew, would you tell me?" I say.

Luda stares at me with her arms hanging uselessly beside her. Dark clouds billow between my temples. My face flushes with heat. Mildred frights and clutches my gown with her fingers.

"Why did I come here?" I yell.

My breathing sounds within my skull, as though someone else blows wind into my ears. It must be Luda: she stares at me with no hint of sorrow in her eyes.

"You came here for Myrah," she says, "but you have forgotten her aldorman."

"He is gone and did not come back to my thoughts until your words bore him hither," I say. "And now Myrah's words have brought me to her once more so she can tell me of the next wretched man she will wed who says he is Mildred's father but is not."

"Myrah's mother is dead," says Luda. "Myrah is not herself. She has said so many things to so many men that I no longer know what is true and what is not, nor do I care. But let me go and fetch Myrah for you so you may hear her words for yourself."

Luda wipes her hands clean on her gown and walks off towards the many houses that from this far away look like longboats berthed on the shore, the same ships the northmen kept at that battle.

"I go to the houses," says Brant. "Do you come?"

Shall I stand closer to the water and see whether the reeds are thin enough for a boat bearing Myrah's next husband to come to us? Here is my answer: a black-clothed shape walks from the houses with slow strides. Brant leads his horse to meet whomever this is, but I will not go with him. They share words and leave one another. Myrah's forehead shines with sweat, which she wipes away with gold-banded fingers; blue gems swing from golden rings around her ears. The many-hued beads that hang from her neck are shaped like the tall handled drinking pots one might keep in the cooking room of a mansio.

"Where did you find those beads?" I say.

Myrah's eyebrows twitch.

"I should have been glad to see you after having been away from you for almost a year," says Myrah, "but let us speak instead of my dead mother and the only memory I have of her."

My fingers take mother's amber beads at my neck.

"I know not whether my own mother has suffered the same," I say.

"If she has," says Myrah, "it is your words that would do it to her before anything else. Luda came here to greet you as one would a sister she has not seen for many months, who bears a child we have never met. You, in your kindness, talk to her as if she came here from her homelands yesterday."

"Brant says she—"

"She has found a husband among her kin, the Geats. They abide with their kith, the Danes, along the northern shore. Their harvests flooded. They wintered in hunger. They came here in search of food and friends and peace but found only death. Luda wished your blessing for her wedding, as did Brant. He and his wife, Frijona, the wise woman of the Geats, will have a son some months from now."

"Derwen augured this?"

"Frijona did. Derwen is not the only one who knows such things. Luda makes ready to leave as though she will not be here another three years. Did you see your mother and father in that hidden world that you behave so?"

"If I had seen them there, I would not have come back here to listen to you speak to me like this."

Mildred sighs against my back. Her breathing tells me she has fallen asleep. There are no oak trees here to hide the sun from her, so I set her down on her wool amid shin-high grass and lean over her to shade her. Myrah sits beside us with one hand stroking Mildred's forehead and the other on my folded knee.

"Do you wish a child for yourself?" I say.

"Not from any of these wolves, but I will be made to give them one." She takes her hand from Mildred's brow and holds her beads as a child would its mother's gown. "If Derwen were here, they would not ask this of me. She does not love me, Ardelle. She left and does not come back. But you have come back to us from among the dead."

"Without your aldorman," I say. "He fell into the water when the boatman would not take him. I spared him from drowning. He told me I had taken him from a dream of you. He said he is not Mildred's father."

"He would lie to his own mother as she lay dying," says Myrah. "You should have let that snake slither to the bottom of the sea. Derwen sent him there for what he did to you."

"Is that why she left?" I say. "Or did she go to bring my mother and father to Powys?"

"There are none but Derwen who know her mind," says Myrah. "Why she would leave these men who worship her as their queen of old, only she knows. Without her, I am nothing to them."

"And you wish me to find her for you," I say.

"You know my mind," Myrah says.

She draws near to me, as I know she will, and sets her hands on my shoulder and knee.

"Derwen told these wolves that her might also runs through the blood of her sisters," she whispers. "Let them see me open your neck with my knife and drink of your life so they will know I share in your strength."

I turn to her. Her lips are almost on mine. Red spots deep within her eyes flit about as if borne along the wind.

"I have shown Derwen nothing but love," she says, "worshipping her even better than these men who think she has come to them from the heavens. How often did we look up at the night stars together and talk as we did in her sanctuary bedroom before you came to us?"

Whatever words follow, I hear nothing of them. My daughter sleeps in peace, beside her mother, dreaming of only birds and flowers and horses that take us through meadows of red and yellow flowers. And those meadows are washed white with snow that falls from the clouds all at once, leaving a swathe of empty nothingness.

"Constantine told me he wanted what is within me," I say. "I should have asked him whether he truly wanted dreams of the rotting bodies among which I lay and wished that I were like them for having lived to bear a dead man's child. When we sat at that table before him, you said nothing. None of you said anything but Marigold."

Myrah takes my hand.

"If the wolves do not find their queen, they may kill me," says Myrah. "And if they do not, I will kill myself so I am not made to wed one of them. We are thus kindred, you and I."

I throw her hand back into her lap.

"I saw Sithebad," I say. "The boatman would not take her. And I would not drown her so she could dream of Alfred and her son. She struck her own head with a stone and fell limp into the lake's water. I will be made to believe that I have done this, but I have done nothing, and I shall do nothing."

Myrah draws back from me and stares at me for a long while. I wish nothing more than to look away, but I must hold her eyes lest her words writhe their way through the thick shelf of ice beneath which my heart sleeps in frosty stillness. Her tears she may wipe away on Luda's gown and thus wash it clean of the earth from Luda's hands.

"I will not keep you from death, then," says Myrah. "And it is thus that we are kindred, for you will not keep me from death. Take a horse, if you wish. Take bread from the mead hall." She sets her hands against her face. "I should not have asked Brant to wait for you. We set a stone bearing your name in the mansio's bedroom where you left us while giving birth. Isadora took it with her after Sithebad's husband, Alfred, came back from war sick with sorrow over his wife's death. He said many unkind and *untrue* things about us. It was he who made us hew the stones of that mansio asunder for having taken him from his wife and thus driving her to madness. And now …" Myrah stands and strikes her own forehead with her palm. "Now, she abides in bitter loneliness."

"Sithebad told me I am a half-wit and a whore," I say.

"I have lain with none since Derwen left us," says Myrah.

"You did not lie with Derwen?"

"I said I have been with none. That is why the wolves do not like me. If you are a half-wit, I have no brain at all, for I thought you loved me. I thought you loved *us*. See how your daughter sleeps, Ardelle. She may not remember the words you have spoken to her ears. When she wakes, forget all thoughts of saying such things, for she does not know when her mother might be taken from her, and I know you would not have the hateful words of a dead woman be your daughter's last memory of her mother."

Myrah's swaying gown is as black as the boatman's lifeless

cloth. We should not have come back here, my daughter and I. Mildred does not yet understand that knowledge begets suffering, and her mother has not yet learned to harden herself against the words of those who would have her believe otherwise.

BELOVED

Mildred knows not what to make of the brightness that greets her open eyes, so she closes them, as if by doing so she might also send the unclouded sun to sleep in its bed of bright blue. My hair clings to my back and waist beneath my linen, held there by the sweat running down from my neck. Without cloth to hide my burning cheeks, I am of a mind to follow the stone path south back to where trees abide and ask their leafy boughs for better shade than what Mildred's thin-armed mother gives her. I take up Mildred from her woollen bedding amid the blossoming grass and stand—my legs shake and my belly yawns.

"Again we must eat," I say to my half-sleeping daughter. "Let us go to Myrah's mead hall and fetch bread. You have more than enough teeth for it. I only wish you would learn that you do not need them when you drink your milk."

East of the houses stands a great hall without walls under whose thatched roof sit three long tables and six long benches. They have become home to men and women in earthen hues who sit as still as oak trees as they heed the words of their brown-clothed herdsman. He still speaks when I am sat at the end of one of the tables, where I chew on soft wheat bread warm from the hearth. Has Myrah taught this man to use so many words? These wooden bowls of honey must be hers. I can not help but take some along with fresh cow's milk and wedges of sheep's meat on thin wooden rods and two eggs for Mildred when she wakes and—

"Have you come to take the blessings?" whispers a woman to my left.

She leaves her man to sit beside me so closely that one might wonder which of us is Mildred's mother. Her frown softens into a smile on seeing how Mildred sleeps with her mouth open.

"Blue?" she whispers and takes Mildred's bedding-gown between her thumb and forefinger. "You should eat berries, not wear them."

"Your breath smells of your man," I tell her.

She stares at me, then slides back to her husband's brown tunic and whispers into his ear. Whatever she says drowns itself in the loud and deep words of a man in clothing as black as Myrah's. Is this one of her aldormen? Unlike his brown-clothed friend, he does not stand still before the long rows of men and women, but walks between the tables as heads and eyes follow him.

"Your lauded queen has not left your memory these many years, for you have been faithful to her," he says. "So, too, does your beloved Budig ask for your steadfastness as she walks alone far and wide in battling the black death. None of us among the living can bear her burden. Only she who has gone to where the dead abide and returned unscathed can hope to win against our faceless foe."

Shaven head, sunken eyes, broken nose, a shadow for a beard. Gerahard. He holds my eyes as if I have said his name aloud. When he looks at Mildred, I must hold my own wrist to keep my hand from hiding my daughter's face. Gerahard's words follow him to the head of the hall, where he stands until he has emptied himself of all that is within him, whereafter the men and women strike their palms against the tables and rise. They walk, one by one, in rows to four empty chairs that face the gathering. Soon enough, the chairs meet their masters: a well-fed woman with reddish cheeks and ringed hair that matches her brown clothing stands beside her fair-faced, slender-armed friend, who wears nettled green. To their right sits a golden-haired, shoeless child in undyed linen on a high-backed chair; on their left, a grass-gowned woman with fire for hair looks to the heavens from her seat.

Annette, Rosamond, Florentina, Marigold. Men and women kneel before them, taking hands on their heads for the length of a short song and rising with smiles that bear no mark of falsehood. I will wait to see whether our sisters will set their hands on my head willingly; when Florentina has given me her waters, I will ask her whether Luda can not be made to tell me where Derwen has gone with my mother and father.

"Why do this half-wit and her child stand so close behind us?" says the woman who spoke of Mildred's berry-gown.

"Why must you speak like that?" says her husband.

A rush of wind sweeps her hair from her face and takes five or ten empty cups from their tables onto the earth. Annette and Rosamond look through the faces of those gathered as the men and women turn to one another and whisper. Mildred is awake and clutches my gown as if my arms might fall to the ground and take her with them. Through the rows walks Marigold, striking with her walking stick against the ground.

"Ardelle," she says loud enough for all to hear.

"Here," I say.

Marigold stands beside me, sending the woman who cursed me to hide behind her husband.

"This is how you tell us you are here," Marigold says. "Silence would have been better."

She takes my elbow and holds it while the woman and her man kneel before Florentina for their blessings. As I come before her, Florentina's eyes widen into spotted goose eggs amid a nest of golden straw. Annette marks my feet but does not see me. Marigold holds out her arms to my daughter; Mildred will not go to her.

"She has been given a fright," I say. "Let her take the blessing as well."

I kneel down and bow my head. Florentina sets her fingers in between thick strands of unwashed hair. Long has it been since I felt the soothing waves of the sea washing over my flesh and limbs—

A shrieking yell deafens me. Marigold's searching hands take Mildred from me. The ringing within my head gives way to the honeyless words of those who have stopped eating long enough to ask Gerahard of who I am and what I do here. Myrah is at his side in haste. She must have been hiding under a table. Rosamond stands with Marigold and speaks soothing words to my daughter in Frankish. Mildred stares at Rosamond in open-mouthed silence.

"What have we done to earn your wrath?" the woman says to me. "You see no other children here, do you? We leave them out of such things. I will not bind myself to your evils." She strikes her husband's ribs with her hand. "Talk to the aldorman and ask him to make her leave."

"If that black hand had not driven us so far north," says Myrah, "we would not be here, nor would your queen have come to you with us. And yet never have you loved your queen so dearly but when she was gone from you."

Myrah reaches for Mildred with her hands under my daughter's shoulders. Mildred goes to her as if I were the one who takes her. Myrah smiles. Mildred laughs. Myrah kisses her on the cheek and blows the wind into it.

"Gerahard," says Myrah, "I need to speak to them."

"Men of the salted marshes," bellows Gerahard, "hear your sister as you eat."

Myrah walks between the tables even as men and women still stand in rows to await their blessings. Some of those seated speak as if she does nothing; others eat while watching what she does; and yet others sit without stirring as they await her speech. She waves me to her with her hand at her waist.

"This woman is Budig's sister come back from the dead to seek a reckoning for her stillborn child," says Myrah. Her words bring meat and bread to their plates and cups to their tables. "She is the one who called the wind you felt. This is the wrath she shows to those who would take her daughter from her again, even in death. Ardelle." She stands close to me. "Tell us what we must do for you that you will leave us in peace and send your sister Derwen back to her kin."

"Do you really believe—"

The benches beside the tables empty. The woman and her husband kneel before me, as do their many brothers and sisters. I take my foot from the lips that kiss the earth from it. Gerahard stands with folded arms among kneeling men taller than Myrah's father ever did.

"What would you have of us?" says Myrah.

"To know who my child's father is," I say.

"I am," says Myrah. "You may take me wherever you wish and I will look after her. What else would you have of us?"

"Where are my mother and father?" I say.

"I will find them for you," says Myrah. "I will go to Derwen myself if I must and bury myself beneath the earth at her feet so that she will return them to you. Give us your strength and we will do whatever you wish. Will this be enough?"

The eyes of these men and women look up from the earth and into the heavens through the back of my head. My own daughter takes my cheek with her little fingers but does not reach for me from Myrah's arms. I have become someone else, someone who is not there—a ghost who shows them whatever they wish to see, even if it is themselves they see when they are no longer among the living.

"I would not have you remember that I was here," I say. "Show me where my mother and father abide and I will have no mind for anything else, not even that which stands before me."

"As you wish," says Myrah. She turns to the woman who kneels beside her husband. "You, ask forgiveness for your unkind words."

The woman throws herself at my feet, dragging her husband down with her by the shoulder of his tunic. Her words fall from her mouth onto the earth as misshapen half-thoughts.

"You are forgiven," I say.

"This man who follows her so faithfully must be of like mind," Myrah says. "You have chosen your wife well."

"She is not my wife," says the man.

"And she will not be if you are so soft," says Myrah. "From this day, let your words keep her from doing such things. And you, young woman, you might wed this man and learn from him."

The woman looks up at her with wide eyes.

"He is my brother," she says.

Gerahard's bellowing laughter sends birds from the far-off reeds in flight. The gathered men and women meet his laughter with their own soft mirth and find the benches once more. Gerahard sits down among them, staring at me for a time before eating alongside his wolf-kin friends. Myrah walks away from me with my daughter in her arms.

"Ardelle," whispers Marigold. Her hand is on my elbow. "Myrah asks me to set fire to things. Her father said I would not have to. Nobody does anything to stop her, that man Gerahard least of all."

"Why do you think so much of him that he should be the one to stop her?" I say.

"You might ask the same of Myrah," says Marigold. "When you do so, tell her that she spoke an oath to her father on your behalf. It seems that with her father gone, Gerahard wishes to keep him and his oaths from Myrah's memory. See where Myrah goes with your daughter."

I follow Myrah to the houses in sight of the marsh—it looks more like a sea—and hasten after her through a narrow opening in the tallest of the houses, wherein the hearth's embers glow with Marigold's fire but do not burn. Myrah sets Mildred down on the cool earth beside a short-legged table bearing a sheaf of half-written parchment. A golden wrist-ring falls from within the sleeve of her black gown as she strokes Mildred's hair away from her forehead.

"Where did you find her?" Myrah says.

"On the floor of that bedroom in the mansio," I say.

"She has grown as much as a child of two years," says Myrah.

"How would you know?"

"Do you think I have never seen or dreamed of children before? I write of my own wishes there on the table. The women here have many. They do not bring them to take their blessings. And now you have shown them why they are right to do so. We thought you had fallen asleep when you gave birth. Annette took your daughter from your legs and wiped the blood from her. Sithebad helped her. When you and your daughter were no longer there, Sithebad ran from the room. Not in fright, Ardelle. She said she was the one who had done it to you."

"What are the words of a dead woman worth?" I say.

"They were worth a great deal from the mouth of her husband," says Myrah. "And they will be everything to these wolves whose hearts forgot their hatred for us when their queen stood among them. You are the only one I have left, Ardelle."

"You have Derwen."

"She was never mine."

"Gerahard?"

"He loves himself more than any other. I help him when he has need of it."

"With what?"

"Things."

"Such as the gathering in the mead hall, where he spoke to your wolves as if he were their king?"

"I spill his seed on the ground, where it belongs. He will nonetheless ask me to lie with him now that you are here lest he take you in my stead. What would you have me tell him?"

"To go and do not return until he has found my mother and father," I say.

"And if he does not return, he will understand your meaning," says Myrah.

"That is not what I meant."

"He need not know this. I will tell him what you have said. He will understand your need. He does what must be done, as do I, as do you, yet neither he nor I can ask the wind or the earth or the sea or the hearth to help us." Myrah's hand goes to my knee, but she stops herself. "I want what you have. I wish to be one of you."

"If I knew how to make this so, why would I do it for one who lets others speak ill of her sisters?"

"They have nothing but words, so let them have their words."

"That woman—"

"Are her words so dear to you? Listen to those who show you strength. It is the strength of those like Derwen that allows us to stay here among these wolves. It is this strength that keeps me in this house with you and your thorny words after not having seen us for almost a year."

My hand goes to my daughter's ribs. Her heart beats with quickness; her breaths are soft and steady. Myrah takes my knee.

"Do you love me?" she says.

My hand rests on hers. I keep my fingernails from clawing into her flesh.

"What do you know of love but when you need something from me?" I say.

"If I had no need of you, you would leave my thoughts, yet you are a ghost who follows me without end, even into my dreams. What do you know of this?"

"Constantine—"

"May rot into worms and dust. Mother heard my heart when I spoke father's oath beside you. She knew my thoughts when I took your letter to your mother and father and read it to them. Isadora, your mother's friend—"

"Sister."

"—sister, saw the redness in my cheeks in the light of a fire as dim as this. I knew my own thoughts when I lay alone in darkness after our talks in your sanctuary bedroom and could not keep my hand from going beneath my gowns. I took your life-breath for as long as I could in the grove among the stones, which are as empty as Marigold knows they are. I thought I knew your heart when you said you would shield me against my foes. I thought I knew your strength when you and Derwen struck down the serving maids father sent to anger you so he would have cause to war with the northmen anew. I waited for you through a long winter, only to have you taken from me for twice as long, and on your return, you greeted me with the memory of my dead mother."

"You could have come to me earlier," I say.

"No, I could not."

Myrah sits beside the hearth. She turns her back to me as she lets fall her black gown, then the linen beneath it.

"Feel this with your own fingers," she says.

Against her spine where it bends to the left rests a thick welt the length of a finger, a wretched reddish ridge amid the smoothness of her brown flesh.

"One of Florentina's hair rods heated by Marigold's fire," she says. "Father did this after I told him I went to your bedroom so often out of love for you."

"And this after your father told her she would not have to set fire to anything more," I say.

"Did you hear me? Have you nothing of your own to say?"

"You spoke with Derwen in her bedroom before I ever came to the sanctuary. So, yes, I know of that which does not leave one's thoughts."

Myrah bows her head.

"I did that with her—for her—after she lost Hugo," she says. "She saw in him the son she might one day have. Father warned her away from me by speaking to her of the arm she had lost before he took her in, but he had none such to make you listen. He told my mother to speak with me of this in his stead. Where mother's thoughts spoke to me, my heart spoke to her. She understood me. But she could not make my father understand why she did not do what he asked her as she had always done before. That is why, after having won a great battle, he left for his imperium to shed himself of us. He cares for nothing else but the old ways that still live on in the hearts of the men of the west, and yet father fights with them for being wrong in their understanding of what he knows better than anyone else."

"Was it other than the black death that took your mother?"
I say.

"Gerahard told me my father has another wife in Francia.
And a son by her. One whom I might call brother if I had ever
seen him. One who will be called atheling to win the hearts of
our own men who have no love for me."

"Are Gerahard's words so dear to you?"

She turns to me; her gowns rest on the earth around her
waist.

"When my father sees how I have kept his kingdom and
freed his daughters from their bonds, he will know the truth of
our love."

Myrah sets her hands where my back ends and pulls me
into her waist. My arm takes the back of her neck without
asking me; my eyes do not show me that her nose is against
mine; my thoughts bid me tell them of the colours of the eyes
that might watch us. It is only Myrah's lips and their fullness
against mine that yield life and breath into an earthly body
made weightless and without substance.

She stands to let fall her black wool and hueless linen in a
heap at her feet. Where her face is soft and fair, her body has
been hardened by bruises that must have been given to her by
unkind horses. Without her clothing, her right shoulder and
hip rest higher than all else on her upright body; her belly has
become fleshier.

"Do you still eat honey with every meal?" I say.

"That is one thing I did not give up when we left the sanctuary," she says. "Now, give up your gowns."

I stand to shed my arms of their linen. Myrah takes it from
my feet and throws it down onto hers, where it rests next to
Mildred. She smiles at me, takes my hands, and lies down
with me against our earthen bed, where she kisses me until
my breath has left me.

"Long did I abide in loneliness," she whispers to my ear. "Show me how you have mastered this foe."

Her hand runs along my neck and down my ribs and between my legs, where it tells me of how the water flows softly against the white cliffs not far from the sanctuary that was once our home. My hands are on every part of Myrah, whose lips have not left mine, even when I seek to draw my own away and gather my breath—she does not allow it, nor will she allow me to still her hand with my own, grasping my wrist tightly until my arm falls to rest beside me. Whatever feelings of false kinship I had for her must at length yield before the swelling waves of truth and wisdom that wash over my body with ever greater strength. My hand takes Myrah's chin as her lips seek to draw my life-breath into hers so wholly that I no longer live but from the life she gives to me. And I give myself to her willingly as beneath her hand mighty winds sweep up the waters of the sea and send them rushing onto the shore and against the cliffs, striking with such strength that the stone should yield to them, yet it does not, but withstands the heaving tides that thrust themselves against the cliffs' walls over and over. My whitened knuckles grip Myrah's neck and hip even as the waves leave us and threaten to become still once more. She calls them anew, telling me with her eyes how the mist of their swells reaches the clouds as they rise to meet the cliffs and rush up over the ridges onto the hills and into the sanctuary, where they flood every room and empty it of all who might have lived there. When the water ebbs, Myrah's hand lies still, as does mine on hers, weary as I am and bathed in my own sweat, which Myrah kisses away from my cheeks and forehead and temples.

We lie there for a time in one another's arms and sweat and smell and breath. My daughter sleeps on her blue woollen bedding, her hair and flesh still dry in the cool shade of Myrah's house. Myrah rises from my arms, fishes among her gowns, and returns to my breast with her mother's many-hued, pot-shaped beads woven between her slender fingers. A slight stinging at my neck follows my shoulder to its bone, sending blood running down my flesh onto the earth. Myrah kisses the wound into stillness. I look into her brown eyes—nothing but the hearth's dim embers live within.

"Do you not fear the black death?" I say.

"Why should I? Do you know to whom this name has been given?"

I slide my fingers along the length of her arm from her elbow to her shoulder.

"You?" I say.

That same arm strikes its palm against my forehead softly.

"*You*," she says. "You, who died while giving birth to a child who grows too quickly for her years. You, who thereafter made that mansio shake and took its aldorman with you to the next life. You, whose wrath swept through my father's kingdom and took from mothers their unborn children, and those mothers, and their husbands, and their children among the living, and even their pigs and sheep and oxen. You are Derwen's sister come to bring her back to abide among the dead, where she belongs. If these men kneel to you well enough, you might spare them from death and let them keep their queen for a time."

"How can anyone believe that I have done this?"

"Men fear many things," says Myrah, "but they fear nothing greater than that which they can not see. Thus, they have given the black death a name and a face, and you are it."

Myrah sets her beaded hand on my shoulder and the other on my waist.

"You have come back to us from that hidden world bearing the gift of death," she says. "There is, then, but one thing I can do: I shall wed death, and death will be my queen."

"Are you not your own queen?"

Myrah shakes her ringed hair against my shoulder.

"I have no king," she says. "My father's *wise* men say they do not understand how I am to be a queen if I am not wed to a king. The wolves speak ill of them for not upholding their own atheling."

"They wish one from among themselves to be your king?"

"They need no king. They listen to the howling of their kindred wolves over the sea at night. Derwen knows better than they of what those wolves speak. They asked me, once, to tell them what their kindred wolves say. I had no answer for them, yet they listened to Gerahard, who speaks as if his words were runes carved into a stone and he has but to read them aloud. Many of them even did what he said."

I sit up, sending Myrah to the ground. She throws her arms around me as if I stand at the edge of a cliff overlooking the sea and threaten to throw myself from it.

"So he believes his words to be the truth whether they are or not," I say. "I shall own you in body or in spirit. That is what he said to me."

"He will own *me*," says Myrah. "Let him believe that. I will do everything to make him think this. He understands that when I lie with him, my heart does not."

Myrah takes Ziri's beads from between her fingers and winds them around my right wrist. From my gowns she takes mother's beads. I fasten them around her neck.

"Gerahard has never seen me without my mother's beads," she says. "When he sees them on your neck, and yours on mine, he will know."

Mildred lies on her belly with her fists beside her head and her mouth half-open. Does she dream of her mother? Of Myrah who held her and made her laugh? Let her dream of these things and know nothing of love that only abides in deepest fullness when one has become a ghost to men. I fasten the ends of the leather string bearing Ziri's beads behind my neck. Myrah sends me to the ground and holds my wrists against the earth as she kisses me about the face in earnest with lips that still bear the blood from my shoulder.

"Ask of me anything you wish," she says, "and I shall see it done, if I am able."

"Find my mother and father," I say.

"We shall find them," says Myrah, "and when we do, they may come with us wherever we go."

Myrah steps into her linen and threads her thin arms through its sleeves. I do the same while Myrah takes Mildred in her arms and sings to her the old song we once sent to the clouds as we stood before our sanctuary's runestone. Mildred sighs into her breast.

"I should not have asked you to come to the mansio," Myrah says. "I should have found another way."

"And I should have not have gone to the mansio," I say. "I should have gone to your father before anyone else."

"Had you done so, he would not have learned of Constantine's wish to bear one of our children and make a king of himself. But you need not worry about this any longer. I will bear Gerahard's child for you."

She stands with Mildred, leaving her black woollen gown on the earth. She bids me come with her to the meadow far from the watery marshes and sit with her among tall green stems bearing spindle-like shafts of purple leaves.

"Florentina calls these *marsh orchis*," says Myrah. "I know where her mind is even when her face does not tell me. The minds of these men are with their queen, Derwen, for they feel some bond with her that goes beyond all else." She takes my hand. "They said they will follow her to where the dead abide. I will tell them that I shall do the same with you. When next your boatman comes to you and asks for your blood, I will give it to him from my own."

I set my fingers between hers and hold her hand against my breast.

"To these men you are dead," says Myrah, "but let us show your sisters that you yet live, as does your daughter; and we shall show them that you and I now share a bond that goes beyond all else—even death."

IV

SHE WHO MAKES KINGS

2 4

KINSHIP

Mother sits before the hearth with her back to me as I braid her long brown hair into three thick strands whose tail will rest in my lap. Father sits on his bench, warming his feet while he carves a walking stick from a fallen birch bough. Mother's quickened fingers run waxed linen thread through a hood and a grey woollen tunic. Father will wear this to shield him from winter's earliest winds when he goes with his ax to gather wood for our fire some months from now.

I wake with the hearth's warmth wet against my temples and clinging to my gown beneath my shoulders. Mildred sleeps soundly in her linen; Myrah wears her black wool. She holds the back of her hand against her sweaty forehead with her reddened eyes half-open.

"Would you not sleep better without your wool?" I say.

"I would wake three times at night to wear it when I am cold, then three times again to take it off when I am too hot," says Myrah.

"I dreamed of my mother and father before the hearth," I say. "Mother had her hair. Father had his feet."

Myrah stands in haste and leaves through our house's opening. She blesses its outer walls of timber with her vomit. When she has nothing left in her belly, she drops handfuls of small grey stones onto the filth. Her gown takes the dust from her hands as she lies down beside me.

"I had no such dreams," she says. "Now, help me sleep before my wise men come and ask me of this and that endlessly."

I turn over onto my left hip and rest my arm on Myrah's shoulder. She still sweats, so I offer my linen sleeve to wipe the sweat from her brow. In doing so, my elbow comes up against her breast. She grunts as if she had taken a blow. I set my palm against her forehead the way mother does when I have been too long in the sun.

"Do you feel hot?" I say.

"Yes, and when next you ask, my flesh may be ice."

"When you slept, did you have nightmares?"

"I did not sleep. I do not have your dark dreams, if that is what you mean, but my thoughts are as swift as a steed that rides along the stone paths all day and all through the night. Your words do nothing to help."

I lie down beside her and stare up at the thatched roof until the sound of her breathing and her fluttering eyelids tell me of her restless sleep. I hie without, stepping around Myrah's small mound of stones. I have not yet learned which of these many houses so close together are home to our sisters and which are home to Myrah's wise men. I look within each one, shying away from unkind faces until I find Brant and Luda. They sit before their hearth and speak to one another; Florentina sleeps on the bedding behind them.

"Brant," I whisper. "Will you come to Myrah's house and look at her?"

Brant stands and comes to me wordlessly.

"What is this?" says Luda. She follows her brother and stops me with a hand on my shoulder. "You need my brother but not me?"

"Will Florentina not yell at you if she wakes and you are not there to be her horse?" I say.

"Yes, and we will hear her from wherever you take us."

We find Myrah with her eyes fully closed, breathing softly with one arm around Mildred as they dream together. Brant kneels down and sets his hand on Myrah's shoulder.

"Have you seen this before?" I ask him.

Luda unfastens the golden bird that holds Myrah's gown together at her neck and slides her hand beneath the wool, feeling with her fingers along the linen on Myrah's belly. Myrah frowns and growls but does not wake. Luda withdraws her hand.

"Her head is hot, and she has not slept well," I say. "You spoke of this when first you found me, Brant."

Brant takes Myrah's hand and looks over her fingernails, then slides her black gown sleeve up to her elbow, feeling along her arm with his fingertips. He shakes his head.

"I do not see that on her," he says.

"See what?" says Luda.

"The black death," Brant whispers.

"Shut your mouth," Luda hisses. "She is with child. You two go and fetch Annette lest your endless talk wake her. Leave Mildred here, Ardelle. She must learn to know us better. Now go off with my brother as you so wished."

Brant leads us through morning's dewy grass to the short-walled house that Annette shares with her man, Wilfrith. He and Annette are awake, but we must wait for them in the field nearby. I ask Brant what they do; he does not tell me. Annette comes to her door in her linen and waves us within. She sweats as well as Myrah does though her hearth's embers glow only weakly. Wilfrith stirs them to life with an iron rod.

"Luda asks for you in Myrah's house," I say. "She thinks Myrah is with child."

Annette runs without her shoes through the opening. Wilfrith watches her as Brant tells him of what goes on. Wilfrith grins and claps Brant on the shoulder.

"You will know the same happiness some day," Wilfrith says.

"May I live so long," says Brant. "And you?"

"Annette says she will find a way. It may be that you and I leave these lands together."

"Where is my horse?" calls a woman from a nearby house.

"Florentina is awake," says Brant. "If one of you knows, all of you will know. You might be the one to tell Florentina of Myrah's child so she does not learn of it from another."

Brant kisses me on the cheek. His rough beard leaves behind the mild stinging of nettles. Beneath morning's waking clouds, Florentina sits in her green-grey linen with her unringed golden hair bound into two tails. I run to meet her and offer her my back.

"Why did you not come to me as soon as you heard me?" she says.

"I did not know it was you," I say. "Your hair is not the same."

Florentina breathes out sharply through her nose.

"Myrah took my hair rods," she says, "and nobody will dig up good clay for me to set in my hair while I sleep. I am to meet Rosamond in the meadow, where she will bind my hair well enough that my rings may stay until dusk. We shall see whether this yet happens. Swiftly, dear mother."

I bear her through purple moor grass towards feather-light white meadowsweet swaying in the soft wind. Rosamond meets us with a wave of her hand and Marigold on her arm.

"*Bone manum*," she says. "Let us do this in your house, Florentina. I do not like the way that man Gerahard looks at me as he rides around on his steed."

"Fetch a steed of your own to ride, then," says Florentina. "To my house, *aithei*."

Within Florentina's house, Marigold lends her reddish-blue fire to the hearth, brightening many short, dark blue and black pots along the walls, which Florentina says are for keeping Myrah's ink. Florentina and Rosamond speak to each other in Latin while Rosamond winds thick lengths of Florentina's hair around her middle and forefingers. She dampens it with water from a clay pot and sets the strands in place against Florentina's head using long brass pins. Marigold says nothing to me, only holds my knee with her hand as she listens.

"Of what do they speak?" I whisper to her.

"They talk of the hidden world in which you stayed for so long," she says without whispering. "They wonder whether you will leave us again."

"Why does Myrah now let you speak Latin?" I say. "Did she not once threaten to shear your hair?"

"Her father did," says Florentina. "He no longer speaks through her mouth."

Her hair is a bed of blooming flowers with its many tightly wound day's eye blossoms yet unopened.

"You should take these little strands at the nape of your neck," says Rosamond.

As she reaches for them, Florentina squeezes Rosamond's fingers. Rosamond cries out and withdraws them from Florentina's grasp.

"I shall keep all of my hair, dear sister," says Florentina. "The men here speak Latin, some of them, though their words sound as if they have not spoken their own tongue for a hundred years. Gerahard speaks it with them as well, that fox-faced man who wishes to slither his way into everyone's hearts and be the king of all snakes."

Florentina makes a claw with her hand and hisses, then bites into the linen on Marigold's shoulder. Marigold sighs.

"The wolf lies with the sheep often enough," says Rosamond. "I should have expected a lamb by now."

"What do you mean?" I say.

Rosamond laughs.

"Myrah shares Gerahard's bed whenever he wishes," she says. "It is a wonder that Myrah is not yet with child."

"She told me she lay with none," I say.

"None worthy of our thoughts," says Rosamond.

"Luda thinks Myrah is with child," I say. "She has asked Annette to help her watch over—"

Florentina climbs onto Rosamond's back, strangling Rosamond with her forearms as Rosamond stands up in a green gown too short to hide her white-dyed hose.

"Away, horse!" Florentina yells.

Rosamond strides through the house's opening as Florentina's socks strike against her waist. Marigold's hand is on my arm above my elbow.

"Let us go and see Myrah's child," she says.

When we reach Myrah's house, Myrah pulls at her own hair while her sisters talk loudly of whether she will bear a son or a daughter. Mildred still sleeps soundly. Marigold sits down beside Myrah and feels along her woollen gown. Myrah frowns at Marigold and sets her hand aside.

"Ardelle, how is it that your daughter sleeps so well?" Myrah asks.

"She has learned to sleep peacefully as she lies beside you," I say.

Florentina falls over laughing to herself. Rosamond groans. Luda stares at me wordlessly. Myrah's sigh bears the hint of laughter.

"And did you sleep so little among so many?" says Myrah.

"I was with—"

I was with mother and father, who helped me find sleep.

"You were with whom?" Myrah says.

"I was with you," I say. "In my dreams. In the sanctuary before I told you we should not be together."

Rosamond laughs beneath her breath. Florentina upbraids Rosamond with a sound from her tongue. Annette sits beside Myrah's head, running her forefingers along Myrah's eyebrows and her thumbs over Myrah's eyelids. Myrah's breathing slows; her words become soft.

"You have told me two things," Myrah says. "One of them is a lie, but I know not which. Tell me another truth, then, or a kind lie, if you wish: is my child a son or a daughter?"

"A son," says Luda. "Like mine shall be—would be."

"I am with Luda," says Annette. "A strong boy who will outrun you when he grows tall."

Myrah smiles.

"I think we would all have daughters," says Florentina.

"I need no children," says Rosamond.

"Myrah asked of herself, Rosa," says Marigold. "She will have twins, a boy and a girl, like the children you watched over in Parisius."

"She is too small to bear twins," says Florentina.

"Am I?" says Myrah. "Derwen would tell me whether I am, were she here. If she were to tell me that I have a son, I would not be the only one made glad."

"Derwen has never needed anyone to show her whither to go off by herself," says Rosamond, "nor has she ever asked for anyone to come and tell her when she should wish to return."

"She would not ask *you* to tell her," says Luda. "She has enough sense to know that your words are not the world. Ardelle, have you had any thought for where Derwen might be?"

"At times, I think," I say.

"At which times do you think?" says Rosamond. "I would like to be there for this."

"She has gone to Deva Victrix," says Luda. Myrah's eyes open; she sits up. "She said she wished to go there with your mother and father and Isadora ahead of the ..."

Florentina hisses at Luda. Myrah strikes Luda's bent knee with her palm.

"Why did you not tell me this?" Myrah says.

"I was not to tell anyone but Ardelle, and then only if Ardelle asked me where Derwen was," says Luda.

"You know we keep no secrets from one another," says Myrah.

"Would you have me speak of such dark things to your child?" says Luda. "To Ardelle's?"

Myrah wakes the blood in her cheeks with her palms.

"I would have none of you speak," she says as she lies down. "I only wish to sleep. Come back to me with Derwen and you may thereafter leave with your man who awaits you on the northern shore." Luda's eyes widen. "Brant may leave with his Frijona whenever he wishes."

"Who told you of this?" says Luda. Her words rise with her as she stands. "Brant?"

"I heard this from Annette," says Myrah.

"Wilfrith told me," says Annette. "He speaks with Brant often enough. Do you think they should say nothing of what weighs on their hearts? Sit down."

Luda folds her arms and walks along the wall.

"They could have kept this to themselves," she says. "Myrah could have done the same with her child so we would not have to sit here and call to each other like geese about whether she bears Gerahard's gander."

My eyebrows fall to the earth. Annette pulls on my arm so that I sit upright again. She wipes my forehead clean with her fingers.

"Why did you not tell me this when you met me?" I say.

"I did not want to make your dark words to me any darker," says Luda.

"Do not be so unkind, Luda," says Annette. "We must do many things we do not like, all of us. We should stand behind one another when each of us is called on to do so."

I take my linen down at my left shoulder and lay bare the thin red wound on my neck.

"Myrah cut me with her knife and drank from it wishing to be one of us," I say.

Luda stops walking and lets her arms fall to her sides as she stares at me. Marigold feels my wound with her fingertips. Annette takes Myrah's neck in her hand and searches Myrah's half-open eyes.

"What sore sickness has befallen you?" says Annette.

"Ardelle and I are bound," says Myrah.

"In madness?" says Rosamond. "She has sworn no oath to you."

"Would you have Ardelle swear one now?" says Marigold.

"No," I say. "I would have her swear one to us."

"What?" says Rosamond.

"If Ardelle is the one who asks it, I will do it," says Myrah.

"You will?" says Rosamond.

"What would you have of me, my queen?" Myrah says.

Rosamond makes a face as though she vomits.

"Stop lying to me," I say. "Stop lying to *us.*"

"I will," says Myrah.

"I do not think so," says Rosamond.

"I shall," says Myrah.

"Then let her be one of us if she so wishes," says Rosamond, "but you must be her keeper, Ardelle."

Luda shakes her head and breathes out through her nose.

"If Ardelle lied half as well as Myrah, she would not have

needed to bring my brother here to see whether Myrah bears the mark of the black death," she says. "Rosamond was right: you are still a barefoot maid who knows nothing beyond the fields in which you clung to your mother's gown."

Luda strides through the house's opening wearing bitter grimness on her face. Where is the smiling sister who taught me to swim while Florentina looked on in laughter?

"Rosamond," says Annette.

"I did not say those things," says Rosamond.

"And if you said them using Latin words she does not understand," says Marigold, "none of us would be wiser or stronger as Myrah's man would have us believe."

I dig my fingernails into the flesh under my hair.

"Myrah needs to sleep," I say. "Let us leave her in peace."

Annette bears Florentina, made lighter without her words to weigh her down. Rosamond takes Marigold's arm; Marigold will not yield it to her. Rosamond sighs through her nose as she follows Annette. Myrah's eyes close once again. Mildred does not stir. Cold fingers take the life from my wrist.

"Why do you not go with Rosamond?" I whisper.

"She has no need of me," whispers Marigold. "I have told her once too often that our dreams have always ever been of those who go to the hidden world. She does not like that I do not dream of Gerahard."

"I dreamed of my mother and father last night," I whisper.

"I should not have told you this," Marigold whispers.

She rests her head against my shoulder.

"Have you dreamed of Myrah?" I whisper.

She lifts her head.

"No," she says. "Never. Why should I?"

"If ever you do, think of us sitting together with her like we do now, but in a many-flowered meadow beneath a spreading oak tree on a fair summer's day. Think often enough on this and we may keep her from our dark dreams."

Myrah sighs. Mildred yawns. Marigold takes a long stick from where it rests against the wall.

"Let us go out into the meadow with your daughter and think on this," says Marigold.

My daughter opens her eyes to the sun that wakes in the east as we walk towards the meadow, where Rosamond sits by herself among white and yellow flowers.

"Rosamond has not been herself of late," says Marigold. "Having heard Luda's wish to return to her homelands, Rosa talks of nothing but going back to Francia. Whether she wishes me to come with her, she has not told me."

"Why would she not take you?" I say.

"I told her I wish to have children," says Marigold. "She cares little for men who are not fair and wealthy, children less so. I would be a burden to her and her friends."

"Did you and she not both take men in the sanctuary?" I say.

"We lay with the watchmen so they would be kind to us," says Marigold.

A black steed bearing a rider clothed in the same dark hue runs towards us, slowing only when he is almost on top of us. Mildred clings to my linen as a man with a broken nose takes his friend's brown-sleeved arm from his waist and stamps the grass flat with heavy shoes. He walks to Mildred and holds her face in his rough hands, turning it from one side to the other as though he looks in his horse's mouth for missing or blackened teeth.

"She is not mine," says Gerahard. His bald head and craggy cheeks bear but a shadow of dark hair. "Had you given birth on that battlefield, she might be so old. No, Luda." He turns to face her as she draws up beside him. "I understand little of what I have seen your sisters do, but this … this goes far beyond that."

Far off to our right, Rosamond leaves the meadow, her

green gown swaying with swift strides. Luda makes a sound to Gerahard's horse and rides off after Rosamond. Gerahard goes down on one knee before me.

"You are too keen for me to keep this from you," says Gerahard. "Better that you learn it from me than someone else. I took you on that battlefield, Ardelle. The aldorman Cyneric allowed this so he could take your child as his. Where you have found the little one you hold, I do not know, but I will not forswear your right to soothe your loss however you wish. I only ask for your forgiveness. I had thought Myrah would have told you this by now, but I do not know her mind as well as one who wears her mother's beads."

Mildred turns to look at Gerahard's bowed head—she hides her face when Gerahard looks up to meet her eyes. He grins.

"Her hair is as dark as mine would be if I wore it," he says. "Her face is as fair as your sister Rosamond's. She even flees me as readily."

"So she should," I say. "Myrah must have met her match in you, for her lies are as nothing when faced with yours. What am I to forgive? You speak the words of one who has gone mad. Be at peace in your madness and I shall ask nothing but that you leave me out of it."

"I thank you," says Gerahard as he stands. His teeth are not as white as mother's. "Let us see whether Myrah is now also a mother."

He walks off towards her house. Luda comes to meet him on his steed with Rosamond's arms around her waist. He does not climb up onto his horse, but bids Luda lead him hither with a wave of his hand. Luda glares at me before walking Gerahard's horse away.

"Marigold," I say, "do you think Rosamond would go to fetch Derwen if Myrah were to thereafter let her return to Francia?"

"No," says Marigold. "Is this what they do?"

She leaves my arm and strikes her walking stick against the soft grass in earnest. I take Marigold's wrist with the hand that does not hold Mildred and lead her whither Gerahard goes, though I would on any other day follow Marigold as far from him as she would take me.

Within Myrah's house, Gerahard's queen lies with her eyes open; her faithful sisters Rosamond and Luda say nothing. Myrah sits up clutching her head in her hands. Gerahard grasps her beneath her shoulders, lifts her to her feet, and swallows her mouth with his. I step back through the opening and look for Myrah's mound so that I know where to bend over and retch.

"Ardelle," says Myrah from within.

My arms are so weak that I must set Mildred down on the ground and let her run straight through Luda's legs to the small, dark blue pots that sit on the ground against the wall behind Myrah. Let her wash her hands with as much ink as she likes if in doing so Gerahard shortens his stay among us. Rosamond sits down behind Mildred and takes my daughter onto her lap.

"Myrah would have Derwen tell her whether she bears a son," says Gerahard. "I shall ride day and night to Deva and return before the last of the aldormen have come to us. When these sons of the wolf learn that I have brought Derwen back to them, they will learn what a king is worth. And when the king's wife bears a son, she will show him to the Cantware and make them kneel before her among those they say they have bested."

"Is that why you knelt before me?" I say. My tongue and teeth burn with bitter breaths. "Did you think Constantine had given me a son? Is my daughter less worthy of love than this?"

"Were your daughter a year younger, I would hold her even as we speak," says Gerahard. "It is better that the wolves see Rosamond hold her, for they will come to know that Myrah's sisters are in sympathy with the dead. They will crawl to you on their knees and beg you to spare them; and when you send Derwen back to them, they will show you kindness for the rest of their days."

"Kindness borne out of fear," Rosamond says to the wall.

"You are keen," says Gerahard. "That is how we shall win Derwen."

"I will talk to Derwen," says Luda. "She listens to me."

"She will listen better to one she hates," says Gerahard. "Myrah, shall we bind Rosamond's ankles and tell Derwen that if she does not return, Rosamond's wrists will also be bound and she will hang from a tree?"

Rosamond stands with Mildred so quickly that Mildred nearly falls from her arms. I rush to take my daughter from her; Marigold helps me in such earnest that I give Mildred over to her hands and the reddish, beaded hair with which Mildred plays in glee.

"Tell your beloved *marhskalk* to go by himself," says Rosamond. "I shall run away with Luda."

"Bind her ankles, then," says Myrah.

"Does she ride with me?" says Luda.

"What?" says Rosamond. "Do I not stand here that you speak of me so?"

"You are the one who came here, Rosamond," says Marigold. "Derwen also chose to go where she will. If Gerahard and Luda wish to find her, they should each take a horse and ride with the wind so the hand of death can not match their stride."

Luda bows her head. Gerahard lifts her chin with his fingers. Luda strikes his hand away.

"What Marigold says is true," says Luda. "You know this, Myrah."

"And you know that if you wish to be free from your oath,

you must do as I tell you until I have freed you from it," says Myrah.

"What of me?" says Rosamond. "I wish to be free. Must I first be bound? Did you not say she is one of us, Ardelle? Why would she then do such a thing to her own kin? Why would you let her do again what she did to you when first you met her?"

"My father did that," says Myrah.

"And who does this?" says Rosamond. "Whom will you say does this in your stead?"

"I lie on the ground weary with child while I listen to one who has sworn an oath to me tell me how unfaithful she is," says Myrah. "When you return with Derwen, the binds will be taken from your ankles."

"You bind yourself to wretchedness, Ardelle," says Rosamond. "The two of you may lie together in filth and whisper dark words to one another."

"Myrah," I say, "would you give Rosamond the same kindness that you give to Luda when Rosamond has done what you ask of her?"

"You would have her go to my father and his false wife and tell them of everything we have done here?" says Myrah.

"How do you know that Gerahard does not lie?" I say.

"You have a brain," says Rosamond. "I may have been wrong about you."

"Many men seek strength in their own way," says Gerahard. "Myrah's father, in his singular wisdom, goes to greater lengths than any king I have ever known to grasp the hilt of a sword he himself has thrust into the ground and left for another to take. When he comes back to his kingdom, he will find that his daughter, whose own men would not call her atheling, has taken it up in his stead."

"I need no sword," says Myrah.

"You wield it so that others do not," says Gerahard.

So would he wield it against Rosamond while her ankles are bound in the tall grass where Luda can not see him—or does not look.

"I will go with Rosamond and watch over her," I say.

"You will watch me walk away from this madness," says Rosamond. "There is nothing to keep me from doing so."

I go to Rosamond; she shies from me as one would from a bald-headed asp who bares his fangs.

"Do as they wish," I whisper, "and I will tell Myrah to let you go back to Francia with Marigold."

"Shall I believe the words of a child who tells me she will make her mother bend to her will?" Rosamond says. "Or am I to heed the words of a madwoman who lets her queen drink the blood from her neck along with her midday meal?"

Gerahard's laughter sounds throughout the house.

"I might do the same had I my sword's thirst for blood," he says. "We leave tomorrow when the sun rises."

He does us the kindness of not swallowing Myrah's lips with his mouth before he leaves. Luda offers Rosamond her hand. Rosamond walks ahead of her in haste. Mildred sits in Marigold's lap and talks to her in a tongue that not even her mother understands. Myrah waves me to her side; when I sit, she draws me down to the ground and bids me hold her in my arms while she lies on her hip with her back to me.

"If you must go hither," she says, "know that I can not follow you though I said I would. Leave Mildred with me so she will grow to know me."

"Who will give her milk?" I say.

"I will give her mashed fish and soft fruit and warm bread," says Myrah.

"And who will watch her when you are weary with sleep?" I say. "I must take her with me."

"I will watch her," says Marigold. Mildred does not speak so well with Marigold's hair beads in her mouth. "When Rosamond returns, Myrah will free her from her oath and let her go back to Francia."

"I will?" says Myrah.

"You will," says Marigold, "for if the houses and the mead hall and the wooden horse stalls and the walls that keep the sheep were to burn to the ground, I would tell the wolves, truthfully, that you were one who told me to do this. And I am faithful to your wishes."

Myrah sighs and draws my arm around her waist.

"As you say," she says. "If this is the truth that burns within your heart, let none keep it from turning all else into ash while you yet stand. When Rosamond goes to Francia, you may go with her whether she loves you or hates you."

"Come, Ardelle," says Marigold. "Let us go to the meadow and sit in peace for the first time this day while Myrah sleeps. We may think on what we talked about."

"She stays here with me until she leaves tomorrow," says Myrah. "Her arms help me sleep. You will need to learn to watch Mildred, Maria, for if the black death you fear so much should set upon her mother, I shall have at least one daughter."

"Her daughter followed her mother when she was born," says Marigold.

"And if Mildred leaves us, I will know to follow her mother as well," says Myrah. "She is my daughter, in this life and the next. Now, let me sleep and dream that we have never talked to one another as we did today."

ROSAMOND

Between dark blue ink pots against a heap of folded bedding, I lie with Myrah's shoulders on my ribs and her hair's little rings kissing my cheeks until my fingers tire of sweeping their fickle strands away; they come to rest on her rising and falling head. All through the night and into the morning, Marigold's hearth warms Myrah well enough to let her sleep soundly. My weary eyes and falling eyelids show me nothing more and nothing less than the ashen-fleshed men among whom I lie on a field awash with the sea's gifts of foam and brine. A wan horse bearing a hooded rider in white wool strikes its hooves beside my ribs, yet my body will not stir, so heavy does it weigh against the earth. The horse's rider swings his legs from his steed's belly and straddles my hips; there, he lifts my red and white gowns above my waist. My hands do not stop him—only my eyes are free to mark the boatman, who watches us far out amid the swelling waves. The rider draws back the folds of his hood: Gerahard's raw, worm-ringed eyes stare through me from the lifeless face of Constantine's stone forefathers made hueless by the sand that blows in from the sea. The boatman shows him a bony forefinger. Gerahard's eyes burn my neck with stinging, salty tears that soften into mildness as he grasps my shoulders and thrusts himself between me under darkening clouds and a moon that runs blood red.

"Ardelle," says Luda.

She shakes my shoulder though my eyes are open. Myrah still sleeps in my arms. Marigold and Mildred lie beside one another not far from us with their heads resting on linen pillows filled with dried eelgrass from the fens' many salty banks.

"We leave now," Luda says.

"I had a dream," I say. "I think I should stay here with Myrah."

"Think all you like," says Luda. "Rosamond awaits us."

Onto the ground she drops green wool and large brass rings cleft in half by thin rods. Her feet are as bare as mine.

"Wear these," she says. "Do not be long, else Gerahard will leave without you."

I leave Mildred with a kiss for her cheek; I bid farewell to Myrah's lips though it might wake her. She answers with only a throaty sound that sends me without. Chilly dew washes my feet as I step through white and yellow blooms whose fairness lies unseen amid the morning's grim fog. Beyond them stand Gerahard, Luda, Rosamond, and three dark horses. Rosamond wears iron rings on her wrists ill-hidden by her gown sleeves.

"I thought her ankles were to be bound," I say.

"They are," says Gerahard. "Help her onto your horse. We ride."

I take the third horse's leather straps and swing my leg up over her back. Luda lifts Rosamond with wiry arms that bear the strength of two oak trees. Rosamond's head is bowed so far forwards that her chin rests against the bones of her neck. If this is how I must remember her, I have earned it.

"Ardelle, hold your fists beside your chin," says Luda. "Rosamond, set your arms over her head. Hug her from behind and do not let go, else your mare will think you weak and throw both of you."

Rosamond's head rests against my spine. Gerahard swings one leg over his horse's leather seat held in place by many straps along the length of its belly. Luda's horse wears no saddle, yet she sits on his back better than Gerahard.

"I have heard your kind ride horses well," Gerahard says to the grey-clouded heavens. "You will have to show me how this is done."

"Lead us to the stone paths before I grow a beard," says Luda.

Rosamond's wrist irons take the breath from my belly as we hasten after Luda and Gerahard. Our horses' hooves strike swiftly against the stone path that takes us south through green grasslands whose few clusters of wind-blown trees shy away from us as we ride by. We stop once at midday to eat bread and salted pike from Gerahard's leather bags and drink river water from where it flows clearest. Our mare stamps against the earth and breathes out through her nose many times to ask Gerahard for her own hay, but Gerahard does not let our horses eat and rest until the sun begins to set and we have reached a place where two stone paths run through each other.

"Ardelle will read the marker and tell us where we go," says Gerahard. "If she leads us away from Deva, my wise men will have to learn from the wolves how to lead cows to water-grass while they await us."

"Your wise men?" I say.

"Their own words," he says. "And now I will wait for a time to hear of your wisdom."

Gerahard walks his steed towards the westering sun. Luda leaves her horse's back and leads it behind her so that it stands between us and Gerahard's hairless head. She speaks to our knees.

"Brant goes north along the shore to tell our kin of the men who gather," she says. "He will ask them to flee."

"Whither would they go?" I say.

"They need time to talk of this," says Luda. "Something swells out on the sea that keeps our ships from leaving the shore."

"The boatman would find them," I say.

"And they believe you, else they would follow the rivers inland," says Luda. "The wolves welcome those who come in peace to live among them, but *that* man ..." She nods towards Gerahard. "... does not come in peace. He will come back with Derwen and send his men—men who once fought for Myrah's father among them—against my kin on the shore for having brought the black death with them this far north. When we lie slain with the sea's waves washing over our bodies, he will tell the wolves that Derwen wishes him to be their king."

"You speak as though Derwen has no words of her own," says Rosamond.

"She will not when she lies dead among us," says Luda. "Our ghostly friend Ardelle will have sent her fallen sister back to where the dead abide. Whether Gerahard sends Ardelle hither thereafter will mean nothing to the wolves, nor will they miss any of the rest of us."

"Why do they not go along the coast or through the marsh?" I say.

"The coast does not lead us north but through the marsh, which is a little sea unto itself," says Luda. "Along that sea is where Brant's wife, Frijona, has foretold that we should make our new home."

"Would Frijona not find much to speak of with Derwen?" says Rosamond.

"No," says Luda. "Derwen leaves. Frijona does not."

"Would you have Ardelle forget how to read the letters on the stone markers, then?" says Rosamond. "You wish to keep her from her daughter for your own sake?"

"She left her daughter with Myrah willingly," says Luda.

"Why, yes, my dear Luda," says Rosamond. "Is there anything Myrah could not make Ardelle do?"

"Which way?" calls Gerahard. "The sun makes its bed and so shall we."

"I do not know where Deva is," I say to myself.

"I will help you if you watch over Maria," says Rosamond.

"Does Maria not have her own words?" I say.

Rosamond lifts her head from my back. Her wrist irons draw a grunt from my belly. Her head finds my spine once more.

"She knows you will not take her to Francia," I say, "yet she won your freedom from Myrah by threatening to burn down her house."

"It is not the first time Maria has done this," Rosamond says, "but I will have no more of this. She wishes for a husband and children. I will have neither. Let her take these things and live her own life. She does not need me."

Gerahard turns his horse around and walks towards us. Luda digs her fingernails into the wool on my leg.

"Then let us not need one another," I say.

I walk our horse to the stone marker. Venta is east; Camelodonum is south. When at night my eyes were closed but would not send me to sleep, mother would hold me in her arms and tell me tales of her homelands in the far northwest until they became my dreams.

"The unmarked path to the west," I say.

"Good," says Gerahard. "You know the way as well as I do. Follow me into the trees and we will bed down in the shadows."

Amid a grove of birch trees, I help Rosamond from our

mare. Gerahard takes it with his steed into the fields to there let them eat of the tall grass and drink from the nearby river. My belly growls though I have no hunger—Rosamond takes her bound wrists from my waist by lifting her arms up over my head.

"Why does he ask me to read the markers if he knows the way?" I say.

"He wields strength like any good king," says Rosamond as she sits down. "And if we take the wrong path, he will burden you with this guilt like any good husband. It is five days there and five days back if our horses do not fall over from weariness for having walked without stopping while the sun is awake. Luda's brother should have enough time to warn his kin if he walks with a manly stride."

"How do you know these lands so well having never been here?"

"In Francia, we read books instead of burning them."

Rosamond lies down. I rest beside her with my shoulder on hers. She looks to me with a frown, holds out her iron-bound wrists before her, and sets them down against her waist.

"I lived in northern Francia near the sea until I met my friend Rigunth," she says. "She came to us one day to drink our wine. I drank only water. While her drunken friends took their men, I kept Rigunth from hurting herself. When she woke the next morning, she remembered that she liked what I had done for her, so she took me with her to Parisius. There, I watched over noble children during the day and Rigunth at night, when she and her friends would often drink themselves to sleep. While Rigunth dreamed, her mother would choke her or put ink in her wine."

"What kind of mother is that?"

"A queen who hates her daughter for going off to be wed to a man in Hispania and coming back without bride-gold to a dead father. She blamed her daughter for her husband's death. I set myself before her mother and asked her to strike me instead, which she often did. When, one morning, I sang to Rigunth, she vomited up her mother's ink-wine and thus did not die. Her mother thereafter kept me bound at the bottom of a well for a month while she thought on what to do with me. I was too useful to kill, yet I would not sing for her or share her husband's bed, so she sold me to Myrah's father."

"Her husband loved you? Is that why she hated you?"

"She wanted whatever is within me, nothing more, and I would not give it to her or her husband. You might sleep close to me this night to keep Gerahard from doing the same."

"Shut your mouths," hisses Luda from amid the darkening trees. "He comes back. If he has needs, I will see to them. Now, sleep."

Rosamond turns away and sets her back against me.

"Whatever dreams you have," she says, "I hope they are more peaceful than mine."

Our second day on horseback finds our legs aching though our mare treads a smooth stone path through grasslands whose softly sweeping hills do little to hinder us. Rosamond's head lies heavy against my back. She will not eat Gerahard's dried bread rounds well and takes only half a wooden cup of his water before spitting out a mouthful onto the ground at his feet. Gerahard threatens to make our mare run swiftly—with two on her back, she would throw us both. Rosamond talks to herself with words that sound as though she reads from one of Isadora's parchments.

The sun leads us west to where our path ends at the meeting of two of its brothers. Left takes us to Londinium and Camelodonum, while right would bear us to Lindum. Lindum must therefore be north, but I know not which of north or south brings us nearer to northwest, having gone south from the fens before we could go west. I know only that the still waters of the river to our left quicken and foam whenever I look at them, as do its cliff-headed banks grow taller.

"Why have we stopped?" Rosamond says to my back.

"The path becomes two," I say. "One of them leads north. The other leads somewhat less north. Which one should we take?"

Rosamond answers by vomiting over her right shoulder as our mare steps away from her filth.

"We will go right, then," I say.

I take our mare's leather straps and make a sound with my tongue, sending Luda's steed from the path to Gerahard's bellowing laughter.

"Are you so keen to leave one sister behind in reaching another?" he calls.

When the sun beds down and we have come to where our northern path branches off to the northwest, Rosamond wakes with a groan. Gerahard rides off the path into the grass until we are in sight of a wide river. I do not follow him hither, but lead my horse into a grove of ash trees that hide the river's water from my eyes.

"Unless you mean to make spears to hunt fish," bellows Gerahard, "your horse comes with me."

"Must we go to the river?" I say.

"We must. Bring me your mare while the sun still lights her way."

I step down from my horse and help Rosamond to the ground. Gerahard takes our mare's riding straps and leads her away. I bed down on the earth beneath stretching, leafy boughs. Rosamond moans beside me in her green wool. I take her in my arms; she buries her face in my breast as Mildred has often done. A man's laughter from among the trees lifts my head: further down the river, in the waning light of the setting sun, Luda takes off her brown tunic and leggings and follows Gerahard's clothing to the ground. I turn away and close my eyes lest what I have seen follow me into my dreams.

On the following morning, Rosamond shakes without the sun to warm her. She takes neither smoked goose nor boiled duck nor any of our small green apples flushed with a redness that has left Rosamond's face altogether.

"I have never seen her skin so snowy white," Luda whispers to me.

"Must I milk a cow for you?" says Gerahard. "Steal eggs from a hen?"

Rosamond shakes her head and waves her bound hands before her slowly. Her eyelids fall as though she has not slept.

"We have three days of riding before us," says Gerahard. "More, if one of you will not do something for her."

"Rosamond is the only one of us who can do this," says Luda.

"Why does she not heal herself, then?"

"We can not do these things to ourselves," I say.

"*Ardelle*," hisses Luda.

"Good," says Gerahard with a smile that shows his teeth. "I am glad that you find my ears as worthy as Myrah's of such knowledge. Who can heal her?"

"Derwen," I say.

"Three days," says Gerahard with a grin. "Come, let us have the horses walk the dung from their hooves."

By midday, the horses have ground their hooves well against the hard earth of rocky hills; where the old path climbs, its stones become too rough to tread. They yield at last to forgiving grasslands, wherein the road becomes smooth and rushes off to meet a bridgeless river hidden beneath the shade of bushy-boughed alder trees. Rosamond's lips find my ear.

"I must sit," she says.

"You have done so all day," I say.

"Over the river," she says.

Where Gerahard's horse walks through the water up to its knees, I tie my mare's straps around an alder's body and wave Luda over to us.

"Can you break her binds?" I whisper.

"A hundred years of water might break stone," she says. "I can do nothing for iron. If I could do this, I would have done it not long after we left. And unlike your dear sister Rosamond, I would have asked nothing in return."

"Would you speak of her so if she were your daughter?"

"None of us but you and Myrah have need to think of any such thing."

"Then I will not ask you to think of living with your own son away from all other men in a place where only snow and winter's winds tell you that you are not dreaming. You need not think of Rosamond in that hidden world, standing on the shore beyond the aldorman's mansio, where the sick who do not heal go to dwell."

"I must do it now," says Rosamond.

Luda blows a burst of wind through her lips.

"How do you wish me to help you?" she says.

"Hide her from Gerahard," I say.

Luda walks her horse through the shin-high water, setting herself between us and Gerahard where he looks out at sweeping hills from the other bank of the river. To my right and left stand trees clumped on grassy banks in the middle of the river—no boats would come to us here. I face Rosamond away from Luda, lift her gowns above her waist where she can keep them in her bound hands, and hold her with my arms. She leans against me as though she sits in a chair and breathes out through her nose loudly.

"I feel no better," she says.

I look down at her legs.

"Green," I say. "I should find something of like hue with which to clean you."

"Take some of that soapwort along the bank," she says.

"We saw this ten years ago, did we not?" says Gerahard as he walks his horse around Luda's. Luda grasps its straps with a frown. "How many of us did this take?"

"I was not in Parisius ten years ago," says Rosamond. "I would not know."

"Yet you must have heard of it," says Gerahard. "Does that *dysenteria* come to us again? Would you have me believe that the black death itself has followed us this far north so quickly? No, I think the three of you wish me to believe something else. What might that be?"

I will not ask Luda to fetch Rosamond's soapwort, so I wash her legs clean with my own hands as I did Mildred in the months after she was born. Gerahard makes a sound deep within his throat.

"Onto your mare," he says. "We ride until the horses can no longer see their own legs."

"Let us rest here until tomorrow," I say. "Rosamond will feel better when she wakes."

"*If* she wakes," Gerahard says. "That is why we ride straight to Deva. I will not ask you to read the markers for me. If you do not bring her to Derwen, you will bear the burden of whatever befalls her."

"We could bring her back to Florentina," I say.

"And thus the wolves will know that Derwen's dead sister has betrayed them," says Gerahard. "They will seek a reckoning."

"They will?" I say.

"*He* will," says Luda.

She and Gerahard stare at one another while Rosamond's weakening legs ask her to sit down in a river that rises to her knees. The boatman will bring me here in my dreams and show me her gownless body floating face down. You have done this, Ardelle. Who else could it have been?

"Then I will go with her to Francia and bury her with my own hands," I say. "I will tell Maria that I am the one who has done this to her dearest friend."

"That much will be true," says Gerahard. "She will not have died by my hand or at my wish. Come to us when you have cleaned her and we will bed down though the sun does not."

He walks off to the west. Luda does not follow. Rosamond shows me the reddish-white leaves of soapwort flowers along the river to our left. Luda holds Rosamond while I soak the leaves into a lather that cleans Rosamond's legs and my hands. Luda leads us on horseback to a stand of yew trees shrouded by waist-high bushes among which Rosamond lies down in her brine-soaked hose and watery shoes, shaking as she waits for sleep to find her. And should Rosamond's dreams take her to that river beneath the boatman's blood moon, I will be the one to draw her up from its mossy bed and return her to the waking world.

In my own dreams, I walk hand in hand with Mildred through a field of summer's brightest purple corn-cockles under billowing white clouds that ward us against the sun's strength. Mild winds cool us as far-off men swing their long-bladed scythes through great swathes of wildflower-dotted hay. Amid them stands Rosamond. I sing her name; Mildred runs ahead of me; Rosamond walks to meet her with the slow steps of ankles still bound by iron. Before Mildred stands a blade-bearing, shirtless man with his head to the ground. I call to my daughter sharply, bidding her return to her mother, but she does not listen—the scythe's haft sends her into the tall hay. I run to where my daughter lies amid the tall grass drying beneath the summer sun. I take her neck in my hand: her cheeks have become high and angled where they should be soft and round; her hair is brown and tangled where it should be black and wavy; her open, lifeless eyes are the colour of oak trees where I have always known them to be hued as the southern sea. Her mouth opens, as do her eyes, as do mine.

I have seen this high-cheeked face before, though not smeared with earth and glistening with sweat that stinks of leaves. Her wild, unbraided hair has been shorn not far below her shoulders; her long fingers thread sharp nails into the strands of hair hanging over my forehead and sweep them away.

"Derwen," I say. "What have you done to your hair?"

"I buried it beneath the broken stones of Constantine's mansio," she says.

Rosamond sits beside me resting her forehead against her folded arms on top of her bent knees. At her feet lie the shards of her iron binds. Gerahard steps out from where he stood hidden.

"How is it that we are so fortunate to meet your sister Derwen on the stone path but three days after leaving to find her?" he says. "She even wears the same green hue as you and Rosamond. Your sister Luda says you do not speak to one another through the heavens. What am I to believe?"

"I felt as though I should come back," says Derwen.

"Where are my mother and father?" I say.

Derwen stares at me.

"I do not know," she says.

Luda turns away from my eyes. Darkening clouds above weep misty tears.

"Luda would not tell me," I say, "and now you say you do not know. Take me to where they are in Powys."

"They are not in Powys," says Derwen, "nor is anyone else. Men speak of the death that comes to them from the sea. I did not stay to welcome it, yet I have found it in the houses south of the stone path from which I took hens' eggs and cooked hare. Do not go looking for death, Ardelle. Wait until it has left us."

"As we were made to wait in our sanctuary bedrooms," I say. "Tell me again the wisdom of having done this."

"Myrah's father's greatest wisdom was in leaving," says Derwen. "His mind shows him a world that is other than what everyone else sees. He has gone to it. Do not follow him there. You will see your mother and father again in time."

"Derwen is wise," says Gerahard. "The kin of the wolf await you. They have missed you dearly."

Black clouds shower us with heavy, stinging drops.

"I go to them for the sake of my sisters," Derwen says. "Nothing more."

Gerahard almost falls from his horse. He bends one knee before Derwen. I swallow in earnest to keep myself from vomiting. Luda hangs her head.

"Forgive me for having spoken so," he says. "I know not which of you has brought this rain to us, nor will I ask. The wolves and their queen only wish you to stay the hand of death that has driven them from their homes in the uplands."

"Myrah is not their queen," says Derwen. "Has she fallen ill that you wet yourself before us?"

Gerahard stands; the black wool on his left leg bears the gift of rain-soaked grass.

"Myrah is with child," Luda says.

"Whose?" says Derwen.

"Gerahard's."

"Willingly?"

"So Myrah says."

"Then I will go to them and bless their worship for Myrah's sake," Derwen says.

"So you will do nothing to him even after he told Myrah he wished to hang Rosamond in those binds from a tree?" says Luda.

"Mere words," says Gerahard. "I have nothing but words to make you see the truth of what needs to be done."

"Words and iron," says Derwen.

"Myrah let him do this," says Luda.

"As did you," Rosamond says to her knees.

"When first I came to Myrah's father," I say, "Myrah sent Annette to do the same to me."

"I should not have given her that name," says Rosamond as she stands in haste. "Let us go back. I will ask Luda's kin to leave me in Francia when they sail away along the coast."

"They have gone," says Luda with quickened speech. "There are none to ask."

"Francia?" says Derwen.

"Why do you care?" says Rosamond.

"Has the black death taken your oaths as well?" Derwen says.

"Myrah frees us," says Rosamond. "We have only to bring you back to her. But you, Ardelle, I know not how you would free yourself from one who cut open your neck and drank of your life-water. Myrah says she is thus one of us, Derwen. She and Ardelle are bound together by madness."

"Timor mortis," says Derwen.

"So you say," says Rosamond.

"No," I say. "Myrah will follow me and my daughter unto death."

Derwen looks into my eyes as the rain soaks our hair and clothing. She steps towards Rosamond, who holds her hands up at her waist as if to yield. Derwen sets her arm around Rosamond's shoulders. Rosamond's wary hands find Derwen's back. Derwen sets a kiss on Rosamond's cheek and rests her chin on Rosamond's shoulder. Rosamond looks to me with wide, frowning eyes.

"Where is Ardelle's child?" Derwen says.

"With Myrah," says Rosamond.

"And Marigold," I say.

"Why is Marigold not on your arm?" says Derwen.

"She did not want to be bound at the wrists and ankles," says Rosamond.

"Shall I kill him for what he has done?" says Derwen.

"Yes," growls Luda. "Do it."

Gerahard steps back from us and draws his long hunting knife from its belt sheath. Thunder from afar shatters its iron into shards that fall to the ground among chilling raindrops. He tosses the bladeless hilt to the earth. His eyes meet mine; his face wears a grimness I have not seen on him.

"Should I?" Derwen says to Rosamond.

"Yes," says Rosamond. "He is the one who made me ill."

"I have not the strength to turn weapons into dust," says Gerahard, "nor to call flooding rains, nor do I have the blessing of death to do to you what you would do to me."

"Ardelle?" Derwen says over her shoulder. "Shall I kill this man for what he has done?"

So that I may stand on the shore with Gerahard's flesh rotting beneath his wool hued as the boatman's clothing? He will tell me that I have slain yet another in his stead and must therefore sit with wrists and ankles bound in his boat as he brings men from the shore into the mists beyond the sea forever.

"Gerahard," I say, "where is your mother?"

"Beneath the earth in Tornacum," he says. "Sickness took her ten years ago, the same one I saw in your sister Rosamond. I thought Derwen somehow knew and thus came to us, but it seems your good fortune is not to be mine."

"What fortune?" I say. "We have done to this ourselves. The men you call the wolves did not send us here. Myrah did. You did. The northmen did. Our own men did, the ones who will not take Myrah as their atheling. So let us give them their king, even those who have no need of one."

Derwen sets her hand on Rosamond's cheek, then goes to Gerahard and takes his hand.

"Stay away from Rosamond and Luda," she says. "I will ride with you to Myrah."

"Good," he says and helps her onto his steed.

Gerahard leads us through the rain so swiftly that it no longer touches Rosamond. Our mare does not throw us as Gerahard threatened, but matches the strides of her brother and sister with seeming glee.

"Why does he still live?" Rosamond says to my ear.

"I am not his keeper," I say. "I will not stand before the boatman with him."

"Would you have been my keeper?" she says.

"I would be in the hidden world with you even now. My daughter would follow me. Myrah would wake without Mildred and use her knife to follow us. Together, we would board that boat and sail into the mists."

Rosamond grasps her own wrists and holds them tightly against my waist.

"You have learned to lie so well that I believe you," she says. "Whatever bond you think you share with Myrah, you are welcome to believe in kind, but know this: the only gift she bears is that of binding others to her will."

OATHBREAKER

Thick raindrops soak our woollen clothing, weighing down our mare's steps against broken stones that no longer stab into her feet. The path's rough rocks instead swim in their own little pools of rainwater given to us by thundering black storm clouds that darken the summering sky into nightfall. Derwen helps us empty Gerahard's leather bags of the last of their bread and meat, whereafter he and Luda head off to hunt the hares who hide from the weather in their shallow dens. Our mare rests beneath the thick-leafed boughs of a thirsty oak tree while we warm ourselves beside a stone-ringed fire of dead twigs. Luda and Gerahard return with hens and chicks—they would not have taken these from men who still lived.

"Luda has not murdered him," Rosamond hums to my ear.

"Why do you bring the children?" I say to Gerahard.

"Children?" says Gerahard. "These little hens will die without their mothers. They live to be eaten."

"You know nothing of hens," I say. "They do not need their mothers."

"Forgive me," says Gerahard with an arm-sweeping bow. "The fields are not my home. Take them back, if you wish."

"I do not know where you found them," I say.

The chicks thus cook with their mothers over our fire. I take less than half the flesh of one grown hen; Derwen takes the other half. Rosamond will not eat them, but colours her lips red with the strawberries she picks from green-stemmed yellow and white flowers. As we ride again, I tell myself I must not dwell on whether those chicks would have grown to be as fat as their mothers if I had not brought Gerahard here to meet them.

By the third day of our return, our horses' steps have slowed from weariness amid rain showers that come and go. Our mare's neighing and bucking hind legs tell us that we are to walk beside her lest we learn from her whether we fly as well as birds. Gerahard's ash-hafted spear lands in wet-haired hares who must have mistaken the day's dark clouds for dusk's feeding time. He takes their hind legs for himself with glee; Rosamond softens her meat with strawberries. Derwen says nothing as she chews, nor does she look at anything but her own hands. Luda sits with her back to us as her horse wanders through tall grass, eating its fill where its rider will not.

At midday, the rain leaves us and does not return. Luda stands with her arms folded before the stone marker at the meeting of two paths whose northern road leads to Myrah.

"The wolves have named those houses Queen's Rest," says Gerahard.

"Who gives a name to a house?" says Derwen.

"Men who do not live there," says Gerahard with a laugh. "They built those houses and that mead hall without walls where the hard rocks rest above the sea for you and your sisters. When they flood during this year's harvest, they wish us to be elsewhere."

"You lie well," says Luda over her shoulder, "but we will make it truth."

"You and they are of like mind," says Gerahard. "Let us go to your kin and see whether we do not hear their howling in the evening's dusk."

We do not, for Gerahard has need of Luda's legs once more, and what we hear is enough to make Derwen sleep with her palm over the ear that does not rest against the earth.

Morning's sun drives the clouds from the heavens and lets our woollen gowns breathe in the mild winds that blow in from the little marsh-sea. Here and there, cows eat from watery grass watched over by brown-clothed men bearing long rods of the same hue. Beyond them stand great wooden walls on higher ground in which the cows must sleep at night. Where the stone path comes to an end, the western sea's shore greets us much closer than I remember. There, on the grassy fields before our houses, stand and sit many men bearing spears and shields and long knives as they talk to one another amid a sea of horses and carts and pots and barrels. Gerahard rides off to meet them with Derwen on his waist; when he alights from his horse, he bears Derwen to the ground so softly that she seems to float. The men stop speaking and listen as Gerahard's words call out to them.

"Give me your horse," Luda says with her own mare's straps still in her hand.

"Take it," I say in weariness. "This time, leave Rosamond with me."

Rosamond waves away Luda's offered hand. As soon as Rosamond's feet are on the grass, Luda is on her mare's back holding the straps of ours. She makes a sound with her tongue, sending her mare walking east away from Gerahard and his brothers. Our mare neighs and sways her head but follows her sister soon enough.

"Ma ma ma."

Mildred's words come to me over the field from Myrah's black-sleeved arms. Myrah runs to us, meeting my cheek with a hand warmed by Marigold's fire. Mildred stares at me but does not take my arms, even when Myrah stands close to me and places Mildred's hand against my face. I talk to my daughter's ear and give kisses to her cheeks; Myrah answers for her by kissing my lips with an earnestness that sends a shaking through the ground. Mildred clings to Myrah's gown. The men gathered before Gerahard's outstretched arms yell oaths to the clouds as they go down onto their knees. Women step down from the raised floors of their houses; on seeing Derwen, they run to her and kneel at her feet. Some of them hold her legs or set their hand on her back; others take her wrist and kiss her fingers. Gerahard rests his hand on Derwen's shoulder as one would a horse's saddle. Derwen heeds nothing of what they do—her eyes burn holes into Myrah's wool until Gerahard speaks to her. Derwen turns away and sends mother's tongue into the heavens.

"Do they understand her?" I say.

"If she speaks slowly and uses small words," says Myrah. "Annette understands them well enough but will not speak their tongue."

"Nor would I among men who had kept me for twenty years," says Rosamond.

"Let us take Rosamond to Florentina," I say. "She fell ill as we rode."

"I am not ill," says Rosamond.

"Nor will you be if I must bear you to the southern shore," I say.

"As you say," says Rosamond with a sigh.

Within the timber walls of Myrah's house, Annette sits beside a table and reads to Marigold in whispered words from a sheaf of bookfell. Opposite her, Florentina's inkless fingers wield a white writing feather with long, flowing strokes.

"You write again?" I say.

They look up as one. Only Florentina smiles.

"I am glad to see you as well, dear mother," she says. "The northmen were kind enough to bring us those things our own men would not."

"When we are north of the northmen, they are not northmen," says Annette.

"Forgive me for having forgotten that everything is north of Hispania," says Florentina. "Shall I howl like a wolf for you?"

"My dreams are dark enough," says Annette. "Where are your shoes, Rosamond?"

Rosamond sits down with her back against mine and her bare feet on the rock-strewn earthen floor. Marigold does not stir. Florentina, however, sets down her writing feather and sends herself from her chair towards me. Mildred stares at her from Myrah's lap. I take Florentina onto my legs; the yellow rings of her long hair rest against my shoulder.

"Mine," says Florentina.

"No," says Mildred.

At once, Mildred leaves Myrah's arms and shoves Florentina's shoulder with her little hands. Florentina yields to her strength and watches with a smile as Mildred takes back her mother's lap.

"Mine," Mildred says.

Our laughter ends when a mighty sounding against the house's walls shakes the timber. Derwen comes within, shaking her hand at her wrist as if seeking to rid it of something.

"The men have chosen Gerahard to be their king," she says.

"Which men?" says Rosamond.

"Did you not see them when you came here?" says Florentina.

"I must ask him of the wedding," says Myrah.

She leaves in haste. Derwen follows, sweeping her hand to shut a door that is not there. Within me, something also closes, and in doing so opens anew the wound of Myrah's bitter kiss when she told me of the king she must have. He is here now, singing to his men as Florentina does to Rosamond with words whose strength he does not understand. Yet where Florentina holds Rosamond's wrists against her waist and sings to her turned cheek, Gerahard's men bind themselves to him freely and breathe in the life of his speech, as though they had not lived until he came to them.

"Florentina," I say. "Let go her wrists."

"Why?" she says.

"Derwen healed her," I say. "She waits for the black death to leave so she can return to Francia."

"Return?" says Florentina as she lets fall Rosamond's wrists. "To those who sold you so they can sell you again? That is an illness I can not heal. They may even thank you for their wealth by doing you the kindness of not killing you."

When Myrah returns, she does us the kindness of not making the house's walls shake before she steps in through its opening.

"We shall be wed on the morrow," she says. "Though the men are not yet fully gathered, we shall go on without them, for those that are not yet come must have fallen ill."

"And yet you smile," says Rosamond. "Have you no thought for the wives and children of those who have *fallen ill*?"

"Shall I hang my head and still my speech for every man who has died this last month?" says Myrah. "Were I to do so, I might never laugh or sing or wed again. Must I show them that I am their kindred by living as though I, too, am dead?"

"No," says Annette as she stands. "Show them that you will know the same happiness they did when they were wed and watched the birth of their own children." Annette smiles at me. "Live for them the life they will not have."

"I will," says Myrah. "And so will you."

"What?" says Annette.

"Wed your man Wilfrith beside us," says Myrah.

Annette lifts Myrah with the strength of ten men towards the thatched roof. When Myrah's feet find the earth again, she and Annette lead each other about as if they were children stamping through wet grass after a heavy rainfall.

"I must tell Wilfrith of this," says Annette.

"Take me! Take me!" says Florentina.

Annette leaves Florentina without a word and rushes through the door, striking her shoulder against Luda's as she runs. Luda stands in the house's opening with her hands under her shoulders.

"Are we all to wed now?" she says.

"Those of us who do not *leave* may be made to do so," says Rosamond.

"The wolves took my horses," says Luda. "They say they need them to bear food and drink for tomorrow's wedding."

"As though they do not have enough," says Rosamond. "Where is Brant?"

"I only know where he is *not*," says Luda.

"Luda is right," says Myrah. "He should be with his wife. If you wish to wed, Luda, you may do so with us."

"Raginhari has been husband to me since I met him," says Luda. "I need not wed him twice."

"Twice?" says Myrah. "You did not ask me once."

"You said you would let us leave," says Rosamond. "Did Ardelle not have you swear an oath or was that also a lie?"

"You knew of Gerahard and what he does before you went with him on my behalf," says Myrah. "And now you must wait as we did in our sanctuary bedrooms until the threat of death has left us. I will not send you south to Francia and bear the burden for your death, even if you wish it on yourself."

"Am I so dear to you?" says Rosamond.

"I told Gerahard I would bear this burden," I say. "You need not worry."

"*That* is why I worry," says Myrah. "Your burdens are mine, much as your blessings are also mine."

"My husband and I should not need anything more than your blessing, then," says Luda.

"Do you not have ears?" says Myrah. "The men have chosen Gerahard to be their king. If you—"

"I did not choose him to be my king," says Luda.

"Then take your brooding elsewhere," says Myrah. "I wish to be among those who share in my happiness."

Luda offers Rosamond her hand. Rosamond takes it and follows her without. Myrah sits down beside me and tickles Mildred under her chin. Mildred shrinks into herself with sharp laughter.

"I would have everyone share in this happiness," Myrah whispers. I look to her; she kisses me. "I will need to spend this night with Derwen."

Heat floods my body. An unseen hand spins the handle of a quern that grinds my brain into dust.

"Might you speak to her for me?" says Myrah. "I think she would listen to you."

"Why in the world do you ask me to do this?" I say.

"Before she left us, the wolves watched what she did, even when she did not wish them to," says Myrah. "They will know that she and I have done this. They will think me a kindred spirit to her. You know better than anyone else what that means."

Soft laughter comes to us from where Florentina sits beside Marigold.

"There she is," says Florentina. "She had not shown herself

for so long. Her spirit has only now come here from her father's sanctuary."

Myrah's smile leaves her. She turns to Florentina.

"Come and cut my hair," says Florentina with a face of stone. "I will choke the life from you."

Marigold sits between Myrah and Florentina so that neither can see the other.

"Free us from our oaths as you said you would," says Marigold. "We brought Derwen to you."

"I ..." Myrah takes her arms from my daughter. "I mean to have Ardelle speak with Derwen and ask her to tell the wolves that I am Derwen's kin."

"Are you her daughter, now?" says Florentina. "Or another of her dead sisters?"

"How would Ardelle do this?" says Marigold.

"I know not how," says Myrah. "I know that Derwen will listen to her. Ardelle will make her understand. Ardelle, tell Florentina and Marigold that they misunderstand me."

Mildred's sweaty hand takes the heat from my cheek. I hold my daughter against me and kiss her on the temple though my heart aches.

"Fetch the others," I say to Myrah. "I will tell all of them."

While Myrah is gone, I sway back and forth with my daughter as Marigold's waxing fire threatens to throw itself beyond its stone ring onto the earth-hidden rocks. Derwen leads Luda, Rosamond, and Annette through the house's opening. Annette is the only one of them who looks at Myrah. Rosamond hides behind Luda. Myrah takes Annette's waist in her arms. Annette starts, then sets her arm on Myrah's shoulders with a laugh when she sees that Myrah's black gown sleeves are not snakes.

"Tell them, Ardelle," Myrah says.

"Myrah said I am the dead sister of Derwen come to seek a

reckoning among the living for having taken Derwen from the dead," I say.

"And they believe her," says Derwen. "This is why Myrah still lives."

"Luda says Gerahard will kill her kin on the shore," I say.

Luda's eyebrows darken; her lips narrow as she glares through my eyes into the back of my head.

"Your king said that if we could not make Derwen come back, he would hang Rosamond from a tree, much as you sent Annette to me in the hypocaust to threaten my mother."

"Ardelle, I am sorry," says Annette with a heavy outbreath. "Have you still not forgiven me for this?"

"Rosamond would only show me the way to Deva if I would watch over Marigold in her stead."

"Am I nothing more to you than one who must be watched?" says Marigold.

"Derwen said there were many empty houses not far from the stone path that led us to Deva. Myrah said that any of our men who were not here must also be dead. I am the one who went to Deva; I am the one who came north with Brant along the stone path. When at night I dream of death, it follows me wherever I go."

"Do you really think our dark dreams are true?" says Florentina.

"Mine are," I say. "And now we have no secrets, for this is the way of things. Which of you feels at peace for having learned the way of things?"

"I asked you to tell them of how they misunderstand me," says Myrah. "You have told us of how you misunderstand us, and of how I have misunderstood you most of all."

"Our dead kin do not lie in those stone graves," I say. "Your father kept us hidden away to starve us into obedience. He sent me home from that battle for having lain above the earth instead of beneath it. Were I his son, he would love me better than your mother."

"*Ardelle*," says Myrah. "What is wrong with you?"

"Gerahard will do the same to you when Derwen augurs a daughter for you."

"You do not know that," says Florentina.

Luda grunts and lets her folded arms fall to her sides.

"She does not need to," she says. "None of us will bear sons. In this, we are kin."

"No," I say. "We are kin in hating one another. If Myrah wishes us to understand her love, she will free all of us from our oaths. Any who stay with her thereafter may do so out of love."

"What love?" Rosamond says to herself.

Myrah holds her own wrist and looks at her shoes.

"Whither would you go?" she says.

"To the southern sea," says Rosamond, "so that I might at least be within sight of the land of my birth when death takes me."

"I will go with Ardelle to Halja," Marigold says to the ground.

"I should not have taught you that word," says Florentina.

"I stay here with Myrah and Mildred," I say.

"As will I," says Florentina.

Annette and Luda say nothing. Myrah hangs her head.

"I …," she begins.

"Stand tall when you speak," says Luda. "Like your father would."

Myrah lifts her head and straightens her back with a grunt.

"I free you from your oaths," she says.

Luda leaves. Rosamond follows. Derwen takes Rosamond's arm and walks with her. Florentina and Annette whisper to one another. Marigold holds out her hand to me. I take it.

"Shall I go with Rosamond to the sea?" I say.

"Why do you hate yourself?" says Marigold. "You have done nothing."

"Have I? My dreams show me otherwise."

"As did those of Myrah's father show him otherwise," whispers Marigold.

I return her hand. Myrah will not look at me, nor does she mark Mildred, who sets her little hand on Myrah's jaw.

"Myrah," I say. Her eyes meet mine. "When you go to speak to Derwen, you might begin by asking her why she was so willing to call the earth for your king after breaking open Constantine's head with a stone and thrusting a knife into his heart."

Myrah's wide eyes stare at me from beneath a frown. She leaves us to a house whose burning hearth has dimmed to cooling embers.

GERAHARD

At eventide, the wind blows Rosamond into the house and throws her arms around Marigold. Marigold starts but does not lean away from Rosamond's whispers.

"No," says Marigold loud enough to wake my sleeping daughter. "I will not leave."

"She will tell Myrah what we say," says Rosamond.

I take Mildred into my arms and rock her back and forth. Her heavy eyelids close.

"And?" says Marigold.

"And Myrah will forget that she has freed us."

Marigold leaves Rosamond's arms and takes up her walking stick from where it lies beside Myrah's dark blue ink pots. Rosamond reaches for Marigold's wrist. Marigold frowns; her knuckles shake; her walking stick becomes alight with reddish-blue flames.

"Send Myrah here," she says. "I will ask her whether she wishes to keep her house."

"She does," says Rosamond and takes Marigold's walking stick with her bare hand. Her shriek draws a cry from Mildred.

The burning tree bough falls into the hearth's glowing embers. Marigold is beside Rosamond, feeling for Rosamond's gown and arms as Rosamond clutches her own wrist.

"Take us to Florentina," says Marigold.

Rosamond's reddened palm leads them through the house's opening. Thereafter, my daughter finds sleep where I do not. When night comes, Myrah does not return. I should look for her without but find her instead within my thoughts. She lies down with us among the wheat stalks in the setting sun's amber glow and takes off her gowns, yet when I have shed my own and turn onto my hip to kiss her, she is gone. All through the night, I wander the rows in search of her but find only my own earth-caked feet. When morning comes, I should be glad for not having found her body, but I have also not found sleep. The whirling wind that brings Florentina into Myrah's house on Annette's back rushes up towards the clouds along with my endless thoughts.

"Annette readies herself endlessly," says Florentina when Annette has left. "I do not see why anyone should wish to bind themselves to another."

"Is Marigold still with Rosamond?" I say.

"If Rosamond still remembers that they are friends, she may be," says Florentina.

"Did they not come to you for healing?"

"They did not, for they know I have no wish to become as well known among these wolves as I was among wifeless men in Emerita. Now, dear mother, I must ask you something wretched, and you must not fright: have you never shortened your hair?"

Before I can answer, she sits behind me with her hands on my shoulders, as if to calm me. From beneath my linen gown she takes thick handfuls of hair and runs her fingers through them to smooth their many knots. Thereafter, she weaves them together, pulling harder than she needs to against the back of my head. Mildred is awake; she goes to Florentina to watch what Florentina does. I take my daughter into my lap and stroke my fingers softly through her dark hair, letting my fingertips fall onto the back of her neck. She shrugs and laughs, then asks me to do it again.

"I would have my hair grow to be as long as my mother's," I say. "Would you give up yours?"

Florentina makes a sound with her tongue and is thereafter silent. When her hands find my shoulders again, my hair rests pulled away from my forehead into a long, thick braid behind which two thin braids from each ear come together and bed down amid a nest of hair that flows to the ground.

"The rain has washed it well," Florentina says. "Myrah would have us find sea rose or soapwort—any purple flower, I think—and bathe ourselves for her wedding."

"Bathe where?"

"Have you not seen where we are? The sea, a river, a stream, a mere."

"And which of those is too shallow for a boat bearing a man?"

"Ah, yes, your friend."

From without comes a great bellowing: a man speaks loud enough to be heard out on the sea. His answer comes from a woman as loud as he.

"It seems two of them have wed without telling us," says Florentina. "Bear me hither so I can eat honeyed bread and watch them swear their oaths at one another."

"I thought I was not be seen," I say.

"The men come together to drink mead today," says Florentina. "Neither a wedding nor a ghost will keep them from this."

I take her onto my back, leaning forwards as I hold her left leg with my left arm and Mildred's little fingers in my right hand. My daughter's short steps follow us into the morning's wind bearing salt and sheep's wool and strong words that do not come from the sea of men and horses gathered in the meadow, but from the mead hall without walls not far from our houses, which now rest but a stone's throw from the marsh-sea's flooding shore. As we near the open long house, Gerahard and Luda's words become bitter. If they call too loudly, the boatman out on the sea might heed them well.

"Why do they speak to each other so?" I say.

Luda's sharp words take flight over the thatched roofs of the houses. Another man—is that Brant?—speaks to her softly, yet her wrath bursts forth into the heavens once again, sending a flock of cranes in flight. Behind them hides Annette in a blue gown that might once have been mine; behind her, a black shape that must be Myrah.

"I think Luda may be angry that Brant stayed here with Myrah instead of going to his wife," says Florentina.

"Does Luda think he would have lain with Myrah?" I say.

"What?" says Florentina. "Did you lose your brain somewhere in the marsh water? And have you never listened to Luda when she is not yelling? She wants a son, as does Annette. I think … yes, I think Derwen must have augured a son for Myrah."

"So why do they not leave and have their sons elsewhere?" I say.

"Have you seen the swelling waves out on the sea that break ships into timber?" says Florentina.

"No," I say.

"Neither have I. And as well we should not. They will take our houses soon enough."

I quicken my steps. Mildred runs beside me. A great roof shields many long benches and tables from both the sun and the rain, though I know not why they would have forgotten to build walls. Florentina sits down on a bench and lifts Mildred into her lap. From behind one of the long hall's many thick posts, Derwen shows herself wearing yellow and white flowers in her hair. Where Brant stands before me, Derwen comes to stand behind me.

"Why are you here?" she whispers. "None must see you."

"These men think that death comes to us from the south," Gerahard says to me, "but those men near the western stone path from whom we took hens were also dead. They hid from what comes. We shall not. I knew of those Geatish men on the northern shore before Myrah told me of them."

Annette steps before Myrah to shield her from Luda's glare. Among Gerahard's wretched words nests but one truth: we must not hide.

"Myrah," I say. "Luda told you to stand tall."

Myrah breathes out sharply and shoves Annette away with one arm. She stands upright and meets Luda's stare.

"Good," says Gerahard. "This is how you must stand when those men and their Danish friends come to take our harvest after death has thinned us and our strength withers."

"Sledda's aldormen say they traded well with our kin before they came up here," says Brant. "I tell you again: they bear you no ill will."

"Why must one bear ill will against those whom death will take whether they flee or stand fast or fight?" says Gerahard. "Why spend men taking sheep and cows when they are given to you?"

"Their lands have flooded," says Luda. "Last year's harvest was weak. They only seek food and a place to live in peace."

"And they have sought these for half a year, coming to my men only when that black death drives them to us," says Gerahard. "I know what you say is not true, for I saw those Geatish men and their twine-bound beards with my own eyes among Sledda's fighting men. They were to be given your fields when Athelbert yielded to them, yet they took nothing when their lord bowed down before the might of your sisters."

"There are enough birds and fish among the flooded grass here for ten times our men," says Luda.

"Yet you do not tell me that I have misspoken," says Gerahard.

"Derwen is with us," says Luda. "Is that not enough for you?"

"When we found Derwen," says Gerahard, "it rained day and night until we reached this place you call Queen's Rest and you found another horse to take you and your brother north along the shore. And yet on that southern battlefield beside the sea, where Cyneric lost many men and many of my brothers fell to spears, the sea's waves did nothing to swallow those who slew them, for you knew that your kinsmen were among them."

Luda looks down at the ground with her jaw clenched. Brant sets his arm around her waist.

"She was not the one who threw a spear into my breast," I say. "She did not give me a child."

Gerahard will not look at me, nor is his answer meant for my ears.

"How might that day have been brighter if you had done what your king had asked of you?" he says. "It is well that Myrah has freed you from your oath. She should not call 'sister' one who does not love her better than any other yet stays here wishing for herself what will never be." He turns to Myrah. Myrah returns his stare. "Your brother at least knows the truth of this. Brant may take a horse and find his woman along the shore. Ride behind him, if you like, and when you reach your man, tell him that what he would find among the wolves is little better than the black death that sweeps through the south."

"Will you swear not to harm them?" says Luda.

"I will swear nothing to one whose oath is worthless. Myrah, I take the wisdom of our men now. If there are any left among your sisters whose words are better than dung, you might do the same with them." He looks to my neck. "If I were you, I would first ask the one who wears your mother's beads."

Gerahard turns and walks towards the southern meadow in which men stand gathered. Derwen steps away from me.

"If you are not his queen when he is between your legs," she says to Myrah, "what are your words worth to him?"

In the western marsh stands a straight, thin, sturdy black tree like the haft of a spear. It belongs to the white-boned hand of a fleeting ghost given shape by dark wool the hue of Gerahard's black tunic and leggings and shoes. That staff takes what it will without heed for any man's weightless words—only the earth shaking beneath their feet might be enough to make them understand this.

"I need no words to make him listen," I say. "Nor do you."

The wind bears my thoughts to Gerahard. His stone face and woollen clothing return to us reeking of ox hides.

"I hear you," he says to me. "I am listening."

"What do you wish him to hear?" Myrah says.

Her bare words grip my heart and chill my mind's endless dreaming into blissful stillness. Where there is neither thought nor speech nor life, where she and I hold each other in our arms beneath the ice-frosted sea forever, there love abides.

Yet the boatman watches us from above through the ice. His staff shatters the sea's bedding into shards and takes me from Myrah's lifeless arms onto the shore, where I am made to crawl with the end of the boatman's rod between my shoulders towards the fleshless bones of deer that lie on their backs with their forelegs at their sides. Their hoarse cries flood my heart with—no, these are men. The slain men. But they can not be men. Something pulls at my hand. A child. Dark, flowing hair. Green-grey linen.

Mildred.

The boatman waves me towards him with fingers of bone and ice. I take my daughter—no, I will not—and bring her to him. Her face is no longer hers. I will not look at her. Can he make her whole? I will not send her beneath the sea with Myrah. Yes, she might be made whole like Sithebad.

She is in the boatman's arms. I do not want this. He sends his ship from the shore and drifts off into grey, cloudless emptiness. Hands are on my forearms, my neck, the flesh of my face. The men have arisen. Their flesh is whole, their bearded faces smiling. They speak kind words to me, some of them in Luda's tongue I only half-understand. One of them says my name.

"Ardelle."

Mildred pulls at my hand. I stare at her ruddy cheeks and forehead sweaty with the sun's warmth. Florentina lifts her up to me. My arms take her.

"Hateful words make their home in this mead hall, where men should drink and laugh and watch their friends run naked around wheat fields," I say. "This is as it should be, for death watches over them from the sea. Nothing they do will keep him from them."

"We are like to those Geatish men in the end, this is true," says Gerahard. "Luda need not take you to those empty houses and show you the earth whereunder men and their wives and children hide from that which has long since found them. So, tell me: what would death have of me? Am I to wait for him to come to me, or does he call me to him?"

"Ardelle," says Luda. She leaves her brother's arm. Her hands come to rest on my back and my daughter's. Her eyes are wet with the weight of her words. "Tell him that death has no love for him."

"Death has no love," I say. "I need not tell him what he knows."

"What if my kin had found you on a battlefield?" says Luda. "What if your mother were among them?"

"Do not talk to her like that," growls Derwen.

"That is the tale Myrah's father told you," says Luda. "One of many. Your father fought for him and found you among their slain foes. He starved us in our bedrooms. He wished us dead at that battle. Which of those are lies? Do we need know? Tell yourself that your mother and father await you on the northern shore seeking to live here in peace among men who will love them for being kin to strength that makes them whole again after five hundred years of unspoken emptiness within their hearts. What will you tell this man who hates them to make him see otherwise?"

Nothing. There are no words he would not wrest to the ground and choke into breathlessness.

I set my daughter in Myrah's arms. Myrah's knife I draw from its leather sheath on her belt. I take Florentina's thick-braided gift to my hair at the nape of my neck and hold Myrah's knife behind my back against my spine.

"Derwen," I say. "Do to me what you have done to yourself."

The knife leaves my fingers. My hand falls to my side. My hair pulls against the skin on my head once, twice, thrice. Derwen sheathes Myrah's knife. She winds fourteen years of my hair around her wrist. The other five are so light that I feel about my head to see whether they are still there. The little braids beside each ear sway freely in the soft wind. Derwen looks to me.

"Give it to him," I say.

Derwen does not throw it at him, but sets it against his breast until his hands rise to take it.

"This is a token of my mother's strength," I say. "You may

keep it as my blessing for your wedding. In return, you will swear an oath not to harm my sisters or their kin."

Gerahard winds my braid around his arm as Derwen did. He bends one knee.

"I will not harm your sisters or their kin," he says. "This, I swear. I also swear to offer stability in your father's absence, Myrah. Your sister Rosamond's western king would know that his trade with the Cantware thrives under the watchful eye of a strong leader. When your father returns, I shall step aside."

"You need not speak of those who do not wish to be here," says Myrah. "Let us make ready for our wedding."

Gerahard smiles and hastens towards the meadow where men have gathered. He does not wait for Myrah, nor does Myrah follow him. She returns my daughter and takes my earth-caked fingernails in her hands.

"Find some shallow marsh where boats can not come to you," she says. "Wash your hands and face and feet. Pick flowers for your hair and for Mildred's when none are looking."

Myrah meets Derwen's eyes. Derwen looks away. Myrah's lips are on mine and then she is gone, running whither Gerahard goes.

"I will fetch you when the time is nigh," she yells.

"You have made the time nigh," says Derwen. She runs her fingers through what is left of my unbraided hair. "I thought of what you might do in that place whither Constantine went. Those thoughts did not leave me until I shed my hair and even then only when I did not sleep. I sent you there."

"You did not," I say. "I went there of my own will."

"These men will say the same," says Derwen. "Kin of the Wolf, Lords of the Oak, Men of the Salted Marsh. Whichever name they use for themselves, they will call out mine as they die and wait to meet me in the next life. The longer you were away from us, the less I felt I could stay among them without hurting them. That is why I left."

"Did not they not suffer when they looked for you and did not find you?"

"They suffer more when I am here. But they do not understand why, nor can I tell them in a way that they will understand. I will tell them that Myrah's daughter is a son so they do not have to kill her. They say there are too many of us to live among them in the fens. So much water and land and yet they watch their cows and sheep like hawks and bemoan this rainfall over flooded meadows. 'Where will our newborn cows eat grass with their mothers?' they ask me among fields that stretch to the sea. They worship me as their queen, yet I know little more than Myrah of what they do here. Which of us understands them less, do you think?"

"Why do you speak so?" I say.

Derwen looks at her feet as bare as mine.

"I know not whether Myrah or I can keep Gerahard from rushing headlong into his own death," she says. "The men look to us, now. Come."

Derwen takes Florentina onto her back and leads us to a meadow east of the mead hall. Far south of us, many men beat spears against shields and call out to the clouds. Out on the sea, the boatman gives them no answer, for he knows as well as I do that I am the one who has blessed their wish to be wed to death.

2 8

WEDDING

From within the broad-leafed boughs of a blossoming aspen tree I take an old, sturdy limb and help it shed its knotted twigs. Mildred wanders through the meadow, picking sleepy yellow cowslip flowers as Florentina unweaves my hewn braid and threads the strands anew. Mildred holds out her gift to Derwen in her little palm; Derwen sets Mildred's flowers in my hair while Florentina's fingers work. Mildred's flowers become too many and thus find their home on the green wool of Florentina's lap, whereafter I offer my twigless stick to Mildred's hands lest Florentina's legs become home to nesting birds and four-winged flies.

"For one who wishes to leave," says Florentina, "Rosamond walks a winding path."

She comes to us from where the mead hall stands out of sight somewhere in the west. Marigold is on her arm, sweeping a thick walking stick through the meadow's tall grass. The purple moor stalks yield their hidden swarms of butterflies hued as reddish yellow as Marigold's hair to the cloudless heavens. Mildred throws down her stick and reaches up to them, as if her unburdened hands might thus give her the gift of flight. I hold her aloft so that she may flutter for a time the way her winged friends do.

"How fares the wedding?" says Florentina.

"I would wish it fare well did that man not ask us to swear an oath to him," says Rosamond. She wears a long black braid woven with white meadwort over her right shoulder. "He says his 'wolves' must know that we will bind ourselves to unwed men and work the land with them while heeding some unwritten law that tells them where their cows and sheep may eat. They think this more worthy of their thoughts than the growling of their own bellies."

"That is what you have come here to tell us?" says Derwen.

She sweeps Mildred's flowers from Florentina's legs.

"Luda will swear her oath with Annette," says Marigold. Her many thin, beaded braids rest on her shoulders amid wind-strewn hair. "Her husband wishes to live here, as does her brother Brant, but she has brought neither of them to the wedding."

"Why should she?" says Rosamond. "Gerahard would have them swear their oaths to him from beneath the earth."

"They ask you to calm the sea, Derwen," says Marigold. "You might speak to your sister Ardelle and ask her to let you stay among them long enough to withhold the rain so they can drain the water and make the first fodder ready for their cows."

"Why did you never tell me you can do this?" says Florentina.

"Must you free every butterfly that lives within the meadow of your thoughts?" says Derwen. "They think it my wrath for having to return to the dead."

"So do not return," I say.

Rosamond leaves Marigold, kneels beside me, and sets her arms around me.

"You came back to us from wherever that hidden world lies," she says. "If I do go there, I hope you might think well enough of me to find me and bring me back."

"Come, Ardelle," says Derwen as she lifts Rosamond from the ground. "The wolves would hear us tell tales. You and Rosamond may think on how I am to stay here among you and not bring the wrath of my dead sister down on their heads. Rosamond, take Florentina."

Beards and brown woollen tunics and ash-hafted spears and iron-banded leather shields swarm about the grassy field south of the mead hall ever closer to the sea's flowing shore. As one, the men still their speech and legs for a hairless man who wears a shirt of iron over his black tunic and a dark-sheathed sword against his black leggings. He takes the iron helm from between his ribs and arm and lets it slide down onto his hairless head. With his face thus shielded, he spreads his arms wide and yells into the clouds, bidding the birds therein come swooping down from the heavens to acknowl-edge his earthly wisdom with their milky white dung-oaths. From his side, a lithe form in a gold-fastened black gown runs to us with halting strides—Myrah bends over with her hands above her knees as her breath threatens to leave her altogether.

"Let Mildred play in Annette's house while he hears our oaths," she says.

"No," says Derwen, "that is not what we have come to do."

Annette's yellow-flowered, fish-tailed braids await the end of Gerahard's wandering words beside her thatch-haired man. On seeing us, some of the spear-men kneel. Gerahard falls silent and nods as if he has asked them to do this. He turns to Annette and Wilfrith, leaving the eyes of one hundred of his men to see us where he does not.

"I will hear your oaths, now," he says.

As one, Annette and Wilfrith speak words of which I wish to have no memory. As they stand, the kneeling men stand with them, clapping their hands together and stomping the earth with their feet. They become still when, from among them, a brown-clothed woman as tall as Gerahard wearing a yellow-white braid down to her shoulders steps forwards: Luda. She goes down on one knee and speaks the same words with a strength that bears them over the roofs of the houses out onto the sea.

"Enough," says Gerahard. "Your words are no better than dung."

Luda looks up to him with a frown. Derwen takes my arm even as I hold my daughter. Mildred has two fingers in her mouth as she stares at these many unknown faces.

"This, men," says Gerahard, "is the sister in red who was to call the sea for Athelbert at our battle near that southern shore. Her king wished to show you his might so that we would not have to spill our blood. But our friends and brothers died when this woman did not heed the king to whom she had sworn an oath. And thus, the oath she would swear to me is likewise worthless, for I know her to be the hand of death that she and her kin along the northern shore have brought to us from the south. They are the ones who make the great sea swell and the little sea flood. They are the ones who will wreak lifelessness on your fields and meadows and marshes and leave them barren for your children and your children's children, should they live long enough to bear them."

A rush of wind sweeps through my braided hair. Mildred clings to me. Derwen sets her arm around my shoulders.

"Will you not stop him?" I say.

"He tells tales for his men to believe," Derwen says.

"What?"

"Luda wishes to leave," says Derwen. "Frijona does not. Luda's brother and husband listen to their wise woman's tales. Let us make the wolves listen to ours."

Gerahard faces me with his back to his men as he takes his helm from his head. Painted eyes sit on a bent-nosed chair bearing the hues bestowed on it by the man who carved Gerahard's face from the marble stone Myrah's father loved so much that he wished us to see it every day for as many days as it might take Gerahard to find the end of his words.

"This is the sister in red who took a spear on that ridge," he says. "She is the one who brought an end to our fighting. She took flight with the wind and hid from our sight to make us believe she had left us, only to return among our men and horses and show us how to wield strength without drawing the blood of another. It is this strength that kept any more of us from dying that day."

Some men drop their spears or throw them to the ground. Those few of their women who do not hide behind them or stand beside them take them up as they stare at me.

"Her sacrifice may also keep this woman Luda alive today," says Gerahard. "Our beloved Budig's sister has come from the dead to give of herself as Budig did so many years ago. It was such strength that our friend, the great king Sledda, wielded when he forgave our women for striking his serving maids. It is this strength that I have learned from Ardelle in forgiving those who have slain my brothers, and in standing together with the king of our southern brothers, for he is still their champion, and I would not take him from them. It is he who would ask his king whether this wretched woman Luda, who stands before you as if she had done nothing, may not yet be given the forgiveness of kings."

"Wretched?" I say. "Who here is wretched but one whose words drown out all others? Why do none of you speak?"

I turn to my sisters—Rosamond, Marigold, and Florentina have gone. They are right to do so.

"You would have forgiven Rosamond when she was dead and could not answer," I say. "Would you have let him do this, Derwen?"

"I spared him at your behest," says Derwen. "That is what I told the men and women who stand here before you. That is why they chose him to be their king. I have done as you asked. Let me stay here a while longer among them, dear sister. Or shall I give the rain and the sea my strength as well? We might strike them down, all of them, and we will not have to ask them to let our friends share their land, for there will be none alive to ask."

Those who do not kneel sit down on their legs. A fair-haired woman in earthen clothing sets her lips on my bare foot before I can take it from her. Myrah looks about her, stares at Gerahard, then grasps the back of my neck beneath my flowered braid knot and draws my lips to hers.

When in the waking sands a thousand years from now the sun's first light brings warmth to wind-blown stone, its runes and rough-hewn edges will tell no tale of the eternity I spend with Myrah in this moment.

I take Luda's wrist and bring her down beside us. The woman who kissed my foot stares at me with eyes of stone, as do her brothers and sisters. Derwen's fingers rest on my right shoulder. Luda speaks.

"I swear to serve you."

Gerahard takes his sword from its sheath and drives its sharpened end into the ground between his feet. Where his lips part to show his teeth, the sea's waves rise from the shore to meet the white cliffs within his mouth and grind them into chalky dust. Somewhere out on the little sea, a great snake of purple lightning strikes down from a cloudless sky and sends misting water down onto our heads as well as any rainfall.

"The truth is but five words," says Gerahard. "Ardelle has shown us strength unmatched among the sisters in red who would live with us. As you heed your new queen faithfully, so shall you have the blessings of your old queen, whose oath to you needs no words. Stand and let us give thanks for our newfound strength and the peace it brings. We eat and drink this day and night in our mead hall."

His men and women stand as slowly as the dead might rise from their own graves. Where their weighted legs follow Gerahard's forthright strides, their eyes are bound to me. I kneel with Derwen's hand on my hair and my daughter against my breast, where she shakes with the sea-mist's chill. Three or four women come to Derwen as if they are cats who bring a mouse to their master. They kneel before Derwen's legs and kiss her fingers. She sets her hand on each of their heads, then waves them away. Myrah kisses my cheek and follows them.

"You allow this?" I say to Derwen.

"You do," she says. "They are still alive."

Within Annette's house, Marigold's fire brightens the walls for those few of us who stare at them in grim silence. I set Mildred down on Annette's bedding and wipe the rain from her face. Rosamond can not keep her eyes from Derwen.

"Gerahard has taken Luda's oath," says Derwen. "Keep yourself from his sight and I will do my best to make him forget that he has ever seen you."

"So I am to be like Ardelle," says Rosamond. "I leave this man alive who will not do the same for me."

"He would give you a child," says Derwen. "Luda told me of how she lay with Gerahard many times when you came to find me."

Florentina sighs.

"So Luda's husband can give her nothing," she says.

"Have you augured a child for her?" says Rosamond.

"Not yet," says Derwen, "but I need no augury to know

that Luda will learn of her child soon enough. When she does, Gerahard will say she is unfaithful for having sworn an oath to him and thus leaving behind the father of her child on the northern shore."

Our words we keep soft while my daughter sleeps through the day and into dusk's dimming light. Derwen sits with us well into the night as we wait for the men to drink their fill and bed down with their women. Shadowy moonlight plays on the earthen floor of Annette's house where Rosamond has lain down beside Mildred. Marigold quells her fire to keep unwed, mead-bellied men from looking within. Mildred whines as she dreams; her hands and feet are ice. Derwen bids me help her lift a tall row of withy-bound alder beams and lean their top against the timber above our house's opening to better hide us. Marigold wakes the cooling embers with an iron stirring rod well enough to bring us welcome warmth; the hearth's soft light is yet weaker than the moon's.

"I will see whether Luda has left," says Derwen.

She steps through the narrow gap between the leaning door and the house's wall.

"Why do Annette and Wilfrith not sleep in their own home?" I say.

"They drink mead with the other blissfully wedded," says Florentina. "Were they here and we were not, they would do anything but sit. Had I a harp, I would make music for them and their newfound friends while the three of you slept."

A soft sounding against the door brings us a narrow, black-shoed foot that threads the moon's beams between the sleeves of a night-shrouded gown.

"Marigold," says Myrah. The house smells of overly sweet honey and well-ripened strawberries. "The mead hall needs lightening."

"Do your heads not yet swim among the stars?" says Marigold as she waves her hand before her face. "Those should be bright enough for even the most mead-blinded among them."

"I told the men of your fire," says Myrah.

"Have you also been drinking mead?" says Florentina.

"Do you know nothing of weddings?" says Myrah. "Did you never see them in Hispania? Yes, I have taken my share of mead, though not as much as others."

"Not as much as your child?" I say.

"Why do you care?" says Myrah. She holds out her hand to Marigold. "Gerahard will hear your oath now, Maria, and would see your brightly hued flames for himself."

"You may take the embers from the hearth with your hands," says Marigold.

"Ardelle, tell her to come," says Myrah. "I will lie with you tomorrow morning while Gerahard sleeps through his weariness."

Myrah waves her hand towards herself, as if by doing so Marigold would come to her. Marigold turns away from the stench of Myrah's breath and coughs into her gown sleeve.

"Myrah," I say. "We have done this before."

"We have," says Myrah and comes to my lap.

She opens her mouth into mine—whatever she drinks must have been made from ground up bees instead of their honey. My ribs threaten to leave my breast through my throat as I cough into the earth. When my breath is mine again, Myrah and Marigold have gone. I look to Florentina.

"Am I to run after them?" she says and leaves her bench to lie beside Mildred. "I will close my eyes even if I do not sleep. Those men would not take us away from a child."

The hearth goes cold. Only the breath of those who dream at night and moonlight from the little sea abide within our sleeping house. I stand. Ten steps are enough to take Florentina and Rosamond and Mildred from my thoughts: the grassy earth vomits smoke from burning chair legs that have been driven into the ground every twenty steps between the houses and the mead hall. Men walk about waving burning willow boughs to see how the purple hue of their fires draws misshapen runes among the stars. On both sides of the mead hall, a long table stands upended with fiery legs burning. Within the mead hall, the men in the middle, to whom those tables belong, have laden the tops of the mead barrels from which they drink with wooden cups, gilded ox horns, golden-yellow cheese, red-green apples, whole cooked ducks, and salted fish.

"There she is," calls a man. "She comes to send us to sleep."

"We have not yet begun to drink," says his friend on the other side of their mead barrel. "Let us sleep when we are dead."

Loud laughter holds my hand as I walk between the backs of men seated opposite one another at their mead barrels and long tables. Here and there, men take their wives and hie away with them lest the others remember that they have no wives of their own and go off in search of one. At a shorter table overlooking the long tables sits Gerahard with seven of his best-bearded men, one of whom holds Marigold on his lap. Her face says nothing to me of her mood. Annette and Wilfrith and Derwen and Myrah are nowhere to be seen—no, there are the rings of Myrah's hair behind Gerahard's black woollen sleeve. She laughs as loudly as if she had a beard of her own.

"I have come to take Marigold to her bed," I say.

"You as well?" says the man who holds her to the laughter of his friends.

"Do my words mean nothing to you?" I say.

"This is a night for many words that will be forgotten by morning," he says. "Drink with us, ghost."

He turns to Gerahard as if I am not there.

"Why do you make her set fire to the tables and chairs on which you would sit?" I say.

"To better see the blood on our faces," says Gerahard.

He drinks deeply from a milky white, silver-gilded ox horn, allowing reddish water to spill down onto his chin. His wise men do likewise, and when they have done, they bare their bloodied teeth with throaty growls that might frighten foxes from their dens.

"You drink blood?" I say.

"Mead made with strawberries," says Myrah. Her face is unbloodied. "Would you like some?"

"You have told her our secret, my queen," says Gerahard. He gives her lips a wet kiss. She wipes the red water from her mouth and cheeks with her sleeve. "Fear not, Ardelle, for your queen has told me of your darkest secrets. I will keep them from those who would wield them against you." He stands with a bellowing call. "Let us drink to the dearest sister of our beloved queen!"

A great cry sounds throughout the mead hall with no walls, whereafter the men hand their emptied cups to those who fill them again from the barrel-tables against their shins. When the barrels are empty, they might fill their cups from between their legs and be no wiser.

"Will you let Marigold go now?" I say.

"We do not hold her here," says Gerahard. "She knows what we do is in mirth. I will let you have your mirth with Myrah when I am not there. If you know love equal to strength, you might let my aldorman share in this mirth with your unwed sister. She may even find in him a husband."

"She will find unfaithfulness," says a woman in mother's tongue.

"What?" says Gerahard. "Who hides behind that beam? Show yourself and drink with us."

Derwen is at my side, her face darkened by earth and her

hair bearing dark green leaves. Laughter dies. Talk stills. A woman leaves her man's lap and sits beside him.

"Did you give Ardelle a child on that battlefield?" says Derwen.

Gerahard is silent. His unblinking eyes would stare Derwen's anger into nothingness.

"Marigold told me of this," says Derwen. "The one you say you do not keep bound."

"She speaks no oath to me," says Gerahard. "She is not bound."

"Why would she give her oath to one who does not speak the truth before us?" Derwen stands with her legs against the edge of the table opposite Gerahard. "They would better learn the truth when these wolves tear his flesh to shreds and show their guests what will become of them if they linger."

"Was it not Ardelle's will that I return here with you?" says Gerahard.

"Was her child not your will?" says Derwen. She shoves the table with her legs. "You did this knowing that we must not have children as your king told you. You speak of the worthlessness of Luda's oath, yet you are silent when asked of your own guilt in bringing my sister here from the dead with her child to show me what was taken from me when I died giving birth."

Gerahard stands from his bench and drinks deeply from a wooden cup.

"Do what must be done, then," he says. "Show them your strength."

His men stand beside him, as do the men and their women at their long benches and mead barrel tables. They meet Derwen's back with the grim, unblinking eyes of those who are dead.

This man lies with an ax wound that has cleft his skull from his eyebrow to his teeth. Beside him, his wife has lost her jaw and the flesh of her belly. Worms crawl about on the sticky ropes within her, gnawing at the wet green flesh with sickening sounds. Their friends on the bench beside them no longer wear their faces, only a reddish mash of skin and bone. About them, their brothers and sisters lie among strewn limbs that do not belong to their bodies. On top of my feet, a shattered skull looks up at me from eyeless holes; its arms and legs are clothed in the dark blue that Constantine once wore. I will not look for Gerahard here, for if I find him, I do not wish to learn whether Myrah lies beside him.

My steps become as soft as when I walked away from Sithebad and her knife-wielding friends. This man's burning bough could have come from that runestone's oak grove. I push my linen sleeves to my elbows and take the stick from his hand with a kiss for his cheek—he runs away and wipes his face as if to take the flesh from it. I hold the bough above my head to one side and stand before Gerahard. Derwen steps away from me; her eyes are bound to his marble head and its stone-edged nose.

"Your queen, Myrah, once asked Derwen to bind us within our rooms in our sanctuary by the southern sea," I say. "We were to hide within as if we were dead while Myrah's father talked of peace with the northmen—king Sledda's men."

"We knew!" calls a man. "We knew he had hidden you somewhere, but we could not find you. We were right."

"Before we went to our rooms, Myrah asked Marigold to quench the hearth's fire, the same that I hold in my hand. She would not, and so Myrah asked me to speak with her to tell her that this must be done. Myrah threatened to put Marigold's hand into the hearth if I would not heed her. Thereafter, I learned what Myrah did not tell me: that she and her kin, Myrah among them, can not be hurt by our fire."

I bring the tree bough to my forearm. My body is fire. The sun lives within me. A thousand snakes sink their fangs into my wrist and leave behind only a bloodied hand-stump. My forearm cooks and burns and melts blood and flesh and bone into ash. I have no thoughts but of aching; I have no knowledge but of suffering.

The fire dies. Marigold throws my stick to the ground. Derwen grasps my wrist. My forearm is hued red and black, carved with a woodworker's knife into knots and winding strands of hair that bleed rivers of fire into my flesh and bone. I choke on thick, sickeningly sweet smoke until the fire within my nose bursts from my mouth and leaves a gift of vomit on the mead hall's rocky earth. Gerahard laughs and slams his hand against the table as he sits down.

"You see, men?" he says. "She has told her tale so well that even she believes it. See how she hides her suffering. *That* is how it is done. We will drink to the strength of your tale. Take your sister and bind yourselves within your house so that your tale may end as well as ours this evening, for we shall drink as though we die in battle tomorrow!"

A deafening roar sounds from among the men. They strike their cups and horns against tables and barrels as Derwen and Marigold hasten away from the mead hall gripping both my arms below my shoulders. In Annette's house, Derwen kneels beside Florentina and shakes her until Florentina grunts in weariness.

"Let her sleep," I say. "I will not ask of her what I kept her from giving Rosamond."

"*I* will ask her tomorrow, then," says Derwen.

Marigold wakes Rosamond and bids her sing to me. She can not see my wounds well in the house's darkness, nor will I have Marigold light the embers so close to my aching arm. Rosamond feels along its crusted ridges with her asp-fanged fingers. The soft waters of her song cool my fire-blood to mild warmness but leave on my flesh the written memory of my harrowing.

A yawn sends me to the bedding beside Marigold. I have not slept these two days. Rosamond gives me a linen pillow to set between my arm and ribs, then lies down beside me opposite Marigold. Derwen sits near the opening between the door and the wall, bathing herself in the night's shadowy moonlight.

"Myrah asked me to tell her why I shook the earth yesterday," she says to us. "I think the mead will help her understand my answer better."

"Wait until Gerahard sleeps lest he think you come for him again," I say.

"As you say," says Derwen, "but I go hither so he does not come for me."

I take Marigold's head on the shoulder of my wounded arm with a grunt.

"What would that man have done with you?" I whisper.

"He would have taken me to his bed," she says.

"I knew a boy named Alfred, once," I say. "I kissed him though I did not want to. I wonder whether he would have asked for my bed as well."

"So what if he had?" says Marigold. "I would not have been there to tell him on your behalf that you will not lie with him. Good night."

Icy fingers take my right hand and hold them until they have warmed.

"She means to thank you for sparing us from the wolves and from our oaths and from whatever else might have befallen us," whispers Rosamond. "Good night."

When I have taken my first step into the boatless river that runs between the land of the waking and the world of dreams, the neighing of horses draws me away from the river bank to the timber of our house's outer walls: Gerahard and his men bear burning chair legs and oak boughs as they help one another onto their steeds. I should not have come out here to watch them, for I have seen more than enough of what they do this evening. I return within and find Marigold's head with my shoulder, then close my eyes and wade once again into a dreaming river with steps that match the softening hooves of midnight's faithful horses.

DREAMS

Slow steps over the sharp stones of the river's bed take me through flowing waves that kiss my bare feet like dead, lipless fish. Beneath midnight's starry black wool, I wander as the water winds until it empties into a half-sunken bed of rough sand and white shells. I rest my aching spine and weary legs before a darkening sea made like to the heavens by the uplifted staff of a boat-bound form. His ember eyes beneath the folds of his black hood redden with fire as they take from my flesh the blood that gives it life.

His boat berths at my feet. I lift my head to meet his eyes, yet my neck bears the weight of two yoked oxen. He steps astride my body, takes his arms from their sleeves, and lets his unclasped gown fall onto my waist: Myrah holds me fast against the ground with amber-brown eyes that glow brighter than the blood moon above. Her elbows she rests beside my shoulders; her nose and lips find mine; her hand takes my gown from my knees to my hips, where searching fingertips call the night sea's waves to soothe my nameless aching. Once, twice, thrice they flow onto the shore with ever greater strength. Her mouth opens mine to bursting; the mead on her breath fills my breast with its warmth; the waves rush over us between the meeting of our lips, flooding my nose and mouth with salty foam that sends me upright to cough up brine onto legs warmed by woollen bedding and the dull embers of Annette's hearth.

Sunlight plays on the stone-flecked, reed-strewn earthen floor through the thatched roof of Annette's house. Florentina sleeps beside my daughter with one arm under Mildred's head. Rosamond and Marigold have gone. Even in the morning chill, I sweat in my woollen gown—it clings to my left forearm. Under a sleeve that yields only haltingly lies a blackened landscape of dead ridges overlooking fields of lifeless blood-grass that ask me to soothe their burning.

Cool wind blows through the meadow wherein men sleep off their drink. In the mead hall, the fires no longer burn, nor do the chair legs driven into the ground stand any longer. My tenth step tells me of the aching between my legs that beset me in my dream; my twentieth step asks me whether Gerahard might sleep in a field somewhere with his wise men; my thirtieth step tells me I must find Myrah's house so she might help me soothe this aching.

Three empty houses show me nothing but dimmed embers where their hearths should be ready to cook the day's meals. These houses can not be like those from which Gerahard and Luda took hens. Men still live here. I must look again until I find—until I find a house that is not empty, yet I wish it had been.

Through the gap between the house's opening and its leaning door, I find what I had sought: Myrah's dark, ringed hair lies atop a pale breast. From shortly shorn, leaf-threaded brown hair hangs a little red-and-white-beaded braid beside a left shoulder that bears no arm. Myrah's hand rests on

Derwen's thigh; two small wooden cups lie near them; the house stinks of mead. Neither of them wear their gowns.

We will need neither clothing nor warmth when we sleep with the dead.

The morning sun's blinding light takes the strength from my knees. The earth yields to my gown little better than the raised marble stone of a sanctuary's bed ever did. An unbidden moan from within Myrah's house strikes life into my shaking legs and hies them into the meadow, where neither the half-drunken grunts of sleeping men nor the river of frosty dew that settles on my shins are enough to slow my stride. Only when my breathless lungs heave with retching do I forget for a time what I have seen, and even then only until I set my eyes on a neighing mare behind a thicket of thick-bodied alder trees whose grey bark streaked with white hides her like hue well. She keeps her hoof steps soft so as not to wake her keepers. Annette's house has no beam for her leather straps; nonetheless, she waits for me as well as any mead-stricken aldorman while I wake Florentina.

"What do we do?" Florentina asks.

"Myrah ..."

My throat chokes before the words can leave it.

"Myrah wishes us to find Gerahard where he lies and give his men your waters," I say.

"Myrah would say that." Florentina wipes her eyes clean. "Even with water all around us. Must you wake me for this? Rosamond has always been better for such ... were she not also always running away from Gerahard. Well, dear mother, let us—what in the world did you do to your arm?"

Florentina wrests the left sleeve of my linen undergown to my shoulder, bringing my seared flesh to fiery life.

"What is this?" she says with a frown. "And do not lie to me."

"I went to fetch Marigold from the mead hall last night," I

say. "The men wished to see how her fires burn. I showed them."

"After drinking mead with them?"

"No. Myrah drank. She did nothing while Marigold sat on an aldorman's lap. Myrah was too drunk to understand anything."

"I drink nothing and I also do not understand." Florentina grips my chin weakly and shakes it. "You are never to do that again. Now, sit still."

Rushing water floods my body and warms my blood where it had grown cold. The black ridges on my forearm soften into brown hills. Between them, the grassy red fields lighten as our woollen gowns once did in summer's sun. Somewhere far away, the boatman drifts along Florentina's water and sends a great stone rolling towards me—even with all my might, I will not be able to stop it.

Mildred stands in my lap and clings to me. She wipes the snot from her nose on my gown. Her eyes are wet with tears.

"I will have to do the same for many weeks before this leaves your arm," says Florentina. "What were you thinking when you did this? You were not thinking. And now you wish to worship at the runestone of thoughtlessness by seeking out sleeping men and waking them so you may make them mindful of that which they might have forgotten had you left them to their dreams."

"I saw Myrah and Derwen dreaming together without their gowns," I say. "They stank of mead."

"Ah," says Florentina. Her frown leaves her face. "I know not whether it is better to understand nothing at all or to understand all too well what goes on. Come, then, my unbound sister, and let us see whether Gerahard wears a golden wreath on his head for having drunk so much mead without wetting himself. Will you leave Mildred with Myrah?"

"Shall I leave you with her as well?"

"The wisdom of motherhood goes far beyond my ken. After you."

I must take Florentina's limp arms and hold them over my shoulders for a time until she wills them to life and grasps her wrists around my neck. When I stand with her, I have only one hand for Mildred's reaching fingers. Florentina thus half-chokes my neck while my daughter walks before me in asking me to bear her. She stops when I lift her onto our horse to sit with Florentina; her fingers dig into my back as our mare walks off bearing the weight of three unwanted riders. Florentina's song brings our horse's legs to a slowing, neighing halt.

"Horses listen to you?" I say.

"In Emerita, I healed so many men that the aldorman Masona thought I could call them back from the dead," says Florentina. "He became angry when they would not listen to me and was no more glad when my waters bade the horses expel the illness from their bellies by shitting on the floor of his patio. Shall we ride, now, my darling sister? Take us whither your queen's king and his men sleep like fallen oaks, and we shall see whether those trees heed my song."

The mare heeds my heels and takes us east beyond the mead hall, where uneaten cow flesh and salted fish sleep forever on their mead barrel beds. If Gerahard and his men came this way, the wet grass hides their hooves. Florentina hums to herself with laughter.

"I will never understand why men live in these wetlands, where the rain greets their ships by sinking them," she says. "And yet I think they would still follow the water if they knew nothing else."

They would follow the shore as Luda's kin do—that is where Gerahard has gone and does not yet return.

"Do we stop for mead?" says Florentina. "Go, before your daughter tells you she is hungry."

As our mare walks, the sun's warmth weighs down the sea's chilling winds and drives them from the shore. The clouds bless us with no rain this day, nor do the smooth stones in the earth strike ill against our horse's hooves. Where the sea wends north, worn grass and trodden earth follow, yielding footsteps that lead us beside the water closer than I wish to be for longer than any of us wish to ride. Where they end, bundles of wool lie unstirring in the fields and berthed on the sand.

"Have we found them?" says Florentina.

"Where?" I say.

"Those men who stretch their arms in that ditch," she says.

I keep my heels from asking our mare to do anything more than walk to meet thirty long-haired, well-bearded men in brown and grey tunics who stand in a waist-high hole in the middle of a shallow hare's den. They dig with spears and hands and boat oars as they bury … as they bury open-mouthed, bloodied men heaped on top of one another like wood hewn for a hearth's fire. Three among those who still live stand up straight and ask me with odd words why I have come to them with two children. A white-braided woman in a brown tunic and earthen leggings runs towards us from the many gathered men out on the open field with her hands clutching her belly; a tall man in like clothing wearing a shoulder-belted sword lopes beside her.

"Ardelle," Brant says. "Did they send you? Do they know?"

"There," whispers Florentina.

Her finger shows me where among the dead lies a shirtless, craggy-faced man with a broken nose. Against his shoulder rests a sword sheath akin to Brant's. His eyelids look as though he still sleeps, yet his innards have been taken from his belly and hang down to his knees like bloody snakes. What Myrah has done with him and with Derwen lies forgotten in houses flooded by the seas little and great, frozen into icy stillness by winter's frost-breathed kisses. There we lie, Myrah and I, in peace and silence that do not leave, for there is nothing to be left and none who leave.

"They know nothing," I say. "I sent myself."

Florentina strikes my back and shoulders, sending me from our horse. I lift Florentina and set her on the ground so I may take Mildred. Florentina creeps to where Gerahard lies. The men who dig with earth-caked hands and dull-edged oars stop and stare for a time, then claw into the ground once more. Florentina takes Gerahard's hairless, bloodless face in her hands.

"Mors tua, vita mea," says Florentina. "He is beyond healing."

"I saw Myrah lie with Derwen this morning," I say to Brant. The words leave me of their own will. "I thought I might find peace by taking this horse elsewhere for a time."

"You have found the same peace that they sought, then," says the woman. "They came to us when the sun had not yet risen. We saw only their fires and smelled the drink on their breath. We took the fires from them and waited as they killed each other. The fire burns so long that we threw it into the sea. We should keep the horses, but we sent them away. Some think them cursed." She shakes her head and sighs. "We have traded with many men who drink mead."

Brant comes to me and sets his hands on my shoulders. His beard has grown longer. His breath smells of ashes.

"What do you do?" says the woman.

"We were eighty," says Brant. "Now, we are fifty."

The woman takes his hands from my shoulders and strikes Brant's breast with the back of her hand.

"My wife, Frijona," he says. "She and my brothers who dig

did not think them worthy of this burial until I told them how I know of these men. Where is our sister Luda?"

"You are kin?" says Frijona.

"If she is not with you," I say, "I do not know."

"I must fetch her before those men miss their king," says Brant.

"We," says Frijona. "We must fetch her."

She bends down and strokes Mildred's cheek. Mildred hides her face in my gown.

"His wound was not made in battle," says Florentina. "Why must you rend him open?"

"I told them of what Ardelle has done with dead men," says Brant. "That is why we bury our foes before our own. And that is why we take Gerahard's innards: so others do not make Ardelle bring him back from the dead to call his wrath down on those he hates. Luda said he would kill Rosamond if he could. She thought he might have mixed something in her food or drink when you left for Derwen."

"Ink," says Florentina. "I know where he would have found it."

She looks as though she might vomit. As she heaves, she closes her mouth and works her lips together, then lets fly white spit that lands on the ground beside Gerahard. One of the men stops digging long enough to grunt and nod at her.

"I hope Myrah's father meets Gerahard some day soon," says Florentina with a look for Gerahard's candle wax flesh. "I threw my hair rods into the sea after I learned of what he did to Myrah's back. It was not enough that he twisted her spine when he gave her to her mother."

"Ardelle," says Brant. "Will you be the one to tell Myrah of this?"

"Do not tell me you go to Halja for this man," says Florentina. "How long will you stay this time? Five years? Ten?"

"None," I say. "I have done nothing to these men, yet if I were to come to them in that place, the boatman would say I have done this to them. I will not go hither to see them wither and rot while I can do nothing for them. At least here, we can hide them from the boatman's eyes and let them see the sun when it rises."

"You will give this man no such thing," says Florentina. Her sun-kissed face does not bear grimness well. "He has not earned a peaceful sleep."

"We might send him out to sea," I say.

"We will not bury him in a ship as we have seen done for kings here," says one of the digging men. "What king is he who knows not friend from foe?"

"Then let us give him a second death," I say. "We will drown him in the water, where he will see neither the sun nor anything at all of this world."

He will see only his dreams of Myrah, if that is what his heart wishes, and the life he might have lived did he not seek his own death in such earnest. He might give Myrah her son as they return to live beside the white cliffs near the southern sea. They walk through their harvest wheat fields; they swim together in winter's iciest water; they smell the blossoming flowers when they wake from their frost and lie amid them in the tall grass on a fair summer's day; he and Myrah drink mead and laugh while Constantine thrusts himself between my legs. Let him dream of that forever where none other shall see him. Let him dream of those who love him best only when he is no longer among them. Let me dream that Myrah and those I call sister will not love their thoughts of me better when I am also gone.

"You think him worthy of this?" says Florentina.

"I should have blown Marigold's fires into nothingness in the mead hall," I say.

"Instead, you do to yourself what you would have others

do unto you," says Florentina. "Brant, which of your boats do you like least? Ardelle wishes to float with the timber and this king's body."

"I will take him out to sea by myself, if I must," I say. "I will leave him there to dream."

Brant stares through my eyes for a long while, then speaks to the digging men with words that sound enough like ours that my ears still understand them. The men stop their digging and turn to look at me for a time before talking among themselves. When they fall silent, eight of them take up their spears from the hole they have dug and lead us to where five great boats lie berthed on the shore. Behind us, six men bear Gerahard by his ankles and waist and wrists as one would a deer slaughtered for a wedding meal; his innards sweep through the sand alongside him like eels gasping for watery breath. With swinging heaves, the fourteen of them throw his heavy body over the breast-high wall of a wide-bottomed boat as long as ten horses.

"Leave Mildred with me," says Florentina. "I will spare her from her mother's wisdom."

Mildred does not sit well in Florentina's lap. I must run from her grasping fingers and cries to meet the men where they sit in their boat. Brant would likewise come to sit with us —Frijona nearly wrests his arm from his shoulder to keep him from doing so. Six more men spring over the boat's wall and take up their earth-caked oars. We are twenty, as are the men on the sand who shove our boat into the water, yet even so many would be too few to stand against the waves that rock against our boat's brittle hull.

"Where do you set him down?" says one man. "Do it quickly. The sea's wrath comes to us whenever we leave the shore."

"Row far enough away that a man can not swim back," I say.

"So the hour of our death draws near," says another.

They row until the shore is but a thin sheet of white foam and the waves threaten to make the bottom of our boat its top. I take Gerahard's golden belt buckle and lift it; eight or ten men lift with me and send his body over the edge of the boat. The sea's salty water sprays our faces with bitter mist—a great swelling rocks the boat to one side, almost throwing three men who keep themselves from falling by clinging to the sturdy wooden beams on which they would otherwise sit.

"He did this to himself," I say. "That is what I will tell Myrah."

And who will have done this to me when Mildred can not find her mother in that hidden world? An unseen hand with the weight of a thousand men thrusts our boat towards the shore with unearthly swiftness. The men who still bear oars have little need to row: their ship is brought to a jerking halt against water-soaked sand. The men throw their oars aside in haste and spring from the boat as if it might swallow them whole. I writhe over the top of the boat's high wall, sliding down the uneven timber beams into my daughter's waiting arms. Brant bears Florentina on his back; Frijona stands beside him with wide eyes and wind-blown white hair.

"I will tell your queen that neither you nor we have done any of this," she says. "She will understand that drunk men did this to themselves."

"She will understand nothing," I say, "but I have no words better than yours to give her."

In that sleeping world where Sithebad has found peace with her Alfred, Gerahard may at last find his love for Myrah. The sea's waves soften into calmness as they take the gift of Gerahard's body below to its mossy bed, where he clutches to his breast the love that death has wrested from my heart. He may keep it close to him as he dreams of Myrah and the son she would have given him. They walk together, hand in hand,

through the high-stalked fields of wheat in Gerahard's homelands in Francia, where his childhood friends, now grown and
bearing children of their own, meet their king and queen with
friendly words and gentle smiles. I will tell Myrah of these
wretched dreams with unkind words that bear no mark of
falsehood, for she will understand little better than I do why
death has chosen Gerahard to be its king.

DEATH

Brant and Frijona leave with the wind to find the horses they sent away. Whether the boatman watches them now, I would not have them know. Let him take our offering of fallen kings and aldormen and leave us in peace long enough for my sister's brother and his wife to bring us Gerahard's horses from among thin-spindled, leafless birch trees.

"They did not wander far," Florentina says from my back.

"They did not wander," says Frijona. "We did not know who you are to Brant. I will tell your men of their king's death."

"Myrah," I say. "You must tell their queen."

"She did not go with her king?" says Frijona.

"No," I say, "nor would I have her do so."

Mildred's back against mine draws a growling from my belly though I have no mind for bread. She throws her back into my ribs and digs her fingernails into my cheeks.

"Eat," she says.

"We found fish and cheese in their leather bags," says

Frijona. "Will you have your daughter take this from dead men?"

"I gave birth to her where the dead abide," I say. "She will take it."

Frijona goes to where her brothers heap earth on the bodies of dead men and takes food from their leather bags. She returns with spotted fish still warm from smoking and a handful of crumbled cheese. Mildred eats it from her fingers all at once and licks Frijona's palm, drawing light laughter from her.

"If the child I bear is a daughter, I would have her be like yours," Frijona says to me.

"Should you ride bearing a child?" I say.

"Myrah will look kindlier upon Frijona's belly than she would my sword," says Brant.

The sun is our faithful friend as we walk our horses alongside foamless water beset with eerie calm. Where the sea wends west, we leave our horses with Brant so the wolves will not see them. I lead Frijona and Florentina further and further from the sea until the sound of talk and laughter brings us to the mead hall, wherein loud men and women clothed in brown and green drink the sight from their eyes not long after morning has left them. The wind bears Luda from among them to Frijona. Whispered words send Luda running whither we came to her. Before I can take Florentina from Frijona, Annette has done so, standing upright with her fleshy arms beneath Florentina's legs. Annette still wears her ringed brown hair woven into a flowered wreath to mark yesterday's wedding.

"Myrah has not left her house this day," Annette says to my ear. "Who is this white-haired woman?"

"Brant's wife, Frijona," I say.

"Where did you go?"

"To bury Gerahard and his men," I say, for my thoughts

offer me nothing else. "Frijona comes with me to tell Myrah of this."

Annette stares into my eyes until her bushy-bearded ox cart of a husband, Wilfrith, takes her arm.

"Go with her and listen through the house's walls," Annette says to him.

"And if I hear something?" says Wilfrith with words deeper than the sea.

"Step within and keep Myrah from hurting anyone," says Annette. "Herself, most of all."

Annette takes Florentina away from the long benches whereunder the mead barrels now rest, as do many hands upon knees and elsewhere. Wilfrith follows Frijona as though he does not follow; Frijona strikes my arm with the back of her hand to take my eyes from him.

"Luda wishes to leave," I say.

"The needs of the many outweigh the needs of the few," says Frijona. "Better for your queen to hear this from us than to have another strike her over the head with it. Give your daughter to her arms to keep her calm."

Derwen's words from within Myrah's house ward the leaning door against my steps. Frijona speaks my name and sets her hand on my back the way mother would when I could not sleep. I step through the gap between the door and the timber wall. Myrah wears her black wool; Derwen, her green. They sit facing one another with their heads turned to us.

"Who is this?" says Myrah.

"I am Frijona, Brant's wife."

"So Gerahard and his wise men went to speak to your kin," says Myrah. "Good. Have they found peace, then, that you come to us?"

Derwen shifts forwards in the sun's dim, scattered light. Myrah's black gown warms her where the hearth's grey embers give us nothing.

"They have," I say as I give her Mildred.

Myrah kisses my daughter's forehead and strokes her little palm with her thumb.

"What do they do now?" she asks.

"Nothing," I say. "He is dead."

Myrah looks at me, to Frijona, at the backs of her own hands, up at the sunlight streaming in through the thatch. It is too bright for her eyes; they flood with water that wets Mildred's hair.

"Gerahard did not come back last night," she says. "Derwen waited for him. We drank mead. We were not ourselves."

"I saw you two when I came to look for you this morning," I say.

"You looked for me?" says Myrah.

"I did. To do the same as Derwen. She had done it in my stead. I took a horse to clear my head but only clouded it. Our men drank mead. Frijona's men drank mead. They were not themselves, and now many of them will never again be themselves."

"Everyone drank mead," says Myrah.

"Everyone," says Frijona.

"Everyone may thus be forgiven," says Myrah.

"Yes," says Frijona.

Myrah looks to me with eyes clouded by thick raindrops.

"Will you forgive me, Ardelle?" she says.

"I will," I say, "though my heart says otherwise."

Myrah nods to herself with fluttering eyelids. She breathes as though her lungs are on fire.

"Your mother and father are dead," she says.

Derwen becomes as still as the stone forefathers that once stood within our sanctuary. Whose arms are these that hold my daughter?

"Tell her, Derwen," says Myrah. "Let us keep secrets no

longer. Tell her how it was that you met them on the path to Deva."

"I walked," says Derwen.

"Tell her!" yells Myrah.

Mildred leaves Myrah's lap and reaches up to me. I come to the floor to meet her.

"Constantine said he gave you Mildred before I knew the truth," says Derwen. "He does not know this leads to madness, nor would he understand if any of us told him with words, so I sent him to where men have no need of understanding. When you left while giving birth, I left to seek death. I told Luda I went to Powys so the others would not follow me. The westward path took me to the homes of men and women who gave me food and warmth in winter in trade for blessings. When the snow melted, the black death took them but spared me. I went to your fields, Ardelle. The men who still worked the wheat and rye in death's shadow set fire to the house and the bodies within so that death would not know who they were, then buried the bodies so death would not know they were there, then took the ashen timber away in carts so death would not know that anyone had ever lived there. I wandered along the stone paths, taking from emptied homes and fields while wishing for death to come to me. It was then that I met Brant. I told him I could not find your mother and father; I would go to Powys to see whether they had fled hither. The Roman roads were my home for a month or more. I came to where many paths meet. Something told me to go east instead of west. It was there that I met you."

"You lie better than Myrah," says a woman who sounds like I do.

"I know," says Derwen. She hangs her head. "I should have gone to them earlier and taken them to Powys with me, where they would still abide had I not hidden myself away for so long. I know that for this, there is no forgiveness, and so I will not ask you for it, nor will I offer you any more of my words no better than dust."

Someone else's hand strokes Mildred's hair. A fair woman with a soft face takes that hand in hers. The dark rings of her hair ward Mildred's body against a cold that comes from no earthly place. Whispered words drift through the sunlight bearing a lifetime of meaning that floats off unheeded into timber beams upon whose hardened flesh shall never be written anything more than the memory of men and women who lie as still as the trees from which their homes were hewn.

"Fire's kiss lends the same hue to everything," says Myrah. She runs her fingers along the brownish ridges of my forearm. "Death has made us one."

Her lips are ash where mine are ice. Her hot breath yields no warmth as she draws away. A hand against her ribs sends her from her knees backwards onto her palms. Derwen hides her from my eyes.

"Why did you not tell me of this, Derwen?" I say.

"I did not want to see the face you show me now."

"That and nothing more?"

"What else is there?"

Nothing.

"I will go to them," I say.

"You will not," says Derwen.

"What would you do?" says Myrah. "What am I to do?"

"You have Derwen."

"Ardelle," says Derwen.

"Derwen will say she sent Gerahard to fight the black death to show that he is true to the wolves," says Myrah. "To show that he loves them as much as he loves me. Tell them this, Derwen."

"They will not believe me," says Derwen. "They will wait as I ask them, but their hearts will weigh heavy with the burden of untruths."

"And?" says Myrah.

"And we are to live among them," says Derwen. "They will become our kin. We should keep no secrets from them."

"Leave Mildred with us," says Myrah. "They will know Ardelle goes in peace if she leaves her child behind."

"You would let her go without speaking a word against it?" says Derwen.

"Yes," says Myrah, "as will you. If, when we wake one day, Mildred is gone, I will go with her to Ardelle. You may come, if you wish, or tell the wolves that Ardelle has forgiven you and returned to the dead."

"It is not enough that the black death comes for you," says Derwen. "You must go to meet it. You *are* one of us, Myrah, if this madness has taken you."

"So I am," says Myrah.

"Mildred comes with me," I say. "I will not have her wonder where her mother is."

"She is *here*," says Myrah. "We will find you, she and I."

"I will not have you find me as Sithebad did," I say. "I can not bear to see you rotting like the slain men in my dreams."

"I bear your blood!" says Myrah.

"I will take Mildred in wool tied to my back on a horse to my fields."

Myrah stands. Her knife leaves its leather sheath. Frijona throws off her tunic over her head and strikes her knuckles against the meeting of her ribs. Myrah's black woollen gown falls to her feet. Derwen stands before Frijona; Frijona shoves her aside. The end of Myrah's knife strikes—not against Frijona, but between where her own ribs meet. It shatters into bloody shards on the wool at Myrah's feet. Mildred cries out and buries her face in my breast. Myrah feels along her wound with fingers that run red with blood. Wilfrith steps into the house. Derwen sets her hands on Myrah's cheeks. Myrah strikes Derwen's arms away.

"Leave my sight," growls Myrah. "If you are so willing to leave me and keep *my* daughter from me and forbid me from coming to you even in the next life, then leave us forever and do not ever come back."

Frijona lifts me to my feet, takes my daughter in her bare arms, and shoves me out of the house. Wilfrith follows her and sets Frijona's tunic over my left shoulder.

"Come," says Frijona as she leads us away. "I have seen such looks on the faces of my sisters before. There is nothing to do but leave as they so wish and wait for their ill mood to likewise leave them."

Out in the mead hall shielded from the midday sun's unkindest warmth, Annette sits between Rosamond and Marigold—my wounded forearm burns in the grasp of an uncaring hand.

"You leave Mildred with Myrah," says Derwen.

"Why?" I say. "I told you—"

"Your daughter knows nothing of this," says Derwen. "She has earned none of this. If you must go, leave her with a mother who has nothing left but the daughter you have made hers. Or have you no love for Myrah? Is Mildred nothing to you that you leave them both so readily?"

"Everything," I say. "That is why Mildred comes."

Derwen draws near to me and looks into my eyes.

"Nothing," says Derwen. "That is what I see. Do not burden Mildred with this. I can not stop Myrah from finding another knife. Mildred can."

Frijona gives Mildred to Derwen without asking me whether she may do so. She takes her tunic from my shoulder and wears it.

"If Brant went to do the same," she says, "our son would stay with me."

Derwen leads us to Myrah's house. Myrah sits in her linen with her back to us. Derwen kneels down and sets Mildred in

Myrah's lap. Myrah takes her, kisses her forehead, and rocks from side to side, singing in her mother's tongue as she does. Derwen jerks her head towards the door with a grim frown. Frijona takes my arm and runs with me beyond the mead hall. She does not stop, even when my breath leaves me, until we have reached Brant and Luda, who wait with the horses. This is how it must be, then.

"I go to my mother and father," I say. "Derwen lied. They are in the earth."

"So leave them there," says Luda.

"I will after I have seen them," I say.

"This mare's bags still have food," says Brant as he walks her to me with leather straps in hand.

"Where is Mildred?" says Luda.

"With Myrah," I say.

Luda shakes her head. She holds me in her arms until Brant bids her stop so he can do likewise. When Frijona takes his arms from me, she blesses me only with a rough kiss for my cheek and a hand for the back of my legs.

"Go," she says.

The wind bears my mare south to the meeting of two paths, where dusk becomes night. Not far from there, an old oak grove lies hidden beneath the moon's shadows. I take us there to make our bed. In my dreams, great, winged birds swoop down from the heavens with claws that grasp at my horse's mane. I swing myself up onto her back before she runs off into the night. She leaves the stone of the old path and thereafter the ground altogether, finding nothing beneath her hooves and my feet but the cold, loveless water of the sea.

I wake to icy, stinging rain drops running down my nose and soaking into my gowns. I have no hood to keep the clouds' gift from my hair; I thus take my morning meal of bread and cheese—my first since the day before yesterday— beneath clumped oak boughs whose weighted, leafy limbs drop their rainy burdens onto my head whenever they wish. When we ride once more, the rain hides these grasslands as well as any fog: our eyes follow the many-shaped stones below us washed smooth by water that flows into earthen ditches on both sides of the path. My mare's strides send us gliding with such swiftness that she might fly a short while alongside her black moorhen kith did the heavens not rest their watery hand so heavily on our wings.

Not long after the stone marker shows us the way to Camulodonum, we take shelter from the rain beneath a stone-roofed opening in its northern wall. On the paths lie many heaps of bundled wool—these are men. Men who do not stir. I squeeze my horse's body with my legs to send her forwards again; my thighs and ankles become weary from asking her to wind us around the bloated and blackened bodies.

"We must not dwell on these things," I say to her neck, "lest they take us with them."

It is among the roughly hewn, dusk-dimmed stone near the northern wall of Londinium that we find warmth. The rain has stopped long enough for the living to drag bodies into great heaps and set fire to them among shadowy houses of timber and crumbled stone. My horse neighs and breathes out wretchedly through her nose; I hide my face with my soaked linen, yet I bring us closer to dry the salted rain from a woollen gown that hangs heavy on my shoulders.

"Are these men?" I ask the dark shape that stands beside me in the sun's waning light.

"They were, once," he says and spits on the ground. The fire gives light to the earth spread over his cheeks and forehead. "We have no weapons to give them, nor can we dig holes wide enough for them without telling death that we stay here. If you have come to help, you should smear blackness on your face so death does not know that you have not yet been taken."

"I go further south to help them," I say as I take my gown from my nose.

"Then you go to help death," he says. "He may not look again where his hand rests so heavily." He waves his spear at the heaps of bodies. "I will hide you as well as any of us is able."

He bends down, takes a handful of rain-softened earth, and spreads it over my face without care for my lips or nose or eyes. He looks me over from my feet to my hair.

"Stay too long in the open beyond these walls and death will find you," he says. "My earth does little to make your face unsightly to him."

The stink of the burning dead does nothing to make his words kinder, nor does their unwanted light help me find the stone town's southern opening. When my horse has wearied of the stench, her hind legs threaten to throw me off. A sunken-eyed, brown-clothed man stretches his arm towards an opening in a great wall that leads to a bridge over a wide river. Thereafter, my mare becomes friendlier: she rides to a field of tall grass and eats from it while I am still on her back. I lie down not far from her amid the hay with an empty belly that needs no bread, nor anything at all.

Naked, burning, blackened bodies send thick smoke into my lungs. Among them are a man whose left leg has been shortened by white worms that eat away at his flesh. Men bear a bound woman who still lives and throw her onto the heap. Her wretched screeching bares her lips and shows me two rows of blinding white teeth that melt my eyes into ashen dust.

Mother? That can not have been her face. Even father would not know her.

I cough myself awake as the sun floods the half-eaten, grassy field with bright light. I whistle loudly though the boatman might hear me from afar. My mare walks out from amid a grove of short, grey-barked ash trees at whose leaves she bites until I call to her again. My dried wool rests lighter on both of us; with the wind at our backs, we tread the stone of the path swiftly enough to bring us to Durovernum before the sun is high among the clouds. When we reach the bridge over the river beyond the western walls, I ask her to walk through the water instead, ever mindful of that dark-hooded man and his long staff. We thereafter follow the outer stone walls alongside high-banked earthen mounds beyond the town's eastern opening to where the earth lies low amid a bed of marshy water shaded from the rainless heavens by the brushy green leaves of snake-boughed alder trees.

That is where Isadora spoke with the thane who was to take us to Myrah's father. Does Isadora yet live? Would she still abide in her house of stone, even after all this time? No, she would not, and yet she can not be nothing more than another body amid a heap of burning flesh. She *must* not be.

The oaks that shroud her house have grown little taller, yet they still stand, as does the unlocked oaken door, to whose back side has been fastened a rusted iron beam that takes its hook from the stone wall when I shove the door open. The wind thus blows ashes from the hearth's dead embers—how long they have been dead, I know not—and nearly sends a thick sheaf of bookfell flying from within the wide, flat wooden box beside the wall. Why were these words not burned? Does Isadora tell of where she might have gone? Mother and father? Do they still live?

I sit with my back against the door to keep it closed as I look over ink strokes at times flowered or angular, rough or fair: Rosamond longs for the painted stone roads and warm baths and flowing aqueducts of Parisius, where she watched over the children of noble men and women who would never permit her return so long as they desire dominion over that which lives within her. Marigold writes of twin kingdoms from her dreams hued bright red and dusky purple, altering themselves whenever she looks away so that they appear anew when she looks back to them. This is all she would ever wish to see were she not bound to her sisters in the waking world, of whom she calls but one her dearest friend. Florentina bemoans the deaths of the fighting men she could not heal for her episcopus Masona, whose volatile temper and fickle religion lauded her on one day and hated her the next so that she never knew whether what she did was right or wrong.

Annette talks of how she has at last broken free from men who painted their faces before battle, and whose tongue she learned without wishing to among sweeping sandstone hills and heathered moors. In coming to serve Myrah's father, she now kneels instead before the painted stone of dead men trapped within lifeless marble walls that still the mother tongues of her sisters. Luda wants to free herself from wretched men and leave for her homelands, where she might bear a son whom she will give the life she took from her aldorman. She swears, however, to meanwhile bear her suffering among us for the sake of her aldorman, who, in his sorrow over his drowned son, threw himself into a battle he could not win and did not return from it.

Derwen speaks of her husband, with whom she left Powys for his homelands in a place called Jutum. The sheet bears dried teardrops upon the ink of the words that tell of the men who met them before they reached the southeastern shore. With their knives and axes and shears, they took her husband's heart and her left arm and a length of her young child's hair. Were she not a mother, they said, they would not have spared her. Her words end in a long, thick line. So great must her sorrow have been that she does not write her child's name, nor does she say whether it is a son or a daughter.

Further down the sheet, Derwen's words come to life in darker ink: Myrah, who had not yet grown into a woman, sought Derwen's friendship after hearing of her tale. Derwen took Myrah's kind hands and soothing words and ... warm lips that breathed life into her as she had never before felt. Myrah's father bade them stop, yet Derwen sought out Myrah wherever they would not be seen until, one day—here, the words end with no line to tell of what has been left unwritten.

The next sheet bears the tall, thick, strong strokes of wandering half-thoughts that leave most of the parchment blank:

> There came to me in that sanctuary
> A wild-eyed maid of tall and sturdy limbs
> With yellow hair that flowed well past her waist
> Head wrapped in linen to shield her sweaty face
> And cheeks warmed to redness by the sun
> No man would speak of her as fair to another
> Yet I would be the one to have her
> As her feet take the earth from the fields
> So, too, does she take my heart
> Wherever she might lie at night
> I would stand against all others to take her in my arms
> And whisper to her of kingdoms beyond the seas
> That she might dream of happiness
> And wake to find the same beside her.
> *Myrah: you may write whatever you wish.*
> *Know that this, too, must burn. —Father*

Derwen's hair is brown, not yellow; she stands a head lower than I do; I have never seen her wear linen about her face but before our now-shattered runestone. Did Myrah write this of *me*? Why did Isadora hide these words away instead of burning them? She must hide *herself* somewhere along with mother and father. I must see whether she has left more such words hidden somewhere in our fields.

I take the sheaf of bookfell and shove it between my leather belt and the gown at my waist. I have only begun to feel the weight of my horse beneath me when we come to stretching rows of knee-high green wheat stalks. My little bread-grinding quern split into stone shards lies half-buried in rain-softened earth at the middle of a great ring of flint-stones as wide as our house once was. I have nothing but my hands with which to dig; as my fingers and nails darken from clawing into the ground, I must thank the endless rain for not having dried the chalky earth into stone.

And yet it should have, for here is mother's damp and greening woollen bedding. My hands dart back from stiff, cloth-hidden limbs. Next to mother's right leg lies a weft board from her weaving loom; at her right arm rest two spindle whorls that bore her yarn. On her left are a row of flint-stones atop straw and grass beside the broken haft of a spear that must be father's. I take the earth from above father until I have laid bare his tunic and leggings. His right foot has been wrapped in linen, while his left leg has been broken off at the shin. Father's head and shoulders hide beneath an oaken shield bolstered in the middle by a silvery fish whose body bears a misshapen square and a full moon of iron.

"Give me your shield, father."

I cough up that morning's cheese at the sight of his white and waxy face. Were his hair and beard not soft against my fleeting fingertips, I might think that Derwen had taken one of our stone forefathers from Constantine's ruined mansio. I give his shield back to him and close my eyes. He smiles, the sweat running from his short brown hair down his forehead as he comes in from the wheat field with scythe in hand. This is how I shall remember him.

And how shall I remember mother? Sleeping under her wool as she sometimes did when she felt winter's night chills more strongly than father or I did. Does she feel them now beneath her bedding? I can not bear to set my hand on her limbs as stiff as tree boughs. I might look at her face as I have done father's only long enough to see that she rests in peace.

A blackened, eyeless face with an open jaw bears nothing of life but two rows of snowy white teeth that knife into my heart. My lungs burst at the stink of rotten eggs and ox shit. Everything I have eaten today and the day before yesterday comes up from my belly, scattering egg whites and mashed apple wedges and milk all over the patchy grass. Shaking hands do not give the bedding back to her, but instead take the shield from father's face. What has done this to them? What is this? How can this be?

I know. I know what happened. Mother died. Father buried her and looked after her. When Derwen came to him, he killed himself while she slept. Derwen woke to the body the next day so she would know all too well of his suffering. She laid him to rest beside mother. She sang to him as she did our sanctuary's marble to keep his flesh whole. This is what must have happened. This is what happened. She did not burn them. She told me that to keep me from coming here so that I would not dig up what she had buried with them, those things we used while we lived together, mother and father and I. Constantine never looked so wan as father even amid those sweeping drifts of snow. Sithebad's ashen, rotting flesh had never fallen away to the blackened blood and bone beneath mother's smile and soft kisses and the warmth of her fingers on my forehead as I lay in bed at night.

Mother's bedding and father's shield lie above their faces once again, stirring little in gusting winds that blow short wheat stalks against the ground. I might lie down in a furrow and become one of them, waiting there in stillness until a scythe comes to harvest me and load me onto a cart to be taken to whichever king is still among the living. Myrah. That is where they would take me. What would she have of me? To stay with her as mother and father lie here in peace. To tell her I will not leave her alone in the sanctuary when her father wished to send me home from his battle. To let Florentina sing to me while my daughter comes into this world and thereafter stays there with her mother. To tell the kin of the wolf that Myrah gives them a son; and if she does not, to flee north with her and our sisters from death's grasping claws until the grassy hills turn to stone and rise so high into the heavens that the great, winged birds have only to bend their legs in taking us onto their backs and flying away into the clouds, where the boatman can not reach us.

But I am here with those who have done no wrong, only what they thought was right, and death has told them that for this they may lie beneath the earth and rot as worms eat the flesh from their bodies.

I bear the stones from between mother and father to a row of wheat stalks laid low by winds that threaten to wrest the leather bag from my belt. I bundle the bookfell into one of the horse's bags, unfasten my belt's iron buckle, and let it rest in my lap. Flint meets flint against the braid-like heads of wheat that none shall ever need, for those who might eat it have neither belly nor tongue to take it. I strike until my fingers ache; the wind breathes life into a spark on my belt bag's cow hide. The wheat heads take this gift from it, as do the stalks, as do their brothers among the fields, spreading their seed in waves that flow in time with the aching in my breast.

I take the bookfell from its leather grave and look through the sheets beneath Myrah's words: they speak of a man named Athelbert—the name his mother gave him rather than the one he gave himself—and how his wisdom showed him the way when his daughter and his wise men and even his thyle did not heed his wishes. Many words tell of how his thyle bemoans having shown her faithlessness by leaving her house of stone to bring her king a young maid taken by the winds who made his foes yield in battle, and yet he did not win. Her last lines are written with shaking letters:

Should you ever read this, Ardelle, know that the guilt for whatever you may have done lies with me for having brought you to Myrah's father. I go now to be with your mother, who left us too soon. In that place, I will hold her to me as I once did you. Do not look for me, my darling child, for when the men find my body, they will take it to where the others lie and burn the mark of death from us. —Isadora

I grasp the upper half of father's broken spear haft and thrust its dulled head into the bookfell. These wretched words I bring to the burning fields and set them alight, then run with them as the wind blows cinders into my gown to the pit where mother and father lie. I set aside mother's bedding and father's shield, throw the fire-tipped spear between them, and kneel with my hands over my eyes as I sing what few words I remember from our song at the sanctuary. The rest I hum as Florentina might have done with her hands upon men beyond healing. I hie away from an unearthly heat: deep red flames billow up towards the heavens bearing a stench that would empty my belly were anything yet within it. They take with them the memory of mother and father's wretched forms, leaving only the ashes of my devotion to Myrah, who has been my queen in the stead of those who brought me into this world. That Derwen forgot my mother and father when she left Myrah means nothing, for I have done the same and worse: I take them from their peaceful sleep and now burn their memory into nothingness. I will offer these bitter tokens to still the hand of death upon men who are only brother to me when their dim and lifeless eyes meet their equal in mine.

The sun makes ready to bed down when the fire has burned itself out and left behind cooling ashes and bone shards. I sweep these up into two dark blue, inkless pots taken from my mare's leather bags—Gerahard stole these from

Myrah; Frijona took them from Gerahard; I took them from her. My horse comes to my whistling with short, fearful steps that lengthen into welcome strides when I tell him we are to ride straight to the white cliffs; and this time, we shall not fall from them.

The dusk-lit path to the shore bears no footsteps from our midday bath so long ago when the northmen did not watch us. There is only one man who sees me now, and it is his hand I seek to take from suffering men as I shed my wool and linen and wade out into the sea. There, I wash clean the earth from my face and spread the ashes of mother and father in water up to my waist. This, too, shall burn; and when the boatman comes for them and Myrah's song and the dreams of my sisters, he may wait in bitterness as they, like Sithebad, remember who they once were and dream, for a time, that they have never been otherwise.

V

A MOTHER'S LAMENT

31

LIFE

The morning sea's calm waters have emptied me of all else but the aching sorrow of the ashes that still lie scattered among the tides. I must leave them there to the one who will take them, yet his bony fingers weigh against my breast so that I can not lift my cheek from the shore's rough sand until the night's wellspring has wrung itself dry through my eyes. My legs are the stone of the cliffs that look down on me from above as I creep up the sloping path on palms and knees. My forehead strikes the sand where it yields to dry brown thatch among dewy green grass dotted with Maria's golden flowers. Neighing lends strength to my neck: my mare stands not far from me, shaking the day's first mist from her grassy nose. I draw myself to my feet, swing my heavy leg up over her unsaddled back, and steady myself against stamping steps that stop when a heavy gale of wind blows her mane from her eyes.

"Take me to my fields one last time," I say to her, as if the truth of my words were enough to make her understand me.

An empty pit, a ring of stone, a broken quern, furrowed

black rows of ash that stretch beyond sight. Nothing here bears any mark of life or love or happiness, yet in Isadora's house I might find hidden a token of her devotion: a writing feather, her hair pin, wax from one of her reading candles.

My mare starts from the burned wheat heads. I cling to her neck. We need not fear the river, now, as we walk alongside it until we find where it is narrowest and shallowest. Isadora's house of stone still stands, though the wind has left the door open and swept the hearth's embers clean of their ashes—

A slight woman kneels before Isadora's wooden box wearing a sleeveless gown of brown fastened with bone at her shoulders. The linen sleeves of her undergown match the pale hue of outstretched fingers spread apart as she shakes a short, brass-clasped tail of thick black hair from side to side. A loud outbreath through my nose shows me her soft jaw and full cheeks too fair to bear suffering well.

"Did you take my parchments, Ardelle?" Isadora asks.

My mouth has no answer. My eyes have nothing left to give her. My heart seeks the bottom of the earth but does not find it. From the stone that dwells where my heart once did, my eyes draw the last drops of water. Isadora's arms become my legs and help me to the ground, where I kneel with my head against her shoulder and wash her gown with my tears as she strokes my hair.

"I saw where mother and father were buried," I say. "I burned your words."

"As you should," says Isadora. "Your mother fell ill in winter. We thought her illness like any other. When the snow melted, she left us. I helped your father bury her beneath the house so he would never be far from her. Your friend Derwen—"

"My sister."

"Your sister Derwen came to us not long thereafter and told us of the black death that crept through the land. This must have been what took Branwen. Your father did not want to leave any memory of his wife for death to find, so he asked Derwen to help him take the house asunder. She did so with her song. She told us she would take us to Branwen's homelands in Powys, but Gildewin would go no further from his wife than to my house."

"You did not see Brant? A bearded man on a horse?"

"We hid from everyone and everything, most of all those among the living who might bear death's hand. Your father ... went out to fish one day, hiding among the reeds as he did so. He did not return when midday became evening. I went off in search of him, thinking to find him in his fields, whither he sometimes went though he knew he should not. There, I found him with his hunting knife in his breast. I knew not how to make my peace with him, so I took his wife's bedding and his shield and buried them together. Thus they would know, wherever they are now, where the other is. I came back to my house and wrote of my misdeeds on the parchment I had stolen from Myrah's father. I would have spoken them aloud before burning them and going to be with Branwen and Gildewin."

She draws back from me to look upon me; her brown eyes and rounded cheeks are wet with tears.

"Why did father look so still?" I say. "Did Derwen sing his body into stone?"

Isadora opens her mouth and steadies her breath. She sets her palm against my neck bone.

"I found him the day before yesterday," she says.

I close my eyes and hang my head.

"If I had come here sooner ..."

Isadora holds my chin upright. Her wan face brooks no hardening even as it bears sorrow and bitterness.

"You could have done nothing," she says. "When your mother died, so did he."

"So did you. I read your words."

"And yet when you found my words and burned them, you still sought me out though I told you not to. Here I am. You are all that I have left." She kisses me. "What we burn, we wish to forget, but we do not often forget. Where do you abide?"

"With my daughter far north of here," I say.

"Your daughter? I was told she did not live."

"She is with Myrah."

"The one who answered your words of love with her own," says Isadora.

"I do not think so," I say.

"Your mother did," says Isadora. "She knew the words you sent with Myrah were not for your mother and father. When Myrah understood this, she blushed so well that I saw it in her cheeks. Take me to her. We shall have each other, at least."

Isadora sits close behind me on my horse with her arms around my waist—she is as slight as Myrah. She leans into me, clasping her own forearms as the wind hastens us southwest to Durovernum. There, the heaped bodies have burned into blackened husks that look nothing like who they might have once been. Do the men who set fire to their flesh lie in heaps of their own? No, the boatman has mother and father.

"We have no need to fear death if we ride with greater swiftness than he," Isadora says to my shoulder.

Our mare's hooves strike lightly against the stone of the open path and the bridges over boatless rivers and the roads that wind through the wood and stone of Londinium. There, some of the dead have swollen to twice their girth, offering us a stench that writhes its way into our noses even under our gowns. Thereafter, oaks, wych elms, alder, birch, beech, hedges, hills—all of these drown in a sea of darkness as mother and father's house and its brightly burning hearth set themselves before me over and over.

Mother gives water to wheat on the cooking stone while father smokes deer meat. I thread wool through my dark green gown where it is torn. Mother's smiling face and long braid warm me better than our fire; father's hand on my knee stills my thoughts as readily as does his kiss before I sleep at night.

I show mother what I have sewn. She has no eyes to look upon it, nor does she have lips to smile at what I have done, only a blackened skull whose white teeth are as snowy as father's flesh where he sits as still as stone with open eyes before the hearth. The fire strokes his leggings, yet he does not stir. I take off my green wool over my head and beat the hearth's burning fingers into stillness.

"Let us bed down here," Isadora says to the setting sun. "When we reach Camulodonum, we will go around the walls."

My mare's leather bags are as full at dusk as they were when I woke beside the sea. Isadora lies down amid oaks with her back to mine and gives to me a dreamless sleep from which I wake unwillingly. Her arms lift my back from the ground and hold me as I sway, so weary am I.

"We shall rest here until you have eaten something," she says.

She holds me as she feeds me what little of her plum-softened bread my aching throat will swallow. I eat little better at midday and nothing at all when the westering sun shines down on the stone marker that sends us north to Myrah's wolves and our sisters. Mother and father's ashes float among billowing grey clouds and fall down onto the brown thatch of empty houses. They burn my tongue when Isadora sets her bread between my teeth. I choke down three mouthfuls of her dried rye bread before taking the last of the boiled river water from her flask.

"I do not want to come upon the men when they drink

mead," I say. "Let us stay here and go to Myrah in the morning when everyone sleeps."

"Only if you eat what is left of this bread when you wake," she says. "That birch grove will do."

"That is where the men keep their horses at night."

"The tall grass, then. Our horse may eat what he wishes for having brought us here so quickly."

Even here with Isadora so near to me, the sea calls me to walk north along the midnight shore and there greet its flowing waves with outstretched arms. The blood moon hangs low in the sky, wider and redder than when it shone down on that river wherein I would have met the same fate as the boatman's thane had Isadora not found me. I cry out for her with words that ring within my head and nowhere else, yet sleep keeps me bound beneath the night stars better than leather string on my wrists and ankles within a hypocaust ever did. The waves rush upon the sand, flooding the grassy earth with frosty foam and soaking my gowns with bitter cold. They ebb and flow in swelling haste until they have grown taller than the white cliffs not far from our sanctuary and come rushing down on top of me with such might that my gasping breaths choke my throat shut and send me upright in the morning's light to vomit up yesternight's bread onto my green gown dyed brown by my own filth.

"Forgive me for making you eat," Isadora says. "I will fetch you water for washing."

Having cleaned my gown and eaten nothing, we leave our faithful horse to the care of bearded, brown-clothed men who sleep soundly beneath the leafless boughs of birch trees that look as though the winds have tried to wrest them from the ground. Four of the clustered houses on their broad, raised bed of earthen stone are now nothing more than fallen timber. To the east, in the dim light of the morning's sun, the mead hall is likewise in ruins. We walk with our gowns held up to our shins in flooded grass that leaves us only when we step up onto the raised floor of Myrah's house. Within, she sleeps near softly glowing embers. Mildred's head rests in Myrah's arm as my daughter breathes into Myrah's chin. They keep one another warm; so, too, does my heart come to life. The memory of mother's smile sends my arms to my sleeping daughter and takes her against me so I may look on her soft, fat cheeks and her sweaty, wavy black hair and her little fingers.

"Who is this?" says Myrah.

Before I can answer, her mouth is against mine; her hands are on my jaw and cheeks. She kisses me twice, thrice on my unwashed forehead and my snot-stopped nose and my matted hair still bearing the stink of burned flesh. I set my nose against her neck and breathe her in until my lungs have grown to bursting.

"The one who kept your words," says Isadora. "Ardelle burned them, yet I see they still live within the both of you."

"Have you seen my father?" says Myrah.

"I have seen nothing of anyone your father knows since he sent me away," says Isadora.

"Forgive me," says Myrah. Isadora lifts an eyebrow. "I thought he might have returned." Myrah speaks to my cheek. "Derwen told the men my tale. They think these mighty winds your gift to Gerahard, blowing first north, then south as he drives the black death from our lands."

My daughter sleeps so well in my lap that her breathing is almost too soft to be heard.

"I have driven it from the lands as well," I say. "I burned your words to me and those of our sisters along with my fields and every memory of my mother and father. I spread their ashes in the sea for the boatman to take so that he might leave us be."

"You did *what?*" says Isadora.

"She did this to share in my suffering," says Myrah. She kisses me. "That is how I know she loves me. And yet when first I saw you, I hated you. I thought my father must have bound you so tightly to keep you from murdering men. When you spoke an oath to him, I wished for your kiss so wholly that I became blind to all else. You could have killed a hundred men and I would have cursed them for having angered you. The men of stone I would have sent to the ground to lie in shards before the only one worthy of standing before mother and father as my equal. Mother hated me for going against father. You know what father did to me. And yet I would have left them behind to follow you had you but asked me. When I told you to run away, you could have done so and taken me with you."

Myrah kisses me until I can not breathe. I gasp and cough, yet my daughter does not wake. Isadora clears her throat.

"I know you must feel the same way," says Myrah. She sets her hand on my neck. "Your heart beats through your flesh."

"That is mother's heart. Father's. I should have given myself along with them, but I have left my daughter so often that she does not know who I am."

"You go where you will with the wind," says Myrah. "You went beyond Durovernum and back in six days where it would take a strong man and a healthy horse four days to go hither. You are right to leave Mildred with me. That is what Derwen says. She stays in Annette's house awaiting you to ask your forgiveness. Stand in our house's opening and call to her. She will come."

My words have no weight, so I send them with the wind to wherever Derwen listens. The green-gowned shape that comes to stand in the house's opening shakes marsh water from her bare feet and sits down beside the wall away from the hearth's mild warmth.

"Forgive me for lying with Myrah," she says.

"You are forgiven," I say.

"Forgive me for not telling you of your mother and father," she says.

"Why did you not?"

"I did not want to hurt you. Nothing more."

"Nothing more."

I shake my head. Forgiveness and nothing more.

"You left Mildred with Myrah twice," says Derwen. "Once when you came for me and once when you went for your mother and father. Gerahard could have killed you. Your boatman could have taken you. Thus, you were right to leave your daughter."

"How is this right?" I say.

"Myrah's father forbade us from speaking Latin though men throughout these lands have not forgotten their old tongue," says Derwen. "He kept us from the sight of trading ships and wandering men and the written words of those wiser than us. These things he thought would take us from him. It is this seed of truth that lives within his law against bearing children among our sisters, for even he knew that we wound our children worse than any other. How many times has Mildred cried out when you sing? When fear or anger stirs within your breast? Had you taken her to your mother and father, your daughter would have died. Think, Ardelle: your sisters have all left their mothers. My mother sent me from her house when I was but thirteen. I sang to trees and sat before runestones instead of heeding her religion. Annette's mother died before her first memory. Maria's mother brought her here from a kingdom called Mide over the western sea and left her with a heartless woman, whom Maria fled. Florentina's kin sent her away on a ship to spare her life. Rosamond was sold instead of murdered. Luda was sent away from her homelands though her mind has never left them. We left our mothers and fathers, all of us, and thus they did not wound us with the gifts they gave to their children. This secret they keep hidden from all others, yet they can not keep it from their children, who, in asking for the love of those who brought them into this world, draw it from their mothers and fathers should they live so long as Hugo. As will Mildred call it from you with greater strength when she grows older. As would my daughter were I able to speak of her without dying. But you, you have learned to spare your daughter from this by leaving her with Myrah. Thus, you have done her a mother's greatest kindness: you can better bear being away from Mildred than Mildred can bear being with you."

"What you say is wretched," I say.

"It is," says Derwen, "but you will come to learn that what you must do is not. Give your daughter over to Myrah wholly and let her care for Mildred. At night, Mildred may sleep with one of your sisters while you and Myrah are together."

Let mother sleep with father in the sea while I am together with the boatman.

Myrah takes Mildred from my arms. I reach out to my daughter. Derwen sets her arm around me to keep me from her.

"Your tears will drown her," says Derwen. "She does not know how to swim. Master yourself as well as you are able, for she knows nothing of what such even means."

"I will," I say. "You are forgiven, whatever that means."

"It is enough that you have said it."

"I will watch her while you sleep," says Isadora. "She need know nothing of these things, nor should she."

"She still sleeps from the mighty winds that blew down the mead hall and some of these houses," says Derwen.

"That was you, Ardelle," says Isadora. "Never have I ridden so swiftly, not even on Myrah's father's strongest horses."

"Isadora," says Derwen, "take Mildred and come with me to Annette's house for a time."

Isadora's arms take my daughter and hold her as would one who had never done such. She will learn how to do so soon enough.

"Stay away from the men," Derwen says to me, "lest others be given a greater share of your heartache than they can bear."

Isadora walks through the house's opening bearing my limp and sleeping daughter in her arms. Derwen kneels beside me, strokes my hair once, and kisses me on the forehead before leaving.

As I weep against Myrah's breast, mother strokes my hair and kisses me before I bed down to sleep, over and over and over. To my daughter I would do the same when she is older, should I live so long that she remembers who I am.

32

FRIJONA

Whatever is left of morning's stillness ebbs into the throaty bellowing of men. If they are newly awoken from yesternight's drinking, their laughter and weighty steps bear no mark of their drunkenness. Myrah wipes the last of my tears from her neck and leaves my arms. She stands up straight, looking about her as though she sees the men through the timber of the house.

"I will go without and speak to them of your return," she says.

"I thought they were not to know of me," I say.

"They have been awaiting you," she says. "I told them you went with Gerahard at Derwen's behest to fight the black death. You return without him. I must tell them the truth, now, to keep them from hating me."

"Will they not hate you for doing this?" I say.

"Less than they would were they to learn of it from another," says Myrah. "I will look in on Isadora and Mildred to see whether your daughter still sleeps."

Myrah leaves our house with a kiss for my lips, lifting her gown to her shins to keep it from the flooded water-grass around the raised bed of stone and earth that may yet keep us from drowning when we sleep. The hearth's embers give me no warmth; I breathe in the frost of timeless rest as mother and father float in a river that flows without end. I stand above them in my boat, clothed in midnight's hue and bearing a long staff with which I turn their bodies over to look on their lifeless faces.

"Ardelle—"

I start into Isadora's breast. She sits beside me with her arms around my waist and shoulders.

"Florentina sings to Mildred," she says. "Your daughter still sleeps. Florentina thinks she may wake later today."

"May I see her?"

"You may watch her where she does not see you so she does not think to ask for you," says Isadora.

"I will see her in my mind whether I wish to or not," I say, "nor will mother and father leave me alone."

"You may wish to give those things a name so you need not fear them so much," Isadora says. "Hatred is what I felt for Myrah's father. Knowing this made me hate him no less, but I was better able to make peace with myself as I spent those first long weeks with your mother and father."

"How were they long?" I say.

"I lived within my mind," says Isadora. "Every day was a year. I would write of my hatred in the earth with a stick and thereafter stamp it smooth with my foot. After some months, I did the same with my spoken words, which became dust as soon as they left my mouth."

"I have no name for this," I say. "I know not what it is, nor where it abides, nor what shape it takes. What does one do against such a foe? I only wish to spare Mildred from knowing the same one day. I think to myself at times that I should die before Mildred's first memory of her mother so she never knows of this."

"No," says Isadora. She sits down in my lap and holds me closer to her than she has ever done. "You will overcome this. I will help you."

She holds me until Myrah, Rosamond, Marigold, and Annette tread the hard earthen floor of our house with feet as bare as mine. Wilfrith is with them; he nods to me as he turns his back to us and stands watch in the house's opening. Marigold grasps my right shoulder and leans into my arm. Rosamond hums sharply but says nothing as she sits down to Isadora's left.

"Before you leave, if that is your wish," says Myrah, "I must tell you the truth of many things you may not wish to hear but you must hear nonetheless. Those of you who would live here among these men may do so, but not until our men have left along with those stranded on the northern shore."

"They are not stranded," says Rosamond.

"Nor do they go elsewhere and live where men can better abide so many of them," says Myrah.

"So let us do what you say and return south," says Rosamond.

Myrah opens the leather bag on her belt and takes from it a folded sheaf of parchment, which she holds out to Rosamond.

"My father sent me a letter," says Myrah. "He returns when the black death has left. He thinks we brought this down on him for having bound us within his sanctuary for so many years and leaving us after winning a great battle for him. He understands our wrath but will not abide it forever. We are to stay away from Dubris and Durovernum and Londinium and the lands of Sledda's men altogether."

"We go where we wish," says Rosamond with a frown.

She takes the parchment from Myrah's hand, unfolds it, and reads it.

"So we may," says Myrah, "but father threatens to send his men to look for us and kill us in our sleep so we can not call the heavens and the earth against him." Rosamond shakes her head. "He knows now that he was wrong to think that he could ever wield our strength in restoring his Roman imperium to the height of its greatness though it has never left our hearts and laws and lands. When he returns, he will bring men together once more with the strength of their own steadfastness and faithfulness to his one true god who lives within the heavens."

Rosamond sighs and hands the parchment to Isadora's outstretched hand. Isadora reads swiftly and gives the parchment back to Myrah.

"Those sound like his words," says Rosamond.

"And those strokes were written by his hand," says Isadora.

"Then let us leave with Brant and Luda," says Annette.

"You know the sea still swells, Ancarat," says Wilfrith from without.

Annette frowns and breathes out loudly.

"Must you use that name before others?" she says. "Let Luda becalm the sea long enough for us to go."

"For how many months, dear?" says Wilfrith.

"Have you spoken with Luda?" I say.

"She speaks to none," says Wilfrith. "These wolves and their friends, least of all."

"Then bring them to me and I will speak to them," I say.

"Would they hear the words of a ghost?" says Marigold.

"I think not," says Rosamond.

"What of Frijona?" I say. "Bring her here and let her speak for herself among us."

"I can not," says Myrah.

"You can not, or you will not?" says Rosamond.

"She is dead," says Myrah.

Wilfrith stands in the house's opening with his back to us, shielding us from the sun's light as his head searches the water-grass for watching eyes or listening ears.

"Where is Brant?" I say.

"With his brothers," says Myrah. "They make ready a reckoning. That is why they have not left."

Wilfrith comes into the house and stands beside Annette with his hairy arms folded over his brown tunic. He bears a sheathed knife almost as long as his leg that would be a sword on any other man.

"The wolves will burn her body in the mead hall where all can see," he says. "Her men will thereafter leave or be made to leave. Some of them have no mind for whether they drown in the sea or die in battle. They think this Derwen's wrath for the death of their king, Gerahard. His queen, Myrah, must be the one to lead them into battle."

"Is Brant not a brother to you?" I say.

"No less than he is to you, though you may have forgotten this," says Wilfrith. "Annette is my wife. I stay with her."

Annette bows her head. Wilfrith sits down beside her and takes her in his arms.

"So you will lead them?" I say to Myrah.

"If she does not," says Wilfrith, "they may kill her."

"They would kill the most beloved sister of the one they call their Boudica?" I say.

"The sea is their neighbour," says Wilfrith. "Where it has given them life for many thousands of years, it now shows them a death that they have never seen, as does the black hand that comes to them from the south. When faced with nothingness on all sides, ice-hearted men may be driven to do a great many things of which they would never have dreamed in any other life."

Father's ashes sear themselves into the furrows of my palm as I take Myrah's fingers between mine. Molten cinders of bone crumble into dust as they fall from my mouth onto the wool of the gown over my legs where I stand beside my queen.

"When we have done this," I say, "let us scatter with the wind as we so wish."

"It is time, then," says Wilfrith as he stands.

"Maria," says Myrah. "You owe Derwen."

"I know," says Marigold. She rises.

"What does she know?" says Rosamond. "Maria, of what does Myrah speak?"

"I …" Marigold clears her throat. "I told Derwen what Gerahard said. He said he lay with Ardelle on the field of battle while she slept and gave her a child. I asked Derwen to make him suffer for this. She stole a horse and knives and gave them to Luda to bring to her kin. When Gerahard and his wise men had drunk their own weight in mead, Derwen bid them ride into the night to face Luda's kin. They were slaughtered."

"And thus Maria has said she will burn Frijona's body in the mead hall," Myrah says.

Rosamond links her fingers and stretches them out before her, drawing from them the sound of acorns breaking underfoot.

"Well done, Myrah," she says. "You are ever your father's daughter. The men in Parisius who spoke such words were grown. When they were not at each other's throats, they read and sang and danced and sculpted and made streets of painted square stones. I felt at home among them, for I knew that when they were not drunk with wine's potency, they would use words to fight with one another. He who spoke best would win, and that would be that. With you, there is no winning, for there is no game to be played with one who breaks the board after she loses. You only ever bested Florentina at playing Latrones when she tired of your false weeping; and she played against you in another room so Luda would not have to carve a new board every time you lost to her. I would tell Maria not to play at all, but I think she knows better than to listen to me after suffering through my obedience to the wretched men you take as your equals."

"Give me your hand, Ardelle," says Marigold. "You said we are to do this and scatter. I need you to stand with me. I will keep my fire from you. Derwen will not be there to send her anger through me into you."

Reddened ridges and flaking black ash rest beneath the linen of my left forearm. Frijona's flesh will not look so kind when Marigold has done this. Isadora takes my wrist below my wound and wrests my fingers from between Myrah's. Isadora's kind face now bears a look of hardness whose bared teeth strike into my heart with the memory of mother's anger when I would not listen to her. Isadora turns away from me and gives Myrah's cheek the back of her hand so hard that it sounds as though a tree has fallen somewhere.

"What has become of you, child?" says Isadora with heated words. "This is not what your mother taught you."

Myrah holds her face with her hand. She says nothing. Isadora turns to me. I shrink away from her.

"If your mother were here," she says to me, "she would tell you to do no such thing."

I take from the bone clasps on my shoulders the blue, red, green, and yellow beads shaped like little pots given to Myrah by her mother. I draw near to Isadora and take her hot breaths on my shoulder as I tie the leather bead string around her neck.

"I know mother would tell me not to do this," I say. "I will take Frijona's ashes to the sea and spread them there so she may sleep as mother does."

Isadora shakes her head. Myrah sets mother's amber beads against Isadora's neck bones and ties their leather string into a knot.

"Ardelle's beads are from my mother," says Myrah, "and mine from hers. They are yours now. You must forgive us for not knowing any better."

Isadora breathes out the winds that bore us from the southern sea into Myrah's ringed hair. She grasps Myrah's reaching fingers once, twice, then frees them so that they, along with their arms, may rest on Isadora's back as Myrah holds her.

"Ardelle," says Marigold. "Wilfrith waits for us."

I take Marigold's hand; she leads me, with her walking stick, through the house's opening and into water that wets the bottoms of both of our gowns.

"This way," Wilfrith says as he walks before us.

"I have done this before," Marigold says to herself. "For Myrah's father."

"I will not ask," I say.

"Good," says Marigold.

Out on the western water not far from the shore, a white swan rests its long-necked head and feathery wings as it awaits the lifting of night's last darkness. Leather helms, ringed iron shirts, woollen tunics, brown belts, sheathed knives, silver-bound shields, bushy beards long and short, and spears taller than those who wield them turn to greet Marigold as she makes her way over clumped mounds of water-soaked earth. The man nearest the mead hall lowers his spear and strikes it against his shield. I leave Marigold's hand and take her arm, drawing her away from his grim eyes.

"Stay close to me," she says, "else I will not have the strength for it."

"Here," says the spear-man and thrusts his weapon towards the mead hall. There, among rough-edged, broken beams stands Frijona, bound at her wrists and ankles to a tall post of oak that once stood beneath the mead hall's roof. Her earth-caked face is clean beneath her swollen eyelids; her brown clothes are in tatters that ill hide the blue bruises on her legs and belly. I leave Marigold's arm and grasp Frijona beneath her shoulder so hard that Frijona grunts.

"They said you are dead," I say.

"I am," Frijona says to her feet. "We took your king. We must give a wise woman in return."

"Why did you not leave?" I say.

Frijona lifts her head, yet her eyes do not open. Her neck will not bear this weight. I hold her chin for her.

"Brant helped you, once," she says. "He said you would help us in return. I thought you might make these men see that we can live among them in peace. I have foreseen that this place where the marsh meets the sea is best for us, but it may be that I am no wiser a woman than you." Frijona's blood-hued eyes open. "You, with the fiery hair. What is your name?"

"Maria," says Marigold.

"You are to burn me," she says. "I came here seeking your strength. I have found it."

"My mother left me in these lands when I knew nothing of anything," says Marigold. "She gave me to a woman who hated me and walked on me as though I were the earth beneath her feet. Without her, I did not live, so I showed her nothing but love. When I left her on her death bed, I showed her the greatest love of all by taking her from this world before darkness did."

"You need not kill me twice," says Frijona. "Keep your words for one who has earned them."

"I will talk to them," I say. "I will ask them to listen."

"Such is your wisdom," says Frijona and turns her chin from my fingertips, letting it rest against her ribs once more.

I take Marigold's hand to the spear-man who watches over us. Ten of his brothers lift spears from the ground and hold their blades towards us. With slowing steps I walk to this leather-helmed, iron-shirted man who clutches a long-headed spear that would stand taller than he does did he not stop me with its sharpened end. A black line runs from his left eyebrow through a sightless eye and over his nose to the right of his lips.

"What is your—"

"Names are for friends, so I have no need of one." He spits on the ground. "If you think to sway me by showing me your child, ghost, I will show you the bellies of the wives of my murdered brothers. Cenhelm. Hrothgar. Leofsige. Tell me their names after we have slain our foes and I will tell you mine."

"Ardelle."

A man speaks my name as softly as the summer wind bears butterflies. His brown hair looks as though he has run a comb through it this morning; the wool of his tunic and leggings and the leather of his shoes match the brown leather helm he wears on his head. He turns his spear end to the grass and thrusts it into the earth—a child's blue eyes have made their nest beside a thin nose hardened into roughness by dark, short-shorn red hair on his chin and cheeks and above his lips. He smiles at me. Frost takes my heart.

"Do you know my name?" he says.

"I do not," I say. "Am I worthy of your friendship?"

"Oswald," he says. "I came to you in your sanctuary one evening with my brothers Gerahard and Edward. Gerahard was a good man, more forthright than most, but this served him well in battle. I stood beside him many times before he was brought low."

Bitter fear creeps along the flesh of my arms and the bones of my ribs.

"And what of Edward?" I say. "Is he still as kind as you?"

Oswald's smile leaves him, making him kindred to the loveless faces of his many brothers.

"Edward was one of Gerahard's dearest friends," says Oswald. "When we chose Gerahard to be our king, Edward was among the first of us to be made an aldorman. I know that he must have been among those who stood with Gerahard when he was murdered."

"How do you know he was murdered?" I say.

"When their husbands did not come back with you, our wives dragged Frijona from her house and beat the truth out of her."

"This morning?"

"You slept with your mother in the fens last night. Alone. We left you be. Some think we should not have."

"Frijona is not the one who took Gerahard and Edward from you," I say. "Is she not worthy of your friendship?"

"We are only as worthy as you, ghost," says Oswald. He takes my left hand and holds it in his as he looks over the wound hiding under my linen sleeve. "We made the wolves believe Myrah's tales until we learned of the loss of our dear friends. Your flesh is as warm as any of ours."

"As is Frijona's," I say.

Oswald lets go my hand.

"I would have been your friend, Ardelle, if you had let me," he says. "When I came to you in your sanctuary, I only wished to spend the night talking with you and nothing more. Gerahard knew this and left so that the unkind thoughts in your mind might leave with him. But I do not think they have, even now. Friendship left us when Gerahard did. My brothers have been wounded in a way that will not soon heal."

"Did you learn this from us?" I say. "To burn others alive from those who hunted us when we wore red gowns?"

"I have never thought of the hue of your gown, only of your face during the summer that glows bright red in a way that stays in my mind even now. It is what we have not learned from you that does not leave our thoughts: you have not shown us what a sister is."

"A sister is one who stands with her brothers," says Oswald's scar-bearing friend. "Not one who leaves or will not speak to them or when they do speak, lies to them so that they suffer greatly. We would have taken your Myrah as our queen, even without her king, but she withheld the truth of Gerahard's death from us."

"She did not lie about his death."

"Nor did she tell us. Which is worse?"

"I saw in you a kindness that made you fairer to me than any other," says Oswald. "This must have died with you somewhere, as did mine die within me when our brothers left us. This woman must not be allowed to bear her son, for we will not have him come to us fifteen or twenty years from now with brothers of his own seeking a reckoning for his mother and his mother's brothers. This reckoning belongs to us and us alone; and we shall have it this day."

"And if I stood there in the mead hall, bound and beaten bearing your child, what would you say?"

The light in Oswald's eyes flickers and dims. He steps away from me.

"Forgive me, young woman, for having spoken to you so. You look like someone I once knew whom I would have befriended had her heart been open to such."

A raw, throaty, bellowing cry wrests our eyes to the ruined mead hall. Marigold stands with her arms around a bound, writing shape whose legs are wreathed in blood red flames made shadowy by thick, dark, billowing smoke. Her harrowing cries scatter a flock of birds overhead, sending them from the wispy clutches of thorned grey clouds to hide amid misty fog. The sickeningly sweet stench of burning ox hides rushes through my nose and down into my breast, where it clings to my ribs. Behind me, Isadora kneels and vomits between her palms. Myrah stares through me unblinking.

I have taught her this.

My swift strides meet the scar-faced man's spear raised in greeting. Its wooden haft splinters in his hand; the iron head falls away into shards; the unbound rings of his shirt strike against his shoes. A cry from somewhere among the houses knifes into my heart yet drowns itself in a mighty thundering within the heavens' darkening clouds. Out on the little sea, a snake of purple lightning strikes its fangs into the water. The men around us raise their spears, only to have them fall broken to the ground.

"So be it!" says the scar-faced man and rushes towards me.

He loses his feet as the mist over the little sea swells and rises before throwing itself from an unseen cliff onto the burning husk of a woman hardened into stone. A great shower of rain quenches Marigold's fire and soaks the wool of my clothing so well that I am made to shiver in wind that blows cold against my fire-hardened flesh. The tide does not take my legs from beneath me, but leaves my skin with stinging kisses. When it has gone, the men who stir cough up water from their lungs. Some sit up bearing the weight of the heavens' gift. The swan near the shore beats its wings to shake the water from them but does not fly—its toothy limbs bear but those few feathers that were not taken from it. Amid the timber of the mead hall, Marigold sits with her head hanging before Frijona's midnight vomit as thick as ink. Frijona's breast still heaves beneath the bloodied and bruised tatters of her clothing.

"I will do it myself, then," says Myrah.

She walks before me with a knife in her hand. She has taken three steps when I grasp her wrist; she has taken four when she turns and strikes me with the back of her hand so hard that I see stars. When they leave me, Myrah stares at me with her knife's hilt bound in her fingers as though they were carved from the same stone. Her elbow sways in the wind and I am on her, throwing her to the ground, sitting astride her, one hand crushing her knife-wielding wrist and the other on her throat as I will myself to choke the life from her. She did the same to me when I dreamt of her beneath a table on the cold stone floor of Marigold's sanctuary bedroom.

What dream is this through which I now suffer?

Myrah no longer holds her knife. Her hands lie beside her head. Her eyes are closed. My fingers shake against her throat but have no strength. I take my hands from her. Myrah's breast rises beneath my legs as she breathes in with the snoring gasp of a man who sleeps off his mead. She sits up as the men do. Where their eyes hide from me, hers seek my face and nothing else.

"If these men kill me," she says, "you must follow me. Our daughter will know where to find us. She will follow us."

"Ardelle," calls Marigold.

My feet heed her words and sting beneath the heat of the mead hall's dead oak for their faithfulness. Frijona's blood-smeared breast is burned black, bruised blue, streaked green with snot from her nose. She bears but half of her snowy white hair; her tunic hangs from her shoulders like that swan's unfeathered wings.

"Her flesh still lives," says Marigold. "Every other part of her is dead. She asks you to send her to the hidden world."

I set my hands against the flesh of Frijona's belly. My palms burn with a thousand stinging nettles.

"This part of you is not dead," I say. "And you are not ashes, so I am not the one to send you hither."

I take her into my arms—I can not bear such unyielding heat—and sing whatever is left of our sanctuary's song within my mind. I know not how long I sing, only that my words end when Frijona sets her hands on my shoulders, having been freed from their binds by Myrah's knife. Frijona's flesh is no longer blue, but reddened as if from sweating too much; her snowy hair rests on her head as would a bird's nest; her rent and shredded clothing bears the greatest mark of Marigold's fire. Myrah steps before the kneeling men who listen, and those who lie unstirring with their faces beneath the water.

"Frijona bears your mark," she says. "My sisters have spoken. Their words brook no answer. Frijona belongs to me, now, as do you. We go to meet her kin and tell them of what we have done. Whether they answer with words or with spears, we will heed what they tell us and answer in kind. Any of you who do not follow shall become brother to those of our foes who do not listen and stand with them as they drown in the sea's rushing waters."

Men find their feet and search for spears and shields and helms that are not broken. Myrah sets herself between my arms and Frijona's searching eyes.

"I may not be able to make the men listen as well as you do," Myrah says.

"And if you see Brant?" I say. "Luda?"

"If they stand against us, it is of their own doing. Not yours. Not mine. Not any of ours. Frijona, kneel and kiss my fingers."

Frijona sinks to her left knee and takes Myrah's right hand. She sets her lips against Myrah's knuckles where her golden ring would rest had she not given it to another.

"Is that how it is done?" says Isadora as she helps Frijona to her feet.

"I wield the strength that Ardelle has shown me more than once," says Myrah. "Now, I may be the one to send offerings to the boatman."

"What has become of you, child?" says Isadora.

"I love you, too, mother," Myrah says and leaves a kiss on Isadora's cheek. She runs off after the spear-men to lead them unto death.

33

MILDRED

Shaking hands and water-soaked arms lift their blue-cheeked bodies from the water. Some mouths empty their bellies of the marsh's gift. Some breasts sleep without rising or falling. Marigold's eyes betoken the same, though she kneels with her head hanging.

"Marigold," I say.

She does not stir. I rest my chin on her shoulder and take her in my arms. Her left hand comes to rest on my leg.

"Frijona burns and the world burns with her," she says. "Frijona does not burn and the world does so in her stead. I should go with you and your daughter to where kingdoms are red with anything other than blood and fire."

"The wights there dance with snow and dust," I say. "They have nothing for you. They have nothing for any of us."

"Nor do you," says Isadora. Her thumb and forefinger hold the thin length of bone that fastens my gowns together on my left shoulder. "Branwen would give Frijona her own linen and wear rough wool against her skin. Is Myrah so great in your mind that you do not remember your own mother?"

"I remember running from her instead of going to the king," I say.

"So you do," says Isadora. Her hand leaves me. "And I remember taking you to him in your mother's stead after I had shown you the dark dreams I was to keep from all eyes but my own. Yet here I have allowed you to help your sister write them on another's flesh and bone. I will go with you whither your beloved Myrah goes and see to it that you do not do this again."

I take Isadora's arms and kiss her cheek. She blinks and looks beyond me. I kiss her lips. She holds my forearms and frowns at me.

"What do you want, child?" she says.

"Will you take Frijona to Florentina?" I say.

Isadora looks behind her to where the sea's foamy tides flow and ebb beneath darkening clouds.

"I will," she says. "And will you come back here with Myrah?"

"Myrah will come back," I say.

"Only Myrah?" says Isadora.

She clutches my waist with all the strength her brittle fingers and bony arms lend her.

"I have nothing else," she says to my eyes.

"I will bring Ardelle back to you," says Marigold.

Isadora lets go my waist and steps back from me.

"Good," she says.

From her raven black hair, Isadora takes a pin as long as my forefinger. She gathers two thick strands of my hair and slides the pin through them, thus fastening them together at the back of my head. Isadora leads Frijona in her tattered clothing through the ankle-high water to where our houses still stand. At my elbow, Marigold's short fingernails glisten with raindrops.

"Will Rosamond not miss you?" I say.

"I will live on in her thoughts," says Marigold.

Myrah's brown-clothed men thrust their spears into the heavens as they sing. Myrah walks among them. Does she lead them in song?

"Rosa says your eyes look like the sea when the wind blows softly and birds fly together overhead," Marigold says. She sets her forehead and nose against mine. "I see nothing but flickering flames without their candles in a dark and empty room."

Marigold draws back and takes my hands. The smoky clouds that hide the green of her eyes no longer bear the memory of our sanctuary's hearth that burned brightly enough to give life to three great rooms.

"I softened my fire as I waited for you," she says. "I knew you would help Frijona. If I am wounded, I know you will heal me. So let us go to do together what must be done that none who outlive us should ever need to remember."

Marigold and I walk with strides that lose their haste when we come to the hindmost of Myrah's stone-legged fighting men. I know not how long we have walked when the salt marsh ends its easterly path and wends north; it bids us follow its snaking banks towards the great sea. Shield-bearing fore-arms wave fog away from reeds: between rushes and long shoots of water-grass lie the blackened bodies of men with twine-bound beards.

"Why?" I say. "He has taken mother and father."

"As he will take all of us," says a leather-helmed man, "whether we writhe against his binds or smile with outstretched arms. We will at least drive death into the sea before he drowns us. Lead us hither, sister, and show him your might."

"Whether any of us lead or follow means nothing," says a long-bearded man. "See those black bodies before us on the sand, brother. No reeds hide them, now. If I still live at the end of this day, I will kneel before the righteousness of this ghost's queen whether she stands or lies on the shore."

A toothless man spits at the sight of ten or fifteen or twenty dead men whose flesh has been burned to like hue on the open shore unhidden among reeds. His mead-breath turns my face away.

"You might run to your queen now and tell her to find what is left of our foes," he says to me. "You would not wish to see her among the fallen. Your fire-haired friend might have to burn her as well."

Nor would they wish to see themselves fall over with broken spears at their sides as they await a burial that does not come. I hasten with Marigold to a small lake that narrows into a long-flowing river. Men who kneel behind waist-high bushes wave their unbroken spear heads northwards to where Myrah's black gown sits low against the earth. To her left, men creep on hands and knees over the edge of the small slope that leads up from the river to the shore. I bend down in walking to meet them—there are so many more of them than I could wish away from Myrah before they set upon her.

"Myrah," I whisper. She turns her head slightly. "I will go and see whether Brant and Luda are still among their kin."

"No," she says. "They must not know that we are here."

"Did you not see the bodies? What if they are all dead?"

"They must not be." She turns to me. "I beg of you to do as I ask—why are you here, Maria?"

"To do as little as you," says Marigold.

"Stay back, then," says Myrah, "and wait until I wave to you. You may speak with them when we show them our spears from all sides."

The men around Myrah half-stand and whisper in looking beyond me. Derwen comes to us bearing a bundle of linen in her arms. She bids me sit with my legs folded to better set Mildred in my lap, then goes to the men and sets her hand on their many foreheads, speaking soft words to the wind-stirred waves.

"Shield Myrah," she says at last, "for she is the spirit who watches over you this day."

The men nearest Myrah gather around her as they would have once done their own mothers. Mildred's waxy arms and legs lie limp against my gown. Derwen comes to me and kisses my cheek where it meets my lips.

"Florentina, Rosamond, and Annette were not able to heal her," she says. "She is beyond healing."

A deafening roar fills the heavens as a bright purple snake strikes down from the clouds into the sea, sending a thick mist of water over the top of the swell and soaking our woollen clothing anew before rushing down towards the river and flooding its earthen banks.

"Not yet!" hisses Myrah.

"Our men on the other side of the river will not be able to come over," says an iron-shirted man.

"Nor will our foes be able to flee inland," says his helmed friend. "We are two hundred. They must be no more than thirty."

I must look for myself to see whether the heavens stir at my behest. My knees become wet with yellowing grass as they creep up to the top of the slope, where my legs bring me upright though I have not asked them to do so. Foam gathers on the sea's angry, swelling waves while ash-hued clouds come together to shield the water's wrath from the sun's soothing warmth. The lips of a fair, dark brown face open and close, yet I hear nothing of their words. My right arm jerks downwards to the bottom of the little slope, where Myrah steadies my daughter cradled between my breast and my stinging forearm. Myrah's eyes come to life.

"Do not go with her," Derwen says to her.

"They come," calls a man far before us.

Myrah runs to him on bent legs, lifts her head above the grassy ridge for a time, then returns to us.

"Brant and Luda are not with them," she says. "We will have our reckoning for our king, for our aldormen, for the fatherless children our wives will bear, and for my daughter."

"Lend us your strength, Budig," says the man nearest Derwen.

"They are near," says Derwen. "If I call the earth, it will take all of you."

"So be it," says the man who wishes Myrah dead.

A shower of mist from the sea blesses our heads. The clouds darken the sky to a starless midnight, beneath which a hueless wasteland of bellowing thunder and flickering lightning asks men to lie down and sleep and dream that this is real.

"Go forth and meet them in battle," says Derwen, "for the heavens themselves are on our side."

The men stand as one and climb the little hill, calling out to the blackened clouds in the heavens above as they beat spears against shields and draw long knives from belt sheathes. A bellowing roar sounds from above the lip of the swell, and the men rush forwards to meet their foes even as a mighty wave floods down on top of them and throws many of them to the ground. Their brothers do not stop to help them; they lift themselves to their water-bound legs and run along the shore with stone-weighted steps. They should go to the sea, instead, and see whether they find the stilling hand of emptiness when water has filled their lungs.

"Should any come upon us," says Myrah, "we have nothing."

Marigold reaches for Myrah's gown and clutches her black-sleeved arm so tightly that her fingertips meet her thumb.

"You have not eaten," says Marigold. "That is what your father wishes. He would have you starve yourself in weeping for the mother he took from you. You know that is why he left. He did not leave to become king to an imperium. Nor have you."

Myrah stares at Marigold. She wrests her arm from Marigold's grip and stands on the lip of the slope. I stand with her, my stone daughter in my arms, and look down from our nest atop the white cliffs at the many men who go to meet a gathering of rough-hewn shapes too weary to crumble into dust. Luda's kin were not trapped here, for those who are dead abide beyond all earthly binds.

"Whom do they fight?" I say.

"Themselves," says Derwen. An arm takes my waist. My back rests against bone. "But none of them shall win: not those who hurt Myrah, nor he who gives you a child while you sleep, nor he who seeks to kill my sister and finds a blade in his own breast instead."

Thunder sounds. Rain falls. Out on the sea where grey meets blue, a dark shape in a boat is born. Lightning-wreathed clouds bolster the bloody cries of men who kill their hatred by giving it greatest life. I stroke Mildred's woollen hair and kiss her marble cheek. At once, water as high as our heads rushes up onto the shore and washes over us. Marigold and Myrah lie soaked on the sand.

"Marigold," says Derwen, "take Myrah far from here."

"Where would you have us go?" says Marigold.

"Take Myrah to a grove of trees and hide," I say. "If anyone comes, set fire to the bark and cry out as if you burn."

Myrah sets her hand on Mildred's face. Tears wet her salt-kissed cheeks.

"Father was right," she says. Her hand finds Marigold's wrist. "This is how it must be."

"Let us find a grove that is not home to empty stone graves," says Marigold.

They run off into waist-high clumps of nettle-hued bushes

that lie low against patchy grass. My feet take me through wet, unyielding sand; the heaving sea's sweeping waves beset my toes with frost and my gown below my knees with a chilling wetness that clings to my shins. Were I to walk out into the water and stand there for a time, my gowns would float freely and I might not feel so bitterly the wind that threatens to turn my legs into icy stone. Derwen stands before me and sets her fingers on mine where they rest on Mildred's breast.

"She does not sleep, Ardelle."

Where the grim heavens meet frothy waters, a boat and its tall, dark-clothed master follow the long black staff he holds in his right hand. The sea's churning waves flatten into stillness beneath the hull of his boat as he drifts towards us.

"I have given him my blood," I say. "Why does he yet come?"

"Ask this of him every morning when you wake and silence will follow you for the rest of your days," says Derwen. "Let me instead tell you of the lies that live within my own mind that they might lessen your suffering: my daughter I named Gweneira for her flesh as white as the snow. Her face reddened in summer and her hands dried in winter." The chill in my cheeks clenches my jaw; my own hands are wan and shake from watery cold. "I left her with Myrah's father. He said he would find for her a mother who spoke my mother's tongue. That is when I died, as did she to me. Yet I am still here, for death comes when it will; and no man is his master."

Wretched cries sound down the shore and out over the water, where the boatman turns the shadowed folds of his hood to greet the men who send each other to meet him. Derwen stands behind me and holds me against her with her arm around my waist. I hold in my own arms wool-bundled wax-stone carved into my daughter's likeness.

"What do you see?" Derwen says to my ear.

The boat's brow stills the swelling water, yet even the

boatman drifts aside to yield to the black mound that rises from beneath a drowning world whose depths must stretch beyond what any man's mind might show him: they are home to a broken-nosed bird of glistening midnight scales with wings as broad as the seaside ridges on which our sanctuary once stood. Those white cliffs we looked upon in awe are only as tall as the raised marble stone of our beds in the shadow of the long-toothed wings that drape the heavens in night's darkest secrets.

"Mildred's father," I say.

The earth shakes with his mighty call. To our right, the far-off men who still stand lose their feet and find the sand. Derwen leans against my back, keeping us upright even as my legs yell at me that we could walk out into the water if Derwen's arm would but yield to its will. The boatman draws near enough to show me the end of his long staff as he floats without straying amid waves that thrust themselves against my waist and breast. I set Mildred's hanging arm on her linen, and my hand on her resting elbow, and my lips on her forehead above eyes that will not open again. Gerahard comes to take his daughter only now when he has nothing else.

How my tears wet my daughter's reddened cheeks among the sea's lingering salt, I will never know, for the waves wash them clean from her face and mine; they take Isadora's brass pin from my hair and throw it to the wind; they take my heart from my breast and offer it unto the sea, where the eyeless glare of death burns it into ash to be swept up along the gales into the clouds. Red rain falls down on our heads and shoulders and feet with icy stones that chill my bloodless flesh to snow-swept frost. The great bird flies up into the clouds and calls out from among them. He shows himself again where the sea meets the heavens; his broad wings beat life and strength into the swelling waters, driving them high into the blackened clouds.

"If you give yourself to the sea," says Derwen, "I will follow you. I will not leave you again."

Bitter gales laden with frost and snow and ash dry our salt-rimed linen and wool in answer, yet they do not send us to the ground as they have the men who no longer bear the strength to take life from others, for it has been taken from them.

When you were born, I held you against the softness of my linen while you slept. I dreamed with you, then, and when we woke, I gave you my milk and my love and my life so that you would grow to be as old as your mother. I watched as you learned how to find your belly from your back, how you played with the wool in our bedroom as if it were your own brother or sister, how you found your knees and crawled along the length of the gowns I set down for you on the hard stone of the floor, how you climbed up against the legs of tables and taught yourself to stand, and to walk, and to run. And every night, when you and I would bed down to sleep, I would kiss your cheeks and forehead and sing to you, in my thoughts, the words of love you could not bear to hear from your mother's heart. That your own mother's love was your bane is a wound within me that may never heal. A thousand times I would have taken you from Florentina's song like butterflies flitting through poppies or the slowly flowing honey of Annette's strength, but it was when I sang the gift of your life into the wind that blew me to mother and father and into the waters I gave to Frijona's aching soul that you were taken from me. For this, I will never forgive myself. I will only think on when I held your little head in my fingers and sat you up in my lap and showed you those red feather-wights that had come to dance for us while you smiled.

Here they are, now, my darling daughter. They have come to take you home.

The world is water. My eyes close. My throat chokes. My legs bend. My arms weaken. They fall away.

I am nothing. I am less than nothing.

I stand with heaving breaths on an empty shore. The great, winged bird swoops down along the water and takes from it a small white shape in the grip of its spear-headed fingers. He calls out once more as he lifts himself into the clouds out of sight, then dives with folded wings beneath the sea's sleeping water, from which he does not come up again. The boatman turns away from us and drifts off towards the sun's bed. Bony fingers take my chin and show my eyes the bundles of wool that rest without stirring on the lifeless sand.

"Myrah is not among them," says Derwen.

Nor am I, for I have given Myrah all of my love. For my daughter, I had too little; for these men, nothing. It is only now that I know this, after it has been done, when the boatman comes to the shore beneath the battlefield ridge to there take men made whole again. Here, among the living, where the sea lies still beneath grey clouds that drift away like smoke, the wind blows softly against broken shields and shattered spears and the water-soaked bodies of those who would have been Myrah's brothers only when she lay dead at their feet.

34

FAREWELL

My bare feet bear the sandy afterbirth of the death and suffering I have brought into this world. The waves, in their wisdom, no longer come to the shore to wash me clean, for I have become filthy beyond reckoning, broken beyond healing. That my own heart has been taken from my breast is a kindness I have not earned—something should stir or ache or hurt within me as I stare out into the sea, whither my daughter has gone; or when I look upon the bodies resting along the shore; or in watching a kindred ghost walk among the slain men and, on seeing a face he does not like, fall to his knees and take its head and shoulders into his lap. The wind blows through my empty husk and finds nothing left to sweep away. Derwen's hand comes to rest on my knee as she sits down beside me.

"I was the first of us to bear a child," she says. "When I wandered in the snow that winter and sang before our rune-stone, it was you of whom I thought without end. I could not —would not—milden my suffering by burdening you with those dark dreams of ever having been your mother. I gave them to Luda instead. She is the only one of us who keeps such things without telling others. When I killed Constantine, I thought on whether I should go to you, much as I wished to in those first days at the sanctuary with only Florentina to keep me, but I did not, nor do you now go to Mildred in the sea, for you know that you must not. In this, we are kindred."

"I am kindred to that dead man for whom his friend weeps," I say. "I will go to him and tell him what I have done. Let his wrath be truth."

I stand. Derwen takes my hand to keep me from walking.

"That is Brant," she says. "He holds his sister in his arms."

A soft wind from the sea sweeps sun-dyed brown strands of hair over tears that run down high cheekbones hardened by a jaw clenched shut. Derwen's bony fingers are the stone grave wherein lie the ashes of what was once my heart.

"My husband was a Jutish man named Gefwulf," she says. "We left Powys together to go to his homeland over the narrow sea along the southern coast. Men came to us there and killed him for having murdered three of their brothers when they were drunk. When they cleft my arm, you … my daughter cried out to me. That is when they forgot their anger. Where death is master, wrath is but his shadow."

"Then let one shadow meet another," I say and leave her hand.

Yet her fingers now come between mine and hold themselves there as we near Brant.

"You did your daughter the greatest kindness by keeping yourself away from her," Derwen says to herself.

"What do you do here, then?" I say.

"We go to thank Luda for what she has done," Derwen says. "She kept my secret and I kept hers. She did not call the sea at that battle on the ridge so men would not drown in her water. She has only ever wished for us to stay together in a place where we could bear our children in peace, but there is no such place, so she swore to shield us from our foes, even those who live only within our minds, and at the same time murder her own unending wish to have a child which you and I, more than any other, have shown her she must not do."

I kneel before brown wool stretched over broad shoulders bearing a thick leather strap that runs to a hip where it meets a hair-lined, leather-bound wooden belt-sheath without its sword. The arms that would have wielded it now bear another weight.

"Brant," I say.

His grim, sand-blown face and wild hair shroud eyes as blue as the sea once was. He shifts his body—a long, ashy white braid lies draped over a brown woollen tunic whose waist belt bears one of the breastpins we used to fasten our gowns at the sanctuary. Luda's face is hued bluish white, as though she sleeps beneath water. I set my hand on her bare foot and hold it there to give her the warmth of lifeless flesh that somehow still bears heat. Derwen falls to her knees and takes Luda in her arm. Her forehead rests against Brant's knee as she shakes with weeping.

"You have no tears," Brant says to me.

"My tears are there," I say to the sea. "My daughter and mother and father have drowned in them."

Red-ringed eyes look out to the water without blinking.

"She waited for you," he says. "Even as Myrah's men came at us with spears, Hluta thought you might help us. We know why you did not."

"They would have—"

"We would have killed Myrah and her sisters," says Brant. "So Hluta told us. That is her name. She softened it for your tongues sharpened and bloodied from speaking in thorns. Our father told us of how a widow whose husband died in battle brought her newborn daughter to a drunken gathering of fighting men and begged one of them to take her. At first, they would not listen, but as they drank, they heard her words better until at last they fought one another not with weapons, but with riddles. The one who answered them best—or worst—became our father. He named his daughter Hluta, one for whom he had cast his 'lot' and won, so she became his 'lot' in life. Her mother died not long after that, and father, in keeping his oath to his newfound child, wed her dead mother's younger sister. Wodanaz strengthened father's lot when his wife bore him a son who became his faithful sword, his Brant. But now, my sword lies useless in the sand; and my sister's lot in life lies with it."

"Forgive me," I say.

"Ask Luda to forgive you and see whether she answers," Brant says with bitterness in his words. "This is what Myrah's father would have wanted. That man left you to die up on that ridge after the knives of women did not find your hearts, then sent you home to await the burning rushes and stones of men who could not be made to hate you for having slain their greedy foes and made them wealthy again. You and Hluta and all the others lived in white halls of marble to shield you from every man but the one who built them around you in the hope that they would one day crumble down on top of you."

Derwen sets Luda in Brant's lap as she would a newborn child. She kisses Luda's watery cheek, then gives another kiss to Brant's beard.

"I must find Myrah," she says. "Do you come, Ardelle?"

Shall I kiss Brant's cheek as well?

"Stay here, then, until I return with Myrah," she says and runs off.

Brant holds one hand against his sister's unstirring breast and looks out into emptiness.

"You are right to have no love for us after we let you die at that battle," he says. "I set you along the path of madness. Luda followed you too well. I think she must wait for you even now in that hidden world. I would as well, even if you would not do the same for me, until the end of your days brought you back to me."

"Shall I go hither and bring her back?" I say.

"Myrah said you could not do this for her aldorman," says Brant. "Luda knows this, yet still she waits for you."

Do these slain men wait with her? I should talk to them once more.

I set my arm over Brant's neck and, in doing so, slide from his right hip-sheath a willow-handled long knife thrice banded with bone. Which of the blade's two curved edges is the sharpened one, I do not know.

"Will you not wait for Myrah?" says Brant.

"I am not worthy of her," I say.

"Nor I of Frijona, yet she is the who wished to make herself my wife."

"She suffered for having met me," I say, "as do you, as did your brothers for whom death was the only end to their sorrow. I will not walk this earth and see the same befall those whose lives are only fleeting while I abide among them. I will send Luda to you, if I can, and wish her a long and happy life from that place where I can never again hurt her."

Brant closes his eyes and bows his head. I cup his tear-matted beard on the cheek that does not face me and give his spittle-flecked lips a soft kiss.

"Your words are ever thorned," he says, "but let them be truth."

As my unfastened woollen gown falls to my waist, the wind bears my name from the river's slight swelling. I turn away from whomever that might be and with the thoughtless fangs of a snake's fiery teeth thrust Brant's long knife between my ribs. My flesh opens, spilling my blood not onto the ground, but into the wind that bears it out over the sea. There, my life's water blesses the still waves and those who sleep beneath them with the only gift one who has lost everything has left to give: herself.

The bundles of wool rise from the sand and walk in the light of clouds made grey to meet their brothers, who stride in from the sea's shallowest water breathing as though their lungs were never made heavy with salt. A hand as snowy as mine brings my wrist to the earthen wool that rests upon a folded knee.

"I knew you would come for me," says Luda.

She looks more like Isadora than herself now: a smile softens her angled cheeks and chin and brightens the chalk-like hue of her lips. The horse's tail of her long yellow-white braid lies still in her palm. If Mildred were here, she would sit herself down on Luda's legs so she could pull apart the thickly woven strands of hair and hide herself from her mother's sisters among them. Luda's fingertips stroke the linen between my ribs made twain by Brant's long knife.

"Did he do this to you?" she says.

"I did."

Luda takes the wool from around my waist and fastens it to my linen at my shoulders. Around her neck rests a leather string bearing a wolf's tooth.

"Brant's first hunt," she says.

Her smile leaves her as she closes her eyes and breathes in deeply through her nose. Her slow outbreath runs its fleeting fingernails down the skin of my arms—a tall form clothed in starless night bearing the stiffened corpse of a dark-scaled snake drifts towards our bloodless shore in a boat of blackened birch bark. The men stand ready for him, as will they do one day when they have become stone forefathers in the halls of their wives' children. I stand with them on weightless legs.

"I must see whether he takes them," I say.

"You need make no peace with my brothers," says Luda,

"but you might talk to them before they have forgotten the need for thought."

Among the smiling men I walk until I find the one whose scar makes his twain eye sightless.

"Cenhelm," I say. "Hroth … Hrothgar. Leof …"

"Leofsige," he says. "And my name is Beornrad, brother to Gerahard, who sleeps in that sea."

"As does my daughter, Mildred," I say.

"Then we stand as brother and sister among many who name us the same." His foot sweeps against a broken shaft of maple bearing a head of sharpened iron banded at the neck with a thin length of white linen. "We have never needed these spears, have we?"

"We did not know it until we had used them for the last time," I say.

Twenty of his brothers walk with emptied hands to a long-boat that bows to meet them. I take my brother Beornrad in my arms and hold him against me until he grunts and draws away.

"Your flesh burns with warmness," he says. "Come with us to the cooling wind nearer to the sea."

He does not wait for me to walk with him to the water. To his brothers—our brothers—I give my arms for as long as they can bear, whereafter they seek their shore-bound kin, whose flesh has taken the snowy, ashen hue of the marble walls of our sanctuary. The toothless man who stays behind withdraws his hand from mine at once. The lines of his palm and knuckles run red with a quickness his flesh can no longer abide.

"We will meet again on the other side," I tell him.

"We will see you there, sister," he says.

"Ardelle," calls Luda.

She sits behind me on the sand with her legs against mine and her arms around my shoulders and waist. I set my hands on the knees of her woollen leggings as Mildred might have done mine. Our brothers, the Geats and the Danes and the northmen and the wolves and the Cantware, board the boat and look on what they leave behind with eyes that no longer seem to see it. When the last of them have drifted away into the setting sun, Luda kisses my cheek.

"Derwen told me why she wandered in the snow," I say.

"And I did not tell you," says Luda. "Is that why you came here in her stead?"

"She kept me from the sea," I say.

"Or you kept her. She wished to tell you of her motherhood many times, to go to you after she could not draw your daughter from you. It is our children who ward us against harm, and for this we thank them by wounding them bitterly with our love. Where is Mildred? Does she not follow you here?"

"There," I say to the sea. "I have made peace with that boatman."

"No," says Luda. Her arms tighten around me. "That is the madness that takes us for having borne children."

From among the clouds fall red feathers that hang over the sea and offer their blood-hued brightness to water darkened by the return of a longboat empty of men. I take myself from Luda in standing to greet them.

"Do you see the wights?" I say.

Luda's blue eyes search the water and the clouds and the heavens and the sand beneath her feet and the wind around my gowns. She takes my hands in hers and brings her bare feet between mine.

"Where is your daughter?" she says.

"I told you. Does my flesh burn you? Is the warmth too great?"

Her arms are as pale as mine but bear none of the rotting greyness that dusted the flesh of our brothers with ash.

"Let us wait for the wights to come down," I say. "I will show you where they are so you may take one in your mouth and return to Brant."

"And how long would we wait?" says Luda. "How long did you and your daughter abide here while we waited for you? Have you any memory of how long you were gone from us? Almost a year. And now you have forgotten where Mildred is."

"I gave her to the sea," I say.

Luda closes her eyes, breathes in, breathes out, opens her eyes.

"And so she kept you from drowning, as you kept Derwen, for this was my doing. Mildred has none to watch her, there."

She nods at the lifeless folds of soot-wool standing in an oarless boat that rows itself to shore and berths before our feet.

"So you will go with him?" I say.

"No," says Luda. "I will go to Mildred where she sleeps and hold her in my arms and dream with her of the life we would have lived together."

"You are not her mother," I say. "If you will not return, let us go together on that boat."

"Who will watch over Myrah?" says Luda.

"Derwen was with her long before I ever came to the sanctuary," I say.

"And who would be here for Myrah if she comes here in search of you? Or, if she does not, would you wait here on the shore for her for as long as she might live and have her days lengthened by memories of you that cloud her thoughts and speech?" Luda's hands rest on my shoulders. The sea's calm dwells within her eyes. "Let me bear this burden for you. Let Myrah give you her daughter as your own so you may sing to her the words of love I will give to Mildred for you."

"You will not come with me?" I say.

"No. The greatest madness lies within me, for I still want

what you had, what Derwen has, even after I have seen what this has done to us. I can not abide any longer in a world that shows me the son I must not have every morning when I wake to Myrah's belly or listen to Annette's endless talk of mothering or walk out into the wildflower meadows and watch from afar as sons walk alongside their fathers among their cows. I can do this no longer, nor will I give myself to this boatman who has wronged you so deeply. I will swim beneath the water as you have done for others and give life to your daughter."

Luda takes me in her arms.

"Do not worry that your daughter will ever be alone again," she says. "I will be there for her, as I will be there for you and our sisters and Derwen when you come to the shore with wildflowers from those meadows through which we once walked and send them to us where we sleep. You may sing to us the old song from the sanctuary and bless our dreams with the memory of a time when our love for one another was the burden that weighed most heavily upon our hearts."

Luda kisses me as she would have kissed her son before she sent him off with his father to scythe wheat in the fields or hunt deer with spears or angle fish from the river. I hold her against me until I have nothing more than the memory of her smiling face as she looks upon me for the last time.

Luda wades out into the sea up to her shoulders. She swims below and does not rise.

Bony fingers grasp an aspen staff and thrust its fanged head into the shore's fleshy sand. Stone hardens against the bottoms of my feet. Blood red feather-wights float down from the clouds in great throngs to hang above the unstirring sea; they gather around the dusky folds of wool that hide the boatman's face from the setting sun; they flit above my head beyond the grasp of my fingers like shining stars whose light is only as wondrous as it is untouchable. The boatman lifts his staff, scattering the wights along the wind into waking wheat fields and birch tree boughs and berried bramble and hawthorn hedges and swanless fens.

"The wights or the boat," he says.

This shepherd of men stands faceless in a ship of wrought alder painted with the bruised flesh of dead men that has become an island unto itself. Hewn boughs stripped of their skin and beaten into a leafless hull bear no memory of their mothers, those leaning trees near the stone walls of Durovernum whose roots drank life from watery grass and shared it with their children. Had I ever known that they would come to this, I would never have left the shelter of their limbs to stand behind Isadora with my arms around her waist as she spoke to the king's thane. Her chiding words would have been honey to my ears; her sharp-nailed fingers on my palms the stinging kisses of one whom death has made a mother.

"Why am I here?" I say.

An answer does not come, for none is left to answer. I am not here. The boatman can not fathom one who never was. I shall give him nothing, as Luda did, and go to dream with my daughter.

My foot leaves the sand. The boatman thrusts his staff into the water. Ice hardens the sea into flawless stillness. Frost hides what he has done. Among the flitting wights dance whirling flakes of snow. The westering sun rises from its bed to shine light without warmth on a shore whose sand lies heavy with sleep beneath the chill of winter's bitter hand.

"The wights or the boat," says the master of men. "Neither comes to you again."

Frost blows over the mounds of snow through which Constantine bore my daughter to the sea without a thought for why he did so. The boatman called to me and I answered without Mildred to ward me from his grasping fingers. Who is it, then, that keeps me from going to him now? I might wander through this sea of snow as far as my legs will take me in search of an answer and find only the silence that held Constantine in its arms as he dreamed beneath the ice. It was I who woke him from his sweet dreams to a world of sleeping butterflies, whose brittle wings of ice he shattered beneath his feet as he stepped into this boat and left the memories of his life somewhere among the swirling snowflakes.

What will my mind tell me of my own life when winter's hand lifts at last from the little hills and narrow dales? Will I wander along the old horse-roads until my shins ache and I strike my head against the path to show its stones that I know as well as they do how not to yield? My legs would hie me without asking to where Sithebad sleeps so I may draw her from the lake into my lap and look upon … and look upon the warmth of a silvery brown face glistening with the lake's after-birth as my chalky thumb strokes life into Myrah's cheeks. I would listen, with my lips on hers and my fingers between her fingers, as her quickening breaths become heavy with the burden of waking and her eyelids ache with the heat of the flesh of those who are not dead. My arms would give her back to the lake and back to her dreams before she wakes. Is it me of whom you dream, Myrah? Alfred would come bearing flowers and words to keep the memory of his beloved Sithe-bad; and his thoughts would shatter into bloodied, rough-edged shards at the sight of the one who bears the name Ardelle, that half-wit whore who killed his wife and made her suffer in the next life as she drowned herself. I have not earned the kindness of sweet dreams of my daughter; nor of Myrah, whose keeper has ever been Derwen; nor of mother and father, whom I let hatred burn into dust. I am no better than this boat-man; he is my closest kindred. And yet even the gift of his boat to the beyond may be too great a kindness—I should suffer as Sithebad did through endless summers as my reddening flesh clings to my bones and my eyes keep their unclouded sight and my ears their keenest hearing so that I may mark well every aching footstep as I take in the fullness of my wretched abode in this world whose master is nothing and nowhere; and thus, there is none to ask for forgiveness.

Brant, come and sit with me in the summer meadow and tell me why you are not a hairless giant. Let us smile for a time as the sun beams warmth into the tall grass where butterflies nest until Luda sits down beside us and sends them fluttering up into a blue sky to find their midday beds in feathery white clouds. Florentina will tell us of their names and of which blue-winged moth is brother to red and yellow. See how Mildred sits in my lap and claps with laughter at the flitting shapes beyond the reach of her little fingers. On my knee rests Myrah's hand; in her lap lies her linen-swathed newborn daughter, brown eyes aglow as she beholds such wondrous sights for the first time. My neck takes the soft warmth of Myrah's lips; her hand is on my cheek, bidding me give her the life of my breath through her mouth unhindered. My heart returns to my breast from where it lay scattered among the sand and beats once more, flooding my limbs with life to bursting. The striking of hooves draws our eyes to Annette where she rides her dun mare alongside Wilfrith's black steed. Rosamond and Marigold walk behind them, arm in arm. Frijona is with them, bearing no mark on her body of having been burned, leading by the hand a little boy who wields his walking stick only half as well as Marigold does hers. His short, stumpy legs stride twice as swiftly as his mother's to stay at her side. From the fields, Brant calls to him and lets fall his scythe as he kneels with outstretched arms to take up his running child. On my shoulder rests a hand whose wrist bears nettle-dyed linen. Derwen's little ear braid with its red and white beads hangs down my arm as she kisses my temple like mother did when I slept ill on summer nights in heat that would not leave me be. What shall I say to you, Derwen? Do you not see Isadora in her black wool sitting in the shade of that weeping oak tree, how she wears Myrah's hue in faithfulness though she sweats and clasps her gown's neck fold halfway down her ribs to better cool herself?

And as the wind blows through harvest fields of wheat and rye, taking the summer's sweat from our linen, I would look to the blood moon in my dreams and ask the hidden, watching boatman why one who says she loves me so much has gone to the bottom of the sea and taken her love with her. Why did your father want us to die, Myrah? Was I the one who did not love you when I left you at his behest? Forgive me, Myrah. I have left you, once again, when men whose fields have flooded come seeking a share of the harvest of others. Your father taught you that the months before winter were when fighting men set upon their foes with the same blades they would use to fell wheat, for he who wins thus feeds his kin and starves whomever among his foes still lives. When we did atop that ridge what your father told us to instead of what he wanted of us, he sent me away for my faithlessness and kept you from me in bitterness. Here, I keep myself from you so that you may never know of these dark and meaningless dreams of mine that must never come to be.

Let this snow that bears no breath of cold freeze my legs into stone and my heart into the silent ruins of a sanctuary that no longer stands. Let this boatman bear witness to the timelessness of what I am not, for I am not here. Let him lift his staff to meet the clouds and make the wights sleepy in their play; and their red hue wane into bloodlessness; and their weight become too heavy for the wind to bear. Watch as one from among them falls lifelessly into the snow and there makes its bed. There you are, Myrah. Another follows—you have found your beloved, Derwen—and another, and another, and another until they fall like shards of ice by tens and hundreds around my feet and onto the ice-laden sea and against the lifeless timber of the boatman's unyielding abode. This is their lot in life—in death—though they did nothing more than dance and play as the wind would have them. Which of these are you, Mildred? Would you have your mother come to you, now? See, here, at the bottom of the boat how many of these wights dream as you and your father and your mother's sister do. One among them is still quick with redness and comes to dance for you. How often you played in glee with those red and white beads in Marigold's hair, and in Derwen's.

Here she is. Your mother's mother. Sent from her house in Powys by her mother into the trees, where she gave birth to a child whose snowy face reddish with cold looks up at us from the frost-hidden grass and the sea and the palm of my hand. Her arm is taken from her; her daughter she must give to another; she sits in silence for days and weeks and months amid the marble halls she shaped with only her thoughts to tell her that she yet lives. And here I stand, the only memory of what she has left behind.

Derwen. Your life has not been for nothing.

I take the red wight into my mouth. The boatman lifts his staff; I send his boat from the sand with my arms. As he drifts away, the rifts in the boat's wake close without sound. Somewhere beneath this ice, Luda sings to Mildred in her dreams, where her words are as light and harmless as a summer meadow's butterflies.

Forgive me, Mildred. Mother loves you. I know you love me, for you never grew old enough to learn otherwise. I will grow old enough to learn what you never forgot, and I will teach your mother's sisters how to bear the burden of our love as we forget that we have ever known otherwise. When I return to this place, I will never again leave you. Sweet dreams, my darling child.

The melting wight dies in my throat. My breath becomes misty frost. My fingers are dry from winter's kisses. I hold my woollen gown in my arms. My feet ache with the chill of the snow beneath them. Let us walk together, you and I, to those houses near the little sea and see whether they still stand.

They do, and when Marigold calls to Myrah, a hooded shape in a green-hued gown comes forth from them to meet me with a kiss for my lips and her daughter for my arms.

35

REMEMBRANCE

Having found each other again, we gather Myrah's things from the one small house that still stands near the little sea and walk inland over snow-frosted grass to a broad bed of raised stone and earth. Atop it stand thirty clay-bound houses that are home to the wives of men who have become their husbands for not having died. Myrah's house stands taller and wider than the others, not for the sake of housing cows or sheep during the winter months, but to warm her sisters with Marigold's reddish-blue fire. It brightens the timber walls so well that Florentina sleeps in her linen above her bedding rather than beneath it. Marigold kneels beside a narrow-shouldered brown gown.

"Here, Isadora," she says. "I have brought her back to you."

Sunken cheekbones bear eyes alight with dancing flames. I sit in Isadora's arms on the rush-bedded earth. Between us Myrah sets her daughter's ringed black hair and fair brown cheeks hued with the golden bands on Myrah's longest fingers. Her brown eyes ask me who I am—they find a welcome answer in Isadora's arms.

"Athelburg," says Myrah. Her daughter looks to her. "Named after my father and the sanctuary in which we lived. We call her Tata for what she says when Florentina plays with her."

Myrah sits in my lap to better hold her nose against Athelburg's. Myrah's daughter does not shrink away, but leans her forehead against her mother's and turns it from side to side while Myrah does the same. Myrah's green gown is fastened at the neck with thin, bead-topped rods of bone.

"From my comb," she says. "The one for which Derwen struck my bedroom door asunder. And this is her gown."

"Where has she gone? Does she live?"

Myrah bids Marigold fetch folded parchments from a locked wooden box opened by an iron key on Myrah's belt ring. Myrah looks through many of them, then hands me one whose damp edges I must unfold with care lest the sheaf break into four.

Ardelle,

In another life, your song to the wind would kiss your mother's eyes to sleep and rest with her as she lay beneath the stars with her dreams of you. But I have gone to Deva with Annette and Wilfrith and their child, a boy taken from one of our dead brothers and his wife who went to be with them when she died while giving birth. We will take him as our own to the hills or to the dales or whithersoever the earth lies still and does not listen to my words. Should you ever read this, know that my last memory of you is calling to you from that little hill above the stream and taking you into my arms to hold you and listen to you tell me that you love me as much as I love you. The sea beneath the setting sun is too small to bear the fullness of the love I have for you, so let it flood with the tears that I have shed in leaving you behind for the last time. In that hidden world, I shall go to where I must, and I bid you do the same.

Derwen

"Where are the others?" I say.

"Brant knew his sister would not come back from the hidden world," says Myrah. "We went with him and Frijona and Luda's wool-bound body south along the rivers to the old, broad path the wolves' forefathers carved into the earth. There, Derwen left them with her blessings and told them you were at peace."

The house's leaning door stands upright to allow a willowy, hooded shape in black bearing a basket of light brown oak apples. She bears Myrah's golden bird at her neck and Luda's gold-worked clasp in her hair. Rosamond hands her basket to Marigold and kneels beside me to give my cheek a kiss.

"Are you queen now?" I say.

"Almost two years you are gone and when first you see me, you greet me so," says Rosamond. "I wear this hue so I may be seen well amid the snow by cows who stray from their wooden walls."

"I have told her many times to wait until the weather warms to seek out her oak galls," says Myrah with a yawn.

"She must have something to do when her ink dries," says Isadora. "As must Maria when her husband is off feeding cows or horses or whatever he does when he is not warming himself by a fire or elsewhere."

Myrah's head rests on my shoulder. Her breast rises and falls with the steady breaths of one who sleeps. Isadora brings a linen pillow for her head and takes her from my arms. I hold Myrah's hand while the hearth's soft embers warm her dreams.

"Bearing a child wears on her spine," says Isadora with a hand for my shoulder, "and being a mother has made her weary."

"*Mundus stercoris*," Florentina says as she sits up with eyes half-open. Her golden, ringed strands of hair fall away from her face. "Ardelle. Am I awake? Too often my dreams of you have kept me from sleep."

Rosamond sits down in a chair before a small table that slopes slightly. Against a wooden hedge near its top Marigold sets a clay pot that is not dark blue.

"And now she is here, so you may sleep in peace," says Marigold. Florentina lies down and hides her eyes with her forearm. "The mark of fire did not leave Frijona's body until last winter."

"Winter?" I say. "How did they keep Luda's body so long?"

"Derwen," says Rosamond. She dips the sharpened end of her writing feather into the pot and withdraws its ink-darkened tip. "You may read of this darkness later. When Florentina has slept in silence, she may be so kind as to sing and play her harp for you."

"And thus Myrah has chosen her thyle with the greatest of wisdom," says Florentina as she lifts the bedding over her head and hides beneath it.

"When you healed Frijona, did you also heal Rosamond?" I say.

"I told her not to drink ink," the bedding says. "Good night."

Isadora takes a bundle of wool from beside the house's

wall and sets it down at Myrah's head. I lie down with Myrah, thread my fingers through her fingers, and send my breaths with hers to the roof's smoke-shrouded thatch.

Darkness falls over my eyes. The sun wakes them. I sit up in a meadow near our sanctuary. Mildred sits in Luda's lap. They smile and laugh together as Mildred plays with Luda's long yellow-white braid. Butterflies flutter up from the tall grass, shedding thorns from their many-hued wings. One lands on Luda's shoulder and kisses her cheek. Mildred reaches for it with little fingers that can not keep the butterfly from flitting away into a cloudless summer sky. Her mirth is mine, and so we laugh together, the three of us. I lift my hand to stroke my daughter's hair—she is not there, nor is Luda. I am alone in summer's meadow.

You were right, Marigold. We often dream of those who have gone to the hidden world.

I wake to Rosamond, who takes the tears from my eyes and the sweat from my brow with a length of linen. A woman sings and strums a harp—Florentina. Her words are as light as though they have been written on the clouds in the heavens. On seeing that I wake, Florentina breaks her song and speaks with words not half as fair.

"When the snow melts," she says, "we will go to the sea and sing to Luda and Mildred."

Rosamond sits down at her table. Marigold is at her side.

"Did you dream?" says Marigold. "What was your dream? Rosa, we should write down her dream."

"I shall when this tale has been brought to its end," she says.

"What tale do you write?" I say.

"It is my tale," says Marigold. "Rosamond walks alone into a meadow one day and is chased away by a swarm of bees who are angry that she did not bring me with her."

Florentina sighs with yawning laughter.

"That is your best tale thus far," she says.

"You spend your ink on this?" I say.

"I write down all of our tales," says Rosamond, "and those of our men so that they will not be forgotten should the black death come again some day and take the rest of us."

Myrah sits up from her pillow and holds me as she twists her spine until it makes the sound of twigs cracking in fire.

"Those who come after us may find what we have written and remember that we once lived," she says. "This is what my father would wish for us."

"And so your daughter bears his name?" I say.

"He calls himself the king of these fens and whatever else he sees," says Myrah. "I will let him do so, as will our men who live here and have never seen him. Let him say and wish what he may to keep him in happiness. I must have some memory of him as I do my mother. Marigold, fetch me her letter. Florentina, recite your song for Rosamond to write so Ardelle may learn it this long winter."

"It was twelve years ago," says Florentina, "when Myrah's father thought to tell the seaside cliffs that their stone would look much better if they were hewn asunder and set one on top of the other ..."

"Athelburg asks for your milk," says Isadora.

"Come here, *sabibir*," Myrah says.

She sheds Derwen's green wool to her waist and slides her right arm from its linen. Mildred never took her milk so hungrily as Myrah's daughter. Myrah bids me look within her belt bag for a sheaf of parchment whose folds are still soft.

"I can not bear to look at it more than once or twice each year," she says. "Mother wrote it before she died. Father sent it to me this summer after keeping it for so long. Those are her letters and her words. She made her peace with my father, as my father wished to do with me, and so I have done this by naming my daughter after him, much as you named your daughter after Constantine's mother. Read the words without speaking them lest Athelburg drink in her mother's sorrow."

I unfold the parchment, whose tall, thick-stroked words I must hold close to my eyes to learn of their meaning.

Beloved daughter,

In my dreams, my heart is still made warm when I see your smiling face; your flowery words are made sweeter by the honey of my name from your lips; I set my fingers in your hair and my forehead against yours as I take in the life your breath gives to me. Your birth marked the beginning of my own life—I was not whole until you came to me. Your cries were my tears, your sighs weighed on my heart, your dreams were the heavens I would bring down to earth to see them made truth. Now, in this place, your father has found his heart's desire among men who look on us with kindness and understanding. Though I share in his happiness, I find no lasting peace, for you have gone from me. I know I must not return to you, and that you must not return to me, yet I wish for it without end; and my longing shall never leave me until we are reunited in that place where we can never again be taken from one another. These words are the last I shall give to your memory, for it causes me such suffering that I can no longer bear it, and I must ask your forgiveness for having inflicted this upon you as I seek to dispel my own clouded thoughts. Remember me always, dearest daughter, for I will forget the beating of my own heart ere I permit the memory of your face to slip from my mind.

Your loving mother,

Ziri

The ink of Ziri's letters runs together where Myrah's eyes have made them wet. Their thick strokes tell me of many fair words that Isadora never taught me, yet I understand their meaning fully. For a time—I know not how long—my mind's eye beholds my own daughter as she rests in my arms in the aldorman's mansio, where neither words nor wights can take her from me.

"I knew," Myrah says. "I knew that father went to his imperium to take mother from me. She knew this as well. He meant for her to die there, and still she went with him."

"You have not burned her words," I say.

"They live forever within my thoughts," she says. "And I know of no fire that sets alight the emptiness between words. They do not leave us, so we must wear them."

Myrah takes one of her hook-ended earrings bearing linked golden circles from her left ear and sets it in the palm of my hand: a hanging blue gem rests in the middle of a ring of little white beads.

"My mother gave me these when I went to live at the sanctuary," she says. "The blue stones she called hyacinths. We will take them to the sea when the chill has left it and sing to those who sleep there."

"I will sing to my mother and father," I say.

"And I will do the same," says Myrah.

"My dearest queen," says Florentina, "we have written our song. Shall I have your thyle take Ardelle's tale now?"

"Let her hear ours first," says Myrah. "She will learn of how we have shared the darkness in our minds with one another."

None will speak, so Marigold does: she tells Rosamond of her dreams of the two of them living together in one of those red-hued kingdoms, wherein Rosamond is queen and Marigold the queen's dearest friend.

"Only half of that is a tale," says Rosamond.

With those words, Rosamond leaves a kiss on Marigold's temple, whereafter Marigold leans so heavily against her friend's shoulder that Rosamond's elbow does not leave her ribs as she writes their tale of the evil queen who sought to end their friendship by forbidding them from going to Francia together; and of how Marigold would have burned the evil queen alive had she not looked within her own heart and found that she herself must show others what she wishes them to become. It is thus that the evil queen's icy heart melted and she found a husband for Marigold from among the wolves so that Marigold would wish to stay among them and Rosamond, on seeing her friend's happiness, would not soon leave her.

"Why are you not with him now?" I say.

"Sawine digs ditches or feeds hay to horses," says Marigold.

"His kindred," says Rosamond with a half-hidden smile.

Marigold strikes her shoulder. Rosamond's laughter fills the house.

"When he and I are ready," says Marigold, "we will find a son and a daughter who have no mother and father. Rosamond will watch over them while we are together."

"If you are much kinder to my shoulder, I may," says Rosamond.

"What of you, Rosamond?" I say.

"I sleep well enough alone," she says, "and there are few, if any, whose bearded kisses would make me wish otherwise. Why do you not ask Isadora such things?"

"My tale," says Isadora, "is one in which my sister's daughter had forgotten what her mother taught her and learned to serve one who only served herself." Myrah looks away. "And yet I must now take them both and love them as if they were my own, for this is what my brother and sister would do."

Isadora kisses Myrah's cheek.

"Where is my kiss?" says Florentina from her bedding. "Or must I wait until our queen is gone and the memory of our sisterhood has left with her?"

"No," says Myrah, "you must not. We have lived beyond my father's reckoning in lands he thinks empty of life and men but those who steal from others and curse them in Derwen and Annette's tongues. Let his mind lead him whither it will so long as it harms none of us, for he bought and sold us seeking the strongest among us to thrust the greatest might of his imperium and his Frankish wife's religion on them, as if they had never known anything of either. Let him thus build these kingdoms in his mind; and let their earthly forms crumble into dust when he and those he has betrayed are long beneath the earth. We shall stay here, where men look upon one another with kindness, for death has taken all else from their minds. Rosamond, write what I have said."

"Frankish wife," Rosamond says to herself. "I shall write that you are queen and that your father may eat the shit that birds drop on Florentina's head."

Florentina's laughter bursts through her nose.

"I was wise to have made you my thyle," says Myrah.

Through that long winter, we tell one another what lies within our hearts and minds; and I am among them. When the snow melts, the men who brought us bread and dried meat in the bitterest cold now share with us the fish they hook from the sea. The wives they have taken, many of whom have come here from afar seeking life wherever it is to be found, plant flax for our linen and help us with the shearing of sheep before the summer sun dries the fresh hay that our horses will eat. Together, we bring our cows to the grassy fields to eat, and our iron shovels to the rivers and meres to dig ditches that drain away flooding, and our axes to the oak trees, whose hollowed bodies bear water better than any of our wide-mouthed clay pots. When we are weary, Myrah's words lift our thoughts and Florentina's waters our limbs so that we may work longer. When we ache and can not sleep, Rosamond's song softens our arms and legs and slows our breathing until dreamless sleep has taken us. Marigold's fires warm the houses of those who have lived long enough to watch over the fatherless children of our women as they help with the day's work. Whether any of them remember that I am a ghost, their eyes do not tell me, nor do I give life to any such thoughts with my own words.

On a day of rest before summer brings the sun's brightest warmth to us, Florentina weaves golden wildflower leaves into braided strands that have grown halfway down my back. Myrah, who wears like flowers in her blossoming rings of hair, leads us and our bare feet to where the little sea yields to a great sea whose waves once swelled yet have lain in stillness these many months. There is no boatman here but in my own mind, for I will not soon forget the one who took everything to the sea in which my daughter and sister dream and whither Myrah must also one day go. I leave Myrah's hand and take Isadora from her so we may walk alone for a time.

"It was here the boatman told me I must go with him or come back to you," I say to Isadora.

"How many times must you leave us?" she says. "How long must we wait for your return when next you do?"

"Neither he nor the wights will come to me again," I say.

Isadora stops. Myrah looks back at us as she leads Marigold and Rosamond, who bears Florentina, to the softly foaming tide.

"So you will stay there?" she says.

"With my daughter," I say.

"And your mother," says Isadora as she grasps my hand.

"And my father," I say. "Among those slain men only Luda's flesh did not rot and bring her suffering. She might have waited with me had I not told her of Mildred."

"She has found peace, then," Isadora says. "Let her abide in it. And you, you will stay with us out of the sun and share your thorned words with those who know how best to keep them from others. The only wind that need cool your face is that which comes in from this sea."

Isadora takes my waist and walks with me towards Myrah where she stands in ebbing water up to her ankles.

"Have you told Myrah of this?" says Isadora.

"I have not," I say.

"Neither she nor I can stay there with you," says Isadora. "What would you have us do, then?"

Under the water of the lake where Sithebad lies, I set Myrah to rest on a bed of moss and stones and there behold her for as long as the breath within my lungs will let me. Whether she dreams of me or of her daughter or of her mother, I do not know—I have only the peaceful stillness of her eyelids to show me whatever I wish to see. And I may see this, whenever I wish, by swimming beneath the water to look upon a face that glows with the sun's radiance even in a place where life and love have crumbled into meaninglessness. I may take Myrah, in my sorrow, from her sweet dreams beneath the water and hold her in my arms until the boatman calls her flesh to aching life. I may kiss her until her blood-hued eyes open to the breathlessness of drowning before drifting away into a sleep from which I had taken her, and to which I sent her anew for the sake of my own heart's longing.

Her suffering is mine. When she dies, the last flickering flame of life within me also dies. I would have Myrah here with us among the living in love and laughter for as long as the wind sends breath into her breast and the sun shines life into her face.

"My blood runs within her," I say. "Let her believe that this will keep us together in that hidden world. And when she does come there and does not see me, she will remember the words of Derwen's letter and know that she must go to where the boatman awaits her. This secret, we must keep."

"I will keep her for you, Ardelle," says Isadora.

Myrah wades out into the sea up to her waist in her green gown. Rosamond is at her side. Marigold comes between them, giving one hand to her dearest friend's elbow and the other to her queen. Myrah sings with words so soft that they can not be heard over the wind that blows through our hair, yet they are enough to keep the greying clouds from weeping. Florentina strengthens Myrah's song with the sorrow of one who has laid a lifetime of guilt at her own feet for not having healed men who were beyond healing. Marigold sings to the heavens of the one friend who is enough to lighten the burden of having kept others from hurting her by taking them from this earth. Myrah chokes on her own halting words when they speak the name of the mother who has been taken from her, yet whose face looks back at her from the water of a sea too shallow to bear the fullness of their love for one another.

Where I thought I had emptied myself of all sorrow, it springs anew from somewhere within me and withholds nothing of itself as I sing of the place I once called home, and of the mother and father who raised me from the earliest memories of my childhood, and of the wheat we grew, whose tall stalks swayed in the summer wind, and of the golden flowers that grew in the fields, and of my daughter, who would pluck their leaves from among the strands of my hair and blow them into the wind, laughing with glee at the sight of those fluttering feathers filled with life. I take those flow-ered leaves from my hair, one by one, until I have gathered all of them into my hand and send them along the sea that they might, when I am gone from this life, find their way beneath the water to the mossy bed where my daughter sleeps in the arms of her mother's sister; and they may come to rest within her palm so that she may keep with her, as she dreams of the life we shared together, a token of her mother's love.